T0365933

Crossroads

Robert Fisher

authorHOUSE®

AuthorHouse™
1663 Liberty Drive
Bloomington, IN 47403
www.authorhouse.com
Phone: 1 (800) 839-8640

Published by AuthorHouse 07/28/2015

ISBN: 978-1-5049-2159-6 (sc)
ISBN: 978-1-5049-2158-9 (e)

Chapter One

Many boys of almost fifteen years of age believe they know it all. And he was no exception. After all, he had already displayed his intelligence by constantly being top of his class in school. However, standing in the bright sunshine with his father's consoling arm around his shoulders, he recognized his appraisal of the depth of his knowledge was far from extensive. Like most young boys at that time, he had never heard of cancer. Not until that awful day six month's ago, in November 1935, when his mother had told him of her illness. And he certainly had no conception of its quickness in spreading and only later did he learn of its ultimate conclusion. The tears swept down his face and his body shook with uncontrollable grief as his mother's coffin was lowered into the earth. The mourners filed past muttering their condolences and shaking his father's hand. A few tried to shake his but he seemed incapable of moving his arms from his side with his fists tightly clenched. Finally when they were the only two remaining, his father spoke to him in a hushed voice.

"Let's go home, son."

'Home?' he thought desolately. 'How could his father call it home when he was now without a wife, and he was now without a mother?'

He gave a last tearful look at the grave and the moment was too much for him. He almost collapsed as his entire being was wracked with the most pitiful shuddering anguish. His father quickly supported him and he allowed his father's strong arm to guide him as they trudged from the cemetery. The man kept his arm around his son's shoulders as they walked the mile to the place where they lived. The boy wondered if he would ever be able to call it home again.

It was the first funeral he had attended and was unprepared for the reception that tradition dictated would follow. A large number of mourners crowded into their small house. His Aunt Jenny had arranged sandwiches,

1

cakes and biscuits, along with an unending supply of tea. The noise of chatter resounding around the small living room was more than he could bear.

"Would it be all right if I go for a walk, Dad?" he asked plaintively.

"Of course, Alex, would you like me to come with you?"

"No thanks, Dad. You had better stay with all these people. Anyway I would like to be alone, if that's okay," he said tentatively.

"Go ahead, son. Take your time. I'll scrounge up something for supper when you return."

"Bye, Dad."

"Bye, Alex."

He walked slowly through the single street of the village, past the little post office, the florist, the general store, the other six small shops and on into the rolling hills of Berkshire. His head was down and his ears deaf to the words of sympathy offered of passers by. They could plainly see his bereavement and were not offended at his lack of response. They looked at the young dejected figure and their hearts shared his sorrow. After an hour of slowly walking over the green grassy slopes the sun disappeared behind the darkening clouds, and he turned back in an effort to beat the oncoming rain.

Back at the house, his Aunt Jenny had taken her brother-in-law into the bedroom, where they could talk in private.

"I saw Alexander go out. Is he all right, John?"

She, like her just departed sister, Helen, had always referred to the boy as Alexander. He had been named after his father's father, a Scot born in Edinburgh. When only in his early twenties John had discovered to his dismay that jobs were hard to come by in Scotland. So he had moved south like many other Scots, looking for work in England. There he had met Helen, married and settled down. John was the second of three children and the only boy. Adding to his father's dismay at his leaving Scotland, John had not retained his Scottish brogue. Nor did he display a strong attachment to his homeland; instead, to his father's disdainful way of thinking, he appeared to have adopted his new land and its dialect. Almost as an act of supplication at his father's obvious disappointment in him, John had named his only child, Alexander – Alexander John MacMillan. The old man had been delighted. His lineage was being perpetuated, and it was being done with *his* name. In his grudging Scottish way he came ninety percent towards forgiving his son for his transgressions, but never for his newfound foreign accent.

John had always called his son Alex; he liked the nickname. However his beloved wife, Helen, always called their son Alexander. Therefore they had agreed to disagree and left it at that.

John stared mournfully into space as some of those memories were going through his mind. Then, guiltily, he realized his sister-in-law was still waiting for a response to her question.

"No, he's not all right, Jenny. I believe it will be a long time before he gets over Helen's death. That boy adored his mother. You know, when he was only eight, Helen complimented him on a good report card, and he said, 'If it pleases you so much, Mum, then I'll try even harder.' And since then he had had nothing but A's and has been top of his class."

The tears welled up in John's eyes.

"What will you do now, John?" asked Jenny wiping away her own tears.

"Well ever since we were told that Helen only had a few months left, I discussed that very subject with her. She begged me to sell our house and move east, closer to London."

"Move away? Why would Helen want you to do that, John?"

"Your sister was a very smart woman, Jenny. She said there was nothing in this tiny village for a young boy. Also, she knew Alex was bright but she felt he could benefit from some real competition at school. If we lived closer to London he would mix with other intelligent children and the competition would further spur his learning. Helen and I studied possible new locations and selected Croydon as our first choice. We did so as it has an excellent school. She made me promise not to delay too long in looking for a job there. A few weeks ago, when we both knew the end was near, she urged me to fulfill that promise and start looking. I kept my promise and to my amazement I was offered a job almost immediately."

"Have you told Alexander?"

"No. I intend to sit down with him and discuss it man to man. I'll only accept the job if he is in agreement. I told Helen that was a condition of moving."

"That's very considerate of you, John. Most men would only tell their young son of their decision."

"No, Jenny, it's not just considerate, it's the only thing to do. That boy is all I have now. He is my life from now on. And he is growing up quickly and deserves to be treated like a young man. He will be consulted, not ordered."

That night, as they were clearing the dishes from the table, John found the courage to talk to Alex about Helen's wishes. The unexpectedness of the thought of moving initially stunned Alex.

"What do *you* think, Dad?" he asked quietly.

"I think your mother was very wise, Alex, and it will be a good thing for you."

"But how about *you*, Dad?" insisted Alex. "You've had your present job for many years and have lived in the village for a long time. You have so many friends here. Won't it be hard to leave?"

"To be honest, Alex, and I hope you don't think me selfish, but I believe a move will help me get on with life without your Mum. As it is, it's going to be extremely difficult, I loved her so much."

The tears began rolling down his cheeks and he took out his handkerchief and blew his nose. Once he had regained some semblance of control over his emotions he continued.

"But seeing everything in this house, each and every day, will continually break my heart. I will never forget the slightest thing about my life with your Mum, but a fresh start in a new house and a new job will give me a chance to move on. And I will always have you."

John looked apprehensively at his son, afraid of seeing a rebuke in his eyes. But what he saw was relief.

"I hadn't thought it all out, Dad, but I believe you are one hundred percent correct. And Mum *was* a very intelligent lady. One day when we were discussing one of my report cards she asked me what I would study if I got the chance to attend university. I told her I didn't know yet and she said I still had time to think about it and she added she had confidence I would make the correct choice. That's when she said I would discover that the journey through an interesting life was one of endless crossroads. Life could be a journey full of opportunities if you had the courage to seize them. The trick was to pick the correct path when you reached one of those crossroads. I think this is one of these times and if it's okay with you then I'm all for it."

Although he was not yet fifteen, he had harbored the belief he knew it all. Part of this pretense was always to try to act like a man and never show weakness. This mandated one must never show deeply held emotions in front of one's father. That would be unmanly. Apparently he had inherited more than a few of his grandfather's traits. But now he forgot all that nonsense and acted like a grief-stricken boy. He rushed over and threw his arms around John, his tears wetting his father's shirt.

"I love you, Dad," he said in a choking voice.

"And I love you my son," responded John as he stoked his son's head while fighting back his own tears.

The next day they visited Helen's grave and it was only then Alex noticed the grassy space alongside. John saw him stare at it.

"That place is for me, son. I reserved it to be with your mother," he said in a solemn voice.

"I understand, Dad. I'll see to it when the time comes."

The quiet determination in his voice indicated he had once again assumed the role of a mature young man.

Two weeks later, on a rainy day in May, 1936, they bade farewell to Berkshire and headed for Croydon. Time would show Alex had reached a crossroad in his life and had chosen the correct path.

Chapter Two

One year later it was just as Helen had prophesized. Alex was no longer top of his class, he was third, and had to study diligently to maintain that position. But, in fact, he was not utilizing his full potential. Something was holding him back.

John had a good job as an ambulance driver at the main hospital and from time to time had to work nightshift. He hated that as his need to sleep during the day took him away from his beloved son. He lived for the boy.

Although the move had definitely been the correct path to follow, it had not yet eased John's sorrow and his heart still ached for Helen. And the increasingly perceptive Alex recognized it. In the evenings, once John had cleaned up after dinner and Alex had finished his homework, they would sit close together and laugh at the comedies on the radio or they would play chess.

He was sixteen and his thoughts and actions clearly exhibited his high intelligence. But now he was sufficiently mature to recognize he was no longer a know-it-all. Nevertheless he was confident in his abilities and had been astounded at his father's capability at chess. Alex had learned it at school from his bright classmates and one night in a fit of regression he had rather high-handedly offered to teach his father. John smiled as Alex set up the board and explained the rules. It was Alex who was dumfounded when five moves later he was check-mated. Believing he had taken the game too lightly he proposed a rematch and was again quickly beaten.

"You know how to play, Dad!" exclaimed Alex in a challenging and utterly surprised manner.

"Yes, son, my father taught me. He was a canny Scot from Edinburgh and never allowed anyone to understand just how clever he was. Keeping one's personal life confidential was a widespread Scottish tradition in those days. He taught himself chess from a book and joined a club to hone his skills. But he had another Scottish trait of those times and never displayed his true feelings of love for his children. He always maintained an air of strict discipline. When he began teaching me, he told me I had to earn a victory at chess and he would never deliberately let me win. I still remember the first time I managed to beat him, he just stared at me and used the excuse that he had been tired. Next day it was my mother who let me know he had told her how proud he was of me."

"That was mean of him."

"No son those were different times, and although he was naturally clever, his only experience in raising children sprang from his own boyhood. His father was a drunkard who beat him often with his walking stick. But your grandfather never beat me and probably thought that by not doing so he was being enlightened, and I suppose in his own way, he was. However, he just couldn't bring himself to show the love he felt for his children."

"That's so sad, I'm so glad you're not that way, Dad."

"I try my best but you make it easy for me, Alex. I'm so proud of you."

It was then Alex understood just how much he meant to his father. It was not transference of his love for Helen, it was simply that she wasn't there and John was giving all his available love to his son. That realization was the reason Alex didn't spend extra time studying; time that may have gotten him to first place in his class. He wanted to spend as much time as possible with his still grieving father. The bond that had always existed between father and son had become even stronger. However it took another six months before John caught on to Alex sacrifice. It was a snowy night in January, 1938 when he decided to finally mention it.

"Listen son," he said after a game of chess, "I know how much you love me and I appreciate all the time you spend with me; but you will graduate from high school next year and I really would like you to spend a bit more time on your studies."

"I'm doing well in school, Dad. I really don't need more time to study," he responded gallantly.

John took his son's head between his hands and kissed him on the forehead.

"Just spend a little more time on your studies, Alex. It will help you get into a good university, that's where you will really learn about the world. It's a golden opportunity that I wish I had. Will you do it for me?"

"Okay Dad, if it means so much to you, I'll do it."

There was a seemingly long period of silence as though each of them wished to add something but was incapable of finding the right words. It was Alex who spoke first.

"You were completely correct when you said I love you. But that's not the only reason I want to spend as much time as possible with you. For a long time, Dad, I've hoped that one day I can be like you and being with you I am gradually learning how to do that."

"I don't know what you mean son. I've done nothing special in my life and have only had menial jobs."

"It's not about your job, Dad. It's all about you. You have always been a considerate and caring man – to everyone. You give so much of yourself and never ask for anything in return. You're not just my Dad and my best friend – you're my idol."

John couldn't think of a quick response so he just held his son tightly and kissed the top of his head. That night he had trouble sleeping. His son's words kept rolling around in his head. Only when he decided he would talk about this to Alex in the morning, did his mind clear and he was able to finally fall asleep.

The morning did not greet John cheerfully. It often rains in England but this morning it poured. To say the sky was leaden would have been an insult to the color of that pure metal. The low whipping clouds were a dirty black and gray combination forming a mosaic that made one shiver just to look at it. To add to the depressing aura, the whistling wind whipped along seeking out any smiling face it could find and delighting in wiping away any semblance of happiness. John heard Alex approach the kitchen and turned away from the window where he had been studying this ugly sight, almost mesmerized by its ferocity.

"Come and have a nice hot cup of tea, son."

"Thanks, Dad, that's just what one needs on a morning like this."

John hesitated before speaking to Alex again. He wanted to ask him about his comments of the previous night but wasn't sure how to approach the subject. As he sipped his tea pensively his son recognized that something was troubling his father.

"What's wrong, Dad?"

"I was thinking about what you said last night, son. To be truthful I thought about it a lot while in bed. What did you mean exactly?"

"Well without being overly philosophic, I have thought exhaustively about all Mum said about life and have read a few books relating to that subject. And I have reached the same conclusion she did. Life is not a single journey, but a succession of journeys. And between each of them we are faced with choices - like coming to a crossroad as she said. One can either go left or right. And it is not always obvious which one is the better or the right one. I have decided that when I come to make these decisions I will try to think which one you would select. I am absolutely certain you would never compromise your principles of right and wrong. And I know you always take time to carefully consider important decisions. So my goal is to be like you, Dad and that will make my journeys have a greater meaning and never be self-serving or greedy."

Alex suddenly stopped there, noticing the strange look on his father's face. It was not a look of misunderstanding but one of wonder.

'I could well be listening to a university graduate and not a sixteen year old boy,' John thought to himself.

Hoping he had not confused his father by not making himself clear, Alex quickly added, "I hope I have explained it well."

"Yes, you have, Alex - very well. The only piece of advice I can give you is some decisions one takes in life seem like the best ones at the time, but later turn out not to be. If you ever find you have taken the wrong path, don't do anything hasty. Stop and consider whether it is better to retrace your steps or to make the best of it and wait for another crossroad. Experience can be a great teacher and it is the smart man who learns from his mistakes. Does that make sense to you?"

"Yes, Dad, it does. Thank you."

John was to look back on his son's words many times. And each time he felt pride in their content and in his son's eloquence.

He prayed Alex would find happiness in his journeys and mostly chose the correct paths at life's crossroads.

Chapter Three

In May 1939, Alex not only graduated top of his class but he was well ahead of the second placed boy. His achievement was so outstanding he was awarded a scholarship to one of England's most prestigious universities – Cambridge. But he was disinclined to accept it.

"I can go to a university close by, that way I can still live at home with you Dad," he said.

John was greatly touched at his son's concern for him but he was also horrified at the prospect of Alex not taking advantage of this wonderful opportunity. He shook his head vigorously.

"No, no, my son, you have earned this honor and it would please me greatly to see you attend Cambridge. You must accept the scholarship, Alex – please! I'll visit you often and we will spend your holidays together."

He paused before adding, "And it will fulfill your mother's greatest wish."

So, even though he had lingering doubts, Alex accepted the offer. However, world affairs clouded the issue. On September third, 1939, a few days before starting university, Britain and France declared war on Germany. That night as they sat at the dinner table, Alex said, "Perhaps I should join up and forget university for now."

"No, son, you must promise me you will finish your education," pleaded a distraught father.

Alex thought for a moment before replying, sensing a crossroad and wishing to respond carefully.

"Who knows when or how this war will end, Dad? I could never make you a promise that I couldn't keep. All I can do is promise not to go into the army now. I *will* start at Cambridge. How's that for a compromise?" he said, satisfied it was the correct path.

"That's good enough, Alex," replied a relieved father.

But as John responded, the observant Alex caught a glimpse of a fleeting strange look in his father's eyes; a look that troubled him.

"What is it, Dad?"

"Eh, nothing son, I just don't like the idea of war," John replied.

However his father wasn't telling the whole truth, as he would learn later.

Alex kept his promise and began his studies at Cambridge, but his heart wasn't in his new endeavor. An undefined worry nagged at him and it affected his grades. When he returned to Croydon for Christmas break, he had achieved good grades but definitely not ones up to his usual standard of excellence. On his second day home, the anxiety he had felt, but could not define, took terrible shape.

As they sat around the brightly burning coal fire after dinner, John could contain himself no longer and blurted out his secret.

"I have joined up, son," he said.

Seeing the horror on the face of Alex, he hurriedly continued.

"I'm too old to do any fighting, Alex. But I can still drive an ambulance. I am to be posted to France in a few weeks time. I hope you are not angry with me son, but I have to do something to aid our country. I just can't sit by and be an observer."

Not for the first time, Alex hugged his father.

"Of course I'm not angry, Dad. I know how you feel and I'm so proud of you. But of course, I'm concerned. You will be in the thick of it by ferrying our lads from the front to field hospitals. And, so far, nothing seems able to stop the German army. They obviously have been preparing for some time because they appear to be highly organized and effective."

"I know, Alex. But we have the best navy in the world. We'll box those Nazis in if they ever attempt to cross the Channel. But I wish we had listened to Churchill earlier. He said this would happen but that wishy-washy mob in parliament only called him an alarmist. If they had paid attention, we would have been much better prepared. Still that's water under the bridge now. There's no point in complaining, we just have to get on with it. Anyway let's have a good Christmas. I managed to get my hands on a superb goose and a bottle of excellent wine."

"That must have cost you a fortune, Dad. You'll have no money left."

"I'm not worried about that. You see I have a secret plan. I know my son will get a high paying job when he graduates from Cambridge and he'll take care of me in my old age. I'll just sit back and let him pay for everything I need."

He said this with a twinkle in his eyes and enormous pride in his voice.

"Don't you believe it," shot back Alex. "After three years at Cambridge, I intend to lay back with my feet up and let my father take care of me."

This time the twinkle was briefly in his eyes. He stepped forward and hugged his father again. Holding on tightly and hoping his father would not see the tears of worry welling up in his eyes.

But there was no mistaking the tears that flowed from both sets of eyes when they said goodbye two weeks later. Alex headed for Cambridge and scholastic challenges and John for France and the dangers of war.

Initially the worry Alex felt for his father caused his grades to lower. After being called to the master's room on two occasions and being told he was not coming close to his potential, he buckled down and his grades improved. By the end of May he completed his first year final exams with good results. They were good but not excellent. He felt a modicum of satisfaction at the improvement and determined to really work hard during his second year. He was surprised, therefore, when he was again summoned to the master's room. It was with some trepidation that he knocked on the door.

"Enter."

Whatever Alex expected it was not this. The master was not alone. There were two other men in army uniforms. Instantly he knew what had happened and he sagged against the door

"I'm afraid I've got bad news, MacMillan. You had better sit down."

Alex collapsed into a chair and one of the army men handed him a glass of water. The other, an officer, took over.

"I regret to inform you that your father, Private John MacMillan, has been killed in action," he said in a solemn voice, one that was well practiced. He had used it on too many occasions.

"But he wasn't supposed to fight, he was only to drive an ambulance," protested Alex in a hoarse whisper, as he choked back his tears.

"That is correct. He was transferring wounded troops from an army hospital to the beaches at Dunkirk for evacuation, when a German Messerschmitt strafed the area killing everyone in the ambulance."

"Aren't medical personnel and vehicles supposed to be off limits?"

This time the cool, collected, practiced voice of the officer cracked with emotion.

"Yes they are, but the Nazi bastard didn't observe the accepted code of behavior!"

His eyes blazed with fury as he spoke. Then with a great effort he calmed his voice.

"You should know that your father exhibited great courage during the tragic events at Dunkirk. For three days, with virtually no sleep, he continually drove the wounded to safety. He has been awarded the Military Medal. I deeply regret his death. He was an outstanding soldier."

The officer came forward, handed Alex a silk lined box with the medal inside, stood to attention and saluted. It was only then that tears of grief ran down Alex's face.

Several days later, there were more tears as Alex fulfilled his promise and had his father buried next to his mother. That night he lay awake for hours in his Aunt Jenny's house staring at the bedroom ceiling. Finally he made the decision that he must undertake another journey. The Nazis killed his father, he would kill Nazis.

Next morning he gave a spare set of house keys to his aunt and asked that she look in on his house from time to time. Then he went home to Croydon, wrote a letter informing Cambridge he would not be returning, carefully stored his books, tidied the house, walked to the recruitment office and joined the army.

He did not have long to wait until his orders arrived. He packed a few things, locked the doors and headed towards the train station.

Chapter Four

The camp Alex entered for his basic training was a miserable looking place. It was located ten miles from the nearest small town to discourage any 'second-thoughter' from deserting. One would never reach the town before the Military Police caught up with you. The huts were all the same dull green color and as the rain beat down on the corrugated roofs it seemed to play a tune. 'Welcome to hell.'

The many conscripts and the few volunteers descended from the buses and most shuddered at the sight that greeted them. They were lined up on the parade ground. Of course there were several who could not wait to go to war and their faces wore expectant, almost happy, looks. Most would lose those looks quickly. The man who would dispel those looks strode out to face them.

He was an imposing figure. Over six feet tall, with broad shoulders and a body that appeared to want to bulge out of its uniform. But all eyes were fixed on his face. He glared at them in a bone chilling menacing manner and his deep brown eyes seemed to penetrate their souls. His face wore a scar that cleft his left cheek - the result of gang warfare on the docks of London. Tough was not a word that first sprang to mind in studying him. The word was frightening. Those who had appeared happy to be here joined the others in shuffling uneasily at this sight.

Sergeant Nichols was an uncompromising man. He had to be in his job. His unenviable task was to take newly conscripted and newly volunteered young men and make them soldiers. It had long since failed to amaze him that some of them appeared not to be able to distinguish between their right and their left. Neither did it surprise him that for the first few nights many cried for their mothers. However, none of this deterred him from 'knocking them into shape' as he put it. Very few failed to at least look the part of soldiers after six weeks with him. Some only looked the part and he could tell they would not last long in war. But that was not his concern. That duty would be passed to their commanding officers; or more probably, their regimental sergeants. His was a cold-hearted, lonely job and one for which he was eminently qualified.

Therefore, ten days later, his commanding officer, Major Grant, was quite astounded to see this hard-bitten rock of a man stand uncomfortably in front of him. He had already asked him what he wanted and so far had only heard the hems and haws of a befuddled man. Not in the least like the sergeant he knew so well.

Major Grant was a disillusioned and bitter officer at being posted to this ignominious position. Frankly, one good look at his face should have made those at the officers' training school question his ability to be in the army at all. His narrow forehead was already deeply furrowed indicating a worrier, not a leader. His eyes seemed to water permanently and his thick lips were continuously licked by a flicking tongue. All these unfortunate features were capped off by a significantly receding chin. But he had managed to scrape though university which had legally qualified him (inaccurately) as an officer. However this error had been quickly spotted and it was recognized he would never become a leader of men. In addition to his other traits, the man had no empathy for his fellow humans. He was given his present posting as a way to keep him out of real soldiering. And actually he turned out to be better than expected at this task.

His job was to turn out fodder for the war machine. Hopefully qualified fodder but fodder never-the-less. And so long as he was supported by the services of competent non-commissioned officers he could do a reasonable job. Like Sergeant Nichols, he was inured to personal feelings and didn't particularly care what became of the men when they left his camp. That was not his responsibility.

In effect he had become a paper pusher. Papers came across his desk with all recruits; weekly progress reports were submitted to headquarters; and final papers were completed when the men left. His dyspeptic nature tended to focus on the recruits' shortcomings rather than any merits they may have possessed. Headquarters recognized this, but good officers were in short supply and none would wish to be assigned to this job. So they put up with his idiosyncrasies and did not interfere with him. So long as the men were trained and the reports came in on time the army was content.

However since he never received feedback on his performance he lived in constant fear of making a mistake. Perhaps in compensation for his disillusionment and his dread of committing a serious error, he had developed a simple but strict routine which while not drawing praise from his superiors, at least did not draw criticism. Therefore he stuck religiously to it.

A tongue-tied sergeant definitely did not comprise a part of his well practiced routine. Therefore, he was highly displeased, as well as perplexed, at Nichols' unusual behavior.

"Sit down, Sergeant!" he commanded. "Now let's start all over. And for God's sake take your time and tell me what's troubling you," he barked.

"It's Private MacMillan, Sir."

"Is he proving to be a problem? Your first report did not indicate one," he snapped officiously, his voice betraying his concern. It would not look good if his just submitted report proved to be erroneous.

"No, no, Sir, he's not a problem, quite the opposite. The fact is, Sir, I don't think he should be here."

"Shouldn't be here? You're not making any sense, Nichols. Explain yourself man!" snapped an agitated Grant.

Recognizing Grant's displeasure, Nichols took a deep breath before continuing.

"He does everything perfectly, Sir. He's obviously way smarter than any of the others. They even recognize that. But he doesn't flaunt it. Everyone likes him and they look up to him. He's too good to be a private, that's what I have been trying to say. Would you please interview him, Sir, I think he may be officer material."

That was the last thing Grant expected to hear and it caused him to speak without thinking.

"In all the time I've known you, Nichols, this has never happened before. You had better not be wasting my time, I have reports to write."

Then his brain engaged and he stopped to think. This was unprecedented and he had better tread carefully. Better not make a mistake. Caution must be the watchword.

"Well all right," he relented. "I'll get his record out. Send him to see me in half-an-hour."

"Yes, Sir!"

The sergeant saluted smartly and left with a mixture of relief and anxiety. He had never come across anyone like MacMillan. He had noticed his attributes almost immediately but it had taken him until now to pluck up the courage to approach Grant. He could only pray his assessment was accurate as he dashed off to find Private MacMillan and tell him of the appointment with the major.

Alex stood at the open door and saluted. Major Grant returned the salute.

"At ease, MacMillan, sit down."

"Thank you, Sir"

"I have been reviewing your file. You could have claimed exemption from service for another two years by remaining in university. Why didn't you?" he began aggressively.

"I wanted to serve my country, Sir."

Apparently Alex had inherited his grandfather's trait of not wishing to let others know everything about him. His father's death had left him totally devastated and his spontaneous reaction was to exact some measure of revenge on Germans. But he had not mentioned this to anyone and chose not to do so now.

"I see. I have read your grades at Cambridge. They were good but not exceptional; nevertheless, if you were determined to serve in the army you could have applied for officer school. Why didn't you?"

"No particular reason, Sir."

Once again he was unwilling to admit his first impulse was to get front line duty in order to kill Germans. However after his week-and-a-half of training, his ardor for retribution had cooled a little and he realized he had acted impetuously. He was still willing to live with his hasty decision but now he did have regrets at leaving Cambridge. He had come to a crossroad and taken the wrong path. He knew his father's greatest desire was for him to graduate and now regretted not doing what would have pleased his father most. Having recalled his father's advice not to act hastily upon discovering he had taken a wrong turning, he had decided it was impossible to retrace his steps; therefore he must wait for an opportunity to come upon another crossroad. Little did he then know he was rapidly approaching just such a crossroad.

Major Grant was puzzled at Alex's attitude and sensed there was more to his story than he was willing to divulge. He thought for a few seconds then decided it would be the smart course of action not to make a decision. That could be too risky; it would be wiser to pass the buck.

"I am sending you to an evaluation center, MacMillan. I want you to undergo a few tests." Seeing a look of protest he added. "This is not a request, MacMillan, it is an order!"

"Yes, Sir," replied Alex resignedly, still not recognizing the signpost indicating the oncoming crossroad.

Two days later he was driven thirty miles to an officer training camp where a Captain Jones sent him for a full day of psychological and intelligence tests. The next day the results were sent to Major Grant who immediately telephoned Jones.

"Something went wrong with your tests, Captain. The results are definitely erroneous. Did you administer the tests personally?" he demanded in an accusatory tone.

"No, Major, one of my men did them. Why do you ask? Do you have reason to believe they aren't correct?"

"I reviewed MacMillan's record at Cambridge and while it was good there is no correlation with the results you sent me. If your results were correct this private should be a brigadier general!" he exclaimed in a sarcastic voice that dripped with acidity. "I would like you to do the tests again and, this time, please conduct them personally."

"Of course, Major," responded an aggrieved Captain Jones.

Jones was a proud man and confident his center had done a thorough job. And he was annoyed at Grant's belligerent comments. Very early the next day Alex made the journey once more. This time is was almost midnight before he returned to the barracks. The following afternoon Major Grant received a visit from Captain Jones.

"I brought the results in person in case you should have any questions. I not only administered the usual tests but also one we reserve for those aspiring to become one of the highest ranking officers in the Intelligence Corp."

Grant studied the results for several minutes.

"My God, this is astonishing," he gasped, at last being convinced that no error had been made.

"Yes, all of us at the center were equally astounded. Your Private MacMillan is close to the top of the best one percent of anyone in the Armed Forces. You were right, Major. He should be a brigadier general!"

The last comment was made with some relish and just a touch of acerbity. But, for once, Major Grant did not take offence. Instead his voice had an unusual conciliatory tone.

"With all your experience, Captain, where do you think we should send MacMillan?"

"Well certainly not to the front lines as a private. That would really be a waste of a valuable resource. And not even to the regular officer training school. I would suggest you contact Intelligence."

"Thank you Captain, that's an excellent idea. I shall note your recommendation."

Grant said this with relish and a great deal of relief. He had found a way to avoid making a decision. And true to the Army code, Grant first went up the chain of command to his colonel. The colonel was a seasoned, capable, officer and immediately grasped the potential importance of this Private MacMillan. He contacted his opposite number in the Intelligence Service and strongly recommended he interview MacMillan.

In late July, Alex was sent to London, to an impressive old building in Westminster where he was ushered into a very large room with a very long table. He was seated in the middle of one side of this table and given a coffee. The door opened and in trooped a panel of six men led by a colonel. They had read his file which now contained the results of his tests. And like Major Grant, they found it difficult to believe those results, but were determined to get to the bottom of this matter. They sat opposite Alex and without preamble began peppering him with questions.

One hour later they told him to wait outside.

"Well, what do you think?" the colonel asked his once skeptical team.

"I say we grab him before someone else does," said a now convinced major.

Four of the others agreed, but not one of the lieutenants. The colonel had a high regard for this member of his staff and looked at him with arched eyebrows and a slight tilt of his head.

"I don't disagree that he would be very valuable to us, Sir ---," began the lieutenant.

"But?" interjected the colonel.

"Well it occurred to me one of the greatest needs we currently have is the ability to crack German codes. We are making good progress and Lord only knows we have a large number of Ph.D.'s working around the clock. But this man has more than just intelligence; he has a uniquely inquiring mind and an ability to look at problems in ways I have never seen before. Perhaps he would be a real asset to Bletchley Park."

"You are suggesting I deprive myself of this valuable man and hand him over to the code-crackers?" responded the colonel in a gruff voice.

One of the reasons the colonel liked this young Lieutenant Baxter so much was his courage. And once again he did not back down.

"As of last week we are all connected to the SOE, Colonel. And yes I believe the war effort would be best served by having him at Bletchley."

The SOE or Special Operations Executive had just been approved by the Cabinet on 22 July, 1940 and was led by the Minister for Economic Warfare, Hugh Dalton. It combined several secret departments and its mission was to conduct espionage, sabotage and reconnaissance against Britain's war enemies. And like any new amalgamation of groups, each head of his group was still parochial enough to protect his own territory. The colonel was no exception. Therefore the lieutenant had risked the renowned wrath of the colonel by suggesting he give up Private MacMillan.

The others in the room held their collective breaths as the colonel considered Baxter's proposal.

"That's a damn good idea, Lieutenant. I'll arrange it. And I suppose we had better not send out a private to Bletchley. Major Simms, would you arrange for MacMillan to be promoted to sergeant?"

"May I suggest one other thing, Colonel?" requested Lieutenant Baxter.

The colonel nodded his head jerkily. He liked this young man but was not in the habit of allowing constant interruptions to his decisions.

"Bletchley has its fair share of people who are filled with their own importance. Therefore I would suggest we make MacMillan an officer. They are apt to pay more attention to an officer."

The colonel had to hide a smile from his crossing his face. The young man was again right. He put an affected scowl on his face.

"Oh, very well," he grumped.

Then he turned to one of his staff, "Make him a lieutenant, Major Simms. And would someone ask him to rejoin us?"

Alex had left the room as a private but little did he know that he now returned as a lieutenant. A lieutenant, who did not yet know, he was approaching a crossroad, one which would lead him on a new journey. He entered the room, stood at attention, and saluted. Finally the colonel looked up from, his papers and returned the salute.

"Sit down, Lieutenant MacMillan," he instructed.

Alex remained standing with a look of astonishment on his face.

"It seems you so impressed the members of my staff that they insisted I promote you. So, you are now a lieutenant."

"Thank you, Sir," said a still reeling Alex.

"Major, would you kindly pass two copies of the official secrets act document to our new lieutenant. Thank you. Now, MacMillan, sign both and keep one copy. You can read all the fine print later. In essence it says if at any time in your entire life you blab any of the secrets you learn from now on, I have the right to have you shot. Is that sufficiently succinct for you?"

Alex did not flinch. He just returned the colonel's stare. This made

Lieutenant Baxter smile. He had been right about the man who came to them as a private. He would not be bullied, he had guts.

"That was very delicately put, Sir," replied a smiling Alex.

The colonel's head rocked back; and one could clearly hear the intake of collective breath from the others at this young man's audacity. But the colonel was not angry, he was grinning. The others relaxed and also broke out into smiles.

"A sense of humor will serve you well in your next assignment, MacMillan. Have you heard of Bletchley Park?"

"No, Sir."

"Good. You're not supposed to know anything about it. You will report there tomorrow. Lieutenant Baxter will drive you down there in the morning. Meanwhile he'll find a place for you to sleep tonight and arrange dinner for you. You'll do all that, won't you Lieutenant Baxter? Since this was all your bright idea."

"It will be a pleasure, Sir."

Chapter Five

On July 29th Alex was driven from the war torn city of London, north westward towards the bucolic splendor of Buckinghamshire, where it was difficult to believe war existed. The sun shone brightly as they entered Milton Keyes and Alex saw for the first time his new home, Bletchley Park.

The previous evening, over dinner, Baxter had told Alex all about this place.

"The estate grounds at Bletchley have been converted to house GC&CS, the Government Code and Cypher School. The place was last owned by a Liberal Member of Parliament, Sir Herbert Samuel Leon. He died in the mid-twenties and his wife died in 1937. The following year it was sold to a builder who intended demolishing the existing buildings and constructing a housing estate. However before he could do so, Sir Hugh Sinclair the head of two departments, Naval Intelligence and MI 6, bought it for its current purpose.

The main building is a beautiful old mansion and there are other more recently constructed buildings for specific sections of the operation. The purpose of the establishment is to decrypt enemy codes. But we also use it to create codes for our forces. If we are to win this war, it will be absolutely essential we crack the enemy codes.

Before beginning his war efforts, Hitler astutely built up his armed forces. Unluckily for us Commander Karl Donitz was appointed to build the Nazi U-boat fleet. He did an outstanding job. Being an island nation, we depend of the sea to bring us much of our food supplies, and now, for materials to build our armaments. The brand new U-boat fleet has been highly effective in disrupting all that by sinking the ships carrying those supplies. We must decypher their codes in order to locate and destroy them if we are to survive.

The center at Bletchley has a large number of the best brains in the country working on this task. That's why you have been picked to work there."

"But I don't know anything about cryptology," protested Alex.

"Don't worry; most of the people at Bletchley were in the same boat when they arrived. You'll learn."

But Alex was worried and it took him some time before he could sleep that night. Just before he drifted off he recalled something that Professor Manning had said at Cambridge. His message encapsulated the same advice his father, John, had offered.

"Life is an unending series of experiences: some good - some bad. What you learn from each of them will determine how effective you will be as a member of the human race."

'Well this journey will definitely be another experience,' he thought, as sleep finally overtook him.

As they got out the car, he recalled his last thought of the previous night and determined to give this experience his best effort. They were ushered into an office with the name Dr. Joshua Kind stenciled on the door. Inside a stooped, prematurely gray haired man, of only thirty nine years, stood up from his desk. He was only five feet six inches tall. His spectacles were almost falling off his nose and he pushed them up as his short legs strode rapidly as he came to greet them.

"Welcome to Bletchley. Which one of you is Lieutenant MacMillan?"

"I am, Sir," responded Alex.

"I'm pleased to meet you," said Dr. Kind shaking his hand.

"And you must be his escort, Lieutenant Baxter."

"That's correct, Doctor."

"Well do sit down; I'll have some tea brought in."

He picked up the telephone to do so and while he spoke, Alex studied him. He had the appearance of the archetypical absent minded professor. His tie was askew, one shirt sleeve was rolled up and the other was buttoned at the wrist, and his mop of wiry hair looked a though it had never been combed. His sleeveless cardigan seemed determined to slip from his narrow shoulders. But a keen observer would not miss his most important feature. His gray eyes were unmistakably intelligent and never missed a thing. Alex would quickly learn that while Dr. Kind's appearance was disheveled, his brilliant mind was razor sharp.

"Your colonel called me last night to tell me all about you, Lieutenant MacMillan. Oh, would you mind if I called you Alex? We tend to just use first names around here."

"Not at all, Sir."

"And please don't refer to me as sir. It makes me feel like a headmaster at grammar school. Everyone calls me Josh. I must say that from the colonel's description of you, Alex, I consider it most magnanimous of him to allow you to leave his group. I detected a note of regret in his voice at that decision."

The sharp Kind saw the look on Baxter's face and knew he had been correct.

"Not exactly a unanimous decision among his staff, eh Lieutenant Baxter?"

"That's correct, Doctor."

"Well then, that makes me particularly pleased to have you here, Alex. Ah, here's the tea. Please help yourselves to biscuits. Now tell me about yourself, Alex while Lieutenant Baxter enjoys his tea. Then we will let him get back to his busy job and I will introduce you to the people you will be working with."

Baxter took the subtle hint to quickly finish his tea and get on his way. He did so and with a firm handshake bade farewell to Alex.

"Good luck, Lieutenant MacMillan. I hope we meet again."

"It would be my pleasure, Lieutenant," responded Alex, not knowing he was bidding farewell to the man who had led him to a path that would change his life irrevocably.

"Well now, let's get started," said Dr. Kind when Baxter had left.

"Sometime in the next two days please fill out these forms. The government files them away in case future reference is required. The information is seldom thoroughly checked and I know that more than a few of my associates were not completely forthcoming with the entire truth. I know of several of them who seem to have developed amnesia over the number of times they have been booked for speeding. I even know of one man who indicated he had been married twice but failed to indicate it was at the same time."

Dr. Kind's eyes lit up with merriment and he winked at Alex. Then his face turned serious.

"I only have two rules. The first is you must always do your job to the maximum of your ability. The second is you must never become a spy for the enemy."

Alex looked startled at the second rule.

"Oh, I am certain the enemy has agents in Britain and they would like nothing better than to know what goes on here. Initially I believe you will find, because of my rules, the people you work with are a bit suspicious about you. I encourage this initial attitude. Trust takes time and I cannot risk my rule number two being broken. So don't feel you are being unfairly singled out by such treatment at the outset. I will not be betrayed. Anyone who does so will be hanged – by me!"

He emphasized the last comment but it was the look in his eyes when he said it that told Alex underneath his amiable façade was a will of steel.

The first few months passed vey quickly. His training was entirely engrossing and Alex threw himself into his work. Dr. Kind was kept informed of his progress and was pleased and very surprised at the unusually high praise Alex got from his instructors. After only three months Alex was transferred to a team dedicated to the most difficult tasks. A sure sign he had been accepted by the establishment.

Time seemed to fly past.

Alex found it difficult to believe he had been at Bletchley for almost three years. However one morning, as he was shaving, he took a good look at the reflection in the mirror. The face looking back at him was definitely older than that of a twenty two year old man. A few lines were noticeable around the eyes. He had thrown himself into his work with an intensity that was beginning to show.

His colleagues noticed this some time ago and had repeatedly asked him to take time to relax. He always responded with a sheepish grin and promised he would do so. But he saw his job as saving lives and he could not let up. The successes he and his colleagues had achieved were like a habit forming drug. The more you had, the more you wanted.

It was about this time he received a message to see Josh Kind.

"You sent for me, Josh?"

"Yes, Alex. I'm very cross with you. Oh don't look so apprehensive. It's just I have asked you several times to take some leave and you have yet to comply. Working twelve hour days takes its toll and your health will suffer if you don't ease up for a while. So this time it is not a suggestion, it is an order. Take time off! I cannot pretend we won't miss you; your work is breathtaking as I have mentioned before but I need you for the long haul, Alex. Therefore, starting on Sunday I want you to go somewhere and relax for a week. Just inform the security officer where you will be."

"Okay, Josh, you win. I think you're right and a week at the beach in June will be refreshing. I can sleep late, drink a few beers each day and read lots of books."

"That's the ticket."

Chapter Six

When Alex returned looking tanned and rested, he immediately reported to Dr. Kind. The observant Josh noted Alex seemed excited.

"You look better, Alex but you seem wound up. What is it?"

"I have something to show you and I would like your honest opinion. It's something I have been working on while sunning at the beach."

"Oh no, no, I told you to relax, Alex," exclaimed Josh, his voice clearly showing his annoyance.

"Sorry Josh, but I have been thinking about this for quite some time. We spend a good bit of our time cracking codes and some of it developing codes for our agents. I have always wondered how our agents in the field manage to handle the complex codes they use. I know they require a code book and I wondered if there was a simpler way for them to operate. Carrying a code book around must be a giveaway if they are caught and interrogated. So I came up with this idea."

He handed a hand written note to Kind who almost instantly began laughing.

"You really had me going for a while, Alex. I thought you were serious. This is a child's code."

But he stopped laughing when he saw Alex wasn't laughing with him. Alex had an earnest look on his face as he explained his invention. Kind's jaw dropped open as he stared anew at the note.

"My God, this is astoundingly brilliant."

He reached for the telephone and called in one of his best cryptographers. When he arrived he handed him the note.

"Alex developed this. Can you tell me the message hidden here?"

The man looked up in astonishment and he too began laughing.

"Is this someone's idea of a joke?"

"Just tell me," insisted Josh.

"It's a kiddy's code, it says, 'Meet me at Elm Street on Sunday at the usual time.'"

"Read the code again, this time drop words two and four and transpose letter three for two in each of the remaining words in a sentence. Tell me what your children's code tells you now."

He wrote the new message on a pad of paper and his open mouth indicated his utter amazement.

"They are on to you – clear out now," he read. "Alex that is the most ingenious thing I have ever seen. Does it works with all messages?"

"The simpler the better. So if the message is sent by Morse code and is intercepted by the enemy, I hope they will do as you did and identify it a child's code, then discard it as a ruse. But the recipient will understand."

"Brilliant, absolutely brilliant! With your permission, Josh, I'll call SOE and have this put this into effect immediately."

"Please do so but keep this top secret here at Bletchley and only inform our most senior team."

He quickly left the room, still shaking his head in astonishment.

"So this was your idea of a holiday?" demanded Josh in a tone intended to infer disapproval.

It failed to accomplish its intent. His eyes shone with admiration.

"It passed the time between reading books," responded Alex modestly.

During the next few days, Alex received knowing looks and pats on the back from the seven other members of the top team.

His reputation was instantly elevated from a highly prized member of Bletchley to star quality. But soon he was back to twelve hour days working as though nothing unusual had happened.

It was the following year, June 1943, when again, Josh called him to his office. He asked Alex to close the door behind him. That put him on immediate alert. Josh's door was seldom closed. When Josh didn't exchange any pleasantries but merely told him to sit, Alex was instantly on very high alert. Josh only tended to speak in terse language when he was very angry or deeply worried. And now he was worried.

"SOE has a problem, one that is causing us to lose too many of our agents. They want one of my best men to go out into the field and assist in finding a traitor. I believe you have all the necessary requisites for this job. I don't have any of the details of this mission. They insisted the man they require must be a genius with codes and preferably a young, fit man, therefore I selected you. I am to escort you to London where you will be briefed. But let me make one thing perfectly clear, Alex. You do not have to accept this assignment. It sounds exceedingly dangerous."

Josh Kind's facial expression coincided with his deeply concerned tone of voice. His sense of duty to his country had forced him to choose Alex since he best met all the requisite specifications. But he didn't like the potential adverse consequences of his decision.

Alex noted his concerned tone and merely nodded his understanding of the assignment with its inherent danger. Ironically his heart beat a little faster as he instantly recognized the possibility of a new, exciting, journey.

"Let's see what it's all about, Josh," he said as calmly as he could.

Next day they drove to London and when they arrived at the appointed address they were ushered into a rather small meeting room. The gray paint on the walls seemed to have been there for decades and was badly faded. Even the table and chairs were flimsy and chipped.

'If this room is symptomatic of the SOE, then this country is really in trouble' thought Alex.

There was only one occupant. He was not dressed in a uniform, but an elegant business suit. He did not rise from his chair at the head of the table and didn't offer a handshake. His entire personage was at odds with the shabby surroundings. His bushy eyebrows, silver wavy hair and steely blue eyes, combined with his strongly built frame, made it clear he was an important member of the SOE. He wasted no time in getting down to business. One more sign he was a busy important man.

"Good afternoon, gentlemen. For today's meeting you may call me Mr. Smith. Do sit down and help yourself to coffee. It was very good of you to come. Let me make one thing clear at the outset, Lieutenant MacMillan, I have read your file and believe you would be ideal for this job. However it could be dangerous and you must not feel compelled to accept it."

He looked at Alex with raised bushy eyebrows, waiting for a response.

"I understand, Sir."

"Good. Then I'll give you a brief outline of the job, and should you decide to accept, I'll excuse Dr. Kind then give you full details of the next steps."

He looked at Josh for an acknowledgement. Josh nodded his head in understanding that he should not linger.

"After Singapore fell in February last year, we had several of what we called 'stay behind units' stationed in Malaya. Quite a few are still operating there, and I may say, very effectively. Some are hooked up with Chinese guerrillas and are causing no end of grief to the Japanese. One of our most prized units has recently lost several of its men during raids. We believe they were betrayed and the only possible explanation is there is a traitor in their midst, who has been giving their codes to the Japanese. And even though our unit changed code after an ambushed raid it didn't take long until they were again ambushed. They have been unable to detect the traitor and have had to cease sending coded messages to other units. Therefore they are more or less stranded and unable to continue their mission. I need someone to go there, set up secure codes and in the process unmask the traitor."

His blue eyes never left those of Alex all the time he spoke. They were almost hypnotic.

"One more thing you must remember at all times, Lieutenant."

Alex returned his stare with steady eyes, sipped his coffee, and waited.

"Up until now only two other persons apart from me knew of this mission. Obviously, there is now a third in Dr. Kind. The other two are the unit commander and the Chief of Operations for South East Asia, based in Ceylon. All others in Malaya will be led to believe you are going out there to augment the unit's fighting strength. If word got out you are a code expert it could reach the ears of the Japanese. You will have to work out a suitable cover story with the unit commander when you reach Malaya. But discuss your mission with no one but him and the Chief of Operations in Ceylon! Are you clear on that, Lieutenant?"

Mr. Smith's voice only rose a few decibels but its intensity seemed to grow enormously as it reverberated around the small room. Once again his blue eyes bored into those of Alex who did not flinch but again only nodded his head.

"One more thing, actually a very important thing you must consider in coming to a decision, Lieutenant. Getting into Malaya will be dangerous enough but assuming you manage that and complete your mission, it may be impossible to get you out. You see, once the traitor is discovered and dealt with, his Japanese masters will know of this as they will not get further information. I am guessing they will call in reinforcements and launch an all out hunt for the unit. The Japanese commander in North Malaya must be very pleased with the results he has achieved by his ability to infiltrate this top unit. I have no doubt his superior in Singapore has received glowing reports from him. Therefore when he is no longer able to anticipate our unit's activities, and begins to suffer serious setbacks, it will be a black mark on his reputation. And loss of face is a life threatening thing to a Japanese senior officer. That's why it may well be impossible to get you back out. You will probably have to wait out the war."

Smith had clearly noted his stern gaze had been met by the unwavering one of Alex. That greatly pleased him. He was even more certain this was the man he wanted.

"I hope I haven't painted too black a picture but I don't believe in sugar coating missions."

"I appreciate you frankness, Sir."

"Well what do you think? Are you going to help me?"

Before Alex could respond, Dr. Kind spoke. He was more concerned than ever for the safety of his young associate.

"May I just say something before you answer, Alex? You have done outstanding work for us at Bletchley. This mission sounds even more dangerous that I had imagined. I would strenuously like to reiterate you are under no obligation to accept it. Your current work is already saving countless lives and is of the highest priority. You are not required to risk your own."

"Thank you, Josh. The people at Bletchley have done marvelous work in breaking many of the German codes, particularly those of the U-boat fleet. Shipping is now reaching our shores in an ever increasing quantity. The Atlantic is much, much safer now. However I can't help but be moved in listening to Mr. Smith talk of all those brave men have done in Malaya for almost two years. Hiding in the jungle in what must be extraordinarily difficult conditions and living in constant fear of discovery. I can't turn my back on such sacrifice if I can be of real assistance. I have to give it a try."

Alex turned to face the man sitting opposite.

"I will give it my best shot, Sir."

"Good man," said Smith with a beaming face.

"However I need Dr. Kind's assistance."

The beam left Smith's face and was replaced by a look of confusion at this request.

"I don't understand?" he said.

"Is there a member of the unit who speaks Japanese?" asked Alex before responding.

"Yes, a few of the guerrillas do and Benson does."

"Excellent! It seems to me that as I will probably spend years in Malaya, I could be of more use if I could crack the Japanese codes. And from my rudimentary knowledge of Japan, they use three alphabets. One is Kanji, utilizing Chinese characters; another is hiragana using discreet Japanese characters of which there are, I believe, forty seven basic ones. And the third is katakana which uses the same sounding characters as hiragana but written differently. And again as I understand, only katakana is used for foreign words including names of people and places."

Now Smith's face showed total admiration at the knowledge of this young man.

"Yes, I believe that's correct. But what are you getting at? Where does Dr. Kind come in?"

"The Japanese will undoubtedly send their messages by a coding machine, rather like a typewriter. I don't believe they will use an English keyboard. And as they will doubtless refer to places in Malaya in their transmissions – foreign words to them - they will most probably use a katakana keyboard. I would like you, Josh, to find out if my assumption is correct. And if it is, make me one. Also I would like one of our coding machines to take out there. And I would like you to construct two fake ones."

Now Smith's jaw dropped and his mouth gaped open. He quickly closed it.

"Why do you need all these machines?" he demanded, annoyed at Alex having taken charge of the situation.

"I think that's better kept secret. Let's just say in my opinion they are absolutely necessary and leave it at that," he answered with a touch of devilment in his voice.

"Now look here, MacMillan, don't dare talk to me like that," blustered Smith.

"I believe you had better give Alex what he wants if you really want him to do this dangerous job," interjected Josh.

Smith relented and as he quickly thought of it, he was secretly delighted at his new recruit's rapid grasp of the spy's guiding mantra – need to know.

"Very well, I agree. Would you please have those items delivered to me as soon as possible, Dr. Kind?"

As he watched Alex whisper something in Josh's ear as he bade him farewell, Smith's face changed again to a very solemn one. He knew the man he had just recruited had little chance of surviving his mission, even with all the items he requested. The jungle of Malaya was a deadly place. If the Japanese didn't get you then disease often did. And this young man would only turn twenty three next month. Smith had sent several men on dangerous missions - missions from which they had not returned. He had not become hardened to this, but had learned to live with it. There were always casualties in war. His face had regained its composure when he again sat opposite Alex after Josh's departure. His previous annoyance had totally dissolved.

"This is the program. You will have three weeks training with us in London. During this time you will learn all about the people you will be working with in Malaya. And we will give you a crash course on the country, specifically the area where you will be located. We will include a few useful phrases in Malay and Hokkien, which is the dialect most frequently used by Chinese in North East Malaya. And we will add a little Japanese. There is no time to give you in depth language lessons, but I'm certain you'll pick up more when you're out there. Also you will learn all we know about the enemy: the senior officers - the troop strength - their location - and their behavioral characteristics. Of course you will receive an up-to-date briefing upon your arrival, but for now this information will give you a pretty good initial appreciation of the mission. And last but not least, you will get a few lessons in the craft of espionage. Following all that you will have another two weeks getting fit and learning to use the various weapons you will have to be prepared to use out there. Have you heard of Achnacarry Castle?"

"No, Sir, I'm not even sure I can pronounce it," he replied with a grin and a shake of his head.

Smith's face creased with a broad smile. This young man's humor would be an asset. He had seen too many initially acceptable candidates later become overly stressed in this line of work, and it inevitably led to disastrous results. One could never be cavalier but a sense of humor always helped to balance the scales of danger and tension.

"Well let me tell you this; you will not only learn to pronounce it but you will wish you had never heard of it. It is in the Highlands about fifteen miles north of Fort William and is the center of our commando training."

"Commando training?"

"That's right. You have to be prepared to fight in addition to doing your cypher work. Better to be prepared now than sorry later."

Alex gulped, this path to this new journey had suddenly become much steeper than he had expected.

Chapter Seven

The three weeks in London were exhausting. He had become inured to the twelve hour days at Bletchley but fourteen hour and even a few sixteen hour days proved to be almost too much. At the end of his training he again met 'Mr. Smith'. They sat in the same room where they first met. The décor had not improved and its gloomy atmosphere only added to the tiredness Alex felt. At least there was hot coffee and Alex sipped it appreciatively.

"Well Lieutenant MacMillan, I am told you have been an exemplary pupil. You impressed our trainers. Well done lad!"

"Thank you, Sir."

The lack of even a scintilla of enthusiasm in Alex voice and his drooping shoulders were signs of his exhaustion. They were not lost on Smith.

"I know it was a grueling three weeks but it'll prove to be invaluable when you reach Malaya. Believe me."

It wasn't that Alex disbelieved him. He just didn't care. All he wanted to do was sleep.

"Looking on the bright side, since you survived it well, you have a fair chance of surviving the commando school at Achnacarry."

That comment brought Alex wide awake.

"A fair chance?" he echoed unable to hide his dismay.

"I have to tell you that not every recruit survives Achnacarry."

"Can you be more precise and define 'survives', Sir?"

"Oh I am not referring to fatalities. We have only had a few of those," replied Smith in an altogether unconvincing tone. "No, I meant that of all those who enter the program, about one third wash out. They just can't take it. It's a combination of physical *and mental* stress."

"And what happens if I wash out? Do I go back to Bletchley?"

Alex had a hint of wishful thinking in his voice.

"I'm afraid not. We really need you in Malaya. Anyway the program at Achnacarry is a modified one. You are not training to be a full-time commando. We only want you to be able to take care of yourself should the need arise. I have given MacTavish strict instructions not to disable you in any way. He can be a bit of an ogre and sometimes allows his enthusiasm for his job to get the better of him."

Now Alex was truly concerned.

"Listen, Sir, I may wish to reconsider this *opportunity* you have given me."

"Sorry, we're past that stage now. You accepted this mission and we have given you top secret information on our operations in Malaya. There is no going back."

Smith's voice was icy, matching the intensity of his steely blue eyes.

"But I already have top security clearance at Bletchley and have signed the official secrets act. I can be trusted."

"Once again, I am sorry. You may have clearance to be a code breaker but in my line of work that doesn't cut the mustard. We deal in life and death. There is no way out. Many more good men will die unless you do this job efficiently."

Alex received the message loud and clear. It was either go forward or the very best he could hope for was to spend the rest of the war in solitary confinement. That was the best case; he didn't dare contemplate the worst. The words he had heard previously reverberated around his head. 'You will be shot.'

"By the way from now on your name is Alex Murdoch. We always keep an agent's first name and his same initials. If we gave an agent a new first name and he failed to respond when someone called it out, it could lead to disaster. Oh and you are still a lieutenant. The surname change is a necessary precaution, I am afraid. In my line of work trust is a rare commodity therefore being hyper suspicious pays dividends. I can't be certain of the loyalty of every man under SOE control therefore it is prudent to send a Lieutenant Murdoch on an undefined mission than an Alex MacMillan whose name may be traced back to Bletchley Park."

For a reason he couldn't explain, that comment really struck home. And Alex came to fully appreciate how deeply he had now become involved in this mission and, of greater significance, just how important it was to the SOE. He shivered a little and attempted to cover this by drinking more coffee. But the ever observant Smith noticed his reaction.

"I told you this mission was dangerous and you agreed to help. My men in Malaya need your skills to survive. So let's get on with it, Lieutenant Murdoch," said Smith brusquely.

Although he had suspected it previously, Alex now knew for certain that this man who called himself Smith was used to sending men into situations from which they probably would not return. He could not afford to be sentimental. He had a job to do and in war one had to accept risk and casualties.

"One of my men will escort you to the airfield. You will be flown to Fort William and driven from there to Achnacarry. I'll see you in two weeks and give you your final instructions."

Smith stood, indicting the meeting was over. And once again he did not offer his hand but merely walked to the door. Outside a man in army uniform waited and led Alex to a large black car with comfortable seats. The driver had the back door open and the escort sat beside Alex. The escort had just started to talk when he noticed Alex was already asleep. Forty minutes later he had to waken him.

"We're here, Lieutenant. Have a good flight."

Actually the turbulence made the flight very bumpy almost the entire time, but once again Alex didn't notice. He slept all the way. He was met at Fort William by a corporal dressed in the uniform of the Black Watch Regiment. The cold air of the highlands brought Alex fully awake and he pitied the kilt-clad corporal. But he didn't seem to mind and chatted amiably to him during the short drive to Achnacarry Castle.

"Ah understand Sergeant MacTavish is goin' tae take charge o' yer trainin' personally. Lucky you, an' ah don't think. He's one o' the few men whose bite is actually worse that his bark."

The corporal laughed heartily at this and the feeling of anxiety that Alex had in the pit of his stomach, shot up. It was confirmed when they arrived and were met by a five foot ten inch bulldog of a man also dressed in a Highland uniform. He glared up at the six foot two inch Alex.

"Ah can see ah'm goin' to hae one helluva time tryin' to get this lang dreep o' water intae shape," he muttered to the corporal. "Take him tae the barracks."

Then, before leaving, he addressed Alex for the first time.

"Be up an' dressed at five o'clock sharp. Ye'll find yer gear in the barracks, Surr!"

Alex decided not to make an issue of the slur over his height or the obvious delight MacTavish displayed in being able to order superior officers to do his bidding. He was here to learn things which could save his life and if that meant putting up with an obnoxious sergeant, so be it. He was on the parade ground next morning at five to five. At exactly five o'clock MacTavish appeared. Alex came to attention, returned MacTavish's salute and called out, "Good morning Sergeant! Lieutenant Murdoch reporting as ordered!"

That shocked MacTavish momentarily. Most officers who came for training made it clear from the beginning that they held a superior rank - usually in a supercilious tone. Of course that only irritated MacTavish and he found ways to exact revenge. But this young man was properly clad and did not display any superior manner towards him.

"Right then, let's start off wi' a nice warm up jog. Does five miles sound about right tae ye Lieutenant?"

There was a note of sarcasm in his voice but Alex responded immediately and with equanimity.

"Whatever you say, Sergeant."

If that attitude in any way caused MacTavish to be a little more lenient, it was definitely not apparent to Alex. At the end of the day he ached in places he didn't even know he had muscles.

Halfway through the fourth day a corporal rushed out onto the course. "There's an urgent telephone call for you, Sergeant. It's from London."

When MacTavish returned Alex thought he saw disappointment on his face. And for the rest of the first week his training was slightly less grueling. Alex reckoned the call must have been from Smith for an update and to remind MacTavish not to be overzealous. He did not wish Alex to return a cripple.

The second week was to be devoted to weapons training and hand-to hand fighting techniques. Alex lost count of the number of times his body was smashed to the ground. Still he didn't attempt to pull rank and chastise MacTavish. Even the irascible Scot was impressed by this.

"Ye huv done no' bad, Lieutenant, no' bad at aw'. The morra' bein' the last day, ah'll gie ye a few wee additional tips on fightin' that I learn'd masel'. Ah hope they'll be useful tae ye. Yin o' them is how tae use a knife. A gun is always a useful weapon, Surr, but in the jungle it's often important tae be as quiet as possible an' the knife is the weapon o' choice."

It was only when he was gratefully climbing into bed that night Alex realized these extra tips were probably MacTavish's way of showing his appreciation of his conduct during the two week program.

At the conclusion of his training he stood in front of Sergeant

MacTavish and stared directly into his eyes. When MacTavish spoke, Alex detected a noticeable change in the sergeant's voice.

"Congratulations on successfully completin' yer trainin', Lieutenant. Ye did verra well," he said as he came to attention and saluted smartly.

Alex returned the salute.

"Thank you, Sergeant MacTavish."

The sergeant seemed to be debating his next move. He admired this young man. In particular he had a high regard for he fact that he didn't bellyache about the training. And - most importantly - not once did he pull rank and refuse an instruction. At last he made up his mind and stuck out his big hand.

"Guid luck tae ye, Surr. It hus been a pleasure."

Alex grasped the hand and held it for several seconds, even though it was like having his hand in a vise. Then with a final wave, he climbed into the car to head for the airfield. He happened to glance back and was astounded to see MacTavish still standing at rigid attention and saluting. He remained that way until the car turned a corner and was out of sight.

Only then did he realize a bond had been forged between them. Not so much one of friendship, but more of comrades-in-arms.

Now he was beginning to feel like a real soldier – a badly bruised and aching all over soldier – but a soldier nevertheless.

Chapter Eight

He had two more days in London filled with final briefings. That was when he first heard of Force 136, a British led sabotage and intelligence agency operating in several countries of South East Asia. One of the leaders of the Malayan branch was Major Freddie Spencer Chapman. His briefing officer gave him details of Major Chapman's achievements since being left behind after the fall of Singapore. Alex was spell-bound by what he heard. It seemed impossible to believe that someone could have survived the incredibly difficult conditions of the jungle, much less accomplish all that Chapman had in creating havoc among the Japanese conquerors. However having its codes compromised had severely curtailed the activities of Force 136 in North East Malaya. His job was to report to an off-shoot team of Major Chapman's main group, led by Captain Chesterton and rectify that situation.

One of his last briefings was conducted by a Major Thomas Pugh, a Welshman with a delightfully lilting voice. To Alex, that was the only delightful facet of this tall, gangly, thirty year old man. His body twitched frequently which appeared to set off jerks from a head that was way too large for his narrow frame. His flaxen hair lay flat on his head, glued in place by hair cream which gave off a strong but not unpleasant odor.

Below his high forehead, two hazel eyes were set far apart and magnified by his thick glasses. The wire frames of which were so tight they had left deep furrows along the sides of his head and on the bridge of his long nose. During their opening conversation, Alex got the distinct impression that Major Pugh was extremely intelligent. Maybe his head had to be so large to house his large brain.

Alex had to concentrate diligently on the words being said to avoid being distracted by the twitching Pugh. It appeared as though he had a persistent itch he couldn't reach to scratch. Worse still it was contagious, and Alex had to sit on his hands to stop them scratching at a non existent itch on his own body.

Pugh looked directly into the eyes of Alex.

"Landing in Malaya is going to be tricky," explained the extremely serious-faced major, with understatement that was about to become all too clear to Alex. "Several of our previous landing areas have been discovered by the Japanese and are now heavily guarded. And a submarine can't get too close to the other unguarded areas of the shoreline due to the shallow waters and multiplicity of small islands. I'm afraid you will have to paddle ashore in a dinghy for quite a long distance. Obviously you would be an easy target for an enemy machine gun if they happen to be in the neighborhood."

'If that is *tricky*, I hate to think what his idea of difficult is,' thought Alex.

"I can't tell you who will meet you; we believe it will be one of the British officers accompanied by Chinese guerrillas. Anyway you'll recognize whoever it is by the passwords exchanged when you land. And most probably there won't be a Japanese patrol nearby as you will only set out after the code flashed from the submarine receives the correct response."

"I understand," replied Alex, his anxiousness definitely not assuaged by Pugh's attempt to pacify him. "What's the password?" he asked tersely.

"You will say, 'Do you like chocolate?' And the correct response will be, 'No, I like lovely lemony lollipops.'"

Alex stared open-mouthed at the officer, thinking it was either a joke or Pugh had lost his marbles. But the man maintained his serious mien.

"Force 136 chose that because the Japanese can't pronounce the letter L. They say it like an R. So if you hear, 'No, I rike rovery remoney rorripops,' shoot, then run like hell."

The bespectacled officer's face broke into what was intended to be a smile. However it more resembled a gas pained grimace which Alex thought more appropriate. He left that particular meeting in a state of giddy nervousness.

On his final day, before leaving for the aerodrome, Alex sat in the same dismal gray room with Smith. After only a fifteen minute meeting, Smith sat back in his chair.

"Well we have made you as ready as possible in the short time we had available. From all accounts you acquitted yourself well. I can only remind you yet again how vital your mission is to the efforts in the Far East. By the way, the special gear you requested is in the car along with all the other things you are to take with you. And here is a confidential letter from Dr. Kind. Good luck, Lieutenant *Murdoch*. You won't forget your new name will you?"

"No, Sir. But didn't *you* forget something?"

"What did I forget?" exclaimed the normally self-confident Smith.

"To advise me that if I ever speak of any part of this mission, I will be shot," said Alex with a wicked grin.

"I'm pleased to note you remembered that," responded Smith with a straight face.

His look unsettled Alex more than a little. Either Smith had no sense of humor or the threats of shooting were real.

'Don't these fellows ever think of anything else but punishment,' he mused.

"Well goodbye, Sir."

"Goodbye," replied Smith, not rising from his chair.

Alex rose, disappointed at the coldness of Smith, and walked to the door. He was turning the handle when he heard Smith softly call out his name. He turned and was startled to find Smith right behind him; their noses were no more than six inches apart. He hadn't heard a thing. Smith must have moved as stealthily as a cat.

"One last piece of advice," said Smith austerely, "on this mission, you must never again turn your back – on anyone."

Then before Alex could leave, Smith did the totally unexpected – he held out his hand. Alex shook the proffered hand.

"Best of luck, Murdoch."

"Thank you, Sir."

In the car, Alex thought about his meeting with Smith and realized he had been taught a truly valuable lesson. Having someone sit opposite you at a table and tell you to watch your back was advice one might remember or might forget. But turning to be nose to nose with the steely-eyed Smith, who had crept up silently behind him, was something he would never forget. It would always remind him not to turn his back on anyone during this mission. This experience was to play over and over in his mind in the future.

He opened the letter from Josh Kind and in doing so wondered just how confidential it had remained. He believed Smith would have steamed it open and carefully closed it again. Alex was delighted to see it was in the code he had devised. He quickly deciphered it.

Josh had used his great supply of sources to confirm the assumption of Alex regarding the Japanese code machine keyboard was correct and enclosed a schematic of it. He also indicated the changes they had made to the two special British code machines to render them useless. And he had added a particularly useful complex feature, one designed to aid Alex in uncovering the traitor. They were now very sophisticated fakes. Alex smiled to himself and said a silent prayer of thanks to Josh.

He closed his eyes but found it impossible to sleep. Too many thoughts coursed through his mind regarding his upcoming mission in Malaya and unfortunately, most of them were dismally negative. He hadn't realized the car had stopped, so deep in thought was he. However his reverie was abruptly disturbed when the driver opened his door and spoke to him.

"Here we are, Sir. I'll load all your gear in the aircraft. Have a good flight, Lieutenant."

"Thank you, Corporal," he replied but in his negative state of mind even the driver's last words of well wishes seemed to have a dreadful finality to them.

Upon boarding the converted air force plane, he noted there were three other passengers. Two of them were obviously friends and sat together chatting. After only exchanging a brief greeting Alex chose to sit alone. He had been warned by Smith not to get too chummy with any of the passengers.

"Friendships begun on a long, tedious, flight can lead to slips of the tongue. And it is imperative that under no circumstances must you discuss any part of your mission. In my line of work it is an unfortunate characteristic that you must always start out by trusting no one."

Almost immediately after he was seated the chief pilot came into the cabin.

"Our first leg will take us well to the west. We need to be as far away as possible from the German fighters operating out of France. I'll be flying low to avoid detection but in case we run into trouble I'll have to maneuver quite violently. So keep your seat harnesses securely fastened until further notice. Our first stop will be Casablanca. There we will refuel and take a rest. Then we fly across North Africa to Cairo."

Alex noticed the third passenger, in the uniform of a major, stiffen as the pilot said this. His attention was momentarily drawn to the man's face which showed traces of severe burns. Obviously signs of battle injuries and he briefly wondered where they had been incurred. He quickly looked away and listened to the pilot's further explanation of their flight plan.

"Again we will stop for several hours in Cairo before beginning the longest leg of the entire journey, to Karachi, and another stop. From there you head straight to Colombo, Ceylon. We have three pilots on board and we change crew in Cairo. There are plenty of sandwiches and a good supply of coffee and tea. Feel free to help yourselves. Buckle up and we'll get underway."

The pilot taxied out to the runway, revved the engines, released the brakes and the plane roared into the night. As the wheels came up Alex softly murmured a prayer.

"Well my new journey has really begun. God give me the strength to carry out this mission in a manner which would make my dad proud."

Chapter Nine

Alex's mental and physical capabilities had almost reached their limits during his training and he slept soundly for much of the flight. He had wakened briefly after a few hours, eaten a sandwich and promptly fallen asleep once more. He was still in a deep sleep as they approached Casablanca and was brought to a startled awakening when the wheels hit the runway.

"We'll be on the ground for three hours," announced the pilot after bringing the plane to a halt at the Royal Air Force base. "My co-pilots and I need a bit of a rest. And we have a lot of fuel to take on. You may have noticed the rather large auxiliary fuel tanks fitted on this plane. Those are necessary as our next leg and the following one are very long ones. A hot meal has been arranged here in Casablanca and you will have plenty time to stretch your legs. I strongly suggest you do so."

The two friends walked towards the cafeteria on the base. The third passenger could only walk slowly using a cane. Alex fell into step with him.

"Are you going all the way to Colombo?" he asked.

"Afraid so, it's a hell of a long journey. How about you?"

"Yes, me too. By the way my name is Alex Murdoch."

"Tom Shaw."

They shook hands.

"Mind if I join you in the cafeteria?" asked Shaw.

"It would be a pleasure."

Over dinner they chatted about home and their families. Shaw mentioned he noticed Alex had slept most of the way.

"You must have been through a tough period to tire you so much."

"Nothing terribly exciting, but certainly long hours. I needed the rest," he responded in a non-committal tone.

When they finished eating, Shaw suggested they take the pilot's advice and walk for a while.

"That's if you don't mind my slow pace," he added.

"Not at all."

Major Shaw had turned out to be the type of person Alex liked. Judging from all his ribbons and medals he had obviously had seen a great deal of action yet he was unassuming in his manner. As they walked he talked animatedly about his joy of fishing and walking on his beloved hills of Yorkshire.

"Shan't be able to go as fast now," he said ruefully, tapping his leg with his cane.

"Sorry about that, but you seem able to get around fine," responded Alex, not wishing to pry into the reason.

Shaw sensed this and was grateful. He decided that having made reference to his injury he would tell this sympathetic lieutenant about the cause. He paused, striving to control his emotions before beginning.

"This is my first time back in Africa since I was wounded. I was a tank commander in the Eighth Army. My tank took a direct hit from a Panzer at El Alamein. Most men in my crew were killed. I spent six months in hospital undergoing surgery and treatment for my burns. I noticed you saw my reaction when the pilot mentioned Cairo. El Alamein is just one hundred and fifty miles from there. If we hadn't stopped Rommel from taking Cairo, the Nazi's would now have total control of all shipping through the Suez Canal and, more importantly, most of the oil in the Middle East. That would have been a disaster too great to contemplate."

He paused again, and Alex noticed the dampness in his brown eyes.

"We lost a lot of good men in that campaign," he said in a tremulous voice.

"They didn't die in vain," said Alex sympathetically. "As you said, it would have been catastrophic if Germany took all of North Africa. But you should know it was an enormous morale booster for everyone in Britain. We had been taking a shellacking and everything seemed to be going against us. You and your comrades gave us our first significant victory. We owe all of you a great debt."

It was apparent Shaw appreciated those words. He gulped air before speaking. He gazed into space almost in a trance as he did so.

"Fate has so many twists and some of them are destined to be remembered for ever. For example, El Alamein is a tiny dusty town which almost no one in the world would ever have heard of had it not been for that battle. It happened to be a strategic location on Rommel's march to Cairo. It has the Mediterranean Sea on its north and the impassable Qattara Depression to its south. General Auchinlech chose it as the Eighth Army's last stand."

"Auchinlech was replaced by Montgomery, wasn't he?" asked Alex.

"That's another of fate's twists," responded Shaw. "You see, when Churchill decided to replace Auchinlech, he chose Commander William Gott for the job. But on his way out to take command, his plane was shot down by a Messerschmitt and he was killed. It was only then Montgomery was selected. And he turned out to be exactly the right man for the task. He could be a pompous, strutting little peacock, and his egotistical attitude greatly annoyed many senior officers – particularly among our Allies. However one of his greatest assets was his delight in mixing with the troops, during brief respites in the action. He would wander among them urging them on in his colorful language spiced with every known swear word. And they loved him for it. Of course he had the good luck to have the new Sherman Tanks arrive just in time for the El Alamein battle. At last we had a tank to match the Panzer."

Shaw stopped his stare into space and focused on Alex.

"Oh, forgive me, I didn't mean to bore you by going on about my experiences."

"No, no, it was extremely interesting. I can only admire your courage: not only in battle, but in fighting so determinedly to recover from your wounds."

"Thank you, Alex. But courage in the Army is a fickle attribute. Soldiers are awarded medals on the recommendation of their superior officers. They are the ones who determined whether or not a particular act was courageous. And such judgment varies from officer to officer. I have come to the conclusion that courage is when one first takes a little time to evaluate all the options of a situation, and if the chosen option gives one at least a fifty-fifty chance, one leans on one's training tinged with experience and goes for it whole heartedly. Any man deciding to charge single handedly against a heavily fortified enemy position, when he had an option to escape and fight another day, is an act of unthinking stupidity, not courage. You shouldn't sign up for your country's justifiable war with the aim of dying for your country. You should do so to help your country win."

Shaw's words indicated the anguish he had undergone and the time he had spent reflecting on all of this during the past six months. It was the first time he had dared to talk about this to someone, and it had a cathartic effect on him. His lips formed the slightest of smiles.

"After all that pontificating, I think I'll have another beer before we board. How about you, Alex?"

"Sounds like a good idea."

Once back on the plane, Alex resumed his previous seat still thinking of Shaw's words. They had provided one more lesson that he was certain one day would be valuable. He remembered Smith's admonition not to let a friendship struck on a long flight cause him to let slip anything related to his mission. Therefore he decided to sit by himself. Major Tom Shaw was exactly the type of person to whom he felt he could confide anything.

On his way back to his seat, Shaw stopped to speak briefly to Alex.

"If you don't mind I'll sit by myself, Alex. The flight over North Africa is likely to be an emotional one for me. Too many memories of good friends lost in battle. I'm afraid I would not be very good company."

"I understand, Tom."

It was a long, long flight to Cairo. At last, the pilot announced they were starting their descent and were passing over El Alamein. Alex looked over at Major Shaw and saw he had his head in his hands and his shoulders were shaking.

They circled the airfield and landed with a few bumps. The plane bounced back in the air twice before the wheels returned to the ground. Perhaps this was a sign of the tiredness the pilots must have felt. The chief pilot came back to speak to them.

"As I told you in London, we get off here. You will have a new crew from here to Ceylon. We wish you a safe journey and the best of luck in whatever your new endeavors may be. Also I should mention there will be three other passengers joining you here. It should only take about an hour to refuel and again a hot meal has been laid out for you in the cafeteria."

The three new passengers were sitting inside the cafeteria when Alex entered with Major Shaw. One of them rose immediately and almost ran towards them with short mincing steps. He was quite a small stocky man with close cropped hair and eyes that seemed too close together for comfort. This along with his sharp nose gave his face the appearance of a hawk. But now it was wreathed in a happy smile.

"Tom," he called out. "It's wonderful to see you again. How are you?"

Shaw's eyes lit up.

"George, it's good to see you. I'm coming along. It's been a slow process. Are you going to Colombo?"

"Yes, I've been posted to the Far East Planning Group."

"Me too, that's great we'll be together again. Oh, forgive me; this is a new friend I met on this flight, Alex Murdoch. Alex this is George Goodman. We were in the same tank command out here in Egypt."

"Are you heading out to Colombo also, Alex?"

"I am," responded Alex, not offering any further information.

"Let's find a table and get something to eat," interjected Tom before his ebullient friend, George, could ask any further questions.

Major Tom Shaw was an observant person. When he first spoke to Alex, He had noticed the lack of any ribbons or army unit insignia on his uniform. From that he knew Alex had not been in any theater of war and guessed he must be in Military Intelligence. He didn't want his garrulous friend asking awkward questions. He needn't have worried; George's total attention was focused on their service together in Egypt.

When the announcement was made for them to board, Shaw turned to Alex.

"I hope you won't think me rude if I abandon you to sit next to George. We have a lot of catching up to do."

"Not in the least, Tom," replied Alex.

The solitude suited him and he read most of the way to Karachi. As promised by the pilot this was another long flight. After refueling and having the opportunity to stretch, they again boarded for the final leg of the journey. This time it was not a lengthy flight and at long last they were in Colombo, Ceylon. They all stood on the tarmac as their luggage was unloaded.

"It was a pleasure to meet you, Alex. And thank you very much for letting me bend your ear in Cairo. You were the first person I really opened up to about that horrible event. Good luck in whatever you are assigned to."

"I truly enjoyed talking to you, Tom, and wish you all the best in your new duties," Alex replied in a sincere tone.

He admired this brave soldier and couldn't help wondering if some similar fate awaited him in Malaya. They were collecting their luggage when a car drove up. A tall imposing general, accompanied by a major, got out and marched over to the group and looked straight at Alex. Everyone jumped to attention and saluted. The general briefly returned the salute.

"Lieutenant Murdoch?" he inquired with authority.

"Yes Sir!"

"Will you kindly come with me?"

Once again all the others saluted. Goodman recognizing the general's insignia whispered to Shaw.

"Ah, your friend is one of those," he whispered conspiratorially.

Tom Shaw nodded and gave Alex a final wave goodbye.

"Sorry to whisk you away so abruptly, Murdoch, but you only have time for a quick shower and change of clothes before you must board the submarine. I am here representing my superior officer, the Chief of Operations for the Far East. I have some last minute instructions for you. I hope you are not embarrassed if I give them to you while you shower and change," he said, once they were seated in the car.

"Not at all, Sir," replied Alex although he had hoped to get a good night's sleep.

He had wisely considered it imprudent to tell a general that he had spent an exhausting three bloody weeks in London, followed by an even more strenuous two bloody weeks in Scotland followed by an almost unimaginably bloody long flight and he bloody well wanted to sleep in a warm comfortable bed. Instead he forced his tired, foggy mind to clear, and kept an acquiescent attitude. When the car stopped he dutifully fell in step with the general. They marched to a building guarded by a cordon of tough looking commandos. Their task was to prevent anyone else from entering. One of the guards opened the door and they went straight into the shower room. The general began his briefing as Alex undressed.

"You will not be met by Captain Chesterton. We have been told by a messenger who just managed to get out of Malaya that he has had to relocate to a safer camp in Perak. I'll point out the approximate location on this map when you're dressed."

Alex had studied maps under the tutelage of Smith's trainers in London. This information filled him with dismay as he knew the great distance he would have to cover between his landing spot and Chesterton's camp. And he instinctively knew most of it must be done on foot.

The general waved the major away before continuing to speak to Alex as he stepped into the shower.

"Being isolated without the use of coded radio signals has thrown a spanner in the works of our chaps out there. You can't imagine how much your assistance will mean to them. Every hour brings Jap search parties closer to them. The only way all of Force 136 has managed to survive for so long is by going on the offensive and attacking Jap outposts. That tends to keep the enemy close to home to guard their positions. But to be successful our attacks must be coordinated between our chaps and the guerrilla forces. If there is no threat of an attack the Japs can afford to send out more men on search and destroy missions. Now perhaps you understand why we must get you there soon."

The general's words shocked Alex. Smith had told him that only four people knew of his mission. Now it was obvious that the general made five. He wondered how many others knew. He decided it would be wise to be very careful in what he said to this man – general or no general.

"Yes, Sir, I see that," he said as he reluctantly turned off the stream of comforting hot water. "Has it been impossible to send messengers between the various groups out there?" he asked as he began drying himself.

"That's been tried, but with very limited success. I fear there are a few traitors within the groups and they have managed to inform the Japs of the paths taken by the messengers. It is difficult to know who to believe among some of the local population. There is a long lasting animosity between the main ethnic groups in Malaya. Therefore, one group complaining of the alleged actions of the other is not always reliable information. That makes identifying traitors even more difficult. You will soon learn in Malaya that the Chinese and Malays are not chummy and one is quick to blame the other for anything going wrong.

Most, but not all, of the guerrillas are Chinese and are communists. There are some brave Malays among them. It has always been easier to recruit good men from both groups to Force 136 when we are inflicting losses on the Japanese. Not unnaturally, people are drawn to a winning side. However, when it's the other way round, we suffer desertions. Men tend to lose their courage under such conditions and find it much safer to return to their villages and towns. Worse still, those deserters will, for the right amount of money, become informants."

Alex reached for his new clothes as the general spread out a map on a bench.

"As you know this is where you land. And here is Chesterton's camp. You will be met by a small band of men. I need you to take several packages and a few letters to Chesterton. The guerrillas who meet you will carry the heavy gear. Well that's about all. Major Bradshaw will take you to the sub. Good luck, Murdoch. We are depending on you."

Those words bounced around in his head.

'How can so much depend on me?' he wondered. 'I'll be lucky to survive a week in the jungle's inhospitable environment.'

Negative thoughts had once again invaded his mind. They were intensified when Major Bradshaw dropped him off at the pier and he got his first close up look at a submarine. His first impression was that it was an extremely vulnerable looking outsize toothpaste tube.

The executive officer was waiting for him. He saluted smartly to both Alex and Bradshaw before instructing the waiting sailors to put all the gear on board. Bradshaw said goodbye and got back in the car.

"Lieutenant Murdoch, welcome to HMS Yarborough. I'm the executive officer, Charles Waddell. I'll take you straightaway to meet the captain."

Alex took one more anxious look at this incredibly small looking tube of metal before following Waddell into its innards.

He had never felt so much anxiety in all his life.

Chapter Ten

For a second, but only the most fleeting of seconds, his mind played a cruel trick on him and he thought he was in his own comfortable bed in England. His eyes opened and the painful truth crashed down on him with the awful realization he was still inside this claustrophobic tube. After two days he had still not acclimatized to its environment. However, if all went well he would leave his confinement tomorrow night. But then instead of claustrophobia, an affliction of the mind, he would be faced with real danger, not to his mind, to his body. Life threatening danger!

'If all goes well,' he thought wistfully. He had had plenty of time during the last two days to wonder why he had allowed himself to be talked into this crazy deal. 'No,' he had thought, 'it's not merely crazy, it's bloody insane. My chances of survival are slim. What the hell am I doing here? At least I've had two weeks of commando training but will that be sufficient to stave off the well trained Japanese troops in the Malayan jungle?'

Not for the first time had such thoughts entered his head and they always resulted in an emotional see-saw. On the one hand the omnipresent dangers and on the other hand the chance to make a real contribution to his country's war. The initial euphoria at being asked to leave his desk and take on a job which could have a truly positive impact on the war against Japan, had all too quickly given way to those thoughts. On the way from London to Ceylon they had frequently invaded his mind. But his sense of duty had always prevailed and he had pushed the negative thoughts out of his mind - at least for a while. But now he was within two days of life threatening danger and those damned thoughts lost their theoretical quality. This was the real thing and he was scared. He was too inexperienced to know that even the bravest most experienced soldiers wavered before undertaking a mission into unknown territory.

'If you keep thinking the worst, it's bound to happen. Try to stop being

51

a coward and go do something you are skilled at – working with codes. If you can find the traitor, thereby saving the lives of truly brave men, your father would have been proud of you.'

His mental admonishment lessened his negativity a bit. He slapped his head, rubbed his hazel eyes, ran his fingers through his dark brown tousled hair and swung his legs over the edge of the bunk. He reached for his towel, slung it over his shoulders and headed for the showers.

"Good morning, Alex. Bumped into anything new?"

The question from the navigation officer from Newcastle was accompanied by a loud guffaw. The six foot two inch frame of Alexander MacMillan had found it difficult to always remember to duck as he traversed the submarine. It was almost as difficult as remembering his new name for this mission – Alex Murdoch. He would have liked to use his real name but the spy service had decided otherwise. However not ducking produced a more physically painful end-result. His head still had bumps to prove this point. Nevertheless he grinned good naturedly at the jibe.

"I only bumped into a simpleton Geordie," he shot back using the name given to all those from Newcastle.

That riposte brought howls of laughter from the sailors on duty. Alex's inherent sense of humor and normally ready smile had made him popular with the crew. He may not have realized it but these irrepressible qualities were stronger than his morbid thoughts. By taking a liking to him the crew helped make this underwater voyage bearable. In August 1943, British submarine crews did not usually take kindly to strangers on their boats; most particularly those whose mission led them into highly dangerous waters. Strangers usually got in the way of their routines and continually asked stupid questions. But Alex was accepted by them. And the fact that this young man was going behind enemy lines in dangerously hostile territory only increased their respect for him.

They had set out from Colombo on the west coast of Ceylon and traversed the Bay of Bengal. These waters were relatively safe to navigate, and they did so without incident. However they were now approaching the Malacca Straights between Sumatra and their destination on the coast of Malaya. And these straits were extremely dangerous. They were narrow and constantly patrolled by the Japanese navy. One could now feel the tension aboard the boat escalate during the last few hours.

After showering and shaving, he returned to the cabin he shared with the Executive Officer. His Newcastle tormentor met him with a grin and thrust a steaming mug of tea in his hand.

"Thanks, Sam," Alex said appreciatively. They had struck up a friendship almost immediately and their banter only served to intensify the bond between them.

"When you're dressed the skipper would like to see you, Alex."

"Right away."

He quickly dressed and still clutching his mug of tea, knocked on the wooden frame of the curtained captain's cabin.

"Enter."

"You wished to see me, Sir?"

"Ah, yes. Come in Alex. Things are apt to get pretty hectic tomorrow so I thought we should go over our plan and our contingences one final time."

"Yes Sir."

"Just wait a minute while I call the Exec."

As if by some form of ESP, the Executive Officer appeared in the doorway clutching a map.

"Ah, Charles as usual you're just in time - come in."

"I thought you might want to review things and tomorrow could be a bitch."

"This man reads my mind, Alex. It's dashed worrying. I hate being predictable."

"I only know your routine because we've been together for two years, skipper. And, as for being predictable, there are thousands of tons of enemy shipping, including naval vessels which would disagree with that."

"To get right down to it," said the Captain, modestly waving away the reference to his exemplary record. "As I have told you before, Alex, my instructions are to get you close to the Malayan coast just south of Alor Star. As you know, last month the Japanese gave the four northern states of Malaya to Siam as a token of appreciation for their cooperation in the invasion of Malaya. The spot you are aiming for is now under Siamese control and may not be so heavily patrolled. But I wouldn't bet on it. According to intelligence reports, Japan has kept an airbase at Alor Star and will no doubt have kept some form of surveillance at points along the coast. And just to make things more interesting for us, fifty miles south of your drop point is the island of Penang where there is a significant base for submarines of both the Japanese and German navies."

He paused to allow that point to sink in.

"Sorry to put you to so much trouble," was all that Alex could think of saying.

"That's okay. It's what we're paid to do. Your target landing spot is here."

He pointed to a spot on the map on his desk. It was a small inlet about seventy miles south of the border that had been Siam before the four northern Malayan states were gifted. The map still referred to the country north of Malaya as Siam as did most of the free world. The fact that a fascist government had, four years ago, decided to change the name to Muang Thai, or Thailand, was not recognized by Great Britain. The Captain looked at Alex while still pointing to the tiny inlet.

"And I am to do this without endangering my boat."

His emphasis on this remark had a chilling affect on Alex.

"I understand, Sir. Should there be enemy activity once I am in the dinghy, you cannot come to my aid. I'll be on my own."

Alex's perception that his worried thoughts about his mission made him a coward, were not shared by Captain Carson. He was used to assessing men. It was one of the qualities that made him a successful leader. He had studied this young man for the past few days and now as looked into Alex's eyes, his judgment of him was confirmed. He knew he was looking at a brave man.

"Sorry son, but those are my orders. I am not privy to your mission details. I can only assume it is vitally important otherwise the British Royal Navy would not risk my boat and crew. One last thing, we have a coded message to flash to shore once we arrive. If I do not receive the correct response I am to offer you the opportunity not to proceed and to return to Ceylon with us."

"I would like to request you to do me a favor, Captain."

"If I can, Alex, what is it?"

"Do not flash that signal."

Both the Captain and the Executive Officer were stunned.

"For heaven's sake why not?" exclaimed the Exec.

"I have two reasons," replied Alex calmly. "The first is it will give away your position to any unfriendly watcher on shore. Any light out at sea can be seen from a long part of the coastline. It's too big a risk on the lives of your men. The second relates to my mission. I can't give you details but I can tell you I have been informed there are probably traitors in the guerrilla forces. As of right now I do not believe I should trust any message until I can verify its source. I'll just take my chances when I get ashore. Hopefully I'll be met by the right people."

"And if not, what then, Alex?" asked the Exec in a hushed voice.

Alex gave him a wan smile.

"Then I suppose I'll just have to use my initiative like any British Officer," he replied with a slightly sardonic voice that was tinged with anxiety.

Captain Carson was quiet for a while during which time he amended his appraisal of this young man. He was not only brave but very smart.

"Okay, Alex, I will disobey my orders. But if you report me I'll hunt you down and bust your nose."

He made the last comment with a smile and extended his hand which was shaken with a firm grasp.

"That's all, son."

Alex saluted and left the cabin.

"By God, skipper, I suddenly feel really proud to be on the same side as that man. First he worries about our crew, and only then does he worry about himself."

"Yes, Charles. You've got that right. By his unprepossessing manner, I don't think Alex realizes how special he truly is. But whatever his mission may be, I feel certain he will do our nation proud."

Chapter Eleven

The next evening two fateful orders were issued.

"Charles, take us to periscope depth," the captain instructed the executive officer.

He peered through the periscope, carefully scanning the surrounding area and only when he was entirely satisfied did he give his next command.

"Surface the boat, then lower the dingy and load it with all the Lieutenant's gear."

The long trip to Malaya had come to an end.

'One journey completed and another about to begin,' Alex thought.

When the submarine had surfaced the captain shook hands with Alex.

"Good luck, Lieutenant."

"Thank you, Sir," replied Alex and saluted.

There were shouts of goodbye from the crew.

"Don't go bumping your head on low lying branches," called out the Geordie navigation officer.

Because their new found friend did not rejoin that remark with a typical smart quip of his own, it indicated to the crew it was now time for danger in the life of Alex. There was silence as he climbed the ladder to the hatch. A few of the crew crossed themselves and muttered a prayer for him. On deck he was met with an inky blackness. There were no lights opposite the submarine but in the distance to the north he could see the lights of Alor Star, the capital of the state of Kedah where the Japanese had a small fleet of airplanes. His target location was a tiny bay ten miles south of there.

"We are a little past the appointed time, but you should be all right," said the Executive Officer before he stood to attention and saluted.

Alex returned the salute before setting out to paddle the almost two miles to his destination. He had not gone far before hearing the gurgling of the sea as the submarine submerged. He was now completely alone.

When he had covered three quarters of the way he stopped paddling. He had two reasons, firstly to listen intently for any sound and secondly to get his bearings. His eyes had become adjusted to the darkness and he could make out the coastline quite clearly. He identified what he thought was the target inlet and quietly paddled to a spot about one hundred yards south. He dragged the dinghy into the shrubbery close to the water's edge and made sure his revolver and knife were easily accessible. He remembered Sergeant MacTavish's advice during one of his night training sessions. Interestingly his memory had stored it in plain English and not in the broad brogue of MacTavish.

"Never creep around in the dark with your hands full of weapons. You are apt to stumble and drop one of them. The noise will alert your enemy and could lead to your death. Keep you hands free as long as you can."

He moved stealthily, in a crouched position, through the shrubbery. He had been told to meet his welcoming party on the south side of the inlet. He hoped to come up behind them and ascertain they were in fact friends. He stopped and listened for a few minutes. His heart was beating rapidly and he had the insane thought anyone close must be able to hear its thumping. Suddenly he heard someone whispering. He edged a little closer. Now he could make out the words.

"The submarine should have signaled by now, Sir. It is already half-an-hour late."

"We will give it another hour, Chin. If we see nothing by that time we will leave. That gives us plenty of time to reach our first stop before daybreak."

Alex took a deep breath, took out his revolver, and spoke in a clear but low voice.

"Do you like chocolate?"

There was a clatter as someone dropped his rifle on the rocks at the shock of hearing a voice. This was followed by several moments of silence during which Alex's heart pounded even faster and he readied his revolver. Then to his immense relief he heard the reply, "No, I like lovely lemony lollipops."

Those words that had sounded so idiotic to him in London were like sweet music to his ears now. A man stood up twenty yards from him.

"What happened to the submarine's signal?" he asked in an accusatory tone.

"Sorry, I didn't want to take any chances," replied Alex walking towards him.

"You're a canny one," was the response in a decidedly Scottish accent. The name's Steve MacDougal. And hopefully you're Alex Murdoch come to join our merry band."

"That's right; I'm pleased to meet you," he said extending his hand. MacDougal grasped it firmly.

"I'm happy to know you and pleased you have decided to join us. We can use all the help we can get."

Then MacDougal introduced him to the other three members of his party. All were Chinese. Their names were Chin, Wang and Yuen.

Then he asked Alex, "Where's your dinghy?"

Alex led them to his landing spot. The packages were unloaded and strapped to strong Chinese backs; the tracks made by the dinghy were erased from the sand; and it was deflated and also taken along. As Alex slung on his backpack he sniffed the air. Since meeting up with the team he had been aware of a distinct odor.

"What's that smell?" he asked MacDougal.

"What smell?" MacDougal responded.

"It's like incense."

"Oh, I see what you mean. That's from the joss sticks the Chinese use to ward off mosquitoes. It's a particular type of joss stick that is extremely effective. They light the tips and stick the long stems in their hair. The only trick is not to let them burn too long otherwise they'll set your hair on fire," said MacDougal with a grin. "Here try it. Believe me you need as much protection as you can get out here. Malaria is not a pleasant disease."

He lit two and positioned the long ends in Alex's hair at the side of his head.

"There you go. But you must remember not to use them when we are on a raid. The Japs know about them and one whiff gives your position away. Are you ready to move out?"

Alex nodded his head gingerly so as not to dislodge the joss sticks.

"We have a four hour trek ahead of us. Don't talk unless absolutely necessary," warned MacDougal.

After two hours of fast walking through the rice fields of Kedah, MacDougal called a halt. He signaled by holding up the outstretched fingers on both hands that they would take a ten minute rest. He came close to Alex and whispered in his ear.

"You seem to be fit, are you feeling okay?"

"Yes, no problems."

"We're about to cross the railway line. We'll do so one at a time. I'll go first then you. As we've made good time are you up to walking for an extra hour? The further away from Alor Star we are, the better."

"I can manage that."

MacDougal left him to pass on the word to the others. At the end of the break he rose and led the way. Once over the railway the pace increased. This didn't worry Alex as the ground was flat and they were still using the paths along the edges of the many rice fields. The sky was turning from black to gray when they halted beside a narrow river. They had actually walked an extra hour and a half which greatly pleased MacDougal.

"I didn't know what to expect from you in terms of fitness and whether or not you would be able to keep up so I had arranged a hide-out some miles back. But we can rest along the embankment of this river for the day. It's too risky to travel in daylight. The farmers around here are Malays; therefore, even the sight of my Chinese men would arouse suspicion. I've posted guards so you can get some sleep. The men will cut some of the vegetation along the river bank to make a cover from the sun."

In a remarkably short time, one Chinese man, Chin, who spoke perfect English brought him a cover woven from the tall reeds along the river bank.

"This will help prevent the sun from burning your white skin," he said.

"Thank you. You speak English very well."

"I went to an English speaking school where my father taught."

"Does he still teach?"

"No, he and my elder brother were killed by the Japanese. The idiotic soldiers who ravaged our area thought anyone speaking perfect English must be a British agent. I was not at home when they raided my parents' house otherwise I too would be dead."

"I'm sorry to hear about your father and brother. Where is your home?"

"In Ipoh. That's in the State of Perak, west of Pahang. I hope you can visit Ipoh one day. It is an interesting place. It's renowned for its famous huge caves nearby in the chalky hillsides, which are adorned with ancient paintings. It also has the best Chinese food in Malaya. But now you should try to sleep before it becomes too hot."

Alex slept well for six hours. When he awoke he was bathed in sweat. It was early afternoon, the sun was directly above them and the air was heavy with humidity. MacDougal came over to him.

"Welcome to Malaya; land of sunshine, rain storms, humidity, and of course, mosquitoes. Did you bring anti-malaria pills with you?"

"Yes I have mine in my backpack and I brought a large supply in one of those packages."

"Good man, take one now and I'll explain where we are going."

Alex offered pills to the others however they had their own. He put one in his mouth and gratefully accepted the canteen of water offered by MacDougal.

"You don't want to drink the muddy water from the river," he said. "Up in the mountains the streams flow rapidly and the water is clean, but not down here in the plains."

He then spread out a map.

"You arrived here, and we are now approximately here," he pointed out. "We leave at dusk and head to this road where we have hidden a small truck. It's the one we came up on. Then we brazenly drive south through Baling and on to Grik. There we will be met by another guerrilla group. They will take us in their vehicles to within forty miles of the camp. That's forty miles as the crow flies; the actual walking distance is much more. I'm afraid it's a devilish two day hike up the mountains."

"How about Japanese patrols?"

"Our guerrilla friends will give us an up-to-date report of Jap activity. There are several different guerrilla groups in this area. Most of them are communists. The communist movement was gaining a lot of support just before war broke out. The Japs were rightly worried about them and stamped out as many as they could find. The rest fled into the jungle."

"Are they all friendly to Britain?"

"Many are, because we are both fighting the Japanese. Some are only friendly when it suits them. And that's mostly when we can be useful to them by supplying them with arms. Unfortunately our communications with them have become more difficult of late, but our leader Captain Simon Chesterton will brief you on all that when we reach camp. We're glad you're here; we need all the trustworthy help we can get. We hope to again begin our raids on the Jap munitions supply depots. Every guerrilla becomes our friend when we share the spoils of these raids."

"Quid pro quo," said Alex.

"Exactly. But when this war is over and we have driven the Japanese out of Malaya, don't expect the communists to still be our friends. Their main loyalties are to Moscow or Peiking. They are not fighting the Japanese because we are at war with Japan. They are fighting them because they are occupying their country."

"Not a totally comfortable situation, is it Steve?"

"It's the old adage – the enemy of my enemy is my friend. But take away the common enemy and there is not need for friendship at war's end. Both the communists and Britain will want the same thing – control of Malaya!"

"Is that because of its rubber and tin?" Alex asked.

MacDougal looked at him appraisingly.

"You're well informed," he said. "And you're right. I was a rubber planter before the war and was recruited to Force 136 because I had a good knowledge of the territory. As a planter I know the value of rubber on the world market. I also know the value of tin. And Malaya is a leading supplier of these highly prized commodities.

That's what the Japanese are after. They desperately require both of them to feed their industrial requirements. And with Malaya's huge resources they can gain control of the world markets thereby holding many industrialized countries to ransom. This is all part of their desire to be a respected world power.

Before the war Japan came up with the idea of 'The Greater East Asia Co-Prosperity Sphere'. Under this slogan they promised to join other East Asian nations in overthrowing colonial rule. As the self proclaimed leader of this idea, they entered Korea, Formosa, Laos, Vietnam and Cambodia and much of China, ostensibly to aid the local population. But did they give those people freedom? – Hell no! They put them under the boot of Japan. Anyone disagreeing with Japan was wiped out. Just look at what they did in December 1937 in the then capital of China, Nanjing. They slaughtered over three hundred thousand Chinese.

And now they are up to the same trick here. They profess their only aim is to free the oppressed Malayan people from the yoke of the colonial power of Britain. But their real objective is to replace one colonial power with another – the Empire of Japan!"

Chapter Twelve

At mid-afternoon everyone stripped completely and bathed in the river. It may have been somewhat muddy in color but it was water, and it proved to be refreshing. With the soap that MacDougal had brought along they also washed their sweat-sodden clothes and left them on the bank to dry. That did not take long under the hot sun. At five o'clock a cold meal of rice and fish was served, then everything was again carefully packed and the ground scoured to ensure no trace of their presence was left. Being so close to the equator, darkness falls quickly in Malaya, and it was barely light when they set out. One of the Chinese, Wang, took the lead and once again set a rapid pace. They travelled through the night only stopping twice for a brief respite and a drink of water.

It was still dark when Wang stopped and held up his hand. Everyone crouched low to the ground, while Wang crept forward into the trees ahead. A few minutes later he returned walking upright.

"Everything okay," he said to MacDougal in Hokkien. That happened to be one of the phrases Alex learned in London.

"Let's go," instructed MacDougal and strode towards the copse.

The small truck was so craftily hidden that Alex didn't see it until Wang began pulling away the thick cover of branches. It was a beat up old vehicle with a canvas cover across the back section. Chin took over as driver with the third Chinese, Yuen, sitting beside him. Yuen had a sub-machine gun under his seat. Everyone else climbed into the back. The truck lumbered across the rough ground for half a mile until they reached the road. Those in the back sat with the canvas cover placed along the side of the tubular frame, but not fastened. If they should happen to pass another vehicle they would pull it over the top to hide them.

The road was smoothly tarred – one thing the British did well in Malaya was build a good road system – and soon Alex dozed off. An hour later his sleep was disturbed as he heard weapons being made ready and the cover was pulled over the top as the truck began slowing. A rifle was thrust into his hands.

"This is the border between Kedah, which is now under the control of Siam, and Perak in Malaya. Keep your head down and be very quiet unless I give the order to fire," whispered MacDougal.

Two men dressed in Siamese Army uniforms approached the truck. Two others stood by the barrier blocking the road. All had rifles. The senior soldier, a sergeant, stopped at the driver's open window and addressed Chin.

"Where are you going?"

Chin was delighted to note he was Malay and not Siamese.

"We are returning to Grik, Sergeant," he said in Malay. He did so in a subservient tone.

"What do you have in the truck?" demanded the sergeant.

"My family has very little food so we went to Kedah to buy rice. It is severely rationed in Malaya by the Japanese," whined Chin.

"Let me see."

Chin got out of the truck and as he did so four fifty Malayan dollar bills happened to fall out of his pocket.

"Ah, Sergeant, I think you dropped something," whispered Chin.

The Malay looked down and hurriedly scooped up the money which he surreptitiously counted before stuffing the notes in his pocket.

"Let them pass," he called out to the two at the barrier.

Once safely well past the barrier, Alex let out a sigh of relief.

"Phew, that was a close call."

"Not at all," responded the unruffled MacDougal. "It is not unusual for the Chinese in North Perak to cross the border to buy foodstuffs in what is now Siam. The border guards expect a bribe and are happy to let them pass once it has been paid. It's only when there is an officious Siamese officer present that trouble can occur. Usually that results in an even greater bribe but sometimes the Chinese are refused entry. Tonight we were lucky, the guards were all Malay, conscripted into the Siamese Army. We have about another hour to go, so try to get some more shuteye."

Alex tried, but initially found it impossible, as he contemplated the border incident. There would be many things he had to become accustomed to in this new land. And the one he had just experienced, of being in a group ready to gun down border guards, was one of them. Somehow that seemed a long way from life in the idyllic countryside at Bletchley Park. He knew there would be many others and once again he hoped he would be up to the challenge. Some time later the constant snoring of his companions proved soporific and his eyes closed. He fell into a deep, deep sleep and dreamed of his happy childhood living with his mother and father.

"Wake up, Alex, we're here," whispered Steve with some urgency as he shook his shoulder.

Alex had trouble focusing on his surroundings, so real had been his dream. It took another few seconds before he fully realized he was no longer in England.

"Sorry, Steve," he muttered. "I guess I was really out for the count."

"That's okay, but we need to get going. We'll spend some time in a safe location, where we'll be briefed by the communist guerrillas. If they give us the green light we will be driven to the starting point of our trek."

"Will the guerrillas come with us?"

"No," said Steve with a grim look. "They are our friends but not our *trusted* friends. I don't want them to know the exact location of our camp. Are you ready?"

"I'm ready," responded Alex.

He hoped his voice did not betray the anxiety he actually felt at the thought of going into the jungle. That was a completely unknown environment to him and one filled with all types of dangers.

Chin stopped the truck in a backstreet outside a warehouse with double doors. Yuen hopped out and unlocked the doors. Chin drove in, shut off the engine and they all got out.

"You check ahead, Wang," commanded MacDougal, again speaking in Hokkien.

Wang padded out silently while they waited in the warehouse with guns at the ready. He returned in less than five minutes and merely nodded his head. At MacDougal's signal Wang led them along darkened back streets until they reached what looked like a general store. They entered through the unlocked back door and were met by three Chinese.

The leader was slightly built, five feet eight inches tall and wore a white singlet with black shorts which clearly displayed his thin bowed legs and knobby knees. The other two were similarly dressed as though it was a type of uniform. They had rifles slung over their shoulders, however the leader was unarmed. His flip flops clacked on the wooden floor as he came forward to greet MacDougal. His hair was sparse and almost pasted to his scalp and his intensely brown eyes appeared shifty to Alex. It was only when he spoke in Hokkien to MacDougal that Alex noted he was missing several teeth and those he had were brown with tobacco stains. His appearance did not give Alex a first impression of dislike, but definitely one of distrust.

His loud aggressive tone so shocked Alex that he involuntarily reached for the pistol strapped to his side. Seeing this MacDougal quickly signaled to him that there was no problem and sharply responded in the same tone. Alex could only understand a few words in the rapid-fire staccato exchange. The communist leader then shrugged in what seemed to be an agreed bargain.

"Don't be concerned, Alex, Cheung was up to his old tricks again by renegotiating the price of the truck rental. Weren't you Cheung?"

The Chinese flashed a grin showing his remaining stained teeth and executed another shrug of his shoulders. He obviously understood English very well.

"Must make little money. Am a poor man. Must feed family," he said in his broken English. "Please to sit," he added pointing to the metal chairs.

He nodded to one of his men who understood the signal and handed out cups of hot Chinese tea that had been sitting on a nearby table. He then faced MacDougal and began speaking to him in Hokkien. As he did so his beady eyes watched Alex face closely in an attempt to determine whether Alex understood Hokkien. Although he had picked up a few words here and there, he kept a blank look on his face as he stared into space, apparently disinterested. Alex had been strenuously advised as part of his training in London not to let anyone see he understood any of the languages he had been taught.

"Better to keep your knowledge secret. You may pick up something you were not meant to hear. Always keep the advantage," had been the advice of his trainer.

After a minute, Cheung spoke in his broken English.

"You no speak Hokkien?" he asked Alex.

"I'm afraid not."

"Maybe I speak Malay, better for you?" he persisted.

"No, I don't speak that either."

"S'cuse me I speak MacDougal Hokkien. Easier for me."

"By all means."

The Chinese nodded, apparently satisfied and continued talking to MacDougal in Hokkien. But Alex got the impression that Cheung's broken English was an act. And from the look on MacDougal's face he fancied he had the same opinion.

They talked for about fifteen minutes. And only when MacDougal appeared satisfied did he bring out a wad of money and pass it to Cheung. The careful Cheung counted the money and nodded his head with contentment. Then MacDougal motioned for Alex to join him at one end of the store's back room. He didn't have to involve the other members of his team as they had understood Cheung.

"Cheung confirmed that the Japanese still only have a very small contingent here in Grik. Their daily routine is to parade at seven when they raise the Japanese flag. Then they casually patrol Grik and the surrounding area. They never venture into the jungle, that duty is left to the main group based in Ipoh, about a hundred miles south of here. That group also parades at seven for about thirty minutes during which time they receive the day's instructions from the lieutenant in charge. The jungle patrols, there are normally two, then collect their gear and start out around eight o'clock returning by five, unless they discover something to keep them out all night. Cheung advised me that recently they have been intensifying their searches. The good news is if they only patrol during the day they will not come close to our camp. It is at least a two day trip from Ipoh and that is only if you know which direction to travel. The bad news is our first day of travelling could possibly bring us in close proximity with the Japs: particularly if they have been out all night and not merely on their normal one day search. We must be careful."

MacDougal looked at his watch, and then signaled the others to join him. He gave out instructions, first in English then in Hokkien.

"I'm afraid it's too late to rest, it will be light soon. We will be driven for about forty minutes then make our way to our base. If we make good time we will stop for the day at five and camp for the night. That should allow us to reach base camp before nightfall the following day."

The Chinese members of his team understood the reason for his equivocation. They knew everything depended on the new Englishman being able to withstand the pace through the jungle. There was no grumbling from the Chinese. They strapped the packages to their backs ready to follow MacDougal back to the truck. Cheung handed Wang a few provisions for their journey but did not accompany them; instead he left it to his two subordinates to escort the group.

As they walked back to the truck, Alex fell into step with MacDougal.

"I didn't get a good feeling about Cheung. For example I didn't buy his clumsy effort with his pigeon English. Do you trust him?"

"Oh, he's a crafty one for sure. And you're right; he can speak very good English when he chooses. That was just part of his act, mainly for the other Chinese. He knows he doesn't fool me. But to answer your question, yes I trust him. You see I know all about him. He owns a modest house here in Grik but he has two mansions - one in Ipoh and the other in Kuala Lumpur. In KL he keeps a second wife and has a Mercedes Benz in the garage. He also keeps a large amount of money under a false name in a KL bank. And – he has a stash of gold hidden in another location in KL."

Alex looked amazed.

"How did you learn all that?"

"I have a mole in his guerrilla organization. The guerrillas may be communists but they are Chinese first and money talks in any Chinese dialect. I pay my mole to keep me informed. I haven't told Cheung all that I know, but once I did tell him that if he ever double crossed me I would make certain that the Japanese learned of his KL mansion. That would really arouse their suspicions and who knows what else they would discover once they began interrogating him. And just to punctuate that point, and stop him from thinking of ways to kill me, I told him I had left a letter detailing all of this with my boss to be opened at my death. So you see he has a vested interest in keeping me alive."

"Wow! I see I have a lot to learn about life in Malaya."

They had reached the warehouse and MacDougal only gave him a grin in response before he clambered into the back of the truck. The others followed, leaving Cheung's men to drive. Once they were seated the engine started up and they slowly proceeded back to the main road.

The first rays of dawn lit up the road as the truck stopped. The group stood at the side of the road as the truck did a ponderous u-turn and set out back to Grik. Yuen took the lead into the brush at the roadside. Chin followed in front of Alex. MacDougal came behind and finally Wang.

"Just stay close to Chin and for God's sake do not stray from his path. And don't touch anything. Several of the jungle plants aren't people friendly. When you think you can't go on any further just raise your hand and I'll call a halt. Don't talk unless it is a dire emergency – remember there will most likely be Jap patrols in the neighborhood."

As though he was not nervous enough, those words only diminished what little confidence Alex had.

Chapter Thirteen

The initial march was over uneven ground but with very little undergrowth. Alex had no trouble keeping up with the fast pace. However they hadn't gone far before they came to the first obstacle - a river.

"This is the Perak River," Chin told him. "Up here it is very narrow and quite easy to cross. Further south it is much more difficult."

Alex eyed it with some concern. It certainly wasn't very wide but it was flowing rapidly.

"Hold on to this end of my rope and when I get to the other side, you follow. It will not be dangerous. But if you wish, tie the rope around your waist for greater security."

Alex decided to do so before he waded in. It was provident he had tied the rope around his waist, for when he was half way across a large branch of a tree came floating at him rapidly. It tangled around him and spun him around as though it wanted to dance with him. He finally managed to disentangle himself from it and proceeded across with no further trouble. Nevertheless this incident disconcerted him, particularly as it happened so early on the trek. He was trembling slightly when he climbed up the river bank. There was no sign of concern on Chin's face. In fact he and Yuen had broad grins on their faces. Apparently they seemed to think it funny. In time he would learn that Chinese humor and British humor were often poles apart.

Once all were over, the terrain soon changed. The flat ground gave way to a gentle upslope and the underbrush grew larger and thicker. Yuen picked his way carefully and when the bushes became too thick he hacked his way through with his parang – a long curved blade. After an hour the gentle upslope became less gentle and the bushes changed into trees. The jungle was almost upon them. All the trees were covered in vines and Alex noted that in some trees their braches had reached the ground and had taken root. He had read of this phenomenon occurring in mangrove swamps but had not expected in on mountainsides. The slope of the ground had increased sufficiently for him to realize they were now on the beginnings of a mountain.

In between the trees were ferns and other plants, the tendrils of which clung to his legs. When this became a problem for him, MacDougal called a halt and handed him a parang from his backpack.

"Be careful with that; it's extremely sharp. Don't miss," he warned.

After another hour, Alex found the trek was becoming quite strenuous but as yet he wasn't laboring. It was then Chin pointed with his parang to a thick leafed bush and whispered, "Very dangerous."

On closer examination he saw the sharp needles on the edges of the leaves and nodded his understanding. An hour and a half later, Yuen suddenly threw up his hand and everyone stopped. Just as suddenly Yuen motioned for everyone to take cover. Alex copied Chin and flung himself under a large bush. MacDougal landed beside him and put his finger to his lips for Alex to remain quiet. It was then he heard it - the unmistakable sound of an aircraft engine flying low overhead.

"Damnation, it's a Japanese spotter plane," hissed MacDougal in his ear. "They use old single engine, slow aircraft. They are searching for movement in the bushes and trees. If they see anything they radio to the foot patrols. It must mean there is at least one patrol within five miles of us. We'll have to be extra careful. It also could mean they were tipped off to be on the lookout for us. Cheung did mention they had intensified their patrols. Once we are further along the trail the trees are taller and their planes are not nearly as effective."

After five minutes MacDougal signaled for Yuen to start out once more. And although the overhead plane had initially caused Alex some anxious moments, his body found the five minute rest to be very welcome. He started out feeling much better and was able to keep up for the next two hours without too much trouble.

MacDougal gave the signal to halt and they ate the cold food from Wang's backpack. It was now one o'clock.

"We'll rest for another thirty minutes then push on until just after five. At that time it will become too dark in the jungle to go on any further. I'm a bit concerned one of the Jap patrols may not return to their camp. They may stay out. And if we attempt to go on through the jungle in the dark we would make too much noise and risk giving ourselves away."

MacDougal said this in English first then repeated it in Hokkien for the benefit of Yuen and Wang. All three of the guerrillas nodded their heads in agreement. When their thirty minute rest was up, MacDougal told Wang to take the lead. Chin still took second place with Alex next and MacDougal behind him. Yuen brought up the rear. Alex recognized he was being sandwiched between the two English speakers in case some warning was necessary.

The path was now much steeper and Alex was really grateful when they at last stopped for the night.

"You did remarkably well, Alex," complimented MacDougal.

"To be honest I don't think I could have gone on much further, Steve," he replied.

"I'm afraid we will have to eat cold meat and cold rice again. I can't risk a fire in case the Japs are somewhere out there."

"That will be fine."

They ate in silence then talked in whispers for a while. Alex saw Wang and Yuen disappear into the jungle. They reappeared fifteen minutes later and signaled to MacDougal – a signal that Alex didn't comprehend. He waited for McDougal to enlighten him, but when he didn't, Alex thought it better not to pry. Instead he brought up a subject that had plagued his mind since he first learned this mission would take him into the jungle.

"Are we likely to run into any unfriendly creatures during the night?" he asked, trying not to appear too worried.

"Normally we would have a fire which keeps them away. Since we can't do that I'll have a guard posted throughout the night. Chin will take the first three hours, then Wang and finally Yuen."

"I don't mind taking my turn," said Alex with more bravado than he actually felt.

"Thanks, but you don't have the experience to recognize the danger signs. You'll probably hear a few noises during the night as the jungle animals go hunting. But don't be concerned. Whoever is on guard will keep us safe."

That was another of those confident assurances that only made him more nervous. The Chinese made him a makeshift bed with branches and ferns. They would eschew such a luxury for themselves and sleep on the ground. Before going to sleep Chin took a large mosquito net from his pack and wrapped it around Alex.

"We can't use our joss sticks so you had better use this," he said.

Alex recalled MacDougal's warning that The Japanese might smell the incense if they were within range. He thanked Chin and settled down on his somewhat uncomfortable bed. He thought he would have trouble sleeping but that proved not to be the case. The strenuous trek had exhausted him. He was awakened by MacDougal shaking his shoulder and lifting up the mosquito net flap that covered his face. He had his finger to his lips requesting silence.

Alex didn't have to strain his ears to hear the loud noises.

"Elephants," whispered MacDougal with a worried look on his face.

"Wang has gone to patrol our perimeter. Better get out of your net in case we have to make a run for it."

The bellowing of the elephants grew louder and suddenly they heard a very different noise – it was a roar. To his astonishment Alex saw MacDougal's face break into a contented smile at this sound.

"It's only a tiger annoyed at having his hunt disturbed by the elephants. You can rewrap your net and go back to sleep. It's four o'clock; you can have another hour or so."

He wrapped himself in the mosquito net and clambered on top of his makeshift bed but he would not sleep again this night.

'Only a tiger,' he thought, 'and the bugger actually grinned at that. Good God, *only a tiger!*' and he shivered at the thought. He lay there staring into the darkness with wide eyes until five-thirty and it was time to get up.

"Sorry no coffee this morning as we can't light a fire," said Chin. "Try some of this cold Chinese tea. I'll get you some rice, I'm afraid we have no more cold meat."

The tea was really bitter but he didn't complain. He now fully realized that his life would be entirely changed for the foreseeable future. He should forget life as he had known it in England. Forget that he once had a comfortable bed inside a building and a bath and toilet and there were no elephants bellowing in the nearby woods and definitely no tigers wandering nearby. Oh and not to forget the other jungle experience he certainly hadn't enjoyed – the tearing of leeches from his skin.

'I suppose compared to those things, eating a slab of cold rice for breakfast isn't so bad,' he thought.

He looked around for the others but only saw Chin and Yuen. A few minutes later MacDougal and Wang appeared.

"Just been having a quick look around," said MacDougal. "Sorry about wakening you last night but it could have been serious."

"You mean a tiger wasn't serious?"

"Only one that has tasted human flesh causes a problem and there are very few of those."

"Then what would you call serious?"

"Elephants can be the most dangerous animals in the jungle. If they have baby elephants in the herd and you get too close, they will charge. And, believe me, elephants can move through this jungle much quicker than any man. Your only hope is to reach a high outcrop they can't climb. But as soon as I heard them I checked the wind direction and it was coming from their direction so we were safe. They couldn't pick up our scent. The second danger could have been from a careless Jap patrol disturbing them as they searched for us."

"Is that likely?" asked Alex.

Hopefully not; you see when they are on night patrol and have no reason to believe they are close to an enemy they light a fire to cook and to keep animals away. You may have noticed Wang and Yuen leave our camp last night after dinner."

"Yes, I did."

"They went a few hundred yards out in different directions and climbed the tallest trees they could find. They were looking for smoke from a Jap campfire. They didn't see any. But if the Japs believed they were close on our trail they wouldn't have lit one. That's why I was relieved when I heard it was a tiger that disturbed the elephants."

"Would I be correct in guessing there could have been a third danger?"

"Yes, and that would have been a panther. They are much better hunters than tigers and have no compunction in attacking humans if they have young to feed and have been unsuccessful in hunting. They are much more silent hunters than tigers. A tiger will grunt while hunting until it sees its prey. A panther won't make any noise. And if it had been a panther that disturbed the elephants its warning growl is distinct from the roar of a tiger."

"Thank you, teacher," said Alex.

"What?" exclaimed MacDougal, with feigned surprise.

"You have just given me valuable lessons in jungle craft."

MacDougal grinned with pleasure at the fact that Alex had paid attention to his detailed explanations. It was exactly what he had intended.

"Try not to forget them. They could save your life one day," he said.

Chapter Fourteen

If his first day in the jungle had been arduous, Alex found the second torturous. McDougal explained they had to set a rapid pace to reach the camp before dark. Although rapid was a relative term as they hacked through the jungle.

"I'm concerned by the increased activities of the Japs and I want to warn those at the camp. I am hoping we don't have to relocate our camp again. This one has stood us in good stead for almost six months and a lot of work has been put into it."

His concern was validated by the same low flying plane passing over them several times during the day. But as MacDougal had prophesized, it remained high above them due to the tall trees. It was dusk when they finally reached their destination. They all were exhausted, hungry and soaked in sweat. Alex was too tired to consider which affliction to address first. It was the seemingly indomitable, MacDougal who took command.

"First thing to do is get out of these clothes and clean up."

Alex followed his example and waded naked into the nearby stream which was surprisingly cold. Before scrubbing with rough soap, came the painful task of removing the leeches. After toweling himself dry he found that fresh clothes had been brought to them though those supplied to him were tight fitting on his large frame.

"Now I'll introduce you to the boss then a quick bite to eat then sleep. All the other introductions can wait until morning."

Although the cold stream had been refreshing, the aching he felt all over appeared to affect his mind. Alex could barely remember shaking hands with the boss and certainly had no idea what he had eaten before he collapsed into a gloriously comfortable camp bed.

The next morning Alex was awakened from his still deep sleep by MacDougal shaking his shoulder.

"Wakey! Wakey!"

"What time is it?" Alex asked guiltily, thinking he must have slept till noon.

"Seven o'clock," said MacDougal. Then seeing the look of disbelief on Alex's face at being wakened so early, he explained. "This is our normal camp wake-up time. It is better you get used to it from the beginning. Anyway after breakfast the boss wants to get started with your briefing. But before that you'll get at a tour of the camp and be introduced to the rest of our group."

As he was dressing Alex noticed four other camp beds around the walls of the roughly hewn cabin. Each had a mosquito net and a night stand. A small table with four camp chairs took up a central location. Last night he had been too tired to pay attention to his surroundings but now he was impressed by the skill it must have taken to chop trees into logs and build this cabin. Once dressed, he followed MacDougal out of the cabin. What he saw greatly impressed him. The camp consisted of another five cabins, a cooking area next to a large mess tent, a laundry area close to the river and what looked like a parade ground in the center. And at the edge of the parade ground was a flag pole that flew the communist flag. They walked to another large tent set back from the parade ground. Inside there was an impressive large table where two men were sitting. Alex noted the skillfully constructed wooden floor which formed the base of the large tent. One of the men rose and came towards him with an outstretched hand.

He was about five feet ten inches tall, with a slim but muscular build. His face was round and his brown eyes emitted strength and leadership. The skin around the edges of his eyes was crinkled and Alex thought that at some time in the past he enjoyed smiling. But now they had a steady gaze. As he approached he flipped back a lock of brown hair that had fallen over his forehead.

"I'm not sure you will remember me from our brief introduction last night. You were really bushed. My name is Simon Chesterton and I'm in charge of this unit. And this fellow sitting here is Anthony Benson but he responds much better to Tony."

Benson continued to sit at the table but waved a greeting.

"Welcome. Excuse me not getting up I've been under the weather recently."

Alex could see by his painfully thin frame and yellow-tinged skin that Benson was indeed unwell. His blue gray eyes had an inquisitive look about them. Alex got the impression they were those of a very intelligent person.

"Like many of us out here in this jungle, Tony is going through a bad patch with a recurrence of his malaria. And to make it worse he had just recovered from dengue fever."

"In Colombo I was given a quite large supply of medicines to deliver to you. Perhaps they will help," said Alex.

"Good man!" exclaimed Chesterton with such enthusiasm that it brought home to Alex just how desperately medicines were needed. He stole another look at Benson and saw the immense relief on his face. And Alex knew right there and then he too would require those medicines at some time. It seemed malaria was an unpleasant and unavoidable reality in jungle life.

"In the past we have been able to get supplies of medicines from the smaller Japanese posts we overran, but our recent communication problems have drastically reduced our ability to effectively conduct raids," explained Chesterton. "Tell you what, let's change our planned schedule. Why don't you get the medicines now, then we'll have breakfast before I show you around and introduce you to our guerrilla friends. I'm certain Tony would appreciate getting some medication as quickly as possible."

"Amen to that, oh great leader," said Benson in a husky, but obviously greatly appreciative voice.

By the time they reached the mess tent, the Chinese had already eaten and were sitting cross legged on the ground listening to a speaker who was gesticulating wildly as he spoke.

"Indoctrination," explained Chesterton. "Every morning they are preached to by Lee Sheng, the leader of the thirty three guerrillas in our group. He is extolling the virtues of the communist party."

"Doesn't that create difficulties for you?" asked Alex.

"Not today. But, at some point in the future, when the Japanese have been vanquished, it will be a very different story. The communists want what the Japanese and the British want – Malaya."

"Yes, Steve explained that to me. Does that mean we will one day be at war with those chaps sitting out there?"

Chesterton stopped walking and gazed pensively at the guerrilla band before answering.

"I'm afraid it probably does," he replied with real sorrow in his voice. "But before that, we have the small matter of surviving and doing as much harm to the Imperial Army as possible. Let's eat, I'm hungry."

With that he strode into the mess tent and sat down. Alex could tell from his manner that Chesterton had a real fondness for his guerrilla comrades.

Once they were all seated a Chinese cook appeared. He was a stocky man with a moon face and just the trace of a beard. The few wispy hairs hung about two inches from his chin. His solemn eyes were widely spaced and unlike other Chinese, they were so dark that they seemed to be more black than brown. Alex guessed he would only be in his late twenties. He carried a large tray with ease and placed a steaming plate of rice with some type of meat in front of each of them.

"It doesn't always do to ask what you are about to eat out here," said MacDougal with a wide grin. "But today you're safe. One of the lads shot a wild boar and we are lucky enough that there is still some left for us. Isn't that right, Wong?"

The Chinese did not smile; his face remained impassive as he answered.

"I always keep food for you, Tuan."

Alex would learn that Tuan was the Malayan word of respect meaning, sir.

"Wong worked with me on the rubber estate and is our chief cook. He has two assistants who are also quite skilled. In addition to being an excellent cook he is a very good shot. He's a good man to have with you on a raid."

Wong bowed at this compliment and returned to the kitchen area. He walked with a slight limp but this did not detract from his strong physique, his arms bulging below his short sleeve shirt.

Alex being keen to improve his knowledge of the peoples of Malaya, asked, "I've been told it is very difficult for a westerner to tell the age of a Chinese. They seem to stay looking younger than we do but when they reach about sixty they age very quickly. For example how old is Wong?"

"He's forty-five," replied MacDougal.

"Well there you are, I would have guessed he was much younger."

"Don't feel badly about that, it took me many years before I even came close to guessing their ages," said Chesterton. "But I have noticed that Wong has not seemed happy for quite some time. Is anything wrong, Steve?"

"I'm not sure, I asked him about that a while back but although he denied any problem he was not forthcoming with any reason. I'm guessing as he hasn't been back to his village for several months, he is missing his wife and son."

They ate their small portions in silence for a few minutes, before Alex had to ask something that was troubling him.

"When you said we were lucky to have wild boar, what do you consider to be unlucky fare," asked Alex with a decidedly uneasy edge to his voice.

It was Benson who responded.

"The Chinese really seem to like eating snake. I don't find it too bad. It just depends on what type of snake. Python is okay but some of the other poisonous ones I'll avoid. That's probably not rational, as, if they are prepared with care I dare say they taste very much like python. But I'd rather be safe than sorry. And when we are really desperate we have to eat monkey. The delicacy is when we are fortunate to bag a deer. But they are deucedly difficult to shoot. They are very timid and usually can spot us and be off before we even have a chance to raise our rifles."

"I suppose, out here in the jungle, beggars can't be choosers," said Alex philosophically as he cut into his boar meat.

The other three exchanged glances of approval at their new recruit's attitude. Soon enough he would learn when Japanese patrols were spotted within a ten mile radius of the camp, there could be no hunting with a rifle. Then they could go for days without meat of any kind.

When breakfast was over Chesterton led Alex over towards the group of Chinese. Lee Sheng was just concluding his sermon and there was a loud roar of appreciation from the audience. They started to rise but Chesterton quickly signaled for them to remain seated.

"Gentlemen, I am pleased to introduce you to a new member of our team. This is Lieutenant Alex Murdoch. Please help him become accustomed to our way of life. This is his first time in Malaya. So please be kind to him and do not indulge in some of your usual Chinese pranks, like putting a scorpion in his bed."

That brought a titter of laughter from the guerrillas who spoke English. However it sent a chill down the spine of Alex.

When Chesterton repeated his introductory speech in Hokkien for the benefit of those who didn't speak English, it brought a roar of laughter from the group and an almost universal slapping of thighs. That made Alex more worried although he joined in the merriment by putting a brave smile on his face. Chesterton then dismissed the men. The men left still laughing which caused Alex to wonder what mischievous prank they were cooking up.

"Alex let me give a personal introduction to the leader of our guerrillas. Please meet Lee Sheng."

"I am pleased meet you," said Lee Sheng in good, if a little stilted, English.

"And I am honored to meet a man who has done so much for his country against the overwhelming forces of the invading Japanese," responded Alex.

Lee Sheng flushed at this compliment and Chesterton allowed a little smile to cross his face.

'This man is going to do all right with Malayans,' he thought.

"Please to excuse me, I hope see you later. I must give men orders not put bad beetle in your bed."

With a grin on his face, Lee Sheng gave a slight bow and left.

"Your comments to Lee Sheng were nicely done, Alex. Now let's get back to the tent and you can tell me what your plan of action is. I'll just get Steve and Tony to join us. It's time they knew why you are here."

"I'd rather you didn't, Simon. My instructions were to speak only to you until we find out who is leaking information."

Chesterton bristled at this comment.

"Now let's get one thing straight right from the start. I've battled side by side with Steve and Tony for almost two years. And I can tell you without a shadow of a doubt that they are totally loyal. Yes, I know there are stories floating around concerning Britons working for the Japanese prior to the invasion. Personally I don't know of any such cases but my boss in the High Commission indicated he knew of several of them. I don't know if those bastards were ever caught but if they were I hope they were punished as spies. And by that I mean shot."

The vehemence in Chesterton's voice told Alex three things. He would defend the honor of his comrades to the bitter end and, he had a deep love of his country. And thirdly, he was letting Alex know in no uncertain terms that he was the boss of this group and his final considered decision on any matter was not open to further discussion.

"I accept all you have said, Simon. However, with respect, I must obey my orders."

Chesterton appeared to calm down.

"I've been in the army long enough to know I can't criticize an officer for obeying orders. So let's start out as you suggested with a private conversation. However as soon as I deem it necessary to involve Steve and Tony, I'll do so and take full responsibility."

"I would expect nothing else, Simon. You are in charge out here."

Chesterton looked at Alex as though he was reappraising him.

"I think you will fit in well and I hope we will not only be comrades but that we will also become friends. Now let's get started. This damned business of losing communications is playing havoc with my mission. They said you were an expert so let's see you prove it!"

The last statement told Alex the introductory pleasantries were over and it was time to go to work. His new journey was about to begin on this humid Monday morning.

Chapter Fifteen

When they entered the tent, MacDougal and Benson were sitting at the table. They joined them at the table and Chesterton turned to face Alex.

"You will find within the camp we normally are quite informal. People come and go as needs dictate. That is particularly true in this tent which is the main meeting place. Should there be an occasion for privacy we post a guard to request others not to enter."

"Does the same apply to the cabin?" Alex inquired.

"Not many meetings are held there, however men deliver laundry and occasionally a few other things. As you have already experienced we change our clothes frequently, so there are a few Chinese coming and going during the day. But while we are alone, perhaps I should give you a thumbnail sketch of our backgrounds. I don't know how much Steve has told you, so if I am repeating anything just stop me."

"I haven't mentioned anything, Simon, except I was a rubber planter. I thought it best to leave it up to you," said MacDougal.

Chesterton nodded almost imperceptibly and Alex took that as approval. He was not to be given too much information unless the boss thought it appropriate. Trust does take time to develop!

"Well starting with me, I trained for the army at Sandhurst and was posted to the High Commission in Kuala Lumpur as Military Attaché. This gave me license to travel around the country inspecting our military bases. When Force136 asked me to consider becoming a member of one of the stay behind groups I volunteered. Now Tony has an entirely different background. He is an academic. He was Professor of Philosophy at Oxford and was doing a stint at Singapore University when war broke out. He had become friendly with Spence Chapman, whom you will no doubt have heard of, and over several nights discussing war tactics, he so impressed Spence by his analytical skills, that he too was asked to join Force 136."

"What Simon really means is that Spence and I enjoyed many nights discussing the woes of the world while in an alcoholic haze. I am still not clear why I 'volunteered' but assume I was not totally sober. I have since decided to abstain. It gets one into too much trouble."

Benson said this with another of his wry smiles.

"Don't believe all that," said Chesterton. "Chapman knew exactly what he was doing in recruiting Tony. He has been invaluable in tactical analyses."

"Yes, once we taught the Professor which end of a rifle the bullet comes out of, he has been okay," chimed in MacDougal with a wicked grin. "And as for abstention, that's only because we can't get the bloody stuff."

"And as for our token Scot," continued Chesterton, "he knows more about the peoples of Malaya than anyone I have met. And *he does* know how to use a rifle. Equally important, by managing a rubber estate he has developed a leadership style with the local population which is respected by the guerrillas. They follow him without question."

MacDougal lowered his head in embarrassment. But Alex had already noticed his leadership skills and was just beginning to understand how important this was.

"Well that's about it. Steve, would you kindly have some of the men collect the packages that Alex brought and bring them here."

MacDougal nodded and went outside. They could hear him call out instructions in Hokkien. While they waited Chesterton asked Benson if he felt any better after taking medicine.

"It usually takes an hour to act and I'm sure it will work. Thanks again Alex, I really appreciate it."

"You should thank the men in Colombo. They seem to know what one needs in the jungle."

"That's true; many of them have had some experience. But thanks anyway."

Just then three Chinese entered with the packages. Alex recognized Wang and Yuen as two of them. Chesterton thanked the men and when they had gone he faced MacDougal and Benson.

"I would like to speak to Alex alone, chaps. Sorry but he has brought messages he was asked to deliver to me personally. I'll call you when we are through. And would you please post a guard outside, Steve?"

MacDougal and Benson exchanged glances but did not protest.

"We'll be in the cabin if you need us," said Benson unable to avoid keeping the testiness out of his voice.

"I hated doing that," said Chesterton when he was alone with Alex. I have never excluded those two chaps from anything as you could tell from Tony's tone. Well let's get on with it. What's your plan?"

Alex unpacked the coding machines and laid them on the table. He pointed to one of them.

"This machine has the very latest technology. It can transmit and receive. It also has terrific shortwave capability therefore you should be able to communicate with Far East Headquarters in Ceylon. And as you can see it can transmit in code."

"That's fantastic," breathed Chesterton. "But why did you have to bring four of them?"

"Let me turn this one around so you can see the keyboard."

"Good God, it's in Japanese," exclaimed an awed Chesterton.

"Correct. And it has built into it an unusually wide variety of wave lengths. This will allow us to tap into messages sent between Japanese locations. They will undoubtedly send out their signals in code but I can break them once the Japanese is translated. I've been told Tony is fluent in Japanese is that correct?"

"Well I know he can speak and understand most of it. But I'm not certain he is completely familiar with all the military jargon they use. But does this mean we can send bogus messages to the Japs? That would be one hell of an advantage," he said, his brown eyes glowing in anticipation.

"In theory yes; once I have broken their code."

"What do you mean 'in theory'?"

"Well I have to learn a particular officer's phraseology and idiom. An alert communications officer will recognize any unusual phrasing coming from a well known source. One must be very careful. However, if they use simple sentence structure and brief messages as we do, it won't be a problem."

"I can see this is more complicated than first meets the eye. Thank God you are here. And what about the other two machines? Are they duplicates of the first one?"

"No, they are the brainchildren of the brilliant people at our coding group in England. They look exactly like the first one I showed you but they are dummies."

"Dummies?"

"Yes, they are the bait with which I hope to identify your traitor."

"You had better go slowly and explain that," said a baffled Chesterton.

"They appear genuine but will not transmit or receive any messages."

"What the hell use are they then?" burst in Chesterton.

"I should have defined transmit. They cannot transmit a normal message however if someone attempts to do so they will send a signal to my base machine – the first one I showed you. And each of them sends a different signal."

Alex could tell from Chesterton's expression that he was completely mystified.

"Let me explain. Let's start from the beginning. You know someone in your group is a traitor and is in contact with the Japanese. However you don't know how he does it, right?"

"Yes, that's correct."

"We can surmise he must have a routine to establish contact."

"Yes we guessed that must be the case."

"He can't be using a radio from inside the camp. It would be far too risky as it would be almost impossible to avoid being overheard in your crowded conditions. Correct?"

"I agree."

"I have given this a lot of thought on my way out here and have come to the conclusion that there can only be two ways of doing it. One is in fact a radio, but it would have to be hidden somewhere in the jungle. However I doubt that someone disappearing from time to time into the jungle would go unnoticed, and would certainly raise suspicions. Then there's the climate. The radio could easily be affected by monsoon rains. Therefore I have ruled out the use of a radio. The other possibility is the simplest of methods - a drop spot. Your traitor will leave a message at a designated spot for collection by the Japanese. He will also collect his instructions from the same spot. I am guessing the Japanese keep someone posted around the clock, hidden near this spot. They can't know when the traitor will pass by. It must be when you send him on an assignment. Like perhaps taking a message to another guerrilla group; or, going into town to get some desperately needed supplies. Then he could easily make a slight detour to his drop spot. He would pick up the reply on the way back. For this turnaround to happen so speedily; the Japanese lookout must have a radio and transmit the message to his HQ in Ipoh and they in turn must radio him the instructions. He would write them down and leave the message to be collected. They won't chance a face-to-face meeting. They will probably suspect that you may have every messenger followed to see if he contacts the Japanese."

"Well we thought of doing that but rejected the idea. You see once it became known we believed we had a traitor, he would immediately change his habits. And the rest of the camp would become suspicious of one another and that would destroy morale. We have enough problems with only a few desertions but that could lead to a major desertion."

"Yes, I can see that."

"Now tell me, how do we use these devices of yours to identify our traitor?"

"First tell me how many guerrilla groups you are in contact with?"

"Three in the jungle and the one you met in Grik."

"And do you always use the same messengers?"

"As you may have noticed, many of the men are quite thin due to attacks of dysentery, malaria, or dengue fever. There are a few who are pretty strong and I use them. We give them extra rations to keep up their strength."

"That's good. Here's what I propose. You send two men to guerrilla groups; each man will carry a fake code machine. They are to tell the guerrilla chiefs to have their best radio men become familiar with the layout of the keyboard of the machines, but not to attempt to use them. They are at presently locked to prevent use. They will have until the next day to acquaint themselves with the layout and to note down any questions that immediately spring to mind. But it must be stressed they handle the machines with great care as they are very expensive and delicate. We will contact them later to inform them of a date when we can give them a full indoctrination program on how to use the machines. The messengers will stay the night in the camps and the next day they will collect the machines and bring them back."

"I'm afraid you've lost me, Alex. How does that help us?"

"Well I should have mentioned earlier that the signal each one emits only happens when the machine is turned on. There is a well hidden device deep inside the machine that activates it. And it will only transmit its signal when unlocked and someone attempts to use it. You see I am banking on the traitor contacting the Japanese located at the drop spot. He will inform Ipoh and they will immediately recognize the knowledge to be gained on the workings of these machines as a great coup. I'm betting the traitor will be instructed to leave the machine and not deliver it to the guerrilla group. And, as communication between you and the guerrillas has broken down, no one will ever know."

"But if the keyboard is locked how will the Japs be able to test it?"

"Any skilled communications officer will discover how to unlock it within an hour or two. But he will never find the secret signal. And to protect their valuable spy, the Japanese must complete their initial analysis and return it to the drop point the next day. Grik is a small camp and will not have a sufficiently skilled operator to conduct this analysis. The machine will have to go to Ipoh. By the time the machine reaches Ipoh it will be late at night and they will have to leave before dawn to return it. That only gives them a few hours to work on it. And without the manual detailing the coding process they will not discover very much at all."

"I see, as soon as the Japs unlock it and begin trying it out, it will send you a signal. And as each machine has a different signal you can identify who took that machine to the Japs. Ingenious! By God absolutely brilliant! Did you come up with this scheme?"

"I had help from my friends at Bletchley."

"You're a genius, Alex. I requested assistance from a code expert and they sent me a bloody genius."

"There's only one possible fly in the ointment that I can see," said Alex cautiously.

"What's that?" replied a now concerned Chesterton.

"The only flaw I can see is if a guerrilla group has an absolutely brilliant radio man and he disobeys his chief's order not to meddle and unlocks the machine and attempts to use it. That will send us a false signal."

"I wouldn't worry too much about that. When the leader of a guerrilla group gives an order it is obeyed."

"I trust your knowledge of the workings of guerrilla groups. Nevertheless people who work on signals and codes have an insatiable appetite for fiddling with devices. I only hope the guerrilla chiefs' warnings overcome those inherent traits."

"Let's say we do not get a signal from the first two. Do we send another two messengers to the other guerrillas?"

"That's right."

"As I said I literally only use a handful of messengers, five. So we have to hope we get a result from the first four we send. I would be reluctant to accuse the fifth if we didn't get a result. It would be too circumstantial. Maybe the traitor is smarter than we think and uses some other way of communicating with the Japs."

"I suppose only time will tell," said Alex hopefully, as the first seed of doubt was planted in his mind.

Chapter Sixteen

Simon Chesterton rose from the table and stood quietly – deep in thought. Alex sat motionlessly, also lost in his own thoughts, as he searched for any possible flaws in his plan. He was so intensely immersed in this that he was startled when Chesterton spoke again.

"I must bring Steve and Tony into this. Obviously we can't launch your plan without them becoming aware of it. And I will not allow them to find out second hand. Can you leave the four machines on the table while I get them?"

"Can I make one suggestion before you do?"

"Of course, what is it?"

"I am in complete agreement with telling Tony and Steve about the plan. As you said, it would be foolish to do otherwise, they would soon catch on. And I can see the loyalty and trust that exists between all of you. My only concern relates to Lee Sheng. Of course ultimately he must become involved, however, for the time being I would prefer that he does not know my role. I still believe there may be grounds for keeping it as secret as possible. I'm damned if I can think of a good one right at the moment. And maybe I'm being overcautious but it was drilled into me by the people in SOE in London that you keep as many cards hidden as possible until they have to be played."

Seeing the protest in Chesterton's eyes as he prepared to respond, Alex quickly continued.

"What I have in mind is the following story for the benefit of Lee Sheng. My sole reason for being here was to carry these machines out to you for the use of Tony. He is a code expert and the plan is all his idea. And since he will be deeply involved later in using his knowledge of Japanese to listen into the enemy's transmissions and sending out fictitious messages to them, it will all seem plausible."

"Well, well, you are a devious one, are you not?" said Chesterton in a tone that was more one of praise than recrimination. "I think you would make an excellent spy. But okay, I'll agree. You wait here and I'll arrange to have some coffee brought in while I get the others."

"I'll cover the machines until the coffee has been served," said Alex.

Chesterton's eyebrows shot up.

'Yes, you definitely have the makings of a first class spy. You leave nothing to chance,' he thought.

Chesterton left the tent shaking his head in admiration at all he was discovering about Alex. A few minutes later he returned with Benson and MacDougal, the latter two stared at the four covered items.

"What's all this mystery about?" asked Benson and reached for one of the covers.

Alex moved swiftly to grasp his wrist.

"Not yet, Tony. Let's wait for the coffee."

Benson had a puzzled look on his face as he turned to face Chesterton looking for an explanation.

"All will be explained shortly, Tony," said Chesterton.

"This is like something out of Alice in Wonderland – curiouser and curiouser," said Benson.

Just then Chin arrived carrying a tray with the coffee. He placed the tray at the end of the table and looked speculatively at the covered items.

"Thank you, Chin," said MacDougal to the young man, in a voice that indicated dismissal.

They helped themselves to coffee as Chin left. Once they were seated Chesterton began by relating the conversation he had had with Alex. MacDougal let out several cries of, 'Good God!' during the explanation but the intellectual Benson merely nodded his head from time to time and allowed a wide smile to cross his face as Chesterton concluded.

"I thank you, Alex, for imbuing me with the craftsmanship of an expert cryptologist. I shall do my best to act the part," he said.

"Well what do you think, chaps?" asked Chesterton.

"I think it's bloody marvelous! When do we start?" was the response from an eager MacDougal.

"I echo Steve's accolade. May I ask if you intend bringing Lee Sheng totally into your confidence right away?"

Alex shook his head vehemently. But Chesterton demurred.

"You must understand, Alex, we trust Lee Sheng. He has been with us for a long time and has fought bravely at our side."

"I am not, as Simon painted me, a seasoned spy. But those experts back in London drummed it into me that one must trust no one. Anyone can be bought. It is just a matter of how much it takes. And money is not always the only incentive."

Chesterton looked very uncomfortable at this remark but before he could respond it was the cerebral Benson who spoke.

"Do we infer from your comments that you don't trust us, Alex?" he asked with arched eyebrows and a slight smile.

"Trust isn't given, is it Tony? It has to be earned. However by giving you the outline of my plan, I believe it indicates a strong initial beginning of that rare quality."

"Ah, my earlier appraisal of you was correct. You are a bright man and, you are smart enough to know what you don't know. Therefore caution is mandated. I can go along with not informing Lee Sheng at this stage. After we catch the traitor we can decide how much to tell him. That is always assuming that Lee Sheng is not the traitor."

"Very well, I too will agree although I must add it is with some reluctance," said Chesterton. "How about you Steve, what do you say?"

"From the very first time I met Alex, and he chose not to send a signal from the submarine in case there was a trap, I thought him a canny man. Now I have just witnessed for myself that I was wrong. He is a *very, very,* canny man; and I will gladly go along with his proposal."

"Very well then who shall we pick as the first messengers? Oh I should tell you, Alex that our usual messengers are Wang and Yuen, whom you met when you landed; Wong, our cook who you have also met; and two others, Ling and Chen."

"The same Chin who just brought in the coffee?"

"No not Chin, Chen. Chin is dedicated to killing Japs because of what they did to his family, but he is still young and not terribly strong. Our messengers were selected because they are tough men. They can travel through the jungle better than most and they would be difficult to break if caught by the Japs."

"I understand."

"Steve, you know the men well. Who would you pick?"

"I'd go with Ling and Chen first, then Wong and Yuen as the second team."

"Obviously I can't contribute anything to the selection, but merely out of curiosity, why leave Wang out?" asked Alex.

"I hadn't known he had recently been ill when I took him along to meet you. And he performed very well on that mission, but I noticed when we returned he was completely worn out. It was only then, when I rather forcefully questioned Lee Sheng, he confirmed Wang had been ill. I don't think it wise to have him carry one of your machines on this task."

"Please forgive me for asking so many questions; but why didn't Lee Sheng tell you of this before you came out to meet me?"

"Perhaps I can explain," interrupted Chesterton. "Not every one of the Chinese was a communist at the outset. Lee Sheng has always been a rabid one and has forced everyone to pledge allegiance to the communist party. Wang and a few others were the most difficult to convert. And communist leaders do not forgive and forget. Lee Sheng would delight in attempting to put Wang in a bad light with Steve. He would have hoped that Wang would fail in his duties on the mission to meet you. For his part, Wang would never have refused Steve's invitation to join him in meeting you. It would be a matter of face saving."

"But can't you talk to Lee Sheng telling him that such behavior is unacceptable?"

Now it was Benson who explained.

"You will soon learn, Alex, the Chinese are not totally under our command. They work with us but not for us. So long as our goals are aligned, they are pleased to accept our advice and leadership; however they would react badly to interference in their customs. The thirty three we have here working with us haven't yet mastered the fundamental capability in war tactics that we have, thanks to our training in the British Army. Therefore when it comes to organizing raids on the enemy they rely on us and try to learn from us. Furthermore as Simon inferred, not all of them are committed to communist ideals. This, and clan loyalties, results in us having camps within camps within camps. It is a veritable Chinese puzzle. But to answer your question, if Simon were to tackle Lee Sheng on this matter which Lee Sheng would undoubtedly consider within his prerogatives as leader of the guerrillas, one of two things would occur. He would at worst, leave and take many with him, or, at least for quite some time attempt to subtly undermine our plans. Now we would consider such acts as maliciously subversive, but he wouldn't. To him it would be justifiable retribution for causing him to lose face. So you see it's a delicate balance, old boy. But have no fear, time will allow you to use your already demonstrated intellect to come to a basic understanding of all of this. And since you are a recognized expert at solving puzzles, you will soon be teaching us how to successfully weave one's way through the labyrinth that is Chinese custom."

He concluded with one of his trademark wily smiles.

The Scotsman, MacDougal, patted Alex on the shoulder.

"Don't let anything we have said stop you from asking questions laddie. It's the only way to learn out here. And not to discourage you, but you must understand we have only been talking about the Chinese. Always remember in this country there is an even larger population of Malays and a sizeable one of Indians. Both of which have their own idiosyncrasies."

Alex shook his head indicating his lack of appreciation at all of this. But true to his good nature he grinned ruefully as he said, "I look forward to learning from all of you."

He was beginning to realize that even if he were to choose the correct turning at a future crossroad he would have to carefully navigate through many twists and turns on any particular journey.

Chapter Seventeen

"All right," said Chesterton, "let's finalize our plan. I suggest we talk to Lee Sheng immediately then have the first two men briefed and let them leave straight away. There is nothing to be gained by delaying things. And I suggest they go to the camps of Choo and Meng. If we get no signal from either of those then the next two can visit Cheung in Grik and the fourth camp of Tan in the jungle north of here."

"However, Lee Sheng must not be told the machines being carried to the guerrilla camps are dummies. Nor that they have a secret signal built in, designed to identify the traitor. After all we don't know if Lee Sheng himself may be the traitor," warned Alex.

That brought immediate looks of protest from the others, but after a moment's reflection, they reluctantly nodded their heads in agreement.

"But before we invite Lee Sheng here, I would like Alex to take me through what I have to say one more time as I am supposed to be the expert on cryptology," requested Benson.

Alex took his time with the explanation and after twenty minutes and two rounds of practice, Benson said he felt confident. It was then Chesterton rose to fetch Lee Sheng, but before he could leave MacDougal suddenly spoke.

"Hold on a sec, Simon. I just had a thought. As I mentioned to you, Cheung told me when we were in Grik that the Japs had intensified their searches. If they send out one of their patrols on a two day search they could come very close to the routes our men will take on their way to the guerrilla camps. Our two messengers will be slower than usual by carting machines on their backs and may not be quick enough to avoid capture should they bump into Jap patrols. It may be better if we were to cause some diversion around Ipoh just after the fellows leave our camp. That would draw the attention of the Japs away from their normal routine. They might even postpone sending patrols into the jungle while they investigate the ruckus we create. What do you think?"

"That's a splendid idea, Steve. Will you lead that action?"

"Of course, I'll take three of the guerrillas with me. A few well placed sticks of dynamite along with several hand grenades should do the trick. And, if possible, I'll select a target on the south side of town. That should cause the Japs to focus a search in that area and take them even further away from where our fellows will be."

"Excellent, but that means you should leave now and be in position in the early hours of Wednesday, the day after tomorrow. I'll delay briefing Lee Sheng until first thing that same day and the two messengers should be on their way by nine o'clock. It should take each of them just about four days for the round trip."

"That'll work," agreed MacDougal and he stood to leave.

"Good luck, Steve," said Chesterton as he shook his hand.

"All the best, my friend," added Benson with a farewell wave of his hand.

"I wish I could come with you for the experience, but I must stay here and listen for any signal coming through," said Alex somewhat regretfully.

He was anxious to play an active role in this operation; even though the jungle still filled his head with menacing thoughts. But he knew he had to conquer his apprehension and the only way to do so was to face it in the jungle. MacDougal seemed to read his mind.

"That's all right laddie, we each have our jobs to do. You'll get your opportunity to go on a mission soon enough." He turned away from the table. "Well goodbye all; I'll see you in four or five days."

With a final wave he left the tent.

"He will be all right, won't he?" asked a concerned Alex.

"Every mission we undertake has risk attached to it. But so long as Steve doesn't get too ambitious, he should be safe," replied Chesterton.

This was not the confident response Alex had hoped for and his facial expression indicated it.

"Steve knows Malaya better than any of us. I feel confident he will be fine," added Benson reassuringly.

Alex nodded understandingly although he continued to be concerned. Then he spoke to Chesterton.

"I'd like to take a look at the codes you have been using, Simon. I can spend my time studying them and then coming up with a few others for future use. You will need something relatively simple to use yet sufficiently complex to baffle the Japanese. Which language do you normally use in sending your messages, English or Hokkien?"

"We always use English. I'll get the code books. Our largest table is here in the tent but I suggest you work in the cabin. The table there is much smaller but you are unlikely to be disturbed. I'll go along with you as the code books are there."

"Would you mind awfully if I watch you work, Alex?" requested Benson. "It would seem fitting as you appointed me chief code breaker," he said with one of his crafty smiles. "But quite seriously, old chap, I am truly interested in the mysteries of your work."

"I don't mind in the least."

They all walked to the cabin. Alex noticed the guerrillas were busily engaged in hand-to-hand combat practice. Some of them stopped and looked expectantly in their direction. Chesterton called out to them in Hokkien. Then he explained his message to Alex.

"They're just practicing for the moment. I usually conduct a class about this time. But first I'll quickly get the code books for you then change and report for my class."

"Simon is our expert jungle fighter," explained Benson. "He was trained at Force 136 in Singapore."

"I would like to watch you, Simon, maybe even join in the class; however, I had better get working on what I know best. Perhaps I can participate at some time in the future."

"You would be most welcome."

"I would be careful if I were you," interjected Benson. "Those boys don't hold back. They seem to relish winning and some of them have had some nasty injuries. That's why I do not participate."

"But no injury was anywhere near life threatening," responded Chesterton defensively as he entered the cabin.

Alex followed him and turned towards Benson.

"As you were a professor of philosophy, I am surprised you don't follow its tenets."

Benson looked astonished.

"What do you mean?"

"Wasn't it one of the most famous philosophers – Nietzsche – who said, 'That which does not kill us makes us stronger.'?"

"Hah! Well said, Alex. What do you have to say to that, Tony? You have no more excuses not to join in now," crowed Chesterton triumphantly.

"Thank you very much, Alex. I was just starting to like you but now

I'm revoking that impulsive emotion," countered Benson attempting to look aggrieved.

But he failed, and burst into loud peals of laughter.

"God save me, we have another educated man," he said and clapped Alex on the back.

Chesterton was still grinning as he went into a corner next to his bed and began twirling the dial of a small safe. He withdrew three books and handed them to Alex.

"Good luck in developing a suitable code. These are the only ones we had."

He changed into a pair of black cotton trousers and walked bare-chested and bare footed out of the cabin.

"See you in an hour," he called over his shoulder as he left.

Alex sat at the table in the middle of the cabin and laid out the code books.

"May I ask you a question before you get started, old boy?"

"Certainly, professor, but don't make it a difficult one. I don't wish to strain my brain. I'll need all wits about me to come up with a new cypher."

The smile on his face clearly showed he was still enjoying his joke about Nietzsche; and was not in the least concerned over his current task.

"Did you study philosophy in university?"

"We barely touched on the subject. And I left after my first year. However I did some reading in my spare time and found some of it interesting, but to be honest, not all of it."

"What didn't appeal to you?"

"The first thing we learned was the derivation of the term philosophy. It's from the Greek, philosophia, which literally translates to, 'love of wisdom', does it not?"

"That's correct. Go on."

"That intrigued me and immediately caught my interest. However when it came to the most recent philosophers it seemed to me they had strayed from the broad concept of the subject and began specializing in one particular branch of it. This narrowing down of the endlessly interesting subject of wisdom into only one aspect of it left me bored. It was almost as though they were attempting to show just how brilliant they were. This egotism both exasperated and bored me."

"I see. If you have an interest, I would dearly love to explore your other reactions at a later time. You are a very bright young man and I would truly enjoy the mental stimulus of such a discussion."

Alex blushed at this compliment.

"I would enjoy that too, however my understanding of your specialty is wafer thin. I don't wish to leave you with the idea that I have deeply studied philosophy. But for the moment I had better get down to work on something I do understand."

"If I may ask one final question before you begin, Alex?"

Alex nodded his head in a somewhat absent-minded manner as he opened the books. His brain was already focusing on his task.

"Why did you leave university after only one year? It seems to me that a man of your talent deprived himself of a wonderful opportunity."

Alex instantly lost his absent-minded demeanor as he stared outside with a pained look on his face. Benson could not help but notice this.

"Oh, I do apologize. I had no right to pry," he murmured with contrition.

Alex shook his head as though to clear his brain and did not answer for a long moment.

"No, it's all right, Tony. It was a very painful time of my life. My father was killed at Dunkirk. We were *very* close. All I could think of was to kill as many Germans as possible in retribution. So I signed up straight away. But later, during my basic training, I came to my senses and regretted my impulsiveness. You see my dad's dearest wish was I complete university. He never had the opportunity to get a decent education and he saw I had the capability and wanted me to fulfill a dream he had harbored for many years. I let him down by leaving. However, God willing, I will survive this war and I *will* go back to university."

His voice choked a little as he spoke and he had to stop to gather himself.

"I'm so sorry, Alex. Was your dad in the infantry?"

"No, that was the most soul destroying part of it. He was too old to fight, but he had a burning desire to 'do his bit' as he put it. So he became an ambulance driver. He received a commendation for his actions at Dunkirk. He saved so many young men's lives by shuttling them from field hospitals to the beach for transportation by boat back to safety. It was on one of those trips that a bloody Nazi pilot strafed his ambulance. I could not imagine how any person calling himself a human being could stoop to the depths of depravity and strafe a helpless ambulance."

Once again his voice failed him and he gripped the edges of the table till his knuckles shone bright white. Benson kept silent for a while at the sight of this pained young man. Finally he spoke in a hushed and reverent tone.

"I am most awfully sorry for raising the subject. However, now I can see from whence your bravery has sprung. You have inherited it from your father. I know for certain he would be proud of you, Alex. And he will be even more so when you finish your mission in this damned awful war and return to finish university."

And although he really wanted to watch Alex at work on a new code, Benson had the decency to realize he had unknowingly opened a thinly covered wound, and left the cabin. Just before doing so he collected the things Chesterton would require after his class – his clothes, towel and soap.

Alex sat with tears in his eyes for a long time before he could compose himself sufficiently to start his task.

Chapter Eighteen

An hour later Chesterton concluded his training class; he was soaked in sweat and headed for the cabin to collect his soap and towel before bathing in the river. He was mildly surprised to be met by Benson.

"I thought you wanted to observe Alex," he said.

"I'm afraid I inadvertently upset young Murdoch," he replied dejectedly.

"How did you manage that?"

Benson told him the whole story.

"Damn it all, Tony, can't you ever desist from being nosy? You may not only have grievously upset Alex, but you may have caused him to be utterly unable to focus on his task."

"I have no excuse. You know my nature. I am cursed with inquisitiveness. It is an extraordinarily useful asset for a scholar but can be a liability in one's social life. I think it may be wise for both of us to stay in the tent after you clean up. It would give Alex some privacy to work and allow him time to recover from my insensitivity."

"Now you are showing some sense. Really, Tony, sometimes you are just too much."

With that Chesterton stomped off to the river muttering in a highly agitated manner. Benson wondered if the river would evaporate with the heat of Chesterton's wrath. He hung his head in shame and trudged towards the tent. Twenty minutes later Chesterton entered the tent. He had calmed down considerably but was still obviously upset. Instead of sitting at the table next to Benson, he paced around and around the table. Finally he could stand it no longer.

"I'm going up to the cabin to see how Alex is getting along. Are you coming?"

"Yes, the sooner I apologize once more, the better I shall feel."

They marched in silence up to the cabin.

"May I come in without disturbing you, Alex?" asked Chesterton in a quiet voice.

"Oh, by all means. Anyway, I wanted to tell you about my progress. I have developed a new coding system that should work well for you."

It was then he noticed the demeanor of Benson. His head was still bowed. The astute young man realized the cause of Benson's discomfort.

"It's all right, Tony. I'm sorry I got upset. I still miss my father a great deal, he was a wonderful man. I always tried my best to please him. And you were right in what you said, Tony, I do believe he would have been proud of me."

"I am most terribly sorry for prying into your personal life, Alex. Please forgive me."

"There is nothing to forgive, Tony. The more I thought of it the more I realized that talking about his death had a cathartic affect on me. I actually feel better."

Relief flooded through Benson and, by the look on Chesterton's face, it was flowing through him too.

"Let me show you what I have come up with," said Alex.

"I trust it will not be overly technical. After all, I only became an *expert* this morning," Benson said.

"Not in the least. Like most good codes it is relatively simple to use but much more difficult to break."

He described his new code and both men were delighted at how quickly they learned to use it.

"In coming up with this solution I first examined the three codes you have been using. They were very basic. Even so, they would have continued to work for some time before being cracked by the Japanese, had they not been traitorously reported to them. I presume each worked well for a period before the traitor could get his hands on your codebook."

"Yes, our first code had been in operation for well over a year. During which time we had some real successes in coordinating attacks with the other guerrilla groups, attacks or railways, ammunition storage areas and small Jap units. During this time news of our exploits spread and the communist guerrillas told us they had no trouble in recruiting new men. Success breeds success. Then when things began to go wrong and our patrols were being ambushed we thought the Japs had cracked our code. So we changed to the second one. But that only worked for about a month before we experienced the same problem. Even then we put it down to the Japs having brought in more capable coding personnel. So, once again we switched. This was to our third and final code. This time it lasted for six weeks before it was broken. Now we realized it was highly unlikely the Japs were so good. We reckoned we must have a traitor in our midst."

"And that's when you took the risk of getting someone to Colombo to ask for assistance?"

"Yes but our first attempt failed and our messenger was killed. By this time the guerrillas didn't want to cooperate with us. They now believed us to be an impotent force. It was mainly due to the persuasive powers of Steve that Lee Sheng agreed to stay with us. In turn both he and Steve convinced the others. But we knew we had to become operationally successful once again – and quickly - if we were to retain their loyalty. It took a little time but we did manage to persuade someone to once again try to reach Colombo and he succeeded. And here you are. And boy do we need your expertise!"

Alex waved away this compliment, his mind still furiously working on the problem.

"I'm sure you realize there are only two ways for the traitor to have gotten hold of your code books. Either he got them from one of the guerrilla groups - or - he knew the combination to your safe."

"We thought about that. But as I change the combination every week we initially believed it must have been through one of the guerrilla groups."

"Does that mean your traitor would have to have one or more contacts in the guerrilla network?"

"That's where we were stumped," broke in Benson. "You see in every guerrilla group there are two very important positions. One is, of course, the leader: and the other is the head of security. The selection to the latter position is handled very carefully. Firstly the man must be intelligent and secondly he is usually a loner with few friends. The most interesting part is the change that comes over the appointee. He becomes suspicious of everyone and everything, and he trusts no one. Oftentimes not even his leader."

"That's right," said Chesterton. "You see the guerrillas have their own particular method of dealing with traitors within their groups – they execute them. So the head of security is a feared personage. He bribes, cajoles, threatens, and terrorizes men to report to him any suspicious act by one their comrades. And when he finds out something bad about someone he becomes judge and jury. If the offence is minor the man is whipped with a bamboo cane in front of the group. If it is middling serious the man is beaten, scarred with a knife to show everyone his infidelity and then expelled from the group. If it is deemed very serious he is killed."

Benson chimed in once again.

"That's why we find it very difficult to believe there could be several traitors in the guerrilla network - one maybe – but not many. Therefore we had to believe the traitor is here in our group."

Alex pondered this new information for a while. The two others remained quiet so as not to disturb his thoughts. Finally Alex nodded his head indicating he had reasoned things out.

"I have to agree with you. As you told me, the other guerrilla camps are closer to Japanese locations, therefore it would not take a traitor long to establish contact. It could be done in a matter of days. Your camp is much further away and your men are seldom allowed to leave. That only occurs when they are sent on a specific assignment. The combination of those two factors accounts for the relatively long time from the change of coding system till the Japanese took action. It was one month between the first and second code usage and six weeks between the second and third. Furthermore, although some of your men come to the cabin, mainly to collect and return laundry; it would take a well trained man to break the combination of the safe. And even then that would require quite some time. I'm still perplexed as to how he could manage that without being detected. Given what you told me of the power of the head of security, does that mean the one here is not doing his job well?"

"Chua is the name of the one here and he is the epitome of that office. Given that, the traitor must be unusually adept at his job. We have wracked our brains but could not come up with an answer. Let's hope and pray your scheme reveals the bastard," said Chesterton heatedly.

"And I gather from your earlier comments that you have not told Lee Sheng of your suspicions."

"That's right, for the reasons we mentioned to you. Without successful actions against the Japs, the guerrillas begin to lose heart for their cause. As it is, we believe only a flimsy thread holds some of them tied to that cause. If we were to let it be known there was a traitor in their midst many in the group would be likely to desert for fear of their lives. Lee Sheng is a strong and brave leader but he is a blunt instrument. If we told him of our suspicions he would be unable to stop himself from immediately starting a witch hunt which would certainly precipitate desertions."

"When we hopefully reveal the traitor, won't he feel slighted that he was not brought into your confidence earlier?"

"I'll have to think of a way to handle that when the time comes," replied Chesterton.

"Then we're all set. Tomorrow you send out the first messengers and then all we can do is to wait," concluded Alex.

The other two nodded their heads and Alex could discern they were men who liked action. And the inaction of waiting they had endured, during the time it had taken for him to arrive with a plan, had just been excruciatingly lengthened.

More for their sakes than his own, he offered a silent prayer that this journey would have a successful ending.

Chapter Nineteen

It had rained during the night. Well rain was not an adequate portrayal of that night's weather. It had been as though some mystical power had lifted a small lake above them then tipped out its contents. The noise was deafening. However as was the case with many such occurrences in Malaya it only lasted several hours. And as though it had been a bad dream, the morning sky was blue and the sun shone brightly. However the reality was clearly depicted as the river had overflowed and its banks were muddy swamps.

The three Englishmen rose early and with an abundance of caution bathed at the edge of the river; staying well away from the rapids raging along at its center. The Chinese were already there at the center of the river, screaming and shouting like children, completely oblivious to any possible danger. Once the three were dried and dressed they forewent breakfast and went straight to the tent.

They ordered coffee to be delivered and sent for Lee Sheng. He had not participated in the hilarity at the river and arrived almost immediately. He came barefoot carrying a towel. He dried his feet before looking quizzically at the two covered dummy coding machines.

"Good morning, Lee Sheng. How are you today?" began Chesterton.

"Good morning, I am very fine," he replied but did not take his eyes of the two mounds on the table.

"Good morning," chorused Tony and Alex.

Lee Sheng only nodded an acknowledgement, his stare unwaveringly fixed on the mysterious items. Then he remembered the question he had for Chesterton.

"Where Tuan MacDougal go with my men?"

"I will explain that later," countered Chesterton.

Then unable to contain his curiosity any longer, "What these?" Lee Sheng demanded.

He pointed to the covered coding machines and finally managing to take his eyes off them to look inquiringly at Chesterton.

Simon did not reply as just then the coffee arrived on a tray being carried very cautiously by a man with muddy, slippery feet. The Chinese delivering the coffee was also filled with curiosity at the covered items and the cups on the tray rattled loudly as he clumsily set it down, almost missing the table. He too had found it impossible to take his eyes off the covered machines and with his wet feet sliding he almost caused the coffee to spill on the ground. Lee Sheng barked out an order and the man scuttled away but not without one final glance from the tent entrance.

Chesterton took his first appreciative sip of his coffee before he stood and whipped the covers off the machines. Alex thought his dramatic gesture was akin to a magician about to pull a rabbit from a top hat. Lee Sheng stood, leaned over the table, and stared at the machines for a few seconds. Then he sat down.

"Only typewriters," he said disdainfully. His expectations of something spectacular dashed.

"No, not typewriters, my friend. Look more closely."

The Chinese again stood and peered at them. His closer inspection revealed the lack of a carriageway and no slot for paper. He was confused but not to lose face he did not hazard another guess in case this too was wrong. He slowly looked up from the machines and stared at Chesterton.

"Lieutenant Murdoch brought these machines all the way from Colombo. They will help us win the war."

Chesterton let that statement hang in the air until he saw an intense interest spring to Lee Sheng's eyes. The Chinese took two big gulps of coffee and leaned forward with his arms on the table. He was hooked!

"I will let Mr. Benson explain. Perhaps you did not know; he is a code expert."

Lee Sheng's head swiveled rapidly to look at Benson. There was a renewed respect in his eyes as he waited for an explanation. Tony went into his well rehearsed speech, repeating some parts in Hokkien when Lee Sheng looked confused by the English version. When he finished he bit his tongue gently to avoid bursting out laughing. Lee Sheng's mouth was agape. His eyebrows were raised to their maximum and his eyes stared so hard that they had become slightly crossed. Quite suddenly he realized his facial antic and snapped his mouth shut. There was a moment of silence in the tent before Lee Sheng managed to speak.

"This all true?" he asked hoarsely.

"Yes it is all true," confirmed Benson "Furthermore I do not wish to waste any time. We should send Ling and Chen to the camps of Choo and Meng this morning."

"Okay, okay, I agree. I go get them, bring them here. You tell them what to do. Yes?"

"Yes, I will explain everything, but do not mention this to anyone else. Do you understand?"

"Yes, I understand."

But Lee Sheng did not understand. If the two guerrilla camps were to be told of these fantastic machines, why couldn't his troops also be told? However, in his excitement over these new devices, he didn't ask his question - just as well — as Benson would have been hard pressed to come up with a believable answer.

He left the tent and returned very quickly with the two men. All three skidded into the tent not stopping to dry their feet.

Ling and Chen were briefed on their missions. It took quite some time for Benson to have them understand just how powerful a tool the machine really was. When they finally did, their eyes shone with enthusiasm mixed with pride at having been chosen. They stood, bowed, had the machines strapped to their backs, and left the tent to set off immediately.

Lee Sheng accompanied them to the beginning of the jungle trail. And all the way he continued to impress upon them the importance of their tasks. When they had gone Lee Sheng's face had a thoughtful look. Some of his initial excitement had dissipated and his brain had begun to work more clearly.

"How did Benson manage to keep his expert coding knowledge secret for all the time I have known him?" he murmured to himself. "It is very, very, strange," he continued to muse.

The three Englishmen sat wordlessly for almost a minute. At last, Benson broke the silence. His words were exactly what the other two were thinking.

"Well, chaps, I suppose all we can do now is to wait."

This redundant statement did nothing to ease the tension they all felt.

Chapter Twenty

With nothing further to be done, they left the tent and carefully walked up the slippery grassy slope to the cabin. Alex noticed that Lee Sheng was not conducting his usual morning lecture, but was hurrying from cabin to cabin. Chesterton saw the puzzled look on Alex's face and explained.

"As you know, we haven't been able to coordinate significant raids recently. Because of this the Japs have been able to be less on the defensive and more on the offensive. They have been sending out more patrols searching for us. Therefore we have had to take extra precautions. We have already identified another camp site several miles from here, in case we are detected and must evacuate this location. And we have posted extra sentries further out from the camp as an early warning system. Lee Sheng instituted another precautionary measure. Every time we send out messengers he knows there is a chance a Jap patrol will catch one of them. So he readies the camp for quick evacuation. If a messenger does not return in time, we reckon he may have been caught. As I told you the messengers were carefully selected and would take quite a bit of torture before talking. That would give us time to move our camp. Right now Lee Sheng is supervising preparations for just such an eventuality."

"It can't be pleasant to live in constant fear," said Alex.

"You will discover the Chinese are much more sanguine about such a crisis that we Europeans would be, Alex," said Benson. "I hate to say it but they are much more philosophical concerning matters of life, death and danger," he added with one of his wry smiles.

"There he goes – always reducing everything down to philosophy," said Chesterton with a good natured grin

However once inside the cabin Chesterton's grin faded and his face took on a concerned look.

105

"Last night's downpour will make the trails a bit more difficult. I hope the men can make the guerrilla camps by tomorrow night."

"Don't worry Simon. They'll make it. Didn't you see the pride in their eyes at being selected? No matter what, they'll make it," replied a confident Benson.

"I hope so," responded a still unconvinced Chesterton. "Anyway I had better go see if I can assist Lee Sheng. See you later."

"One would imagine that having made philosophy my calling, I would have a reasonable quotient of patience," said Benson to Alex, "but alas I do not. In life in general, and in war in particular, waiting is one of the most difficult things to do. And I have yet to master it. To pass the time, may I return to our earlier conversation?"

"The one regarding my skimpy knowledge of philosophy?" asked Alex.

"Quite so, you were describing your boredom with certain philosophers who, in your opinion, were ignoring the fundamental panoramic view of this science. Would you care to elaborate?"

Alex drew a deep breath. He sensed he was about to get into a subject that was way over his head.

"Well ---," he began hesitantly.

"No – please don't hold back, Alex. I am not attempting to trap you or belittle your views. I am genuinely interested."

"Well it seemed to me the earliest philosophers had an interest in your subject as only one of many of their interests. It was almost as though the pursuit of their other interests led them to think of philosophy. Oh I am not expressing this very well," said Alex in embarrassment.

"Yes, yes you are – go on."

"I mean they came to philosophy as an outgrowth of other studies. They didn't start with the study of philosophy and then later take up other sciences."

"Give me and example."

"At Cambridge they taught us that Pythagoras could well be called the father of philosophy. Most schoolboys learn the Pythagoras Theorem relating to right angle triangles and therefore think of him only as a brilliant mathematician. That he was, however his main obsession in life seems to have been his religious convictions. I believe it was in 530BC he moved from Greece to Croton on the southern tip of Italy. Many Greeks migrated across the Ionian Sea to that region and they named it Great Greece. It was there he set up a religious sect where his followers studied under him. The most important aspect of this was not a close minded restrictive religious system but rather through religion and probably mathematics he was seeking wisdom - hence philosophy. And the same search for wisdom through other pursuits could be said of Plato."

"Bravo, young Murdoch," exclaimed an admiring Benson. "You could have taught my course at Oxford. Did you learn all this during only one semester?"

"It interested me so I did quite a bit of reading on my own."

"Did your reading extend to more modern philosophers?"

"Yes, I was particularly impressed by the writings of John Locke. And here again his basic education was medicine. He was a doctor and surgeon. It was while he was living in the house of Lord Shaftsbury he conducted a delicate operation of Shaftsbury's liver, saving his life. But once again he is mainly remembered as a philosopher not a physician. Also I enjoyed reading about the lives of Rousseau and Descartes."

"As did I. Two great philosophers. Rousseau was also a wonderful composer who gave us such beautiful melodic music. Yet it was Rousseau whose political writings probably inspired the French revolution. And René Descartes, like Pythagoras, was also a brilliant mathematician and was described as the father of analytical geometry. It was his statement 'cogito ergo sum' or 'I think therefore I am' which is regarded as one of the pillars of philosophy."

Benson paused and stared into space as though savoring the accomplishments of those two philosophers. He shook his head as though in awe, then turned again to face Alex.

"How about Bertrand Russell, a living philosopher, did you read much about him?"

"Only a little. Frankly, I can't stand the man."

"Oh, why is that?"

"Perhaps it shows my prejudice against the elite upper class system of Britain. He was born into one of the most aristocratic families in Britain. His grandfather was twice Prime Minister. I don't object so much to his anti-war activities but I totally disagree with his communist agitation. I shouldn't say that too loudly out here. Lee Sheng may have me killed."

He laughed at this. Benson joined in but wagged his finger as a warning.

"Don't enter into a debate on communism with Lee Sheng," he advised.

Alex nodded his understanding before continuing.

"You see it is difficult for me to believe that someone so privileged; someone born with a silver spoon in his mouth; who wanted for nothing;

someone so rich; - would happily give all that up and cheerfully live the life of a peasant. I just do not subscribe to someone rabidly propounding that all others should embrace a way of life he himself has never experienced."

"I doubt Russell wished everyone to be a peasant," said Benson gently.

"No I'm sure he didn't, forgive my hyperbolic lapse. But he does wish everyone to be equal and that's just not possible. Life is meant to be a rewarding experience. I know there are millions who will never see it that way. But if one has the energy and drive to better oneself then he should be allowed to succeed and enjoy the fruits of his labors - so long as he doesn't abuse his fellow man in the process."

"Now that statement is one on which we could have a serious debate. There are many excellent minds that would not agree with your sentiments. They would advocate the end justifies the means; even if it were to result in the sacrifice of one's fellow man. However there is no man who could ever deny you have given more than you need have done for your fellow man. You gave up university to fight for your country in its time of need. Then you gave up a comfortable life at Bletchley Park to come out here to aid our struggle against the Japanese."

Alex shrugged his shoulders modestly at this compliment.

"I apologize if I got a bit carried away. Particularly on a subject I know so little about. I should know better than to attempt to teach my grandmother how to suck eggs."

Benson chuckled loudly at this.

"It's many a year since I heard that phrase, Alex. But you shouldn't belittle your knowledge of philosophy. You obviously have the ability to get right to the heart of a subject, that's a rare quality my young friend, believe me."

"I think the best philosophical advice I ever received was from my mother," said Alex reverently.

Benson arched his eyebrows indicating he wished to hear more.

"She told me life is made up of journeys during which you encounter endless crossroads. The trick to an interesting and rewarding life is to pick the correct path at most of the crossroads."

"Ah! I see your mother was the fountain of your knowledge. Life can indeed be described as a series of endless journeys. But it is essential one does not micromanage the process. By that I mean don't attempt to apply that logic to inconsequential tasks, like should I take the bus or walk. You must save your analytical skills for the important opportunities. But I know you have learned that already. And always remember, Alex, when you reach one of those crossroads and you are in doubt, trust your instincts. I would not give that advice to everyone, but from what little I know of you, your instincts will not let you down."

Benson's shoulders sagged and Alex saw he was still a man not yet recovered from debilitating illness.

"Maybe you should lie down for a while, Tony," he suggested worriedly.

"You not only have excellent instincts but also a keen sense of observation. Yes, if you don't mind, I will rest."

Alex was to recall this conversation many times. And always regret that war would interfere with his opportunity to learn much more from this wise professor of philosophy.

Chapter Twenty One

That night Alex tossed and turned and got little sleep. Yet his body craved exactly that. The combination of an unfriendly climate and lack of nourishing food seemed to have drained him. However it was the upcoming events that mainly prevented his mind from being still. His brain kept going over and over the plan looking for a fault. The one obvious and potentially devastating problem was the Japanese deciding to keep the coding machine. Given that they would be unable to make it work in the short time available if they intended to return it, they may be tempted to keep it to learn more about it. But by doing so they would be revealing the identity of the traitor. He decided they would rather keep their stream of information going. The traitor had provided invaluable intelligence so why disrupt that flow. Yet something was nagging him and as he drifted in and out of sleep he was unable to stay awake for a long enough spell to bring it into focus.

It was four o'clock in the morning when Alex came fully awake. Both Benson and Chesterton were rushing outside. Their ears, sharply attuned from years of war in the jungle, had heard a noise they all too well recognized. Alex ran out to join them and in the far distance they all beheld an orange glow and now Alex heard a muffled roar.

"Good old Steve," exalted Benson. "He must have hit an ammunition store or a petrol dump."

"Looks to me like the latter," said an excited Chesterton. "An ammo store would give off continuous flashes of light."

Then he cried into the night, "Well done you bloody marvelous Scotsman."

Their excitement was shared by all the other guerrillas who had come out to see the spectacle and were now cheering wildly and dancing around in the dark. This brought a satisfied smile to Chesterton's face.

"As I told you before, Alex, nothing breeds commitment more in this type of warfare like a little success," he breathed ecstatically. "But Steve must have taken one helluva chance. Let's pray it wasn't a suicide action."

All the excitement had banished the nagging thought which had troubled Alex - but only temporarily. Once back in bed he found it impossible to fall asleep.

When he arose tiredly at seven o'clock his mind registered it was only Wednesday yet it seemed an eternity since Steve left on Monday. By now MacDougal would either be in hiding or on his way back after causing such a spectacular diversionary action. And starting tonight Alex would be listening for the tell-tale signal indicating the Japanese were tampering with one of the dummy machines.

Breakfast was a quiet meal. The strain of the long hours ahead and the worry over the fate of MacDougal was evident on the faces of all three men.

Just as they were finishing, the dilemma that had plagued Alex all through the night came suddenly into focus.

"I must talk confidentially to both of you," he exclaimed excitedly. "Where is the safest place?"

"I'll post a non-English speaking guard at the tent. We can talk there," replied Chesterton hurriedly.

The eagerness in his voice was caused by Alex's animated tone. They rushed to the tent and after receiving an ordered supply of coffee the two men looked at Alex expectantly.

"I couldn't sleep last night, even before the fireworks, and I finally worked out what was nagging at my mind. The traitor knows the location of all the camps and the names of the leaders. So why hasn't he given this information to the Japanese and why haven't they launched a full scale attack on the camps? We were told they intensified their patrols but surely such action would be redundant if the traitor gave them our locations. I just don't understand it; but the reason must be of great significance."

Benson's face had a wan smile as though he was acknowledging the point, but it was Chesterton who answered.

"We have struggled with the very same point. And we can't come up with a logical answer. That's one of the reasons we have increased the perimeter of our guards and have instructed the other camps to do the same. Tony analyzed the situation and did come up with a few possible reasons. Go ahead and tell Alex," he instructed Benson.

"The first is the Japs have had success in deciphering our messages in the past and because of this have killed many men in ambushes. They may prefer to continue doing so until they are certain our numbers are greatly degraded, rather than launch a head-on assault. Such an attack could cost them heavy casualties. The second is our traitor may not be willing to sacrifice himself. If the Japs first bombarded us then attacked he would most likely be killed along with many others. Therefore, he may claim not to know the location of all the other camps. And if he knew of an assault and suddenly disappeared beforehand such a move would be instantly noticed. That would be a red flag and would cause us to relocate the camp. The Japs are not stupid; they would understand the consequence of their informant's sudden departure. It would negate the element of surprise. The third is they have a plan and the time is not yet ready to launch that plan, but what that plan is, we have no idea."

"However now that we have you and your plan, we will soon have the traitor and Lee Sheng and his men will get the truth out of him before they kill him," added Chesterton with a smile of satisfaction.

They sat quietly ruminating on the problem when suddenly Alex slapped the side of his head and yelled out.

"You idiot! You bloody idiot!"

"What is it?" demanded a startled Chesterton.

"I was delaying using the Japanese machine until we discovered the traitor as I was sure any messages between Ipoh and Grik would be of a standard variety and unimportant. But that was the wrong thing to do. I should be listening in to their standard messages in order to identify their broadcasting wavelengths. And it's possible the Japanese in Ipoh will not even deign to encode messages to Grik since they would be so mundane. But I'll be able to identify their sign-on and sign-off signals. These will be a good start in later helping me decypher their encoded messages. Ipoh will have to report Steve's attack at some point and that will certainly be sent in code. I had better get started right away. I'll need your services as a translator, Tony."

"Gladly, old boy."

"And Simon," said Alex, "I think you should act as guard and keep everyone as far away from the cabin as possible. If our traitor is still in camp, we don't want him to overhear our attempts to listen in on Japanese transmissions."

"Good idea," replied Chesterton.

Benson didn't add a comment agreeing with Chesterton's praise. He just smiled a knowing smile and tapped the side of his head indicating that Alex was always thinking ahead.

Crossroads

Once inside the cabin, Alex set up both machines. The first was the Japanese machine, the second one ready to listen for a signal from one of the dummy machines should it fall into Japanese hands. That signal would only happen at the earliest the next night. He also brought out a tape recorder from his backpack.

"I'll record any messages we get. That will give you a chance to play them back and better enable you to translate them," he said to Benson.

Once again he got a smile from Benson who was gaining an even greater appreciation of this young man's talent. Alex then sat in front of the Japanese machine and began a slow search of radio frequencies. It wasn't too long before Benson raised his hand.

"That's it," he said.

Alex jotted down the frequency in a notepad.

"That's a voice transmission from Grik to Ipoh, merely saying there is nothing of importance to report."

"I'm sure Ipoh will acknowledge. I'll keep tracking."

A few minutes later Benson once again raised his hand.

"That's Ipoh responding. You've got it Alex!" said an excited Benson.

"Are they using a code?" asked Alex.

"No, it's just as you thought, they are speaking normally. They are either sloppy or more likely they have a complete disdain for our ability to intercept."

As Alex noted the Ipoh frequency, his face reflected some concern.

"What's troubling you?" asked Benson.

"Ipoh should have reported Steve's raid, but we didn't pick up the message. They must have used a different frequency to contact their superiors in Singapore or Kuala Lumpur," muttered Alex. "It was probably a short message saying an attack was being investigated and a full report would follow. Anyway I can't worry about that now. We'll just have to wait for them to report again."

Benson went outside to give Chesterton the good news.

"Well done, Alex. You've got the frequencies. Do you require me to continue as a lookout?"

"No thanks, Simon, that's all I can do for now," he said tensely.

The afternoon dragged by. To fill in the time, Chesterton decided to call an unscheduled hand-to-hand combat training session and Alex joined in. He was partnered with Chin.

"I shall try to be careful, Sir," said the well spoken Chin. "I do not wish to harm you."

113

Almost as though he had been reading Chin's mind, Chesterton came by just before the class started.

"Take it easy, Chin," he said.

But after a while he realized such a warning had been completely unnecessary when he saw Chin pick himself up off the grass for the second time.

"Where did you learn these skills, Murdoch?" he demanded.

"I had a few lessons before coming out here."

"That's obvious. I think I had better change your partner before you hurt Chin."

Alex was then paired with a wiry Chinese who didn't return his friendly greeting. His face was set in a smug smile. He would enjoy teaching this Englishman a lesson. The smile didn't last long. He found Alex to be a much tougher proposition than he had bargained for. He had started out too confidently and found himself overcome by the training MacTavish had given Alex. He soon took matters much more seriously and the contest became an even struggle. When the session was over both men were feeling the pain from hitting the grass several times. Alex was covered in grass stains and his clothing was drenched in sweat.

"Time for a dip in the river and a change of clothes," said Chesterton. "You really are very accomplished at jungle fighting, Murdoch. Quite the dark horse, aren't you?"

"I had a brief but intensive period of training," replied Alex in a noncommittal tone.

He hadn't forgotten another part of his spy training – to give away as little as possible – no matter to whom you were speaking.

Once in the river he couldn't help noticing the stares from the other guerrillas. They were looks of respect.

Late in the afternoon Alex sat at the small table in the cabin intently waiting for a signal. Benson brought his dinner to him but he hardly noticed so intense was his concentration. Finally at two o'clock the next morning he gave up. None of the dummy machines had been given to the Japanese.

Chesterton, Benson and Alex went to bed sharing the same mixture of feelings. Relief that neither of the delivery men was a traitor; but deep dismay that they would have to go through the terrible period of strain all over again.

Chapter Twenty Two

Late Thursday night Steve MacDougal arrived back in the camp. He quickly reported to Chesterton before bathing in the river.

"Unfortunately we lost one of our men. I gave the order to stay hidden when the first Japs appeared after the explosion. But he lost his nerve and tried to make a run for it. He was mowed down before he had gone twenty yards. We thought there would have been at least a dozen Japs guarding the petrol dump. Therefore as soon as we were discovered by our man's stupid action, we believed we had had it. But fortunately there were only five Japs on duty. We had to fight our way out and to our amazement it was easy. The Japs were completely disorganized and instead of spreading out they bunched together. We took them out and ran into the jungle. Our man would not have died if he had just obeyed my order."

"That's really strange they would only post five men to guard such a strategic location," said Chesterton.

MacDougal quickly changed the subject to something he had been thinking about all the way back from the raid.

"Any luck with identifying our traitor," he asked eagerly.

"Unfortunately not, we'll have to send out two more messengers," replied Alex.

Before MacDougal could pursue this subject, Chesterton took control.

"You better go get cleaned up and get something to eat, Steve," he advised. "We'll join you in the mess tent and you can finish your briefing there."

By the time Steve arrived in the mess tent, the other two Chinese members of the raiding party were already there, surrounded by a large group. Many were talking at the same time and the noise was almost deafening. Suddenly Lee Sheng appeared with Chua the head of security and the noise stopped. Lee Sheng began debriefing the two men while they still stuffed food in their mouths.

"Go ahead with the rest of your report when you're ready. Steve," said Chesterton placing paper and a pencil on the table ready to log the action.

"The trails were tricky after the heavy rain but we made good time. We didn't encounter any patrols and were on the outskirts of Ipoh at two o'clock. I reconnoitered the area for an hour and discovered an ammo dump to the east but there were four huts inside the wire fence. I reckoned they would be full of Japs so I dismissed that as a target. On the south end of town I came across the petrol storage area. There were two huts and as I said I anticipated many more Japs than we encountered. Nevertheless, I decided to take the risk and blow up the dump. I said there were five Japs but actually there were seven. Two were guarding the gate; the other five were in one of the huts."

Chesterton was writing furiously as MacDougal spoke.

"The two at the gate were squatting on the ground smoking."

"What?" exclaimed Chesterton. "You'd be jailed for that in any decent army. It indicates a complete disregard of duty and as any good soldier knows there is always the possibility of an officer's surprise inspection."

"This is most unlike the Japanese Army we have been fighting," interjected Benson. "They have proved to be highly disciplined. Those troops successfully fought for several years in Korea and China and know their jobs. They proved that by how swiftly they marched all the way down Malaya sweeping everything in their path and proving equally effective in capturing Fortress Singapore."

"Well all I can tell you is the two at the gate were not elite troops. They even fell for the old trick we used to kill them. We lobbed a few pebbles inside the fence and when they jumped up to peer at the cause of the noise thereby presenting their backs to us, we knifed them quietly. That allowed us to plant the explosives and retreat a safe distance."

"Was that when our man was killed?" asked Chesterton.

"Yes. After the first explosion the five guards ran out of the hut and our man made a run for it. Once we took care of the five I sent the remaining two men on ahead into the jungle and I stayed for a while to observe. That's when I got the biggest surprise of all. It was the reaction of the main garrison. Lots of Japs came rushing to the scene but they were running around like chickens with their heads cut off. The officers dithered before restoring some order. And even then they sent patrols to search the town and the road south. No one was sent to the jungle. I didn't understand that, however, I took that opportunity to gallop after our other two men. I am guessing the Japs will be searching around for some time. So our messengers should have no trouble in getting back."

"That was excellent work, Steve," said Chesterton. "Now we had all better get some sleep."

Alex was up early the next day and was scanning the frequencies on the Japanese machine. The noise of doing so woke the others.

"What are you doing, Alex?" demanded Chesterton after looking at his watch. "It's not yet seven."

"It struck me that the commander of the Japanese garrison in Ipoh must report the raid destroying his petrol dump. Even though it will represent a loss of face, he definitely needs to be resupplied."

"Oh, I see. Good thinking! Are you awake, Tony?"

"Unfortunately yes oh great leader. I suppose you want me to stand by to translate, in case your guess proves correct, Alex?"

"Yes please."

"Damn, I was rather hoping you had stayed up all night learning Japanese," said Benson sardonically.

"While you two are hard at work, I'll arrange for some breakfast to be delivered," said MacDougal pulling on his trousers."

"If you don't mind would you bring it here yourself, Steve. We don't want anyone listening in. And would you bring enough for all of us?" added Chesterton as he too dressed.

"Yes master," responded the Scot bowing three times before leaving.

Benson laughed heartily at this.

"No respect for authority, that one," muttered Chesterton but couldn't keep a grin from his face.

Alex kept tuning the machine while he ate a skimpy breakfast. Their food supplies were running low and unless they could mount a significant attack on Grik soon, the situation would become dire. After half-an-hour Chesterton was becoming impatient and suffering from the screeching of the many frequencies Alex was trying.

"I thought you already had the frequency at Ipoh," he said curtly to Alex.

"I do, but only the one they used for Grik. I have labeled that one as A. But they probably use a different one when communicating with their HQ. And that HQ could be in Penang, or Kuala Lumpur, or even Singapore. There is no communication using A at the moment so I have to try for others while periodically flipping back to A."

Ten minutes later MacDougal poked his head in from his position as guard.

"Any luck?"

"No and keep to your post," growled Chesterton, showing his frustration.

MacDougal thought better of making a smart riposte and went back to his duties.

"Temper, temper, oh great leader," chided Benson. "None of us enjoys the waiting, Simon."

"I'm sorry," said Chesterton, and then went outside to apologize to MacDougal.

He had just returned when Alex held up his hand for silence and immediately turned on his tape recorder.

"Ipoh is using a different frequency as I suspected but I've got them."

Benson hunched over the code machine as he listened intently. The transmission lasted for fifteen minutes and at the end of it he shrugged his shoulders.

"It makes no sense – it is all gibberish," he cried in irritation.

"What?" complained Chesterton having almost reached the limit of his endurance.

"Take it easy everyone, it's undoubtedly in code," said Alex in a take charge manner. "Playback the recording, Tony, and write out every word. First in katakana then in Romanized Japanese then translate each word into English. And finally write out the katakana alphabet and the numbers from 0 to 9 in Japanese," he instructed.

Benson looked at him with continued respect.

"Okay, boss," he responded.

Alex was too intent on the task before him to pay attention to Benson's tone. But Chesterton didn't miss it. He too saw that Alex was now in command – at least as far as codes and communications were concerned. And not having to deal with this important issue served to ease his burden as leader. He relaxed and went outside to brief MacDougal.

"Thanks for the update, Simon. Obviously only Alex is an expert in code braking but to my uneducated mind it sounds like a very tall order to break a code in Japanese. And I don't quite understand what good it does him to have the coded Japanese translated into English. Anyway it seems like a long process. I had better get a supply of coffee to keep us all going. Will you takeover as lookout while I am away?"

"Certainly, Steve," replied a disconsolate Chesterton, agreeing with MacDougal's analysis that the task in front of Alex seemed insurmountable.

When MacDougal returned they entered the cabin. Benson put his finger to his lips. Alex was hunched over the information Benson had provided oblivious to everything but his task. Benson poured a cup of coffee and laid it next to Alex who picked it up without taking his eyes off the paper in front of him and without saying a word. The others took their coffees outside.

"That young man is a true cypher genius," breathed Benson. "And you know me well enough that I wouldn't make such a remark lightly."

"How is he getting on?" asked an eager Chesterton, hoping that his prior assessment may prove wrong.

"First he broke down the message into segments. What Ipoh transmitted and what Kuala Lumpur transmitted. Then when the sign-on signal he had previously gotten from Ipoh didn't work he tried various others such as 'Ipoh calling Kuala Lumpur, are you receiving me?' and had me write this out in katakana. He counted the characters in each word and searched the opening of the transmission to see if it matched. It didn't match exactly but many of the words did. So he had a start. Then he asked me to write out the names of the commanders in both Ipoh and KL and searched the parts of the transmissions where names would be used. He found them. He asked me where a new supply of petrol would likely come from. I told him Taiping, Penang or Kuala Lumpur. Again he had me write out Taiping and Penang in katakana. He already had KL then he wanted me to write out the Japanese for petrol storage area, resupply, raid, troops, urgent, report, and guerrilla attack. He grunts with satisfaction when he believes he has found some of these words. And he has accomplished all of this in – what? – only six minutes! Truly he is a genius."

"But why did he want you to translate the words into English?" asked MacDougal.

"To see if the Japs were sloppy and didn't encode proper names, such as the towns. But they weren't. Not one word in the transmission was a real word. Every one was in code."

Just then Alex called out for Tony in a loud voice.

"I need more words translated, Tony. Now!"

Benson rushed back into the cabin. He returned in ten minutes.

"He's back in an almost trance staring at the message. God only knows how long he will be."

They waited in the heat and humidity, ready to obey any command from the master of codes. It was exactly forty-five minutes later that Alex appeared in the doorway. Perspiration had soaked his shirt and matted his hair to his skull but he was completely oblivious of his appearance.

He had a grin on his face that spoke volumes. He was a completely satisfied code breaker.

Chapter Twenty Three

"Please come in, chaps, and my apologies if I appeared a bit of an ogre. Once I get started I am afraid I lose track of everything else."

"Have you cracked it?" asked Benson eagerly, as all three almost ran into the cabin.

The first thing they noticed was the large number of scrunched up pieces of paper that littered the floor: obviously unsuccessful decoding attempts. Alex held the final piece in his hand.

"I believe so but I won't be certain until Tony translates what I think is the decoded message. You see once I managed to get a reasonable number of words, I found the transposition sequence of the katakana symbols."

He noticed the bemused looks on the three faces as they struggled to understand.

"Let me explain. In the simplest of codes you change the first letter in the first word for the letter, say, five moves away in the alphabet. That means you transpose the letter f for every a in the coded message and for example you change the letter h to an m. That's the most basic of codes. It becomes much more complicated when the numerical sequence is altered. For example when the first letter is moved five places but the second letter is moved seven places and the third letter is moved eleven places. The sequence could be moved many times. Then you would need a code book to work out the real message."

"But the Japanese don't use our alphabet," interrupted MacDougal.

"That's true, Steve, but their language is totally phonetic unlike English. Therefore each character is very much like a letter."

"How did you work out the sequence the Japs are using?" asked Chesterton.

"The speed with which Kuala Lumpur responded to Ipoh was too fast for them to have been using a code book. Decoding in such a manner is very time consuming and naturally it requires the same long time to encode a response. Therefore I presumed they must be using a relatively simple code sequence. And I guessed it must be a numerical sequence they would easily remember. Japan like Britain signifies dates in day, month and year. For Japanese soldiers one very important date is that of the start of the invasion of Malaya – 8.12.41. Therefore I tried the sequence – 8-12-4-1, and it worked on the letters I had decyphered."

Chesterton stared in awe for several seconds before he could speak.

"You said it, Tony, he's a bloody genius."

"Let's be sure it works for the entire message before throwing compliments around," warned Alex. "Will you translate the message, Tony?"

Benson took the sheet of paper and studied it before translating.

Ipoh calling Kuala Lumpur. Are you receiving?

Receiving Ipoh. Go ahead.

Urgent from Lieutenant Ito to Major Ozumi. Guerrillas have blown up gasoline store. Must have new supply immediately. Please advise delivery.

This is Major Ozumi. How could this happen? Did they have superior numbers? And have they been caught and executed?

They escaped but we are conducting a search in town and south of Ipoh.

This is a great embarrassment. How could you allow it?

As I told you, Major Ozumi, we were taking a serious risk when you took almost all my seasoned troops and particularly my good officers. The replacements you gave me straight from Japan have no experience and it is taking time to train them. This resulted in a completely disorganized response to the attack. The new officers took far too long to direct their men.

You were informed, Ito, that your experienced troops and officers were required to repulse the American attacks in the Pacific. You must immediately train your new troops and launch the agreed full scale attack on guerrilla installations. No further excuse will be accepted. Meantime I will arrange new supplies of gasoline to be sent from Penang. Out.

"Brilliant work, Alex!" exuded MacDougal.

"We should thank Tony for his invaluable service," replied Alex.

Chesterton grabbed both of Alex's hands and shook them vigorously in a highly emotional manner. His eyes were brimming with prideful tears.

"Thank you, Alex. You not only cracked their code but your fantastic work has answered the question we have all struggled with. Why haven't the Japs forced our traitor to reveal our location and launch an attack? It was because the new troops were untrained. But it can't be too long until they do so now. We must identify the traitor and put him out of business. Then we have to initiate a preemptive strike."

Benson came close to Alex to add his congratulations and finished by whispering in his ear.

"Your father would have been very proud of you."

That almost brought tears to Alex's eyes but he recovered to say, "I don't know if you got the news out here that after a long siege the Japanese evacuated Guadalcanal in February. So General MacArthur is on the move. That's why the seasoned troops were taken out of Malaya."

"I bet MacArthur has his sights on the Philippines. He promised he would return," added Benson.

"Let's get back to our business," said Chesterton. "The messengers should return tonight and if your assessment is correct Steve, the Japs will not yet have organized patrols close to their return routes. We can't do anything further until we have the dummy machines returned. Then we can send out the next pair of messengers."

"Well I think I need to bathe and change clothes," said a drenched but happy Alex.

The rest of the day was again one full of strain-filled waiting until at night Steve's prophesy turned out to be true, and the two messengers arrived safely in camp. They carried their fake coding machines with great care, very proud of their accomplished missions. They could not have known they had been treated as guinea pigs in a serious but fruitless mission. Once again they were rigorously debriefed by Lee Sheng, this time without his head of security but with Chesterton sitting in. He took copious notes and pretended this had been a highly successful assignment. At the end Lee Sheng swore both men to secrecy regarding their mission. No one must know about the coding machines.

When the men left, Lee Sheng turned to Chesterton and spoke in English.

"We call Wong and Chen now?"

"Not yet, my friend. It will be better we do so first thing tomorrow morning," responded Chesterton.

He had given no other explanation but knew the messengers had to leave in the morning in order for the traitor to only make contact with the Japanese in the evening of the second day. The plan of Alex was precise in its timing.

By bedtime Alex thought he would have another night of fitful sleep.

But the adrenaline release after having cracked the code proved otherwise and he slept soundly.

Early next morning Wong and Chen were carefully briefed and dispatched, carrying their precious cargo. Alex and the others attempted to resume life as usual. They bathed, ate breakfast, and with nothing else to do, gathered in the tent. They sat in silence until the tension became palpable. Although nothing was said they all had the same thought - the traitor must be identified – and if it was not one of the two departed messengers then they were back to square one. Not finding the traitor was a pill too bitter to swallow. Almost simultaneously they decided they had to do something. Just sitting around would drive them crazy.

As food was in short supply Steve said he would form a hunting party. Benson decided to rest, he still was not looking well. Chesterton left to meet with Lee Sheng and identify possible targets for attack once communications was restored. Of course he would not mention that nothing could be initiated until the traitor was unmasked. Alex decided to return to the cabin with Benson.

"Will it disturb you Tony if I listen in for Japanese communications?"

"Not at all, old boy. Please go ahead and if you wish any urgent translations don't hesitate to wake me."

He managed to pick up a transmission from Penang to Ipoh and recorded it. He reckoned it was merely indicating when a new supply of petrol would be shipped and did not wake Benson for a translation.

The balance of the day seemed like an eternity to Alex. Even the success of MacDougal's hunting party in shooting a deer, combined with another party's success at fishing, engendered little enthusiasm in him.

If that day was a long drawn out affair, the next was even more agonizing. From late afternoon onwards, Alex was glued to his listening post. His anxiety had ruined his appetite and he had eaten very little. The others had an early dinner at six o'clock but Alex refused to go to the mess tent. All he did was drink coffee. Finally after eleven o'clock, Benson whispered to Chesterton.

"He is apt to stay up all night. I'm going to get him something to eat."

He soon returned with a plate of food, but Alex waved it away. Chesterton knew this to be an unhealthy sign and with a wink at MacDougal he feigned his most authoritative voice.

"Lieutenant Murdoch you will make yourself ill if you do not eat. I am ordering you to do so. If you disobey this command I will instruct MacDougal to hold you down while I force feed you! Now eat!"

Alex turned round and stared at Chesterton. He appeared totally confused and at first seemed not to understand. Then the message sunk in but he still appeared unwilling to accept that Chesterton would roar at him in this fashion.

"I said eat, Lieutenant Murdoch!"

"Yes sir," said Alex in a stunned voice.

The deer meat was excellent and in next to no time he cleared his plate. To his surprise he soon began feeling more alert as he settled down once again to his vigil. The others decided to go to bed but told Alex to wake them should he get a signal.

It was exactly two-twelve when they were wakened by a high pitched piercing signal emanated from the coding machine.

Chapter Twenty Four

For a split second everyone seemed to be frozen in place. Then Alex pressed a key on the machine.

"Is it the correct signal?" demanded Chesterton, his chest heaving in a breathless manner as he attempted to shake off the effects of his deep sleep.

"Yes, there is no doubt," replied Alex

"Well who the hell is it?" cried out MacDougal.

"It's Wong," replied Alex in a hushed voice knowing the effect it would have on MacDougal.

"No, no, that must be a mistake. Check it again," bellowed a distraught MacDougal.

"There is no mistake. I'm sorry Steve. It is definitely the machine that Wong was carrying."

"But he has been with me for fifteen years. I attended his wedding and I know his wife and son. I can't believe it."

"I am sorry too, Steve. All we can do is wait until he returns and question him," uttered a dismayed Chesterton.

MacDougal abruptly rose pulled on some clothes and strode outside.

"Life can hand you no more bitter a blow than to discover a trusted friend has become a traitorous foe," muttered the professor of philosophy.

"What about Steve?" asked Alex. "Should someone go after him?"

"No it's better to leave him alone," replied Chesterton. "And I suggest you get some sleep. You look absolutely exhausted."

The three of them went to bed and at seven they arose as usual, to find that MacDougal had not returned to the cabin.

"Damn," uttered Chesterton. "Let's go look for him."

They found him sitting at the large table in the tent. His bloodshot eyes were sunk in his head and ringed with dark shadows. He was a man gutted by sorrow and disenchantment. He had spent the night searching for answers but had found none. He looked up at them wearily.

"I can't believe it. Not Wong. He has fought the Japs side by side with me. He couldn't have changed allegiance. Why would he do such a thing? Why? Why?"

"Perhaps you should get some rest, Steve. Wong won't be here until tomorrow night, you won't get answers until then," suggested Benson gently.

MacDougal turned his glazed gaze to Chesterton.

"I want to question him first, Simon; before Lee Sheng gets his hands on him," he said in a low but unmistakably assertive voice.

"That will be difficult my friend. You know Lee Sheng will want to debrief both of them as soon as they enter the camp. If you try to interfere he will be instantly suspicious and that could soon lead to Wong's quick execution."

"Then I'll just have to go into the jungle and meet him before he reaches the camp."

"But he will be with Chen," protested Chesterton.

"I'll think of some excuse to be alone with him. I have to do this, Simon," he added determinedly.

Chesterton saw there was no use in arguing with him and reluctantly nodded his agreement.

"Okay, Steve, now will you get some rest?"

"I'll try -- thanks Simon," he mumbled and trudged off towards the cabin.

Alex looked at both men with questioning eyes. Benson shrugged resignedly. But Chesterton answered his implied question.

"Out here in the jungle you rarely form deep, lasting attachments. It's cruel to say but people die too easily – either from the enemy or from disease. It's not that you don't care for your fellow comrades but time and experience teaches you mourning dulls your senses and puts you and your remaining comrades in danger. The only exception to the friendship rule is when you have put your life in another's hands and he hasn't let you down. That bond is intensified by further such occurrences. Then the bond becomes immutable. If you were to combine that with a previous friendship as is the case between Wong and MacDougal then you have something exceedingly rare. I cannot explain to you in words how devastating it must be to have that bond severed by traitorous means. I can only say that Steve MacDougal, the strong almost invincible Scotsman, has had his heart broken."

"Beautifully put, Simon," agreed a greatly saddened Benson.

"I hate to question your expertise, Alex, but can you be categorically certain that signal came from Wong's machine?" asked Chesterton.

"Regrettably there cannot be even a smidgeon of doubt."

Chesterton's shoulders fell in dejection; one last sign of final acceptance.

"Then there's nothing more to do," he said morosely.

The rest of that day and most of the next, they busied themselves in the usual camp activities, except MacDougal who stayed in the cabin the whole time. Each hour seemed like a day to Alex. They were sitting in the tent when Chin kindly brought them coffee at four o'clock.

"I'll take a cup to Steve in the cabin," said Alex.

He returned almost immediately.

"He's gone," he gasped, and was surprised when his news brought no response from the other two.

"He's on his way to meet Wong," said Benson dispassionately. Then changing the subject he said, "I hope you have thought carefully about your imminent discussion with Lee Sheng, Simon. He will not take kindly to having been left in the dark," he added ominously.

"Any suggestions, Tony?"

"Perhaps the truth is most appropriate."

"May I make a suggestion," interjected Alex.

"Please do," said Chesterton.

"I don't think you should mention anything about the entrapment method. On my first morning here you took me for breakfast. It was then I was introduced to Wong. While he was preparing breakfast you asked Steve if there was something troubling Wong. Do you remember?"

"Yes, now that you mention it, I did. And he said Wong had evaded giving an explanation."

"Then I suggest you tell Lee Sheng that Steve had noticed a decided change in Wong's behavior and had not been given a satisfactory answer by Wong. This had been eating at Steve and he decided it could not go on. He would make him tell what was causing his altered attitude. He went to meet Wong to have it out with him and in the process Wong broke down and admitted his sin."

"Hmm, that might work, thanks Alex."

"There is only one slight problem, oh great leader."

"And that is---?"

"You would have to meet with Steve before he enters the camp with Wong, to brief him on this story. And to ascertain if Steve has managed to discover what caused Wong to betray us. Your story and Steve's must be in harmony to fool Lee Sheng and equally importantly, to fool Chua. He will lose a great deal of face. The head of security should not have allowed a traitor to operate for such a long time without being discovered. You can be positive Chua will push for every little detail of Wong's transgression."

"You're absolutely right, Tony. I had better leave camp in about two hours to intercept Steve."

The perceptive Benson noticed the look of the face of Alex.

"Something bothering you, Alex?"

"I was just wondering if Steve would be so upset by Wong's deceit that he would act as judge, jury and executioner."

"Oh God. I hope not," exclaimed Chesterton.

But Benson shook his head vehemently.

"I do not believe so. Steve is too knowledgable for that. He will most assuredly know that such an action without the prior consent of Lee Sheng would create an uprising among the guerrillas. No, he will bring Wong in alive and have him confess his sins to Lee Sheng. He won't like it but he will do it. Nevertheless you must meet Steve well before he reaches the first sentry. It will take all your skill to bypass that sentry. I have no doubt that Steve will have managed that with his jungle craft but you will have to be extra careful, oh great leader."

"You're right, Tony. Perhaps I will leave a bit earlier to allow time to detour the sentry."

At five thirty Chesterton slipped out of the camp and into the gathering gloom of the jungle. In the cabin Benson and Alex could only lie in their beds and stare at the ceiling. Then as they had agreed with Chesterton, at six o'clock they went to the mess tent to collect four trays of food, saying that Chesterton and MacDougal were not feeling well and they would all eat in the cabin. At nine-fifty, Lee Sheng came to the cabin. Benson met him at the doorway putting his finger to his lips for silence.

"Captain Chesterton is sleeping. He has not been well," he whispered in Hokkien.

The inquisitive Lee Sheng peeked into the cabin. Alex and Benson had pushed clothes under a blanket in Chesterton's bed to give the impression that he was asleep in his bed. Satisfied with his quick inspection, Lee Sheng said, "Chen come back but no Wong. Chen say Tuan MacDougal meet them in jungle and stay to talk to Wong. But you tell cook Mr. MacDougal not well and he take dinner in cabin," he said in his broken English but with an accusatory tone.

This was something they had not anticipated and Benson silently chided himself for overlooking this eventuality. But the quick thinking professor had an answer which he gave in Hokkien, ignoring Lee Sheng's prior use of English.

"You know Mr. MacDougal and Wong have been friends for a long time."

Lee Sheng nodded his agreement.

"Mr. MacDougal thought that Wong has been very worried for the last few weeks and decided he must find out the reason. We asked him to wait until Wong returns but you know Mr. MacDougal, once he decides to do something he does it immediately. He wanted to have time alone with Wong and went out to meet him. He believes Wong will talk more freely on a one-on-one basis and not in front of the other men."

He shrugged helplessly.

Lee Sheng gave Benson a suspicious stare. But after a few moments consideration he slowly nodded his head in agreement.

"Please wake Captain Chesterton when Wong returns. I will wait for him and we can debrief both Chan and Wong at the same time," he responded in Hokkien.

It was just after ten when Chesterton returned.

"Steve will be here with Wong in about twenty minutes. I wanted to come ahead to brief both of you. Unfortunately it is true that Wong is the traitor. Steve confronted him straight away and Wong broke down and confessed. However it was not for money. Those bastard Japs kidnapped his wife and son and threatened to kill them. When Wong bravely attempted to call their bluff they sent him a little bit of persuasion – his wife's finger. Wong recognized it by the jade ring. They said the next piece of anatomy he would receive would be his son's ears."

Gasps of horror simultaneously came from both men.

"The inhuman fiends," snarled Benson.

"Wong knows he can expect no mercy from the guerrillas and is willing to take his punishment. However he did plead for one thing from Steve."

"To save his wife and son," blurted out Alex.

Chesterton gave Alex a strange look bordering on wonder.

"Yes, that's right. How did you guess?"

"It seems like it would be the last wish from one old friend to another," he replied.

"And what was Steve's response?" queried Benson.

"For old times sake he agreed he would try."

The next remark from Alex left both of the other men with their mouths agape in astonishment.

"Then Lee Sheng must not be allowed to kill Wong - at least not yet. *We need him alive!*"

Chapter Twenty Five

"What the blazes are you talking about?" exploded an exceedingly tense Chesterton.

"Pardon the idiom, but we can kill two birds with one stone," answered Alex.

"Even to a professor of philosophy that requires an explanation," said Benson with some testiness.

It was evident the strain of the last few days was still having an impact on the two men. Alex took a deep breath before elaborating.

"From all you have told me, Simon, you are badly in need of two things. First is a highly successful raid on the Japanese to re-establish your stature with all the guerrilla camps; thereby preventing further desertions and, hopefully, strongly enhancing the recruitment of new men. Second is to get your hands on the Japanese supply of medicines, food and arms."

"That's correct – so?"

"Here is an outline of a plan that may accomplish both of those things. It's just an outline I'll need more time to think on it a bit more before I can finalize all the details."

When he had finished, Chesterton did an uncharacteristic thing – he hugged Alex. Benson sat back with a look of absolute joy mixed with awe.

"Absolutely brilliant, old boy," he gushed.

Chesterton glanced anxiously at his watch.

"I had better leave now. I'll have to waylay Steve and Wong before they arrive and bring them straight to the cabin. We must be certain Wong will go along with your plan otherwise it won't work. But I'm pretty sure he will. Then we'll ask Lee Sheng to join us. Meantime why don't you and Tony work on finalizing the details of your plan, Alex?"

"Okay," said Alex, relieved at the reception his plan had received.

Twenty minutes later Chesterton returned accompanied by MacDougal and Wong. He had the slightest of smiles on his lips and merely nodded twice indicating Wong had agreed. For his part Wong hung his head and refused to look at any of the four others. Steve MacDougal was grim faced and only gave Alex and Tony a cursory wave of his hand. His action clearly indicated he was still a man suffering from considerable trauma. Wong's confession had not had a cathartic effect on him. If anything it had increased his misery.

"Shall I ask Lee Sheng to join us, Simon?" asked Benson.

At the mention of the guerrilla chief's name, Wong shook visibly. He was evidently dreading meeting him and enduring the vituperative venom Lee Sheng would unleash on him. Not to mention the ultimate fate he would most certainly undergo. He could only hope it would be a swift death and not one at the end of countless hours of torture.

"If you wouldn't mind, Tony. Thanks."

No one in the cabin spoke until Lee Sheng appeared with Tony. On the way to the cabin he had peppered Tony with questions about this unusual procedure, but Benson had refused to answer, merely saying that Captain Chesterton would explain everything.

"I'll stand guard outside in case we have unexpected guests," volunteered Benson.

"Good idea, Tony," replied a grateful Chesterton, knowing that the camp would soon be buzzing with speculation.

"What wrong? Why we no have debriefing?" demanded Lee Sheng in his broken English.

"I had better explain things in Hokkien, Alex. Sorry, but I don't want to risk any misinterpretation."

"I understand, Simon."

"Please sit, Lee Sheng."

The Chinese seemed unwilling to do so. It was only after a second bidding that he sat and looked at Chesterton with a mixture of anger at being delayed and inquisitiveness at something he sensed was of the utmost importance.

"You know we have been unable to conduct significant raids on the Japanese positions because we could not send safe messages to the other guerrilla groups."

"Yes they learned your codes and ambushed us. I lost seven men and the other groups lost eighteen men. And unless we have a secure code and can get all the other groups to act simultaneously it is not possible to coordinate a raid."

"Correct. For some time we believed the Japanese had a new code breaker sent out from Japan."

"That is possible," said Lee Sheng in a tone that indicated it was not the only possibility.

"Or there could have been another reason," said Chesterton ominously.

"I also thought of that but my secret investigations revealed nothing."

Lee Sheng's tone indicated he knew exactly what Chesterton meant. As he uttered those words his eyes swept the room and for the first time he noticed the looks on the faces of MacDougal and Wong. His acute sense of something dangerously amiss was aroused and he half rose from his chair, his hand reaching for the revolver strapped to his side.

"No. Please remain seated," commanded Chesterton.

Lee Sheng obeyed but kept his hand on the butt of the revolver.

"Mr. MacDougal noticed the recent change in Wong and tonight he questioned him. Wong finally admitted he was the source of intelligence to the Japanese."

Once again Lee Sheng started to rise from his chair, his eyes blazing with fury as his hand reached for his gun in a menacing fashion Chesterton quickly stood in front of him, putting one hand on his shoulder and staring unblinkingly into his eyes.

"He did not do so for money," he said, "they kidnapped his wife and son and threatened to kill them."

"That does not matter, he must be killed as a traitor," cried out Lee Sheng still standing half crouched, refusing to sit down.

"You must listen to all I have to say. It is vitally important. Do not act hastily," said Chesterton in a powerful and domineering voice.

Alex watched this drama with alarm. He only understood a few words however he didn't need to understand the words, the actions spoke for themselves. He was greatly relieved when Lee Sheng after a moment's hesitation nodded and sat back down.

"At first Wong refused to cooperate but the Japanese sent him one of his wife's fingers and told him if he continued to be uncooperative they would cut off his son's ears. If that failed they would execute them."

On their part the guerrillas would never hesitate to torture or kill their enemies, but women and children were off limits. Lee Sheng shivered at this news. All Chinese couples longed for a son and the thought of one's son having his ears amputated chilled the soul even of a hard-bitten communist like Lee Sheng. But he quickly recovered from this uncharacteristic feeling of pity.

"Nevertheless he must be punished," he stated sternly.

"We agree and Wong knows this to be true. But we have developed a plan to inflict great losses on the Japanese and we need Wong to be part of it."

Now Lee Sheng's interest was clearly aroused. He removed his hand from his revolver.

"Tell me," he demanded. He gave this unmistakable instruction with as much authority as he could muster. It was his way of reasserting his role as head of this guerrilla camp.

"Wong will take a message and leave it at the drop point for the Japanese. There must be a Japanese soldier close by to receive such messages. The message will read that a large meeting of all the guerilla groups will be held in five days at a place near Grik. The purpose of the meeting is to try to persuade the guerrillas not to continue with the desertions that have been taking place. It will also say a high ranking British officer, who has just arrived, will address the meeting, promising a new supply of arms. Wong will add he will be near Grik that night and will lead the Japanese to the meeting place, but only on one condition – that his wife and son be set free. He will call his wife at his home to confirm this before joining the Japanese at their Grik headquarters."

Lee Sheng immediately saw the plan.

"The Japanese will send most of their seventy men from Ipoh to Grik and we will raid Ipoh. Is that the plan?"

"Yes, partially. We have developed a new code that the Japanese cannot break. We will immediately have it delivered to the other camps with an urgent message from you telling them to be ready for a coordinated attack to occur soon. At this time you will not give them final details of the target or the date. You will only do so one day ahead of the raid."

"I do not understand. Why not tell them to meet us in Ipoh?"

"We do not require the other groups to raid Ipoh. The Japanese will leave no more than ten men on guard in Ipoh. We can easily overpower that number. Once having done so we will wait until two hours after the appointed time that Wong was to go to the Grik headquarters, then send a radio message from the Japanese Ipoh headquarters to Grik. It will say that the meeting of the guerrillas near Grik was a ruse and a few guerrillas attempted to once again blow up the petrol dump. This time the remaining Japanese soldiers captured them and they are being held for interrogation when Lieutenant Ito returns. After having waited impatiently for two hours, Lieutenant Ito will have begun to smell a rat and this message will only confirm his thinking. He will order his men back to Ipoh."

"And on the way back we and the other groups will ambush them," exalted an excited Lee Sheng."

"Correct. Except the ambush will not include the Grik guerillas. They will raid the Japanese headquarters in their town and kill them all."

"But how can you send a message from Ipoh to Grik? The Japanese will undoubtedly use a code."

"Our expert code breaker has cracked their code," said a triumphant Chesterton.

His triumph was severely dented when Lee Sheng next spoke.

"And this expert's name is not Benson, I think. Perhaps it is Murdoch?"

Chesterton was nonplussed for a moment. He had not thought Lee Sheng to be so perceptive.

"Yes, you are right. But I had to keep his identity as secret as possible until we uncovered Wong. I'm sorry for that."

"It's okay," said the Chinese, this time speaking English.

He stood upright and Chesterton prepared to rush at him, thinking he was about to attack Wong. But Lee Sheng turned to Alex and held out his hand.

"Congratulations. You very smart man."

Then he addressed Chesterton in Hokkien.

"I shall take the prisoner with me. We will lock him in a cage."

"No, I think it will be better if we tie him up here and keep him in the cabin. When word gets out he is a traitor some of your men may attempt to assassinate him."

"Do not worry. I will keep him securely bound inside the cage and keep it inside my hut. I will have two of my most trusted men guard him."

"Okay, that is acceptable. But do not hurt him. He must be fit to make the journey through the jungle."

"I understand. There is one more thing that concerns me, Captain Chesterton. It will be difficult to accompany Wong to the drop point without being spotted by the Japanese. And Wong may change his mind and attempt to escape."

A low voice came from the corner of the cabin. MacDougal, without raising his head, spoke for the first time.

"I will accompany him, and if he tries to escape, I will shoot him."

Lee Sheng did not have to see MacDougal's lowered face to see his agony. He heard the pain in his voice.

"That is satisfactory," he said.

Chapter Twenty Six

The small group was left to sit quietly in the cabin. Finally they began preparing for bed. It was only then that MacDougal again spoke.

"I presume this plan was your idea, laddie. You have really been a godsend to us. Well done."

"Thanks Steve, but I was only doing my job. However there is one thing I do not understand. Would someone care to enlighten me?" asked Alex.

"What's that?" asked Chesterton.

"You said you kept the code books in the safe and changed the combination each week. How did Wong manage to open the safe?"

"As I mentioned to you, several of the Chinese come to the cabin for one reason or another. Wong was such a frequent visitor that he almost became invisible. And as you said I changed the combination to the safe frequently. Because I was afraid I would get confused or forget the current combination, I would write it down on a slip of paper and put it inside a book that I kept in my table drawer. Wong saw me do this. One of his jobs was to bring us tea at bedtime. He asked the Japanese to provide him with sleeping pills which he dissolved in our tea on the nights he opened the safe and copied the code book currently in use."

"Very cunning. The drug they used must have been of a high quality. Otherwise you would have felt hung over in the morning or have been left with an unpleasant taste in your mouths."

"You're right. We suffered no ill effects," replied Chesterton. "Well let's get some sleep. You must be exhausted, Steve. I'm sorry to have you go back into the jungle again tomorrow."

"That's all right. It won't be a problem."

The other three knew this would not be so. To have to travel several days with a man who had been a staunch, trusted friend for many years and who had now betrayed him, would not be easy. They had no idea how MacDougal would manage it.

They only knew he would do it better than any other man in the camp. And with that thought as comfort they went to sleep.

Next morning they met Lee Sheng in the tent at seven o'clock. They helped him draw up the letter to the other four guerrilla groups, and they composed the message Wong would carry to the Japanese. Having completed these tasks, Lee Sheng ordered coffee and breakfast to be brought to the tent. They quickly ate the meager meal.

"All right let's review the timetable to ensure we have thought of everything. Tony would you kindly take notes?"

"Certainly."

"And Steve would you translate anything Lee Sheng is unsure of into Hokkien?"

"Okay, Simon."

Day 1 is today. Steve will leave with Wong.

Day 2. In the morning Lee Sheng will brief four messengers regarding their tasks to contact the other guerrilla chiefs. Immediately after his briefing they will then leave carrying his letters. Steve and Wong will arrive at the drop point late afternoon to early evening. Lieutenant Ito will receive the message that night. During the day Alex will tutor our guerrilla radio man on the new code and practice the messages to be sent to the other four guerrilla camps on day 4.

Day 3. We will leave for Ipoh leaving behind one cook and the radio man. We will meet up with Steve and Wong that night. Wong will then be escorted back to camp by two of Lee Sheng's men where he will await our return. During most of the day Lieutenant Ito will, most probably, drill his troops in Ipoh in preparation for his raid on our bogus meeting.

Day 4. Ito and his troops will leave for Grik where they will say overnight. We will arrive outside Ipoh and take up our positions. The radio man will send his messages to the four guerrilla camps. Three of them will leave for the ambush location.

Day 5. We will overrun the small detachment of troops in Ipoh at ten o'clock. We will load all the food, medicine and weapons on trucks either taken from the Japanese or borrowed from the townspeople and drive north to meet the main body of guerrillas. We will leave Alex behind to send his coded message later that day and three guerrillas in case of any unforeseen trouble. At noon the three assigned guerrilla groups will chop trees ready for the ambush. The ambush will take place on the Ipoh road, about thirty miles south of Grik, two miles south of the road to Selama. At four o'clock Alex will send a message to Grik using the Japanese code. Wong's letter will have stated he will be at the Japanese camp in Grik at two o'clock and the alleged guerrilla meeting is scheduled for five o'clock outside Grik. Lieutenant Ito will have been waiting impatiently thinking something must be wrong. Now, having received the message it will confirm his fears and he will leave immediately in order to travel in the remaining daylight. Thirty minutes after his departure the Grik guerrillas will eliminate the small Japanese force there."

"How about the ambush details?" asked MacDougal.

"Just before I answer that, is there a question about the timetable?"

They all said no.

"Okay. About two miles south of the turnoff to Selama the road turns quite sharply. Trees will be placed across the road at that point. And once the Japanese convoy has passed about one mile south of the turnoff for Selama, the main road will be blocked off thereby preventing a retreat. Ten guerrillas will be positioned behind each of the road blocks in case any Japanese manage to make a run for it. Riflemen will be placed fifty yards back from the ambush point on the west side of the road along with our two machine guns and guerrillas with hand grenades. That puts the sun behind them for better light. When they come under attack, the natural inclination of the Japanese will be to either seek shelter at the side of their vehicles or to run to the east. We will have positioned the four machine guns the other groups possess inside the tree line on the east side, along with men using hand grenades. The terrain rises there so they will be firing down on the Japanese. As soon as the men on the west have caused the convoy to stop they will rapidly retreat. Another line of our very best snipers will be located twenty yards behind them. We don't want any of our men to be caught in the crossfire. The balance of the guerrillas will be held as backups at every position in case of need."

"Any questions?"

"Just one point," said MacDougal. "The Japs usually mount a machine gun on top of the first vehicle of a convoy and one on the rear vehicle. We had better make sure our best shots are told to take them out first."

"Good point, Steve, will you kindly arrange that? You know our best men."

Alex was getting his first experience of preparation for war and he was impressed; not only with the attention to detail of the ambush but also with the calmness of every man. He wondered if the same calmness would exist once the fighting began.

Lee Sheng stood and saluted. He was now a happy man. His group would see action again and inflict pain and losses on the nation that had so brutally subjugated his country. Chesterton returned his salute.

"I go brief my men," the Chinese leader said tersely, in English.

MacDougal said his goodbyes and left with Lee Sheng to collect Wong and head for the jungle. Alex sat quietly not knowing what to say or do. Thinking of a plan had been one thing but now it had been set in motion he knew many lives would be lost and many families would grieve. Soldiers were trained to obey orders and not to think of the deaths of their enemy. Suddenly he remembered his feeling when leaving Achnacarry Castle after his training under Sergeant MacTavish. He had believed he was beginning to feel like a real soldier. Now he knew he had been wrong, he was not a soldier, at least not at heart. The thought of a host of human beings being killed, even though they were your enemy, did not fill him with joy.

Chesterton and Benson had been conferring. They both noticed how silent Alex was.

"I should join Lee Sheng," whispered Chesterton. He raised his head and pointed with his chin towards Alex before he left.

Benson nodded his understanding and moved next to Alex. It was several moments before Alex noticed him.

"You were lost in thought," said Benson. "I believe I know what you were thinking. Perhaps you were wondering how many lives would be lost: and maybe even taking that responsibility on your own shoulders."

"How could you know?"

"As a civilian volunteer, I often had similar thoughts. But my experience in seeing the atrocities the Japs perpetrated on the people of Malaya swept away all such thoughts. They claim to do it in the name of their Emperor. But I have long since known this to be an excuse. It's the militarists in Japan who want to conquer the world. And it is their officers here in Malaya who relish their vicious, evil deeds; and who permit their troops to rape and pillage as they conquer. Do not lose sleep over them. Save your sorrow for the men we will lose and for their families."

"I am also thinking there will be consequences. The Japanese may take it out on the civilian populations of Ipoh and Grik."

"Ah, that is a valid point, Alex. But there is another aspect to that. I have seen such acts committed, and in every case it leaves sorrow and hatred. But I can tell you it leaves another emotion – pride. Pride that their countrymen are fighting back and a renewed belief they will prevail. It gives them courage to go through each day by believing that."

"I hadn't thought of it that way," admitted Alex.

"No matter how we evaluate it, war is a horrible thing. Remember one thing my young friend; this time we didn't start it. And another important thing, Alex, it's our job to see we win it."

Chapter Twenty Seven

The following day Alex spent several hours teaching the young radioman the new code he had devised. Fortunately the young man spoke very good English and there was no need for an interpreter. He was also sharp and picked up the code quite quickly. Nevertheless Alex drilled him until he was certain he would not fail in his task. After lunch he and Benson worked on the coded message he was to send from Ipoh to Grik. The message was agreed to by Chesterton. It was short and to the point but later Alex added a final sentence.

"I think that last bit will give us extra security," he said.

Later as he walked around the camp with Benson he noticed the guerrillas were huddled in small groups chattering excitedly and noisily.

"They always talk volubly before going into action," explained Benson. "However once in battle they hardly ever utter a word. This I find most unusual. Many nationalities including ours let out war whoops as they charge or engage the enemy, but not the Chinese. They are deadly serious and completely silent. It is evident they get all their emotional vocalization out prior to battle. And since it has been quite a while since we attacked the Japs, you can hear they are letting out a lot of verbal emotion."

That evening Alex was sitting outside the cabin. His thoughts were focused on how he would react when in action. He knew he was not a coward yet this new experience would certainly test his resolve. He hoped he would not let his friends down. His thoughts were interrupted by a conversation inside the cabin – one in low tones and one he was not meant to hear.

"Tony, I have to ask if you are really up to this action. You have been terribly sick. I can't risk the operation by carrying a passenger."

"Simon, I am going. Nothing will stop me. I admit I am not one hundred percent fit but I can assure you I will not be a burden."

"Sorry, but I had to ask. It would be perfectly all right if you stayed behind."

"Thanks for your concern, but I *am* going."

"Okay, Tony. Well I'm hitting the sack. Do you know where Alex is?"

"I suspect he is pretty tightly wound up. He has never been in battle. He is probably walking around outside trying to calm his nerves. Would you like me to fetch him?"

"No let him be. He'll be no different from any of us and find it difficult to sleep tonight."

Alex crept away from the cabin and waited fifteen minutes before entering. He undressed and slid under the mosquito net. To his surprise he did manage to sleep relatively well.

Next morning the entire group ate a hearty breakfast of rice and salted fish. No one bathed. There was little sense in doing so as their bodies would soon be discharging copious amounts of perspiration as they trekked through the jungle. Finally they were on their way laden with weapons. Alex found he was not thinking of battle. His mind was fully occupied with thoughts of leeches, mosquitoes, spiders, snakes, red ants and poisonous plants. As he had previously learned the jungle was a noisy place, and again his ears were assaulted by the insects, birds and monkeys. They were well into the afternoon when his body gave an involuntary shudder. He heard the trumpeting of elephants.

"Do not worry," said Chin who was behind him, "they are far away."

Somehow those words didn't quite comfort him. And for the umpteenth time he wondered why he had agreed to take on this mission to Malaya. He had come to a crossroad and could have chosen the path to safety. Instead he had chosen the one which he knew could lead to danger. It had all seemed so glamorous back in London. He was being given a chance to do a service for his country - an important one at that. Now a young Chinese was telling him not to worry. 'Worry? Me worry? You're damn right I'm worried,' he thought. 'After all I'm trudging through this thick jungle, my clothes sodden with sweat, concerned about all the nasty things that inhabit this hell, and now there are elephants. Worse still there will be panthers and tigers on the prowl tonight.'

He was startled out of his negative thoughts by Benson who was ahead of him. With his extraordinary sixth sense he knew something was wrong. He turned and said, "Are you all right, Alex?"

"Yes, yes, I'm fine," he lied.

"You don't look fine. Why don't you drink some water?"

"Good idea," he said guiltily, hoping his depressed attitude was not evident on his face.

Gradually, as had been the case on the other times he suffered doubts, his negative thoughts dissolved and he again felt some pride in his mission. This was inspired by staring at the back of Benson ahead of him. This brilliant man had given up so much to fight for his country and had suffered terribly with disease in doing so. Yet he marched on bravely. And once again Alex recognized his initial reason for getting into the war had been emotional and not rational. However he knew in his heart that his father would have been proud of him. This thought chased away the dark cloud that had blanketed his mind and he marched on purposefully, following in Benson's footsteps, until they came to a halt for the night.

They were met at their campsite by MacDougal and Wong. Steve told them everything had gone to plan. That was great news to Chesterton. And to Alex's enormous relief he was not attacked that night by a tiger or a panther and he didn't even hear another elephant.

Next day as he trekked through the jungle, his mind was clear and focused on the job that lay ahead. Although still aware of the incessant jungle noises he didn't allow them to cloud his thoughts. The monkeys still shrieked at them as they passed and the birds and insects continued their unceasing cacophony but the belief he had of his father's pride buoyed him. Benson had taken up a position at his rear concerned about Alex's attitude and was pleased at today's change.

At three o'clock they stopped at a river to bathe and wash their clothes which, as usual, didn't take long to dry. Although now close to Ipoh they were unafraid of being spotted by the Japanese who would be on their way to Grik. They reached their overnight hiding spot at five o'clock and Lee Sheng sent two of his men into Ipoh.

"They will check how many Japs they can spot and the location of their sentries. Also we want to be certain there are no unexpected surprises," explained Chesterton to Alex.

"Unexpected surprises?" echoed Alex with concern.

"Don't be worried. However we must be sure they didn't leave more men than we anticipated. And that they haven't set up machine gun nests. That sort of thing. It's always better to reconnoiter the lay of the land before going in."

"Hopefully the Japanese will not spot our men as they check things out," said Alex.

"Lee Sheng had them change their clothes. Instead of long sleeved shirts, trousers and boots, they are wearing singlets, black shorts and flip flops. They will blend in perfectly with the local community."

Three hours later the men returned to report that all was well. They had seen two men guarding the petrol dump, two at the entrance to the camp and another five lounging on chairs inside the camp. Reckoning on perhaps another few inside the camp huts, everything was as Chesterton had thought.

Alex found it difficult to sleep that night and was happy when dawn performed her daily miracle of gradually lighting up the sky.

"Why do we have to wait until ten o'clock to attack?" Alex asked MacDougal.

"Most probably Lieutenant Ito will check in with the Ipoh camp first thing in the morning to make sure everything is okay."

"Oh my God, I just thought of something," exclaimed Alex. "Won't Ito just use the telephone? Why bother with coded radio messages?"

MacDougal smiled indulgently.

"When the Japs are on a mission they can't be sure their telephone lines have not been tapped. They know from experience that the guerrillas have this capability and indeed have used it many times. Remember telephone lines run from pole to pole along every main road and the Japs cannot possibly cover every mile of telephone line. It is easy for the guerrillas to tap into a line in some remote area. So they never risk using a phone for something important. And they will correctly assume they have been noticed leaving Ipoh in strength and believe this information will have been passed along to the guerrillas. No, Ito will not use the telephone.

But we must get to that radio quickly before a signal can be sent to Grik. That's my job. By ten o'clock the Japs will have sent out a few men on patrol around the town. We will take out the guards at the gate using silencers and I, with three others, will rush to the radio hut and secure it. Yesterday the men we sent into Ipoh were told to identify the location of the radio hut by its antenna. Luckily it is close to the entrance."

It was all over at ten-fifteen. Alex, who was not allowed to participate, could not believe the mission's rapid conclusion when told. He arrived at the Japanese camp at eleven o'clock as Chesterton was concluding his final instructions to the guerrillas. When he saw Alex he came straight over.

"The soldiers Ito left here must have been the bottom of the barrel. They were not in the least alert," said Chesterton, shaking his head in wonderment. "I would have thought given the inexperienced troops Ito complained of, he would have left at least one skilled man to take charge."

Just then MacDougal appeared.

"We have borrowed four tucks and they are being loaded now, Simon."

"Excellent. Have them driven about two miles south of the ambush point. When the action is over we will divide up the spoils between our group and the three others. But remember to keep a good part of the medicine for us. The Grik group can keep the rewards of their action."

"Will do. And as you know, one of our chaps, Chin, lived in Ipoh. He still has an uncle here who has agreed to drive Alex and his bodyguards to join us at the ambush site."

"Very good. Now is there anything further you need from me, Alex?"

"No, Simon. I'll be fine."

"There is one other thing, I have told our lads to let it be known that the local population can take all the petrol they need. Two of the guerrillas staying with you have been advised to supervise this activity to ensure no one is overly greedy and, most importantly, they bring their own containers. When replacement Japs are sent here, one of the first things they will search houses for is petrol. Anyone found with Japanese manufactured petrol cans, will be executed. When the locals have taken their share, the guerrillas will set fire to any remaining petrol before leaving. Oh and one last thing, do not wander around town. Someone may report your description to the future replacement Japs. Better to stay indoors. The third guerrilla will stay with you at all times."

"See you later," said MacDougal as they walked off.

"Good luck," called out Alex.

Chesterton waved an acknowledgement.

Alex had done so before and he did it again. He marveled at the calmness with which these men faced danger.

Chapter Twenty Eight

At precisely four o'clock Alex sent the message to Grik then hung up instantly. The final sentence he had added said some trouble with the locals had just occurred and that he, the radioman, was required immediately to assist the other troops. Therefore he would be away from his post for some time. He had done this in case Grik should send a response to his transmission. Not having a Japanese speaker with him he would be unable to reply and this silence would certainly raise serious questions. And those questions could definitely put Lieutenant Ito on extra alert. Alex had done one other thing - he had not coded the message to Grik. There were two reasons. Firstly he had made the message sound panicky and as such the operator would have decided not to take time to encode it. And secondly when the dust had settled he didn't want the Japanese to know he had cracked their code.

The guerrilla waiting with him asked if he should now tell his comrades to burn the remaining petrol. He was about to agree when he had another thought.

"Tell then to bring the petrol here. We will burn everything in this camp. The Japanese will undoubtedly send replacement troops and I don't want them to walk right into an undisturbed camp. We will force them to first have to reconstruct the entire camp. That may even delay their brutal questioning of the local inhabitants."

"Okay, Tuan," the guerrilla said nervously. These had not been his instructions but he obeyed anyway.

It was four-forty-five when they finally left Ipoh with Chin's uncle who had been instructed where to drop off his passengers. He turned out to be a very congenial old man who spoke good English. He told Alex many things about his home town, which was on the banks of the River Kinta. He was particularly proud of the importance of the Chinese whose labor and skill had been essential in building Ipoh's rich heritage based on tin mining. The largest tin field in the world was discovered in the Kinta valley in 1876.

"And we have a magnificent new railway station which houses the wonderful Majestic hotel. All this was designed by the famous architect, Arthur Hubback."

He went on to describe the many other attractions of his home town. After close to an hour Alex had to interrupt him.

"We had better slow down and be careful, we must be getting close to our destination."

"The Selama road is still twelve miles away. Don't worry we will be there soon."

It was evident to Alex that the man had not been told of the ambush and of the possible danger of getting too close to the fighting. He had to tell him.

"There will be fighting up ahead, so please drive slowly. We must be very careful."

The old man stood on the brake so violently that the three guerrillas, who were crushed into the back seat, almost landed in the front seats.

"You mean with the Japanese?" he asked tremulously, obviously terrified of the Japanese. "Those horrible soldiers killed my brother and nephew. My brother was only a teacher and no possible threat to them. His wife had to leave their home and return to her village for safety."

"Yes, I know all that. Your other nephew told me about it."

"You know my nephew? But how?"

"He is one of the brave guerrillas fighting the Japanese. I have had many chats with him."

The old man nodded his head knowingly.

"Pardon me for not acknowledging it. But I have to be very careful in saying anything about my nephew. I must never admit he is a guerrilla. If it came to the ears of the Japanese they would torture me for information. And because I truly know nothing of Chin's whereabouts I'm afraid the torture would kill me. Do you know if he will he be involved in the fighting?"

"Yes, he will."

"Then perhaps I will see him. It has been a long time since we last met," the old man said with a wistful voice.

"Perhaps," replied Alex, not wishing to be too positive. He was well aware there would be casualties in the ambush. "Let's move on, but proceed with caution."

The old man gulped but did as he was instructed. They had only gone six miles before they heard the faint but unmistakable sounds of battle. The guerrilla who spoke English volunteered to scout ahead.

"The gunfire is still a few miles away. I will go with one of my comrades to investigate," he said.

The two men jogged away along the road with their rifles at the ready.

"Let's move up a little further," suggested Alex.

The old man looked at him as though he was mentally deficient. He had no intention of getting close to gunfire.

"Just go very slowly. And if we spot trouble you can leave us and return to Ipoh," Alex added gently.

Very reluctantly the old man started the car, engaged first gear, and kept it there as they crawled forward. They continued at this excruciatingly slow pace for another two miles. All the time Alex had his head out of the window, listening intently. He heard the gunfire becoming more and more sporadic.

"It sounds like it is almost over," he said.

This was confirmed when the two guerrillas returned with broad smiles on their faces.

"Everything is okay, Tuan. Very successful."

They climbed back into the car and instructed the old man to drive forward. He was still reluctant, but did so still exceedingly slowly, until they reached the ambush area. As they drew to a halt they saw the guerrillas leaping jubilantly as they went about their tasks. The carnage that met Alex's eyes was sickening to him. Bodies were strewn all around. Some of the guerrillas were collecting all the armaments while others moved from body to body stripping the Japanese soldiers of anything of value. Watches and money appeared to be the most prized items but to Alex's horror he saw that each dead man's mouth was being examined for gold teeth.

One of the guerrillas disengaged from his gruesome task. It was Chin. He had seen his uncle and he ran over to greet him, bowing low as he paid his respects.

'At least there is one joyful event among all this bloodshed,' thought Alex.

He went over to where Chesterton, MacDougal and Benson were standing. Chesterton was elated.

"We have captured enough rifles and ammunition to keep the guerrillas supplied for many, many months. And, we got seven machine guns also four mortars. This has been a tremendous haul," he said, his voice bubbling with enthusiasm.

It was only then he noticed the look on Alex's face clearly indicating he did not share his zeal. He realized as Alex had never been in battle before he was probably upset at the cost in lives of this victory.

"You haven't had to witness the many acts of bestiality by the Japs that I have. If you had, your feeling toward all those bodies would be different. There is no way I can help you with that. It is something one must experience for oneself to understand it."

Alex knew this to be true. He remembered his own murderous thoughts at the way a Nazi fighter pilot had taken his father's life. He nodded his head in acknowledgement of Chesterton's words.

"Oh, I should report that I exceeded my remit at Ipoh."

He then explained his reasons for torching the camp.

"That was good thinking, Alex," said Benson and Chesterton agreed.

"Excuse me," said MacDougal, "I'll supervise the dividing up of the arms and send the other groups on their way. Then I suggest we head for camp before it gets too dark. We can use the serviceable Jap trucks to travel along the road to our cut off. A few of guerillas can take the trucks to Grik and hide them. You never know, we may need them again. And I think we should follow Alex's example and have the guerrillas burn the Grik camp."

"Yes, let's do that," concurred Chesterton. "And let's get going as soon as we can."

The journey through the jungle was much slower than usual due to the additional load of arms, food and medicine being carried. But the jubilant guerrillas had no complaints about the extra weight. They had lost three men in the ambush, but that appeared to be a distant memory as they chattered triumphantly. This attitude gave Alex another insight into the Chinese communist mind. During the burial of the three bodies before leaving, there was obvious sadness in some of the guerrillas who had been close to the men. However that feeling soon evaporated to be replaced by the joy of their victory.

Alex would soon learn that mourning must be a short term emotion in war - one that quickly had to be substituted with continued survival.

Once back at the camp and the spoils were stored, everyone bathed in the river and changed into dry clothes. Most went to the mess tent to enjoy some of the decent food taken from Ipoh, but Alex went straight to his coding machine to tap into Japanese messages. There were only a few and he recorded them and later Benson translated them and gave a synopsis for all to hear.

"It had taken a day before scouts from Penang had been sent to discover why Ipoh was not responding to calls. Once the loss was discovered Penang had contacted Singapore to inform HQ and ask for instructions. Singapore decided to send replacements from its own troops and had instructed Penang to send small parties to both Ipoh and Grik to keep order until replacements arrived."

As soon as Benson had finished, the contents of the messages were discussed in the cabin.

"I don't understand why Penang did not instruct Taiping to investigate," said Benson. "After all it is only fifty miles from Ipoh and Penang is over one hundred miles away. Further, why would Penang call Singapore and not Kuala Lumpur where the main Japanese force in Malaya is located?"

It was Chesterton who responded.

"I can make an educated guess since I have served in the army. All armies are probably the same and there is a more than healthy rivalry between unit commanders. Penang would want to show the Commander-in-Chief in Singapore that he was taking quick control of this disaster and not allow his superior officer in Kuala Lumpur to take credit. And to cover his backside, I bet he sent notification of his actions to his boss in KL saying he did this as he thought the C-in-C should be notified right away."

"Is that the way our army behaves?" asked an incredulous Alex.

"You bet it is. Every senior officer is always bucking for promotion. Like every large organization politics is always lurking just below the surface."

Just then a messenger entered the cabin.

"Lee Sheng would like to invite you to the execution of Wong. He asked me to tell you he has convened a court martial and found Wong guilty," he said to Chesterton in Hokkien.

"Tell Lee Sheng I thank him for the invitation but we will not attend. This is a matter for the guerrillas."

"If you don't mind, I'll go, Simon," said MacDougal. "I think Wong would like to see my face before he dies. And I want to inform him when I was in Ipoh I confirmed his wife and son were safe."

"By all means, go ahead, Steve."

When MacDougal had left, Chesterton continued to speak.

"You see that was an example of what I was just talking about. By rights, Lee Sheng should have had me present at the court martial and I should have had a vote. But he wished to assert his authority as leader of the guerrillas and chose to exclude me. I will take bets he will come to me later explaining he was under pressure from his group for a quick sentence to be passed on Wong and could not wait for me."

No one was surprised when thirty minutes later that is exactly what happened. Politics had reared its ugly head.

Reflecting on recent events, it became one more reason why Alex decided when this journey was over and he came to another crossroad in his life, he would avoid the road leading to continued service in the army. Not merely because of political maneuvering, he was sufficiently wise to realize that was almost inevitable wherever he may work.

However the sight he beheld at the ambush would haunt him for a long time. Not just the awful spectacle of so many dead bodies but the guerrillas using the butts of their rifles to knock out gold teeth.

That was carrying the adage – to the victors go the spoils – way too far.

Chapter Twenty Nine

Over the next few days Alex continued to monitor the transmissions between Penang, Kuala Lumpur and Singapore. He came to a startling realization. Lieutenant Ito had told no one of his trip to Grik to capture all the guerrillas. The only possible explanation for such a breach of protocol was he wished to have a hugely successful coup and then spring an announcement of his triumph on his superiors in order to greatly impress them. He came to this conclusion when he heard Singapore raise the question of what Ito was doing so far north of Ipoh with the majority of his command. Neither Kuala Lumpur nor Penang had an answer for that.

The Commander-in-Chief in Singapore was furious at the loss of so many men to a band of guerrillas. Also he was deeply concerned with the reaction in Tokyo once they learned of this disaster. He was still in the shadow of the man who had led the brilliant campaign to invade Malaya and Singapore - Lieutenant General Tomoyuki Yamashita - nicknamed 'The Tiger of Malaya'.

Yamashita's troops, battle hardened in China, had landed in Kota Bharu on the very north east of Malaya and in Pattani and Songkla in Siam, close to the Malayan border. Then in only fifty four days they had ripped through the four hundred mile Malay Peninsula, sweeping away all resistance in their path. A feat thought utterly impossible by the British Army. When they completed their rout by capturing Singapore, the 'Impregnable Fortress', in only fifteen days, the Japanese forces had taken one hundred and thirty thousand British, Indian and Australian troops prisoner.

This conquest had made a hero of Yamashita in Tokyo. While his achievements pleased Hideki Tojo, the Prime Minister and also the Army Minister, Yamashita was getting too many accolades for Tojo's liking. Whether for this reason or some other, it came as a surprise when

Yamashita was taken out of the war and posted to Manchuria in July 1942. However he remained an idol to the troops in Singapore and Malaya. Such adoration was much to the annoyance of the current C-in-C, who now paced the floor at his HQ in Singapore. His staff remained in an outer office, keeping well away from his state of furiousness. They knew all too well that proximity to his flaming temper could only lead to severe burns.

Finally the C-in-C made decisions. Penang was instructed to send many more spotter planes out from their airfield in Butterworth looking for the guerrillas. Butterworth was situated on the mainland directly opposite the island of Penang and was one of the major bases housing Japanese planes. His instructions were, if the spotter planes saw any traces of guerrillas in the jungle they were to report back immediately and bombers were to be dispatched to bomb the area. This method was preferred to sending out patrols. That would entail a long journey to the Ipoh area without back-up. Patrols would be sent in force when reinforcements were in place in Ipoh. He didn't want to risk losing more men until he felt the odds were in his favor.

The other important piece of intelligence Alex gleaned from transmissions was Singapore had decided not to send replacement troops until the destroyed camps were rebuilt. Penang was instructed to do the reconstruction starting with Ipoh – and do so very quickly. This infuriated the Penang commander who felt he could not spare the men; however, he was too smart to vent his anger on Singapore – that would be a terrible, maybe even a terminal, mistake. Instead he poured out his grievances to his boss in Kuala Lumpur. He strenuously requested him to help by sending some of his troops to assist. His boss took great delight in refusing to entertain his request. This was a vengeful way of repaying him for his temerity in bypassing him when reporting the Ipoh disaster. His only advice to his subordinate was to have the Penang troops spend their nights in the safety of the Taiping camp rather that outdoors in tents in Ipoh, where they could be attacked by either guerrillas or adventurous locals.

Chesterton called a meeting in the tent to review this new intelligence.

"The question now is; what next? Do we lay low for a while or press our present advantage? And if we go on the offensive, what target do we hit?"

"There is nothing to be gained by laying low," answered MacDougal. "The guerrillas are now well armed so I say we have to strike again. The only question as I see it is where to strike."

"I agree with Steve," added Benson.

"How about you, Alex?"

"I think Steve makes sense. But with my limited knowledge of Malaya I am not qualified to identify your next target."

"Well the obvious one is Ipoh. The Japs sent from Penang will be well guarded as they rebuild the camp. But a fully coordinated attack by all the guerrilla units could take out thirty or forty of them," argued Chesterton.

"I doubt we would need all of the units. I'm guessing the Japs will send twenty to twenty five men at the most for that job. Remember the commander in Penang complained to KL that he was already understaffed. Also, I have seen the Taiping camp and they couldn't accommodate another thirty men; maybe ten at a push. If Penang were to send, say even as many as twenty five, to bivouac them would be a problem. No, I would guess Penang will send a smaller number of men and compensate by accompanying them with heavily armored vehicles. They will most probably include armored cars and trucks with mounted machine guns, but we now have mortars to take out such vehicles," counseled MacDougal.

"And are you assuming Ipoh will be constructed and manned before they rebuild Grik, Steve?"

"Definitely! They don't need many men to construct a small camp at Grik, and such a small number of men would be highly vulnerable to an attack."

"Okay, that's settled. We will attack the Japs sent to rebuild Ipoh," concluded Chesterton.

"If I may add something, I think we ought to consider doing so when the reconstruction is almost complete," said Benson. "It would cause more damage, and more importantly, if the first part of rebuilding went off without incident, the Japs may be lulled into a sense of false security making our raid less risky."

"Good idea, Tony. Maximum damage is what we want," responded Chesterton. "I'll call in Lee Sheng and tell him the plan."

He was about to finish the meeting when he noticed Benson had raised his hand. Benson had happened to look at Alex at the end of his last comments and noticed he was staring into space, lost in thought. Now Benson pointed at Alex, drawing the others' attention to him.

"I can almost hear the gears whirring in your brain, *Lieutenant Murdoch*. Why don't you share your thoughts?" asked Benson.

Alex started guiltily.

"Oh, it was just a fanciful thought. Probably not really worth mentioning."

"That, I cannot accept. When I see that look on your face I know you have come up with and idea. Now tell us," demanded Benson who was getting to know Alex well.

"Well a couple of things occurred to me. The first thing was the recent ambush was so successful due to the old conjurer's trick of misdirection. Lieutenant Ito was fully focusing on achieving a major coup outside Grik and therefore unprepared for an ambush. The second thing relates to Steve's strong belief that the Ipoh reconstruction troops could be handled by just one guerrilla group. If that's the case perhaps an Ipoh attack could become not the main objective but another misdirection action."

"And what would be the main target?" persisted an intrigued Benson.

"Well once the troops at Ipoh came under attack, they would send an SOS to their home base in Penang. I'm betting the commander would send a huge number of troops to rescue his men. Also he may see it as an opportunity to get revenge on the guerrillas for wiping out so many men with the ambush. And to ensure success I'm betting they would resort to overkill. That's why they would dispatch every man possible. It would be like a swarm of bees angrily leaving a disturbed hive. They may even send planes and helicopters from Butterworth. Now prior to this attack, if every man we could muster travelled to Butterworth in the Japanese trucks we have, we could launch artillery and mortar attacks on the aircraft on the ground. The planes are among the most prized possessions of the Japanese. The loss of many of them would be a devastating blow to the Japanese ego. And this sort of news would travel quickly and would undoubtedly be a huge morale boost to all the guerrillas throughout Malaya."

"A few minutes ago you said you weren't qualified to identify our next target. Where did this idea spring from?" exclaimed a delighted Chesterton.

"It just came to me while you were talking," replied Alex somewhat lamely.

"Don't apologize, laddie, it's a brilliant idea. Destroying their petrol dumps or even their camps is enough to drive the Japs crazy. But to destroy their planes, my God, it would make them absolutely insane. Of course there is one detail we can't overlook," said MacDougal.

"What's that, Steve?"

"We would have to move our camp immediately. The Japs would be so incensed they would send men from all over Malaya to find us. We and the other guerrilla bands would have to disappear."

"Well, it was just a thought," intoned a deflated Alex.

"No, no, it is a most inspired thought," interjected Benson. "We could move south to Jor camp fifteen miles south of Cameron Highlands. It is often used as a headquarters by Chin Peng the leader of all the guerrillas and is a stronghold that is extraordinarily well protected. Simon and I have been there and it would be an excellent haven for a while until things die down around here. Of course it could not accommodate Lee Sheng's men; but I have no doubt they could melt into the countryside. I would hazard a guess that we could not regroup for about six months. What do you say, Simon?"

"It gives me chills just to think of it. If we pull this off it will be the greatest feat our side has achieved since the war began. However I will have to consult with Lee Sheng. He may be averse to disbanding his group for six months."

But as Chesterton explained the scheme to Lee Sheng he didn't have to wait for a reply. The light shining in Lee Sheng's eyes told him all he had to know.

The next few days were packed with detailed planning. Alex took the opportunity to bury the dummy coding machines which had served their purpose. Then a council of war was held with the leaders of the other guerrilla groups. They too were ecstatic and so the date was set for ten days from then.

Somehow the word got out that this was all Alex's idea, and his back ached from the number of times the guerrillas congratulated him by slapping him on the back.

It appeared the Chinese had never heard of a simple pat on the back. Instead they whooped as they smote him mightily with exuberant joy.

Chapter Thirty

The C-in-C in Singapore could not believe his ears.

"Repeat!" he yelled at the quavering major who read out the news.

"The partially rebuilt Ipoh camp has been raised to the ground. Eighteen men were killed in the action." He gulped for air before continuing. "And fif -- fif -- fifteen bombers, te—ten fighter planes and fo -- four helicopters were destroyed at Butterworth," he stammered.

"At Butterworth?"

"Yes, General. It appears the two attacks were coordinated."

"Impossible. The guerrillas are not that competent. These were unrelated attacks carried out by two different groups."

Having passed verdict, the general resumed his pacing, all the time muttering to himself.

"Twenty five planes destroyed and the Ipoh camp again raided. Who is organizing these attacks?"

He stopped suddenly as he thought on this. But getting no inspirational answers, his mind snapped and his whole body shook as he screamed in uncontrollable rage. He shouted every swear word he knew, using some of them several times; kicked over a chair, swept everything off his desk and in blind fury swung around and scythed the air with his riding crop. Unfortunately he did not only hit air, unintentionally his crop slashed his aide across his face. Evidently he had never heard the phrase 'don't shoot the messenger'. With sudden shock he recognized what he had done. The major had been his faithful aide for several years. Now he stood stiffly at attention as blood flowed down his face.

"Sorry, Ishibashi," the C-in-C mumbled. "Stand at ease."

He righted his chair and plumped his fat rear end down heavily.

"Tell me all that happened."

Major Ishibashi steeled himself for a further beating as he was about to contradict the general's belief that the two incidents were not related. He lowered his head as he answered.

"The troops at Ipoh radioed Penang for help when they came under attack. Major Sato dispatched eighty troops with tanks and armored cars. In addition he ordered three helicopters to the scene. He also ordered all planes to be fully fuelled and to stand at full alert, ready to fly at a moment's notice. We believe the Ipoh attack was in fact something of a diversionary move. Because an hour after the troops crossed the straights from Penang to the mainland the attack on Butterworth began. It is estimated there were over one hundred guerrillas. Eight of them were killed along with sixty four of our pilots and men at Butterworth. The guerrillas were very well organized and armed. They had field artillery, mortars, bazookas and heavy machine guns. That is all we know at the moment, Sir."

"And you really believe this was all preplanned and Butterworth was the main target?"

"It appears as though that's the case, General. It seems unlikely that it was a coincidence."

The general had resumed his pacing. Now he stopped as he digested this information. It looked like every time he stopped pacing his control over his temper evaporated. And once again it erupted.

"Where did they get all the armament?" he shrieked at the top of his lungs.

Major Ishibashi again lowered his head, afraid to answer. His chief had lost all semblance of rationality and who knows what he would do next when he received more bad news.

"Well?"

This time he had to answer. Half turning away to avoid any further beating he said, "The armaments are believed to be ours; taken in the ambush north of Ipoh"

This brought another stream of swear word laced invective. Finally the chief's body stopped its shuddering rage and he whispered instructions to Ishibashi - whispered in a hissing manner that was even more terrifying than his intemperate outbursts.

"Tell Sato to leave Penang immediately and come down here. I want to speak to him."

"I regret that will not be possible, Sir; Major Sato committed seppuku."

Seppuku or ritual suicide by slashing open one's belly was an ancient samurai tradition when one was defeated in battle or had dishonored one's master.

"The swine! He did not deserve to die in such an honorable fashion. He should have been shot for the incompetent fool that he was."

"Get as many more details as you can and put a full report on my desk as quickly as possible, Ishibashi. I want to know who was behind this."

The major shot to attention, bowed and as quickly as decorum allowed, rushed from the office. Those in the outer office had heard most of what had been said. They stared in horror at the sight of Ishibashi's slashed face and his blood soaked uniform. No one offered to assist him; they knew Major Ishibashi would take that as an insult. In addition they were all paralyzed with fear. If this was what the chief had done to his most loyal aide, what could he do to them?

"Kawaguchi!" screamed the C-in-C. "Bring tea!"

The young lieutenant's eyes went wide with fear as he ran to obey this command. Fetching tea was not a problem but having to enter the C-in-C's office to deliver it without spilling any due to his shaking body was a terrifying thought. A sergeant sitting next to Kawaguchi thanked the gods he had not been the one called to deliver tea, as he sat upright in his chair in a pool of urine.

They all knew there would be further repercussions over this catastrophe. Heads would be certain to roll. Not figuratively but literally and each of them prayed fervently it would not be his.

The Butterworth raid had been meticulously planned and well rehearsed. When it was over the guerrillas knew exactly what to do. They left for assigned locations carrying their armaments to be hidden in preselected secluded spots. They left in the highest of spirits and couldn't wait to tell of their success when they finally reached their destinations.

MacDougal was at the wheel of a small truck, heading for the Jor camp. Alex sat next to him with Chesterton and Wang behind them. Wang was included in the party as a precaution in case something unexpected happened and they were forced to stop along the route. He could easily mingle with local people in a small town should they require food or supplies.

Unlike the celebratory mood of the guerrillas as they departed, the atmosphere inside the truck was its very antithesis. In the back of the truck lay a blanket-wrapped figure. Tony Benson had been killed in the raid.

The young English speaking guerrilla, Chin, had foolishly run onto the tarmac in an attempt to rescue a fallen comrade not knowing he was already dead. In the course of this action, Chin had been shot twice in the leg and was crawling back towards safety, when a recent Japanese recruit opened fire on him. Being inexpert and terrified at his first battle experience he fired wildly. Bullets peppered the ground all around Chin and although the Japanese was green it could only be a matter of time before he killed Chin. Recognizing the wild shooting and the pause which meant the rifle was being reloaded; Benson took the chance to race out and drag Chin behind one of the vehicles. It was only then, as Chin was pouring out his thanks, that he realized Benson was not replying. He lay on the ground with his eyes wide open but unseeing. The new recruit having spotted Benson had again emptied his magazine in an inept fashion and had only hit Benson once. However once is enough when one's heart is pierced.

Alex sat dejectedly fighting back tears.

"Let it all out, laddie," whispered MacDougal. "I'd join you but I must keep my eyes clear if we are to get there safely," he added in a low grief stricken voice.

Neither of them dared look back at Chesterton. He and Tony had been friends and comrades for a long dangerous time. They could not even begin to imagine how he must be feeling.

The truck was bucking dangerously as MacDougal's foot pressed the accelerator hard against the floor. Even though the road was dark and twisting, they were driving without lights as there could well be helicopters looking for them. And it was essential to put as much distance between them and Butterworth before it became light.

After two hours Chesterton took over from MacDougal who was obviously tiring from the strain of driving at high speed along a dark road with countless bends.

"We are about a third of the way there in terms of miles but the road becomes much worse when we near the camp, it may take another six hours before we arrive," Chesterton explained to Alex.

However they had only gone another twenty miles when Chesterton braked suddenly, but not quickly enough to avoid hitting the deer that was crossing the road. He cut the engine and allowed the truck to come to a silent halt on the grass verge where they could assess the damage. By flashlight they saw the front wing has been bent inwards and was rubbing against the tire. Alex looked around but could not see the deer.

"They can withstand a great deal," said MacDougal. "It may be okay but if it is severely hurt it will end up being some cat's dinner tonight."

With that explanation, he bent over to help Chesterton pull the metal away from the tire. As they struggled with this task, Alex was still looking around for the deer when abruptly he stood stock still. Chesterton let out a sigh as the metal finally was bent back into shape and was about to say something when he noticed Alex strange posture.

"What is it?"

"Are my eyes playing tricks on me or is that the faintest of lights up ahead?"

"By God, you're right," whispered MacDougal. "Wang and I will check it out. Stay here and keep quiet," he tersely added in his lowest voice.

It seemed an eternity to Alex but it was only thirty minutes before they returned looking grim. They huddled close to hear MacDougal's whispered report.

"About a quarter mile ahead the road makes a sharp right turn. And a little further on is a heavily defended Jap road block. We counted fifteen Japs. If we hadn't hit that deer we would be dead now. If we surprised them we maybe could kill all of them. But that's a long shot. Even if we could they will be expected to report in periodically by radio. And without a report a high alert will be sounded and the road ahead blocked. So no matter what, we can't go on in the truck."

"Then we have no choice we must go back a ways, ditch the truck and proceed on foot," said Chesterton making a quick decision.

"Agreed," said MacDougal grimly.

"I don't want to start the engine; it makes a hellish noise as it engages. So we have to push for a bit," said Chesterton.

The difficult part was turning the truck around. Once that was accomplished they pushed it for quarter of a mile before starting the engine. Soon they found a gap in the trees and drove the truck off the road then covered it with branches and ferns.

"We can't take Tony's body with us," said a sad Chesterton. "We have to bury him here."

The others nodded their agreement. This took a long time as the grave had to be very deep to prevent animals from digging up the body. They stood silently, each remembering Tony Benson in his own way. Then Chesterton said his final words to Benson.

"I shall come back for you my dear friend. You deserve a proper burial, Tony, and I shall not rest until you have one."

His voice choked with emotion.

MacDougal took out a map and by flashlight marked the spot where Tony Benson had been laid to rest. He paced out the distance from the road and from the largest tree he could find and marked this on the edge of the map. Then they gathered their gear.

"This is going to be a bitch of a trek," muttered MacDougal as he took the lead.

Knowing he was not one given to either undue pessimism or exaggeration, MacDougal's words sent a frisson of fear down Alex's spine. A voice inside his head told him this journey would be one of the most difficult he would ever undertake, and he prayed for two things.

That they would all survive it and he would be strong enough not to let his friends down.

Chapter Thirty One

"The first thing we must do is skirt that roadblock - and quickly," said MacDougal without looking round. "Experience says where there is one group of Japs, there is usually another not too far away."

"That's right," added Chesterton in a flat tone. His redundant comment indicating the impact Benson's death was having on his ability to fully concentrate. This alarmed Alex. They would need everyone to be at their best if they were to survive.

"Once we are clear we can stop and plan our route. Keep close and no talking from now on," said MacDougal in a low urgent voice.

He set a rapid pace. They kept that up for over an hour before he called a halt in a small clearing.

"Hold the map, Alex," he instructed as he shone his flashlight on it. He took out a pen and after some time marked out a route to the Jor camp.

"I think this is the best way. What do you think, Simon?" he asked in an attempt to engaged Chesterton.

Chesterton took quite some time to focus on the map. His indecision was obvious for all to see.

"That looks okay to me," he finally said. Then as though he recognized his impaired state for the first time he added, "I'd like you to continue taking the lead, Steve. You know this country better."

"Certainly," replied MacDougal gently, clearly understanding that Chesterton was still in shock over his best friend's death. "The first problem we have is, because we had intended to drive all the way to the Jor camp, we have very little food and water. We will have to head to the outskirts of this little town," he said, pointing it out with his finger. "It takes us well out of our way but it is the safest nearby place to get the supplies we must have. We should be able to reach it in about two days and Wang can buy what we need."

"Fine," agreed Chesterton in a detached manner.

This was most unlike the leadership attitude of Chesterton. He had definitely changed since they buried Benson. Alex looked at MacDougal with continued concern. MacDougal responded by lowering his eyebrows and cautiously nodding his head a few times. This signified he understood Alex's anxiety but he felt it would not be a problem. He had faith that Chesterton would shortly recover.

They traveled through the night and rested as dawn broke. Breakfast consisted of the meager amount of dried fish they had and a few mouthfuls of water.

"We'll rest here for a while. Then Wang and I will reconnoiter the area ahead. I don't expect any Jap patrols out here but we can be sure they are licking their wounds over the Butterworth attack and are sending out every available patrol. So, even though I don't expect them in this remote area, we had better be safe than sorry. After we get resupplied we will resume the route I marked out. But as we get closer to the Jor camp we will undoubtedly come close to patrols. And travelling at night increases the possibility of bumping into them. From now on, I'm afraid we will have to cautiously travel as far as we can during daylight hours and spend our nights without lighting fires. That will slow our progress. As I said the Japs will be on full alert. Therefore it will be a case of finding a good hiding spot, reconnoitering ahead, before moving to another hiding location."

"How long do you estimate it will take, Steve?" asked Alex.

"That's difficult to say. It all depends on how many patrols we have to avoid. But at a guess I would say about two weeks."

'Two weeks,' thought Alex glumly. 'I hope I can make it.'

After an hour, MacDougal and Wang set out to scout the trail ahead. They returned in half an hour.

"Just as I thought, no sign of Jap patrols having been in this remote area. I suggest we push on for a few hours. Then after another rest we should go on until dark. Hopefully we will reach that small town late afternoon the day after tomorrow."

"That means two days without food and only a little water," said a worried Alex.

"We've done that before and we can do it again," said Chesterton, at last showing some interest.

His statement of resolve made Alex feel inadequate and ashamed.

But that's exactly what they did. It was an exhausted group that welcomed the halt called by MacDougal. After a brief rest Wang was dispatched to purchase the things they needed. That evening they enjoyed a welcome dinner of dried beef and vegetables, washed down by beer.

"We'll rest here for the night. Two hour watches. I'll go first. Then tomorrow we will head for a small river on the other side of town. I reckon we could all use a good bath," said MacDougal.

"Did you buy any soap, Wang?" asked Chesterton in Hokkien.

"Yes Tuan. We can wash our bodies and our clothes. I bought plenty," he replied.

Alex got the drift of the conversation and was relieved that Chesterton seemed less despondent.

They travelled slowly as MacDougal had prophesized due to their need to be constantly watchful for patrols. With the passing of each day Alex saw an improvement in Chesterton's attitude. His mind was much clearer as evidenced by his discussions with Steve on the tactical aspects of the trek ahead.

Alex was now more worried about his own capabilities. Although he had managed to keep up physically, the jungle environment with all its dangers and uncertainties was having a deleterious impact on his mind. So far he had managed to cope but only by the most strenuous determination not to let the others down. Each day was becoming more and more difficult.

Ten days had now passed and Wang brought good news. He had once again spotted a Japanese patrol but this one was much more lethargic in its search. And when he spotted another one the following day exhibiting the same demeanor, MacDougal opined the Japs were close to giving up the search.

"They have most likely decided we have already found a hiding place and therefore they are no longer on high alert. We should be able to make better time now. All going well we should reach the Jor camp in three days. But as we get closer we have to be on the lookout for guerrillas guarding the camp. They may be trigger happy and not knowing who we are they may shoot first and ask questions later."

As it turned out they came across a guard in two days. MacDougal approached him with his hands raised and spoke to him in Hokkien. Luckily the bamboo telegraph had worked perfectly and the guerrilla recognized his name. He had already heard of their success at Butterworth and was overjoyed to meet them. He speedily guided them through the other checkpoints into the camp where he proudly announced their presence to the head of the camp.

Chesterton having now fully recovered took the leadership role once again as he introduced his team. The camp leader, who had attended university in England, shook each of their hands in an energetic fashion.

"My name is Woon. You are all most welcome. It is a pleasure and an honor to meet the men who have given all of us so much new hope. I have another honored guest in camp, the leader of the Malayan Communist Party, Chin Peng. He will be staying for a few days. And we have three resident Englishmen who have been training my comrades. Perhaps you may even know one or more of them. We have all heard of your wonderful success and will be eager to listen to a first hand account. But you all look exhausted from your journey, so I suggest you bathe and have a meal. I will have our doctor visit you to dispense any necessary medication and then you must rest. Tomorrow will be soon enough for you to regale us with your story."

Then he repeated this in Hokkien for Wang.

The team gratefully accepted his proposal.

While they were bathing, Steve MacDougal whispered to Alex.

"You did very well laddie. That was one helluva trek. And you were smart enough to quickly recognize Simon's condition. However, I know him better than you and I knew he would only need a little time to get over it. If the truth be known, I was actually more concerned about you than Simon. A few days in the jungle is one thing, but two weeks can sap the physical and mental strength of any man. But you came through it with flying colors."

"If the real truth be known, Steve, I wasn't sure I would make it. I didn't want to hold you back. All I could do was put one foot in front of another all the way and hope I would be okay."

MacDougal stared at his young friend.

"Let me tell you something, Alex, I know as much about the jungle as any foreigner. And the way I have survived is by doing just what you said. You hit the nail on the head. It is imperative you take it one step at a time and focus on where you are stepping. Most people can't do that no matter how many times they have been told. They start out full of vim and vigor, not giving the jungle the respect it deserves, and they land in trouble. Then after a while the hell they are living overcomes them and they begin dreaming of a hot bath, antiseptic ointment for their bug and leech marks and sleeping in a comfortable bed. It's when their minds start to wander that they get into serious trouble. I have found that's something almost impossible to teach. One has to experience it. You have learned a very valuable lesson. Always remember – one careful step at a time – and stay focused."

In the days ahead Alex would be eternally grateful for the teachings of both Sergeant MacTavish and Steve MacDougal.

Chapter Thirty Two

They were awakened at seven o'clock by a guerrilla who brought them coffee and toasted bread. Alex's whole body still ached and he would have been happy to stay in bed for many more hours. Before leaving, the guerrilla informed them they were requested to meet with Chin Peng, the three British officers and the camp's main committee. They were all most anxious to hear of their exploits. Of course they could bathe and dress first, and after the meeting have a more substantial breakfast. He then told Wang he was to be billeted with other guerillas and he should follow him.

"I'm afraid that sounds like an order and not a request," said Chesterton. "I could certainly do with a bit more sleep."

They had been given a cabin to themselves. It was not as sparsely furnished as the one in their own camp. In fact, although it wasn't the Ritz, it was quite comfortable.

They got up, picked up towels and soap and were about to leave when Alex had a thought.

"Hold on a minute, chaps."

They looked at him expectantly.

"This man, Chin Peng, is very powerful in the fight against the Japanese, isn't he?"

"He is El Supremo," replied MacDougal.

"Does he consider himself to be your boss, Simon?"

"That's an interesting question, Alex. He would expect me to respect his position and if possible carry out any instructions he has. But he would understand that he has no ultimate authority over me. Why do you ask?"

"As you will not doubt take the lead in telling the group about our recent successes, there is something I must ask you."

"What's that, Alex?"

"I don't think you should mention our coding machines."

"These are our allies, Alex. We should have no secrets from them," responded a puzzled Chesterton.

But Steve MacDougal instantly knew why Alex had made this request.

"I think the laddie is right, Simon. Chin Peng will undoubtedly be infatuated by the machines, particularly the Japanese one. From what I know of him he can be very demanding. And I would bet he will strongly request you turn over the machines to him. And furthermore he will want Alex to go with him to operate them and to teach his people to use them."

"Ah, I see. Is that what you were thinking, Alex?"

"Exactly! After a few days when we better understand the aims of the group in this camp, we can use the machines if you believe it is appropriate. But until we get the lay of the land here, I believe we must keep them secret."

"For a moment I forgot you were indoctrinated in London to be a spy. Now you are showing it again. However, I do believe it would be wise to be cautious as you suggest. But you do realize you have given me a huge problem. How do I describe our recent activities without mentioning the coding machines?"

"As our dear friend, Tony, would have said with an impish grin, 'That's why you hold the rank of captain and are paid so much,'" said MacDougal with a smile of his own.

That arrow struck home. It took a few seconds for Chesterton to compose himself at the mention of his lost friend. Then he nodded his head.

"Okay, I agree. But we had better hide the coding machines. Two of our rucksacks have locks. We will store them there. Remember the Chinese have an insatiable curiosity and I would bet someone will have a quick look over our things, while we are in the meeting."

That having been settled, they left for the river with both Chesterton and MacDougal still shaking their heads in amazement at Alex's forethought. As they walked to the river Alex took a good look at the camp. It was huge, with at least fifteen cabins, many of them very large. Alex estimated there must be over one hundred and fifty men in the camp.

When they had bathed and dressed they were guided to the largest of the cabins, the one used for meetings.

"I hope I can dance my way around not mentioning your machines, Alex," muttered Chesterton.

"Of course you can, Simon. You're the best dancer we have," responded MacDougal with a wicked grin.

"Thanks, that helps a lot you ugly Scot," replied Chesterton unable to keep a grin from his own face.

There were ten people waiting for them. They were Chin Peng and three of his staff, Woon, the chief of the guerrillas, and two of his aides and the three Englishmen. One of the Englishmen jumped up and came rushing towards Chesterton.

"Simon, it's wonderful to see you again. How are you?"

"I'm reasonably well. And it's equally great to see you, Charlie. It's been quite some time since we served together."

"Perhaps I may be allowed to make all the introductions. Later both of you gentlemen can catch up," interrupted Woon in his impeccable English, and proceeded to do so.

Chesterton's friend was Major Charles Lander, next was Lieutenant James (Jim) Rose and then Mr. Arthur O'Shea who spoke in an aggrieved tone.

"Everyone around here continually refers to us as the three Englishmen but I am not English, I am proud to be Irish."

There was a titter of laughter from the Malayans who failed to see the difference even though O'Shea had repeatedly made this point. Then O'Shea looked with puzzlement at the doorway as though he was expecting someone else.

"Where's the professor? We served together in the High Commission in KL and last I heard of him he was with you, Captain Chesterton. Has he gone on to another camp?"

Alex saw Chesterton blanch and for an instant thought he would lose control at the mention of his dear friend. But Chesterton managed to retain control over his voice as he said in a hushed tone.

"My great companion and friend, Anthony Benson, was killed in the action at Butterworth. He gave his life saving one of our men who was under fire," he said.

He uttered his last word just as his voice was about to give out on him.

"Oh dear God, no. Not Tony," was all that O'Shea managed to say before he slumped in his chair.

He used a handkerchief to wipe away the tears that had sprung to his eyes. There was a respectful silence before the guerrilla chief spoke.

"We lose so many good men because of those damned Japanese and their megalomaniacal ambitions."

He allowed another brief period of silence before asking Chesterton to tell how they had managed the ambush of Ito's troops and the destruction of the Japanese camps at Ipoh and Grik. And, most particularly, of their ultimate and enormously successful raid on Butterworth. Simon began a long, detailed account of their actions and accomplished all this without mentioning the coding machines. After almost an hour, Chesterton concluded after describing the attack on Butterworth and the response was a spontaneous and long lasting applause. The applause swiftly died as Chin Peng rose to speak.

"Needless to say your exploits have spread throughout Malaya and have given us renewed encouragement in our struggle against this hideous enemy. You have shown they are not invincible and inspired by you we have already received reports of other successful attacks. Unfortunately I must leave soon but before I do I look forward to having further conversations with you, Captain Chesterton, and the other members of your team."

Then Woon rose.

"Thank you so much for your exhilarating account of such a tremendous feat, Captain Chesterton. Now, if you gentlemen would excuse us we have some further business with Chin Peng and his team."

"Let's have something to eat and we can catch up," suggested Charlie Lander, "I'll show you the way to the dining cabin."

All the way there Chesterton and Lander were engaged in animated conversation interspersed with laughter at recalled events in their past.

Alex was delighted to see this. Simon Chesterton had lost a very dear friend but had just been reunited with another.

Chapter Thirty Three

During breakfast, which was surprisingly good, the two old friends, Chesterton and Lander continued to reminisce. O'Shea took this opportunity to speak to MacDougal.

"Tell me about Tony. Did he adjust well to being left in Malaya? And tell me more about how he died."

Steve MacDougal gave a detailed account of Benson's life with the guerrillas and the key role he played in analyzing situations and making recommendations to Chesterton. He made particular mention of how much he admired Tony's ability to maintain his calm demeanor and sense of humor, even in hazardous situations. He concluded by describing in more detail the circumstances of Benson's death. This was done in a manner and tone of voice which clearly demonstrated to O'Shea how much affection MacDougal had for Benson.

"Thank you, Steve. You perfectly described the Tony Benson that I knew and cared so much for. God, how I've missed him; I have always looked forward to seeing him again. Now I never shall."

He struggled to keep his composure and after several seconds, succeeded. He then looked guiltily at Alex.

"Oh, pardon me for seeming to ignore you, Lieutenant Murdoch."

"Not at all. I only knew Tony for a short time but he soon became a good friend. He was one of the wisest men I have ever met and right from our first meeting he earned my respect. A respect that grew deeper with every passing day."

O'Shea nodded indicating he understood how a person could quickly come to admire his friend. Once again there was a brief silence as they remembered Benson. Lander had overheard the last part of their conversation and noticing the sad looks he took the initiative to change the mood.

"If you have all finished, let's go to our cabin and I can brief you on this camp and its activities. I know you have been here once before, Simon, however your friends haven't."

"It looks like there have been several improvements since my visit. And it was a very short one. So please go ahead with your briefing, Charlie," said Chesterton.

"I tell you what," continued Lander, "I believe you were given that empty cabin because you were so exhausted when you arrived and you would be undisturbed there. But we have room in our cabin, so let's move you in there if you are in agreement."

This they did and Lander ordered tea before he began his briefing.

"You seem to have a very good supply of food," noted Alex as cakes came with the tea.

"Yes, we do. The camp has an extensive vegetable garden and we have cows for milk, pigs for pork and bacon, and hens for eggs. Also we are quite close to Cameron Highlands and although there are a few Japanese there, the guerillas have excellent contacts with local farmers and we get tea, fruit, and occasionally, beef from there. We are quite high up here, about three thousand feet, so the climate is significantly cooler than most of Malaya. One notices this particularly at night. You may have found you slept better last night."

"Yes we did. In fact I didn't want to get up this morning," said Chesterton.

Lander nodded his understanding.

"Well if you like you can go back to bed and rest for a while."

"No, we'll be fine. Please continue your briefing, Charlie."

"The camp itself is located on the side of a mountain and is only accessible by a narrow twisting road. Therefore it is easy to defend. However this has not been necessary as the few Japs in Cameron Highlands are happy to stay there living an easy life and only conduct desultory patrols whenever they are visited by senior people from Kuala Lumpur."

"Don't you get air attacks?" asked MacDougal.

"Let's take a quick walk outside and I'll show you why that doesn't happen."

Once outside Lander pointed out that all the cabins had a one foot coating of earth on the roofs. Weeds were growing in the earth, so from the air it looked like jungle.

"You can see we have quite a large parade ground. The guerrilla chief, Woon, loves to have his men drill. In case of an alarm, the flag pole can be hastily lifted out of its lined hole and laid flat. But the most ingenious protection device is a woven net of small bushes and weeds which they can quickly pull out at the first sound of an aircraft. Woon got the idea when he was in England and saw how the courts at Wimbledon were protected by a tarpaulin when it rained. And as low flying is impossible due to the rugged mountains, high flying bombers can't distinguish this camp from the regular jungle."

"Amazing," said Alex.

"Let's go back inside," said Lander. "It's safer to talk in here," he explained when they were seated. "You see the location of the camp with its inherent and craftily constructed security is the good news. The bad news is the guerrillas feel too secure and we've had a very difficult time attempting to persuade them to launch serious attacks on the Japs in the towns down below. I feel certain one of the reasons for Chin Peng's visit is for precisely that purpose. He wants them to be more active in sabotage operations."

"Is the camp well armed?" asked MacDougal.

"They only have rifles and a few machine guns. No heavy artillery. You see they don't feel they need it. So I intend to follow up on Chin Peng's visit by suggesting a raid on a Jap location."

He pulled out a map from a drawer and spread it on the table.

"I was going to suggest Ipoh, but you chaps have beaten us to that. There is a smaller garrison at Tapah which is at the foot of the road leading up to the Cameron Highlands. We have four trucks and that would only allow us to take about fifty men. However that would be more than enough to take Tapah. What do you think, Simon?"

"I would recommend you postpone any raid for another couple of months. Let things settle down after the damage we managed to inflict. On our way down here we noticed the Jap patrols in the jungle were giving the appearance of losing interest. But Tapah is on the main road from Kuala Lumpur to Ipoh and I would imagine that road is being heavily guarded. What do you think, Steve?"

"I agree. And in the meantime you could get better prepared for a serious raid. You could acquire more trucks for transportation and even send some of your men to contact our men and retrieve mortars and artillery from wherever they have hidden them."

"That sounds like an excellent plan," said Jim Rose speaking for the first time.

It was obvious he was used to deferring to Charlie Lander. Lander was not only his superior officer but also had a much more striking appearance. He was close to six feet tall with a muscular frame but it was his face which gave him more authority. He had been a boxer as his face clearly showed. His nose had been broken at some time, and his eyes peered out form under bushy eyebrows. His square chin, thick lips and cauliflower ears completed his fierce appearance. Rose was five inches shorter and his boyish face was atop a thin build. But whereas Lander was the brawn, Rose was the brains. He had the same pallor as Benson which made Alex think he must have suffered quite badly from malaria. That would later be confirmed.

"Yes I agree, that makes sense," said Lander with a trace of wistfulness in his voice.

He really wanted action and having heard the achievements of his old friend only made him want it all the more. His old friend now spoke again.

"I would be remiss if I didn't tell you, Charlie, that the brains behind actions we took were not mine. They belong to that young chap there," he said nodding towards Alex. "If you don't mind I'd like ask him to give some thought to a possible plan."

Alex felt his face redden as all eyes were turned on him. The respect of Lander, Rose and O'Shea could not have been clearer.

"I'd be happy to," was all he could manage to say.

"I would suggest, however, all of you take several days to recover from your arduous journey before starting any work," said Lander wisely.

Chapter Thirty Four

One week later they met again to hear Alex's report. He had spoken to Chesterton prior to the meeting and received his approval to tell the others of the coding machines.

Lander opened the meeting then turned to Alex.

"Please go right ahead and explain your plan."

"Well it seems to me that everything Simon and Steve said was very sensible concerning an attack on Tapah."

He hesitated and MacDougal took the opportunity to speak.

"You will learn as you get to know this laddie better that there tends to be a 'but' or an 'and' after his initial comment. In this case I sense a 'but'."

That really got the attention of the three members of the camp. One could see them sit forward in their chairs with anticipation. Alex cleared his throat to hide his embarrassment before continuing.

"But," he said with a smile, "my thought is that Tapah is indeed too close to your camp. As was said, it is at the turnoff from the main trunk road from KL to Ipoh and Penang. That turnoff leads directly towards Cameron Highlands and your camp. Such an attack would surely cause the Japanese to swarm all over this area. And whereas bombers cannot see your camp, they could use helicopters which may well spot it. I think it might be better to wait for say three to four months then strike a more significant location; one closer to our previous area of operations. The Japanese are likely to believe it is our group back in business and redouble their efforts much further north of here. From what I have heard I believe a successful raid on Taiping would cause the Japanese significant damage."

MacDougal was now used to Alex's off-the-wall ideas and was not shocked. But he had to bite his tongue not to burst out laughing at the looks on the faces of Lander, Rose and O'Shea.

"That's impossible," said an agitated Lander. By that time the Japs will have re-manned Ipoh which is only fifty miles from Taiping. They would race up there and slaughter us."

"I doubt Alex has finished telling all the details of his plan. Have you, Alex?" said Chesterton with a knowing look.

"That's correct," he said as he pointed to the map. "As you said Charlie, Taiping is fifty miles north west of Ipoh. To successfully attack Taiping we must lure Japanese troops away from Ipoh. To do so we will have our old guerrilla group attack Grik as a diversion. But we will not use many guerrillas in the attack as we don't intend to overrun them, only to scare them. Grik is one hundred miles due north of Ipoh. When under attack, Grik will ask Ipoh for aid."

"But the new commander will certainly be aware of your previous ruse to lure Ipoh troops into an ambush," interjected O'Shea.

"Yes, I am counting on that. I believe he will send just enough troops in a convoy of heavily protected vehicles to assist Grik, keeping the majority of his troops in Ipoh. The convoy will move along the road slowly, sending out scouts to check for trouble. This time we will not barricade the road. That would alert both the forward and the rear scouts. But we will have our other guerrillas hidden in the jungle at the side of the road and they will lob mortars taking out the lead vehicle and the rear vehicle. This will take place about ninety miles north of Ipoh, and only ten miles from Grik. Then I surmise the convoy, being under attack, will radio back to Ipoh and the commander will have no choice but to send out almost all of his remaining force to rescue his convoy. He will not wish to lose face by being tricked by the guerrillas. Importantly, this time he will know, unlike the prior attack, there are no barricades. It will appear to be a relatively simple military mission of sending enough additional firepower to cover the retreat of his convoy. That's why he will send most of his remaining troops."

There was a nodding of heads from his audience at his reasoning.

"Meanwhile, Charlie, your guerrillas will have by-passed Ipoh and be in position to attack Taiping. We will signal them to commence their raid two hours after the main body of troops has left Ipoh. By that time they should be within ten miles of where their comrades are under attack. Taiping will undoubtedly radio for help when we attack, but the Ipoh troops will be too far away to be of any assistance. Simultaneously with your raid on Taiping, most of Lee Sheng's guerrillas will wipe out the small number of troops remaining at Ipoh and destroy the camp. Also, at that time the guerrillas attacking the first convoy will cease fire and rapidly disappear into the jungle. And finally the guerrillas at Grik will destroy that camp.

"Holy Mary, Mother of Jesus," exclaimed O'Shea unable to contain his amazement. "That could work, couldn't it Jim?" he asked Rose.

Rose nodded his head slowly as he came to the same conclusion.

"However there are lots of ways it could not," he said pensively. "To pull it off we would need to know exactly what the Japs were about to do. What happens, Alex, if the Jap commander does not send a convoy to rescue Grik but decides to sacrifice them rather than risk his own troops?"

"Then we call off the raid on Taiping."

"So you are planning to have spies in place to see if troops leave Ipoh and somehow communicate with our men outside Taiping. Is that it?" interjected O'Shea.

"No. I will be listening in to the Japanese communications. But I need someone who is fluent in Japanese to assist me."

"Wait a minute, what so you mean you will be listening to their communications. Just how do you propose to do that?"

It was time for Chesterton to intercede.

"Steve will you kindly guard the door?"

MacDougal did that but kept glancing back into the cabin. He didn't want to miss the finale of this story.

"Please keep this information to yourselves for the time being. During our meeting with Chin Peng I did not go into Alex's background. Actually Lieutenant Murdoch worked for several years at Bletchley Park as an expert code breaker. He was sent out here to uncover a traitor who was giving our coded messages to the enemy. He did that brilliantly. He brought several code machines with him manufactured at Bletchley Park. Two of them are hidden in our rucksacks. One is specially outfitted to allow us to communicate not only within Malaya but also to Ceylon. But it is the other which is truly special; it was made with a Japanese keyboard."

"But even with that the Japs will transmit in code," persisted the bright O'Shea.

Alex looked appraisingly at him. Later he would learn that while O'Shea's position at the British High Commission was ostensibly Secretary for Economic Affairs, his real job was Head of Intelligence.

"That's true," continued Chesterton, "but the brilliant Lieutenant Murdoch used his training to break the codes used by Grik, Ipoh, Penang, Kuala Lumpur and Singapore. That allowed us to know every move the Japs planned and made our attacks so successful."

This time MacDougal could not contain himself. At the sight of the raised eyebrows, bulging eyes and gaping mouths of Lander, Rose and O'Shea, he burst into uncontrollable laughter.

"Bloody hell," exploded from the lips of Lander.

When O'Shea at last managed to close his mouth he couldn't keep from adding to Lander's outburst by using another of his Irish aphorisms.

"Dear God in Heaven," he ejaculated. "Do you think you can still listen in to the Jap transmissions?"

"Yes, they may have changed their wavelengths but I should be able to track them down. And they may have changed their codes, so I will need the services of a fluent Japanese speaker."

"You need look no further than that irreverent Irishman," said Lander crudely attempting an Irish accent.

"Yes," admitted O'Shea, "prior to the Jap invasion several of us in the High Commission were given extensive lessons in Japanese. Tony and I were among that group. We could see it was only a matter of time before Japan moved further into Asia. What we didn't recognize was just how vulnerable our defenses were and how well trained their troops were after their experience in China."

A smile of satisfaction crossed the face of Alex. He had a trusted source of Japanese. Things were falling into place.

Chapter Thirty Five

Chesterton had grinned at the reactions of Lander and O'Shea then his mind refocused on the new potential raid. While he was thinking about this, it was Rose who posed the next questions.

"But how do you propose we explain to Woon why you didn't mention this to both Chin Peng and him. And what if he considers it politically prudent to insist your machines are given to Chin Peng?"

"I've given that some thought," answered Alex. "I propose we say that the machines were commissioned by Lord Louis Mountbatten. And he mandated they stay in British hands. He further demanded we send regular repots directly to him on their use. And by telling Woon of their existence we are conferring on him the trust of Lord Mountbatten. He must not mention it to a soul."

"That should work," agreed Rose. "Lord Mountbatten is revered among the guerrilla leadership."

But Chesterton was still concerned. From his experience with the communist movement he had learned that a guerrilla leader always kept his superiors informed on matters of great importance. Not to do so could easily mean death. He addressed his next comments to Lander.

"The question I have for you, Charlie, is, even with Alex's inspired idea of using Lord Mountbatten's name; can we trust Woon with this information? I don't mean trust in the sense he would give it to the enemy, but would he feel compelled to report it to Chin Peng?"

Lander thought for a moment before replying.

"I don't believe so. However I would wait for a week or so until he gets to know you better. This will increase his trust in you and he will be more inclined to take your advice."

Lander could see that Chesterton was not entirely convinced about Woon.

"You will soon get a better understanding of Woon. When he speaks with his beautiful English, one can get the impression he is a bit of an effete dilettante. But nothing could be further from the truth. He is in total command of this camp and rules with a rod of iron. He rigidly controls the comings and goings of everyone. His sentries will not allow anyone to leave. Any violation of this means death. He is extremely proud of his position as head of this camp, and from a few slips by him during our private conversations, I believe he doesn't take too kindly to Chin Peng interfering in how he conducts the affairs of it. Furthermore, he is a true patriot who loves his country and fervently wishes it to become independent. Undoubtedly he wants it to become a communist state but has told me in confidence he would willingly abide by the wishes of the people in a fair election."

"That does speak well of him," admitted Chesterton.

"I should also tell you, Simon, he respects us for our knowledge of warfare, and for our part we only offer advice when we are alone with him; never when one of his men is within earshot. I know he appreciates this. That's why I suggest you wait awhile before telling him of your special coding machine. Then we can ask for a private meeting and have Alex explain his plan to him. I believe he will be intrigued by it. Even though I mentioned the guerrillas were not inclined to take too many risks, I have always had the strong impression Woon would love to accomplish a truly major victory. Such a success would greatly increase his stature throughout Malaya. And this feeling was confirmed when you gave your prior camp leader, Lee Sheng, praise for his leadership in achieving the magnificent raids. I watched Woon closely and could see the envy in his eyes."

"Politics, politics," muttered Alex, and then hurriedly apologized for his remark.

"No, you are absolutely correct, Alex," interjected Rose. "As I'm certain you have been told, the communists are not fighting the Japanese to aid Britain. They want their country back. But they want it to be under their control. If Woon could achieve a tremendous victory it would greatly enhance his chances of having a significant position in the new communist regime controlling this country."

"Today we are friends but after the war we will be enemies," agreed O'Shea.

"Well returning to our plan, what do we do between now and the time we can speak to Woon?" asked Chesterton.

Alex was happy to see Chesterton back to his usual authoritarian self, but surprised he was taking the lead when his rank was lower than Lander's. Apparently this also suddenly dawned on Chesterton.

"Oh, I beg your pardon, Charlie. You are the senior man here."

"That's all right Simon. You have had much more battle experience. As I said our role has mainly been a training one with very little action. I am happy for you to take the lead."

"Well, any ideas?" asked Chesterton once again.

MacDougal happened to look at Alex and saw his eyebrows raised in a question. These two had developed something akin to mental telepathy and he knew what Alex was asking him to say.

"I believe we ought to have Wang return to our old area and start locating our men and more particularly, the location of our captured armaments. He could also check on the strength of the Japs in Ipoh and Taiping. I would give him six weeks to do all that. For security reasons it would be wise not to advise him of our ultimate plan. However, he must be given license to say he believes we will be planning more raids at some time in the future, and his job is to scout out the territory. To do the job we are asking will require him to ask many questions of some trusted people. This can't be done without arousing curiosity. Better he gives out half a story than nothing. That prevents excessive speculation."

"Good thinking," enjoined O'Shea. "And while that's going on, can you begin checking the Japanese wavelengths and codes, Alex?"

"Yes, if we can be certain there is no one close by to hear the noise of the machine."

"I believe we can arrange that," said a happy Lander.

He was excited they would soon see action.

The day after Chin Peng left the camp two important events occurred. Firstly Chesterton briefed Wang on the mission they wanted him to undertake.

"I regret sending you back into danger, Wang, but this is vitally important," he said in Hokkien.

Alex's Hokkien was improving and he understood most of this.

"That is not a problem," responded Wang. "Anyway I am not happy here."

"Why?" interrupted MacDougal.

"These guerrillas have not accepted me. I am not known to any of them and of course at first they did not trust me. But problems really began when later they asked me lots of questions about the three of you – very personal questions. Then they wanted to know details of Lee Sheng and where he may be now. When I refused to answer they turned against me. It will be a relief to leave."

"I understand," said MacDougal knowing both the clannishness and the curiosity of the Chinese character.

Following this conversation, Chesterton and Lander talked to Woon saying that Wang's role in helping guide them was now over and he wished to return to his family. They asked Woon's permission to allow him to leave and added that if at a later date Wang wished to return to rejoin them, Woon would permit this. Woon had no objection and so with a plentiful supply of food and water, Wang set off.

The second important event was, with Rose standing guard at the door of the cabin, Alex began using the Japanese machine. Some transmission frequencies had been altered but he soon zeroed in on the new ones. He recorded a message from Singapore to Ipoh. After O'Shea had written it out in katakana he used the previous code to decypher it and had O'Shea translate the result. It turned out to be a simple request for an update on how the troops Singapore had sent were settling in. Alex let out a long sigh of relief in learning the code hadn't changed.

"Thank God for that," he breathed.

"What is it?" asked Lander.

"Well I must now confess that I disobeyed an order from Captain Chesterton."

Simon looked at him expecting this was a joke. But when he didn't see a grin on Alex's face, he walked over beside him and stared into his eyes.

"And what order was that?" he demanded.

"I was instructed to send the message from the Japanese camp in Ipoh to Grik in code. I didn't. At the last minute I thought it may sound more authentic if the message was panicky and sent uncoded. But also I didn't want the Japanese to recognize we had cracked their code in the hope they wouldn't change it. And they haven't."

"Well done, Alex!" exclaimed Rose from the doorway.

Then realizing his enthusiasm may not be shared by Chesterton whose order had been ignored he mumbled, "Sorry."

Captain Simon Chesterton's face was set sternly as he looked at Alex.

"Despite your intolerable action, *Lieutenant Murdoch,* you will be pleased to hear I have just given careful consideration to the punishment for your blatant disobedience and decided --- not to have you shot."

His face broke into the broadest of smiles as he said this, and he clapped Alex on the back.

Chapter Thirty Six

After ten days, Alex, with Chesterton's approval, sent a message on the regular coding machine to one of the guerrilla groups asking if they had seen Wang. He used the new code he had developed back at the old camp. The response was disappointing; they had no contact with Wang. They also said the Japanese were extremely active and the group had been disbanded; only the leader and the radioman remained in contact. They requested not to be contacted until further notice.

Not good news!

After a further two weeks Woon informed Lander he was about to begin planning an attack on Tapah and requested his advice. This, also, was not good news. Lander arranged a private meeting between the British and Woon.

When Woon arrived expecting a discussion on Tapah, Lander wasted no time; he came straight to the point.

"We don't believe an attack on Tapah would be wise."

He then explained all the reasons for this opinion.

"I understand and tend to agree with you, but you must realize my position. I am under pressure from Chin Peng to inflict significant damage on the Japanese. It has been too long since our last raid."

Lander did not immediately respond but looked steadfastly into Woon's eyes. Woon's instincts were instantly on alert. He sensed something momentous was about to be said.

"I'm not sure I will like what you have on your mind, Charles. However, please tell me," he said softly.

"We have another plan for you: One which will give you and your men much more glory than a raid on little Tapah. I had better let the architect of this plan explain it to you. But before I do I should tell you something about his background."

He told Woon all that Alex had accomplished before arriving in Malaya. Then he came to the crucial fact.

"Before Lieutenant Murdoch left England, Bletchley Park made a very special coding machine and Alex brought it to Malaya."

He paused for effect.

"It is a Japanese coding machine. Its use made the raids on Ipoh and Butterworth successful by intercepting the Japanese radio transmissions. Lieutenant Murdoch aided by Anthony Benson as translator, decyphered the Japanese codes."

Woon fell back in his chair as though punched. Then something in his brain clicked in and he leant forward quickly. His face changed from wonder to anger.

"Why did you withhold this information from me," he barked. "This is of the greatest importance and you deigned not to tell me."

Now his voice was rising to a hysterical level and Alex was afraid someone would hear. But Woon rapidly regained control.

"You have betrayed our trusted relationship, Major Lander."

Everyone noted the change from the informal 'Charles' to the formal 'Major Lander' used by Woon. It was not a good sign. Chesterton stood.

"I am to blame for that. I believe you know as well as I do what would have happened if we had mentioned this coding machine at our first meeting. The Malayan Communist Party would have demanded we hand it over along with Lieutenant Murdoch to operate it. I could not permit that. Lieutenant Murdoch is under my command."

His last sentence was spoken in a strident tone leaving no doubt that it was not a negotiable matter.

"I regret not informing you earlier however I was under strict instructions not to allow this machine out of my hands. This order came directly from Lord Mountbatten who commissioned the construction of this machine."

Woon sat back in his chair and looked at Chesterton. The anger had disappeared from his face.

"I have nothing but the highest regard for Lord Mountbatten and also for you and all you have achieved, Simon. And now that I see you are a cautious man in addition to being a brave one, my respect has increased."

The smile on his face and the informal greeting of 'Simon' eased the tension in the cabin.

"Now perhaps you will please explain your plan, Alex," said Woon.

Alex took his time to cover all aspects of the action. He concluded by telling Woon that through his recent monitoring of Japanese transmissions he knew their code had not changed.

"This is breathtaking news," responded Woon, at once seeing the tremendous recognition it would bring to him – the recognition he craved.

"But how do I respond to Chin Peng's urgings for immediate action?" he asked Lander with a worried look on his face.

It was Alex who jumped in with an answer.

"You could send one of your most trusted aides to Chin Peng saying you have developed a plan of such audacity that it necessitates allowing the Japanese a few more weeks to fully get over their loses at Butterworth and reduce their degree of alertness back to normal levels. And due to the need for the utmost secrecy you could not entrust your aide with the details in case he was captured and tortured by the Japanese."

The worried look faded from Woon's face and was replaced by a conspiratorial smile.

"Excellent," he breathed. "Having just witnessed your sharp mind in action, I understand why you were selected to come out here. You are a very clever chap, Alex. So tell me, what do we do now?"

"I must admit to one other deceitful action," intervened Chesterton. "Wang did not leave here to visit family. He is actually scouting out the situation in Ipoh and Taiping. In addition he is locating our caches of arms and informing my guerrillas to be prepared for further action. He knows nothing of the plan just outlined to you. He should return here in about three weeks, and after receiving his report, we can finalize all details of the raid."

"And what if I had rejected you proposal?" asked Woon with arched eyebrows.

"Then his trip would have been redundant. The commencement of this proposed action is yours to command – and only yours," responded Chesterton without hesitation.

Woon nodded his complete satisfaction with this answer and stood to leave.

"Of course it goes without saying I shall not mention this to anyone. Please feel free to consult with me should you require my assistance," he said and left the cabin with a smile of pure delight.

He would not only get the raid he desired but he would get personal credit for it.

"That was brilliantly handled," enthused O'Shea, as Rose nodded his agreement.

"Yes indeed," concurred MacDougal. "Now we are back to the waiting game. I hope Wang is being successful."

After another two weeks, the waiting was becoming very stressful. Not knowing if Wang was even still alive created this tension. The least tense person was MacDougal who had great faith in Wang.

"Don't worry, he'll be here in a week," he averred.

While the others fretted, Alex kept busy checking Japanese transmissions. He was doing so one day after his river bath and had not put on a shirt as it was an unusually hot day. Since Alex had skipped breakfast, Chesterton ordered tea and toast to be sent to him. Alex was bending over the coding machine when a guerrilla arrived with his tea.

"Just leave it on the table, thank you," he said over his shoulder as he covered the machine.

Without knowing why, his mind flashed back to the last meeting he had with Mr. Smith of the SOE.

'Never turn your back on anyone,' rang through his mind.

He whirled round in time to see the knife racing towards his back. Thanks to Sergeant MacTavish's lessons he leapt to one side and grabbed the hand holding the knife, twisting it back painfully. His move would have been perfect if it had happened a split second earlier. As it was the knife only lightly sliced down his side. It was not a deep cut but it bled a lot.

The perpetrator cried out in extreme pain as his wrist cracked. In the struggle the tray of tea and toast clattered to the floor like a clap of thunder. Alex wrestled the attacker face down to the ground and was straddling him, still holding his wrist in an agonizing grip, when O'Shea came running in.

"What the hell?" he yelled at the top of his lungs and rushed to Alex's aid.

Within minutes the cabin was full of people who had heard O'Shea's cry. MacDougal and O'Shea speedily had the attacker under control and Chesterton ushered all the others out of the cabin where they milled around outside. Woon pushed his way through the increasing throng and looked in disbelief at the scene inside. He shook off his incredulity and rapidly took command.

"Fetch the doctor – quickly! And lock up Tan. I'll deal with him later," he roared.

"What happened, Alex?" asked a distraught Chesterton.

"I don't know. Simon. I just turned round in time to see him lunge at me. I was really lucky."

"I'll say you were. You must have the reflexes of a cat," said Rose.

"I had a good teacher," was all that Alex would say.

The doctor arrived and shooed everyone out of the cabin while he dressed the wound. While he was doing this, the attacker's screams of agony could be heard. He was being interrogated. The doctor pursed his lips and shook his head. Just after he had finished dressing the wound, Woon arrived back. All the foreigners came back into the cabin to hear his report. Woon looked at Alex.

"Are you all right, Alex?"

"Yes, the doctor said it is not a deep wound. I shall be fine."

"Tan has told me his story. You see Alex one of the negative attributes of we Chinese, is a tendency to be nosy and to exaggerate what we discover. It seems that stories of your involvement in the Ipoh raid were passed from man to man. Eventually it sounded as though you single handedly raided Ipoh killing all the Japanese and setting fire to the camp.

"Of course there were repercussions after the raid. A few known communist sympathizers were beheaded. Your attacker, Tan, and his wife both come from Ipoh and while he is serving with us, his wife was staying with her parents. His father-in-law apparently disobeyed the instructions given out at the Ipoh raid regarding the handing out of petrol from the Japanese fuel dump. In addition to filling an unmarked container he stole a full Japanese container marked in Japanese writing. Unfortunately the Japanese discovered this container and as a punishment they publically shot everyone in the house, including Tan's wife.

"Therefore to Tan's simple mind you were the cause of his wife's death and he sought retribution by attempting to kill you. By doing do he has brought disgrace on this entire camp but more importantly he has disgraced the glorious state of communism. He will be shot."

Alex was dismayed.

"Is it not possible to explain to him that I didn't kill any Japanese and perhaps banish him instead of killing him?"

Woon's face hardened and his words indicated how deeply he believed in his version of communism.

"No, that's impossible," he thundered. "I told you he has disgraced communism. He must die."

Alex had learned another lesson. Extreme believers in any cause have no mercy. Their extremism turns their hearts to stone.

Chapter Thirty Seven

Steve MacDougal was proved correct. Wang returned six weeks to the day from his departure. After he had bathed and eaten, he was summoned to the foreigners' cabin and asked to report. Only the six men and Woon were there to hear his account.

"Will you please take note of all he has to say, Jim?" Lander asked Rose.

"Certainly, if someone will translate."

"I'll take care of that," volunteered MacDougal.

Wang had compiled a complete catalogue of every hiding place of arms, trucks and people. All of this was committed to memory with nothing in writing. He described everything with astonishing specificity. He also gave a detailed description of the camps at Ipoh and Taiping including an estimation of the number of troops. His report indicated the troops now at Ipoh, having been sent from Singapore, were significantly superior to the prior unproven troops and to those at Taiping who were still green. As he stressed this last point he looked straight at MacDougal.

"Are our people still willing to fight?" asked Chesterton.

"Yes, Tuan, they are most anxious to do so."

"You did a superb job, Wang. Thank you very much," said Chesterton.

Wang bowed his head in acknowledgement of this compliment.

Alex and Rose had been given a running translation of this Hokkien conversation by MacDougal, and Rose wrote everything down in a notebook. When the discussions were over it was Lander who spoke to Woon.

"Armed with this excellent information, we will complete all aspects of the plan and present them to you for your approval," he said.

"Thank you, Charles. I look forward to that," responded an excited guerrilla leader.

When Woon had left, Wang looked at MacDougal, Chesterton and Alex in turn.

"Lee Sheng sends you his best wishes and looks forward to seeing you soon."

It was obvious he had waited for Woon to leave before delivering this message. It also conveyed that his loyalties would always be with Lee Sheng and not Woon.

"Thank you," they chorused at receiving Lee Sheng's greeting.

"Now, Wang, I suspect you have been holding something back. What else do you have to tell us? You can talk freely in front of these other three men," said MacDougal.

He clearly recognized Wang didn't want to tell all in front of Woon. Also he probably was uncertain he could trust the three unknown foreigners.

Wang nodded his head at MacDougal's assurances. He trusted his judgment implicitly.

"Only one more item; I heard strong rumors Taiping's forces were to be greatly strengthened soon - by the end of the year at the latest. This timing may be important to you."

Such insight greatly shocked everyone in the room except MacDougal who had a high regard for Wang's intuition and investigation capability.

"What do you mean by that?" demanded Chesterton, deadly afraid Wang may have overstepped his mission and in doing so he may have compromised the intended attack.

Wang shrugged.

"I overheard two Japanese officers talking in a restaurant one night. They had drunk a lot of beer and were indiscrete. One said he had heard it from someone in the communication center and the other said it could not be true otherwise he would have been informed. That's why I said it was still a rumor. But I believed the first man."

The maxim, 'Don't judge a book by its cover,' sprang immediately to Alex's mind. This man was much more intelligent than most suspected.

"I believe Wang has deduced from his mission that there are only a few targets for another attack of any significance. Taiping being the most likely, that's why he took time to find out as much as he could while he was there," said MacDougal in English so that Wang would not understand.

"If he blabbed that, it could prejudice the entire attack," exclaimed Lander heatedly.

"I doubt that he did. But let's ask him," replied MacDougal, which he did in Hokkien.

"No! No! Tuan. I mentioned my deduction to no one. And I asked no questions in Taiping. I only observed the camp and listened to gossip in coffee shops and restaurants. It would have been foolish to do anything other than observe and listen."

That response rocked Lander. In his interaction with other guerrillas, except Woon, he had not experienced such perspicacity. Neither had O'Shea and he gazed at Wang with admiration. MacDougal translated for Rose and Alex and they too were deeply impressed.

After they all had congratulated Wang for his excellent work, MacDougal escorted Wang to the door. When they were outside he put both hands on Wang's shoulders and stared with a penetrating gaze into his eyes.

"You have done very well, my friend. I am very proud of you. Thank you."

Wang could never have asked for higher praise since it came from a man he so admired and respected. He stood back, placed his right hand over his closed left fist, held his hands at his chest and bowed three times. Then he hurriedly turned away. He did not wish the man he worshipped to see the strong emotion he felt reflected in his eyes.

The next few days were filled with meetings as they planned the details of their attack. There was an urgency they hadn't anticipated due to Wang's warning of reinforcements going to Taiping. This was uppermost in their minds as they worked tirelessly from morning to night. At last they believed they had thought of every contingency and presented the plan to Woon.

"This is excellent, but I thought you had intended we move towards the end of next month."

"We decided it would be wiser to move earlier during the monsoon season. The guerrillas are used to the heavy rains but the Japs don't like to go out in that type of weather," replied Chesterton in a carefully rehearsed answer.

"Well I approve. When do you suggest I tell my men?"

"It will take about three weeks for Wang to return and prepare everything. He must inform the guerrillas around Grik and Ipoh of their parts in the raid. Then they must retrieve all the transport and armaments. I suggest you start increased training of your men right away and tell them of the plan in about two and a half weeks. Our departure date will be three weeks from today. It will take almost two days to march down to the main road. Wang will arrange for the trucks to pick up your men five miles north of Tapah at eleven o'clock at night. From there we will proceed to Taiping."

"Very well, now if you don't mind would you go over the plan one more time for me?"

During the next three weeks, the guerrillas were put through exhaustive exercises. They were just beginning to grumble at this when they were told of their objective. Immediately morale rose and they paid close attention to instructions. Only seventy of the men were chosen for this raid. However the rest were drilled in protecting the camp should anything go wrong.

When it came time to set off, they left at dusk and marched down the winding road. Lander had decided it would be safe to do so as the Japanese in Cameron Highlands seldom left camp at night. Their plan was to take the easy way by staying on the road until dawn then strike out through the jungle during the day. After about five hours of marching the forward lookouts gave the signal of approaching danger. Two vehicles were coming up the road. Everyone moved into the shrubbery on each side of the road and lay prostrate with weapons at the ready until the vehicles passed. Luckily they were civilian vehicles, breaking the curfew, and travelling with only side lights.

"Probably black marketeers going to buy fruits and vegetables," murmured O'Shea.

Alex was relieved. While lying at the side of the road he was sure everyone would hear the pounding in his chest. It took a few minutes for his heart to slow back to a normal rhythm - at least normal for someone about to go into real danger. Chesterton took the opportunity to call a halt for fifteen minutes before they resumed their march.

They reached the rendezvous point the following night and climbed into the six trucks. Chesterton was puzzled when Wang ushered him along with MacDougal, Alex and O'Shea into a small armored vehicle at the head of the column. As they took off the driver turned to greet them.

"Good evening," he said in his best English.

It was a grinning Lee Sheng.

After happy greetings were exchanged and O'Shea was introduced, Lee Sheng switched to Hokkien and spoke in a somber tone.

"The last few months have been difficult for all guerrilla groups around Ipoh and Grik. The townspeople and villagers who have hidden us were very brave. Unfortunately several were tortured and executed along with those of my men they were forced to reveal. And after this attack it will become much more dangerous, both for the local population and my men; therefore, I have decided to lead all the guerrillas to the mountains in the north east of Kuala Lumpur. There are several camps there and we will join those groups. I have already dispatched men to contact the camps. And to protect the local people I have given locations of our old camps to their leaders. If anyone is to be tortured he will give directions to the Japanese. When they discover the camps are deserted they will redouble their searches in the surrounding areas but hopefully spare the local population. So I will say goodbye to you after this raid."

"That is a wise decision, Lee Sheng," agreed Chesterton. "We shall miss you and I wish you good luck."

"I shall miss all of you," responded Lee Sheng, but his eyes were on MacDougal. "And I shall certainly miss the tricks played by Lieutenant Murdoch and his magical machine. I think it best if I do not mention this capability to anyone, in case they were to be captured by the Japanese. I am sure you will put it to continued good use," he added with a smile.

O'Shea saw this was a man endowed with not only strong leadership qualities but with good sense. He translated Lee Sheng's comments for Alex.

"Thank you," Alex said to Lee Sheng in Hokkien.

"Ah, you are learning my language."

"I am trying but still poor at it," said Alex in the same tongue.

That degree of knowledge greatly impressed Lee Sheng and he laughed heartily. Then he turned serious.

"Now let's repay the bastards who killed my men. It is time to destroy more of the Japanese Imperial Army," he shouted.

O'Shea had to translate that for Alex who shivered at the words of this avenging warrior.

Chapter Thirty Eight

Observing the raid on Taiping, one could have been excused if he thought this was a well rehearsed play. Alex coordinated everything from his battery operated coding machine. He intercepted all Japanese transmissions. Not too surprisingly those messages were not sent in code because of their emergency nature. This allowed O'Shea to give Alex a running commentary on all Japanese positions. In turn it permitted Alex to send out signals to the various groups telling them when to start their activities. At the end, the Japanese troops at Grik, Taiping and the few remaining in Ipoh, were killed and their camps reduced to rubble. And the main body of Ipoh based troops was stranded on the road to Grik not knowing if it would again come under attack. It too had taken losses from the mortar attacks and waited until the new commander and his troops reached them before making any moves to search out guerrillas. In the end the decision was reached to return to Ipoh. This was done carefully and quite slowly as Ipoh was not answering radio communications and they feared another ambush. When they arrived they discovered their camp had been destroyed.

This delay gave the attacking forces valuable additional time to make their various getaways. Now supplied with more trucks taken from Ipoh and Taiping the guerrillas met up thirty miles south of Ipoh. The trucks and other loot were rapidly divided up, then with little time for goodbyes, Lee Sheng and his guerrillas headed quickly towards their new camps. Woon, his men and the six foreigners drove unobserved back to camp. Both groups passed through the outskirts of Tapah but the Japanese radio operator had been sound asleep therefore the few troops posted there knew nothing of this.

The next few days in Woon's camp were spent celebrating. Part of the loot they had taken consisted of many cases of Japanese sake. This greatly enhanced the celebrations. However Woon was wise enough to keep several sober guards posted around the outskirts of the camp. Included in the loot were several bottles of quite good Scotch whisky and the foreigners laid claim to that.

In Singapore the Commander-in-Chief did not pace around his office yelling expletives as in the previous disaster. Neither did he lash the face of any of his subordinates. He sat morosely in his office, alone. No one dared to enter, except his scarred aide, Ishibashi who brought him tea. The C-in-C didn't even speak and Ishibashi quietly left. The commander looked out of his window at the surrounding green lawns and shook his head.

"Why has every thing turned sour?" he muttered. "I am certain to be relieved of my post now."

The shame of these set-backs caused him to stay inside his office all day. He refused to eat anything until after it was time to leave for the day. His staff watched as he trudged out of the office with his head bowed, not responding to their calls of goodnight. But they too recognized his days in Singapore were numbered.

A few weeks later his gloomy prediction came true and he was recalled to Tokyo in disgrace. He would arrive home just before New Year, a time normally celebrated in Japan with four days of national holidays. But there would be no celebration in his household.

Around that time Alex picked up some startling news.

"The new Lieutenant General is to make his headquarters in Taiping," he told an amazed audience.

"Was there any indication why?" asked Lander.

"No explanation was given."

"It can only be due to the successful raids," opined O'Shea.

"Thank the Lord Lee Sheng and all the guerrillas have moved south," said MacDougal.

"But it also means the whole area north of here will be swarming with Japs. And not the new recruits - experienced troops. That means no more raids," intoned Chesterton sadly.

"I had better inform Woon," said Lander. "Then after dinner, I suggest we put on our thinking caps and decide what our options are."

It was a subdued group that met. The euphoria of recent success had evaporated with the thought the possibility of inactively by sitting out the rest of the war.

"Any ideas?" began Lander.

"Well tomorrow night is New Years Eve or Hogmanay as we say in Scotland and I for one intend to welcome in 1944 in traditional Scottish fashion. And that is one night of glorious drinking followed by two days of head-pounding recovery. So if you wish any opinion from me, you had better get it now."

That immediately lightened the atmosphere.

"Well give us your advice you drunken Scot," said a laughing Chesterton.

"We have to wait and see what sort of man this new commander is. I would hazard a guess he is a seasoned veteran and will not wish to act hastily. He won't fall for any of the tricks his predecessor did. And since the guerrillas aren't in his back yard to cause problems, I would bet he will gratefully accept an initial peaceful life. There is no doubt he will heavily patrol the area at first, but after a few months of quietude he will gradually relax."

"That's around here, but what about the rest of Malaya?" asked Alex.

"We have no control over that. I would guess Lee Sheng and his new friends will also be initially cautious. Perhaps they will wait for two or three months and then they will create as much havoc as possible around Kuala Lumpur. That will force the new commander to focus his attention there. But I imagine he will have enough troops to face that contingency."

But MacArthur's advance in the Pacific will mean he will have to make do with a limited supply of proven troops. And if he keeps them close to Taiping to protect his headquarters, surely this presents opportunities elsewhere where he has mainly new recruits," persisted Alex.

"Aye, your right laddie. Therefore, as I see it, we have three choices. One is to sit here until the war is over. Two is to wait and hope in four or five months things are easier here then attempt new raids on Ipoh or other nearby towns. Three is to move to another area in Malaya and start raids there."

"I believe that succinctly sums up our options unless someone has another idea," said Lander. "Is anyone in favor of either option one or two?"

That brought a unanimous negative response along with a shaking of heads.

"Well any suggestions as to where we should go?"

"I agree with Steve that we should wait for about three months. Then I suggest that half of Woon's men head south with three of us and the rest head east to the state of Pahang," said Chesterton.

"Is it necessary to break us up?" asked Rose. "We seem to be a very effective team."

"That's true, Jim, but the guerrillas need more guidance than they realize. Some of us should be with them to provide that tactical advice. The difficulty may be in having Woon agree to leave his cushy life here to take on more danger."

"Of course Woon would have to agree, however now that he has tasted the fruit of fame after the Taiping raid, he will be more amenable to adding to his stardom and his claim to a significant role in the Communist apparatus after the war. And with your silver tongue, Charlie, I'm certain you can soon persuade him this is all his idea," said Chesterton.

The others laughed at this, but all of them knew it would not be an easy task. Alex looked over at Steve MacDougal.

"What would be the main targets east of here?"

"Well in southern Pahang there is the main port of Kuantan, and all along the east coast there are several airfields. Kuantan is a large bustling town located half way down the east coast of Malaya and as such became a natural site for the Japanese to establish a strong strategic base."

Alex nodded thoughtfully at MacDougal's comment then asked, "And where do you think Chin Peng will be?"

"I would guess he's most probably south of here near Kuala Lumpur."

"What's brewing in that mind of yours?" O'Shea asked Alex suspiciously.

"It seems to me Charlie's task in persuading Woon to move his men would be easier if he had high value targets, like airfields, that were far away from Chin Peng. Then, if he conducted successful raids, he would not have to share the glory with his boss. Furthermore if I went with him he would have the benefit of the Japanese coding machine. Whereas if he went south and Chin Peng heard of this machine Woon would undoubtedly be pressured to hand it over."

"My, my, you not only have a brilliant mind but a devious one," said O'Shea in his lilting Irish voice. "I do believe the lad has solved your problem, Charlie."

And so it proved to be.

They waited until late April before Lander, Alex and O'Shea set off east with Woon and fifty of his men.

Chapter Thirty Nine

This would be the longest, and by far the most arduous, trek Alex had undertaken. For anyone who has never experienced such a trek it is impossible to completely comprehend the strength-sapping exhaustion it induces. Pahang is the largest state in Malaya and most of its topography can best be described as one unending, steeply mountainous, jungle. Because of the terrain they had to zigzag across the state looking for breaks in the mountain chain. The journey took three months, two weeks and four days. Five of those days didn't register in Alex's mind as he was in a fever-ridden state, suffering from malaria. Only the limited supply of quinine saved his life. Obviously the anti-malaria pills he had taken were ineffective on the strain of the disease he contracted.

Nine of the guerillas died on the journey from either disease or accidents. Many more of the party would have died had they not been cared for at various times by friendly groups. Two of those groups were indigenous tribes living in the jungle. One was the Sakai and the other the Senoi. These people had never seen what Alex would have called civilization. They spent their whole lives deep in the jungle. But their cures for jungle diseases, although unknown to western medicine, were highly effective and saved guerrilla lives. The third group was a band of guerrillas camped about twenty miles from the small town of Temerloh, located almost in the middle of Malaya. It was there Alex spent his five days of high fever. He was not the only one to suffer from malaria, over sixty percent of the men did.

Their days of chopping through the jungle were debilitating and soul destroying. Maps were inadequate and if it had not been for the knowledge of the indigenous tribes they would most probably never have reached their destination. On one part of the journey it took four days to cover only five miles, such was the denseness of jungle on a sixty degree mountainside and all this in mudslides caused by the torrential rain.

In addition to the extraordinarily difficult terrain, the disease, the insect bites and the wild animals, one other new danger was to prove terrifying. The first time Alex heard a *Sumatra* he thought he was about to die. This is the Malayan name given to a fantastically powerful gale which sweeps over the central mountain chain. It started as low rumble in the distance and grew in intensity until the noise was deafening, causing great pain in the eardrums. It knocked over trees, but one of the greatest dangers was the raining down of falling branches which had partially rotted through. Several of these big falling branches caused the deaths of two of the guerrillas.

Lander who had previously suffered from malaria had a relapse. He was treated by the Sakai and it only lasted three days. O'Shea seemed impervious to disease thanks he said to the lasting beneficial effects of Irish whisky.

"Your friend Steve MacDougal doesn't know what he's talking about when he extols the virtue of Scotch whisky. Only the good stuff from the Emerald Isle is the true nectar of the Gods," he explained gleefully to Alex shortly after his recovery from malaria.

Somehow they made it to the guerrilla camp in the north east of Pahang. Undoubtedly one of the most important factors which spurred them on was the news Alex received on the radio of the regular coding machine that in early June the Allies successfully landed in France. The liberation of Europe had begun. They hoped it would successfully conclude in several months. Then the Allies would be able to focus their total attention on the war in the Pacific. The only other good thing about this journey was the lack of Japanese patrols. The forbidding terrain kept them close to their camps and to main roads.

When they finally arrived at their destination they discovered the quite large guerrilla camp had only twenty eight men. This group had lost many men in futile raids on well protected Japanese posts. Despite the large size of the camp it was necessary to build additional huts to accommodate all Woon's men. All of the twenty eight Pahang guerrillas set about building new accommodation for the newcomers straight away. Those of Woon's group who could help did so and everyone was under roof in a remarkably short time. However it would take almost a month for many to fully recover from the trek.

The leader of this camp was a Malay, Abu Bakar. Only five of his men were Chinese, the rest were Malays. All of them had lived in the neighboring state of Terengganu which occupied almost half of the east coast of Malaya. Alex knew from information he had picked up the population of the north east coast of Malaya was predominately Malay and therefore Muslim. Abu Bakar was not a communist. He had been a headman in his village and had killed a Japanese soldier who had raped his daughter. This forced him to flee and he was followed by others in his village. The Chinese in his group had lived in the town of Dungun, a small fishing town about two thirds of the way down the Terengganu coast. Its size did not merit a large Japanese occupying contingent. However a soldier had discovered the five Chinese were hoarding food and they had hurriedly fled to join Abu Bakar.

Lander was fearful of a power struggle between the committed communist, urbane Woon, and the relatively uneducated Muslim, Abu Bakar. However Woon showed skillful diplomacy by making it clear Abu Bakar ran this camp. Nevertheless after only a month there was an uneasy atmosphere between the Malays and the now predominant Chinese who firmly believed their leader should be in charge. It was only Woon's iron control over his men that kept the pot of racial animosity from boiling over.

"We need a successful raid to help unify this lot," said Lander to the other two Europeans. "So let's get started." He looked at his youngest member. "Alex we need a plan."

Alex spent the next four days studying maps of the east coast area and talking to Abu Bakar whose knowledge of the area was invaluable. They marked all the Japanese posts and aerodromes on the map and discussed the enemy's strength at each location. One of Alex's main concerns was the lack of heavy armaments in the guerrilla camp. Woon's men had been unable to carry any on their arduous journey, and Abu Bakar had almost none. This left the guerrillas with rifles, hand grenades and one light machine gun.

Lander had given Alex excellent advice, based on Abu Bakar having lost many of his men in poorly planned raids.

"Make certain you identify the safest escape routes. That's a mistake most of the guerrillas make. They are pretty good at planning an attack but often get caught afterwards when enemy reinforcements arrive and the guerrillas find the way they came is blocked. It is important to look for several escape routes before launching an attack. And remember the east coast had quite a few airfields now occupied by the Japs. It would be wise to find out how many helicopters they have. Once a Jap post comes under attack they may call for air support and, as you know, helicopters can pursue our men even when they are in the jungle."

Alex thanked him and out of courtesy did not mention he had already considered all these factors.

Two days later a meeting was called. Attending were Abu Bakar with his second-in-command; Woon with two of his aides; Lander, O'Shea, and Alex. The meeting had been scheduled for eight o'clock but Alex requested a delay until nine-thirty as he was working with O'Shea on intercepting Japanese coded messages. When they did convene it was Alex who opened the meeting.

"Let's start with good news. I have just heard a broadcast from Ceylon, that Trinian in the Marianas has been completely captured. And as you know the attack on Guam began a few weeks ago and will hopefully be brought to a successful conclusion quite shortly. That can only mean the invasion of the Philippines must be soon."

This was greeted by a roar of joy from all there. Alex let this subside before continuing.

"As you know we delayed this meeting as Arthur and I were decoding interceptions of Japanese transmissions from Singapore to both Kuantan and Kota Bharu. Those two camps have been instructed to send some of their aircraft to Singapore for onward duty in the Philippines. No doubt as a reaction to the good news Ceylon supplied."

Once again there was rapturous applause.

"Do you know how many are to be transferred?" asked Lander.

"Four planes from Kota Bharu and seven from Kuantan."

"How about troops?" asked Abu Bakar.

"No troops were mentioned, only the pilots of the aircraft and some support staff."

Woon's brow was furrowed as he astutely posed the next question.

"You said that was the good news – is there bad news?"

"I'm afraid it is not very good. Let me show you on the maps."

He spread several of Abu Bakar's maps on the table. Everyone stood to get a good view.

"There are three air bases, all of them in coastal towns. They are Kota Bharu, Kuala Terengganu and the largest by far in Kuantan. And we are somewhere near here, on the border of Pahang and Terengganu. The precise spot is difficult to ascertain but I would not be surprised if in fact we are in Terengganu. There are no roads anywhere near this camp. As you can see an attack on Kota Bharu in the very north east of the country is out of the question. It is just too far. That leaves two possibilities. Kuantan is the further away base and the most heavily guarded."

"So we attack Kuala Terengganu?" asked an eager Woon. It was obvious to Lander, O'Shea and Alex, that he desperately wanted to enhance his image by another successful raid."

"There are three problems with that. First we don't have sufficient firepower. We will need something much heavier than just rifles and one machine gun. Second the best way to approach and leave Kuala Terengganu is by river. And leaving by river opens us to attack by fighter aircraft or helicopters from either Kuantan in the south or Kota Bharu in the north. It is possible to take a slight detour and travel part of the way by road however we still risk attack from the air. To avoid such an attack we must precisely time our mission which as all of you know is always problematic in any action. And lastly the third thing we need is intelligence on the Japanese strength in all three places plus their one other camp on the east coast located at the town of Dungun. It is foolhardy to make a plan without intelligence information."

There was a deflated silence in the hut. It was the intelligent O'Shea who next spoke.

"It didn't take you two days to come up with that analysis. Not even a few hours. So what is your plan?"

"First we should attack the weakest camp, which is Dungun. Five of Abu Bakar's men lived in Dungun. They told me the Japanese force there was about twenty men. They have three trucks with machine guns mounted in the rear and a jeep. These vehicles are used to travel to nearby villages in order to frighten the villagers thereby keeping them pacified. They also have a motor launch to patrol the shore."

"Do the Japs have any other heavy armaments?" asked O'Shea.

"We don't know for certain but we suspect not. Their heavy machine guns are all they require to maintain control," responded Abu Bakar.

"I estimate the three heavy machine guns along with their supply of hand grenades and rifles are all we need for a successful raid on Kuala Terengganu," continued Alex. "But I can't be certain until we get information from our reconnaissance missions. Abu Bakar has agreed to send two of his men to each of the four towns to gather as much intelligence as possible. He estimates it will take five to six weeks."

"That's a long time to wait, but I agree we must have up-to-date intel," said Lander with a touch of impatience in his voice.

"However in the meantime we can launch two raids. Abu Bakar has three shallow draft boats with small engines. They are hidden close to the end of a tributary of the River Terengganu. That location is only five miles from here. We can send a raiding party to steal another five such craft from Kuala Terengganu. We will need all those boats if we choose to attack the camp and airfield there. The other raid will have a similar mission to steal from Dungun. This time two or three boats will suffice.

"Why all the boats?" inquired Woon.

"Let me explain a possible attack on the Dungun camp first. For our attack to be a total success we must take out their radio first. That ensures there will be no support from any of the other three camps on the east coast. We will attack at twenty three hundred hours when the main camp will be asleep. Normally only two men patrol the small town at night. But I estimate there will be a radioman on duty. It should not be a difficult job to completely take out all of the troops. I leave the number of men we need up to you, Charlie; but the fewer the better in order to escape hastily and safely.

"In that case if we use our best guerillas, we would only need twelve men."

Lander looked in turn to Abu Bakar and Woon for agreement. Both men nodded their heads.

"Once the troops have been taken out we will load all the armaments in the motor launch and sail up the Dungun River to here."

He pointed to a spot on the map.

"As you can see a tributary of this river narrows significantly at this point and will be too shallow for the motor launch. The shallow draft boats we will have stolen from Dungun will be waiting and the armaments transferred from the launch which will then be hidden. The end of this tributary is less than three miles from our camp."

But will the small boats be able to navigate the narrowing tributary?" asked Woon.

"Most of Abu Bakar's men were fishermen and are expert at handling boats."

"And the trucks?" prompted Lander.

"They will be driven about fifty miles north west of Dungun to the village of Berang which is on the banks of the River Terengganu. Two of the boats from Kuala Terengganu will be there to bring the men to the end of the river which as I said is close to our camp. The ground transportation must be hidden in either the jungle nearby or with highly reliable sympathizers in Berang.

"So all this is in preparation for a possible attack on Kuala Terengganu. How about Kuantan which is a much larger and more significant base?" asked Lander.

"As far as we presently know, Kuantan is too heavily guarded for a successful attack."

Then Alex launched into a detailed plan for each of the other targets. When he finished there was a few seconds silence then applause broke out around the table. Once that subsided, Lander spoke.

"Brilliant, Alex, but I fear you are correct and Kuantan may just be too risky and difficult. But let's not prejudge the matter. We must wait, even though impatiently, for the intel to come back before deciding."

As the meeting broke up both Woon and Abu Bakar thanked Alex for his terrific analyses.

However the anticipation of possible successful actions that shone in their eyes was all the thanks that Alex required.

Chapter Forty

On September 6th another meeting was held. The acquisition of boats from both Kuala Terengganu and Dungun had been accomplished without stealing even one. The local populations had loaned the guerrillas boats, hoping to have them returned in good condition at the end of the war. However they had indicated even if their boats were damaged by action against the Japanese they didn't care. Such was the hatred of their oppressors. The reconnaissance teams had returned safely and their reports carefully studied. This, in addition to the information Alex had learned by constant monitoring of Japanese transmissions, allowed him to make concrete plans.

"Each of us has heard bits of information and rejoiced in good news. However I want Alex to give us a complete report and a recommendation of a plan of action," said Lander as he opened the meeting.

"The overall news from our reconnaissance is much better than we could have hoped. The Japanese have been withdrawing men from the east coast. The only potential bad aspect of this is I have not heard it mentioned in their transmissions. This could mean they either know or are guessing their code has been broken. The instruction to withdraw troops must have been done by messengers."

"Could there be another reason?" asked Woon.

"That's possible and could be supported by the fact they have not changed their code. There have been very few transmissions recently. It may simply signify they are closing down most of their operations on the east coast."

"Let's hope so," murmured O'Shea.

"Our reconnaissance missions revealed the following. Kota Bharu has had its troop strength reduced to twenty men and only two small aircraft. No bombers or fighters. Kuala Terengganu also has only twenty men with two aircraft, one of them a fighter, and one helicopter. Dungun is down to ten men. Kuantan, which at one time had two hundred men and twenty five aircraft is now down to eighty men and twelve aircraft - two bombers, seven fighters, one small aircraft and two helicopters. And while the commander normally used to send frequent patrols deep into the state of Pahang, and a few roaming north into Terengganu, now he restricts patrolling to only nearby small towns."

There was rapturous applause after the information on each town.

"Obviously the Allies are making very good progress in the Pacific to cause this redeployment. I would guess the invasion of the Philippines can only be a matter of weeks away. However all the various Pacific battles have taken a heavy toll in Allied lives. The Japanese have suffered much much more, often sacrificing their men in suicide attacks. Over one hundred thousand lives have been lost."

If Alex expected this news to have a somber affect of his audience, he was disappointed. There were cheers at these military successes despite the cost in lives. However Alex did not join in the jubilation. He felt badly about all those deaths. It was one more indication that he was not cut out to be a single minded soldier.

"So what do you suggest we do?"

The question came from Abu Bakar.

"Kuantan remains the biggest prize and in my estimation is now doable. But it would undoubtedly result in significant losses among the guerrillas. I would ignore Kota Bharu, it is now insignificant. And since Dungun is so undermanned, I suggest a two pronged attack on both it and Kuala Terengganu. That means we ignore the previous plan I had proposed on Dungun only. Now I propose it should be taken after dark, around eight o'clock. After which the attack force and the captured armaments should be driven straight to Kuala Terengganu in the three trucks the Japanese have. There they will join the waiting larger guerrilla group and together attack the camp and the airfield. After the Japanese installations have been destroyed the entire group should return to camp. Then we wait to see if Kuantan sends replacement troops."

"What's your guess, Arthur?" Lander asked O'Shea.

"If they did so it would greatly weaken the Kuantan garrison. And it would still leave a re-manned but weak, Dungun and Kuala Terengganu open to similar attacks at a later stage. The smart move by the commander of Kuantan would be not to send troops, but simply to forget about Dungun and Kuala Terengganu. Write them off. And, if he was sufficiently

impressed by our show of strength, he would further protect Kuantan by abandoning Kota Bharu and transferring everyone to Kuantan."

"What do you think, Alex?"

"Those are exactly my thoughts."

"Then what do we do afterwards?" asked Woon.

"I suggest Abu Bakar and his men return to their former lives. They should be safe. Woon, you have three possibilities. One is to disperse your men along the east coast. The second is to build a camp much closer to one of the towns on the coast where you can receive all the supplies you need. You can live there until the war is over. The third is to make your way back towards an area around Kuala Lumpur and join one or more of guerrilla groups there."

"Are you certain we would be safe back in our homes?" asked Abu Bakar.

"Well there is one more thing we could do to absolutely assure that."

"What's that?" Abu Bakar asked eagerly.

"If Arthur is correct and Kota Bharu is told to evacuate. The two small aircraft they have will be flown to Kuantan. Each plane will carry a pilot, copilot and a mechanic. That will leave sixteen troops to travel by road. Rather than our entire group returning to camp after the Kuala Terengganu raid we will leave behind a contingent to ambush the Kota Bharu convoy."

"Yes, that's a splendid idea," exclaimed Woon, anxious to have another feather in his cap.

"Of course we could take an easier path by letting the Kota Bharu troops retreat to Kuantan," said Lander.

"Yes that's certainly an option. But remember the intelligence report indicated the commander of Kuantan had significantly restricted the area of his patrols. If he had the additional troops from Kota Bharu he may feel sufficiently confident to once again extend this perimeter."

"Good point," admitted Lander. "Well does everyone agree with Alex's suggested two prong attack?"

There was a resounding yes vote.

"Okay then let's get down to detailed planning and training of the men."

A few days later Lander met with Woon.

"Have you decided what you will do after the raids?"

"I cannot just sit here on the east coast. I must return to the action."

This was a complete about face for a man willing to live a life of ease at the Jor camp near Cameron Highlands. Obviously a few successful actions had given him a taste for more. And probably he wished to be close to the political leadership to ensure they never forgot his successes. Lander smiled.

"I thought you might choose to do so. We will travel with you and join up with Captain Chesterton. Since we will have eliminated much of the Japanese threat in this area, we can use the trucks to travel a good part of the way. Obviously once we get closer to Kuala Lumpur we will have to ditch the trucks and travel on foot. But I estimate the total journey should take just over a week."

In another two days the detailed planning was complete and the briefing and training of the guerrillas began. Lander was aiding Woon in this training leaving O'Shea and Alex alone in their hut.

"Did you enjoy living in Kuala Lumpur before the war, Arthur?"

"It is a lovely place. Latterly I didn't get much time to enjoy it. For six months prior to the Japanese invasion, I spent most of the time travelling around the country. Partly in reviewing our preparedness for war and some of it was spent in searching out spies."

"I remember Tony Benson mentioned spies. He was extremely angry over anyone British spying for the Japanese."

"Yes, Tony and I worked as a team. We managed to catch nine traitors. But no matter how hard we tried we couldn't get close to the leader."

"A Japanese?"

"No, no we were certain he was British. And he held a pretty important regular job. He must have done so to be able to mix in the right circles and pick up high grade intelligence. Oh how I wanted to catch that bastard. But catching the leader of a high quality spy ring is like peeling an onion. One goes through layer after layer after layer. I never managed to peel enough layers. Tony and I found the outer two layers were locals. We caught some but not all of them. Then we had just started on the next layer when war broke out."

"Were any of them in the armed forces?" asked a fascinated Alex.

"We believed they included businessmen who, like the locals, were probably purely in it for the money. And we also believed there was a sprinkling of a few men in the armed forces. And while they too undoubtedly liked the money they would most probably have harbored anti-establishment resentments. Most likely they were men who had been passed over for promotion and were bitter. However greed was certainly a prime motivation for all of them. Believe me those foreigners would have been paid plenty of money. Given that, the top man must have made quite a fortune. When this war is over, I intend taking up the chase again. He has to be made to pay for his crimes."

"Do you think there are many more spies of the lower layer variety?"

"Oh yes, without a doubt. Many of the locals were thugs. They killed several policemen who were aiding us. I'm sure there are several still out there."

"How about foreigners?"

"Yes, I'm certain there are a few of them still alive. They too will be on my list when I am able to restart my quest. Enough about that, it only gives me dyspepsia. How about you, Alex? What will you do when this is over?"

The sudden change in subject should have alerted Alex. But he missed the clue.

"To tell you the truth I haven't given it much thought. I have been too busy trying to be useful. And sometimes trying to stay alive," he added with a grin.

"I have come to know you quite well and you are just too modest to say you have been up to your neck in important work. We couldn't have inflicted so much damage on the enemy without your particular brand of genius," said an admiring O'Shea.

Alex was about to disclaim this praise.

"No don't pooh, pooh me. It's absolutely true. Do you mind if I make a suggestion?"

"Of course not, Arthur."

Now he was about to hear the reason for the subject change.

"You came out here to help find a traitor and to re-establish effective communications between Simon's guerrilla groups. He told me you did that brilliantly. Since then you have been using that outsize brain of yours to plan highly effective attacks on the enemy. You have exceeded your mission by a hundred miles. I think it is time you went home. And so does Charlie Lander. The Japs are on the run all over the Pacific as you have told us. Soon they will be running here too."

"You two have discussed this?"

"Yes. We would like you to contact Ceylon and tell them it is our strong recommendation they send a submarine to get you out. When this upcoming mission is over we can send you, with a couple of guerrillas for protection, in a truck over the northern route back to Kedah where you first landed."

Alex was dumb-struck. Then a negative thought entered his brain.

"Please tell me the truth, Arthur. I know I'm not a regular soldier and am of little use in battle. Is it the case I would be too big a burden to take all the way to the outskirts of Kuala Lumpur to join the fighting there?"

"Good God no! Don't even think like that for a second! You have proved yourself invaluable. A burden? For such a brilliant man you have suddenly sounded silly for the first time. Believe me Alex, your mission has not only been fulfilled it has been hugely surpassed."

Alex sat in a stunned silence. 'Home?' He was still grappling with this thought when Lander came in.

"I can see you have talked to Alex, Arthur."

"I'm afraid I've flummoxed him."

"Well let me bring you back to earth, Alex. A few things have come up in the training that could be problems. I need you to solve them. We'll talk more on your future after this mission. Okay?"

"Certainly," replied a still reeling Alex.

Chapter Forty One

On September 15th both attack groups set out. The small Japanese camp at Dungun did indeed turn out to be an easy target, and was quickly wiped out. Kuala Terengganu was slightly more difficult because the main camp and the airfield were five miles apart. But the planning and training proved effective and both were destroyed after some resistance was overcome. However two guerillas were killed in the fighting. And precisely as O'Shea had foretold, Kota Bharu was ordered to evacuate everyone to Kuantan. That convoy was successfully ambushed.

Once back in the camp, Alex listened in to the communication between Kuantan and the new Japanese Headquarters in Taiping. Luckily they still had not changed their code and with O'Shea's assistance in translating, he was able to report that Kuantan had been instructed not to send any further patrols northwards to investigate the raids in case of further ambushes. Nor were they to send small spotter planes as the guerrillas obviously now had heavy machine guns and could bring down the low flying slow planes. The commander was further instructed to confine all troops to camp and prepare for a possible attack.

"Well that wraps up our operations," said Lander. "It's time to relocate. Have you considered the advice we gave you, Alex?"

"I hate to leave if I can still be useful," he replied.

"One thing I didn't mention," interjected O'Shea, "Chin Peng will receive a full report of our activities from a jubilant Woon. If you were to stay with us and move close to Kuala Lumpur, it will be extremely difficult to deny him the use of your coding machine and you to operate it. Even after invoking the name of Lord Mountbatten. The machine has simply been too essential to the success of all our operations. With the Japs gradually withdrawing troops to Pacific operations, and by using your capabilities, Chin Peng will believe he can be much bolder in his raids. Perhaps he will even be a bit reckless. I believe that is his nature. Risky missions to well entrenched Jap positions will not only endanger the guerillas but also we advisers who will be expected to go with them."

"Are you serious?"

"Yes, Alex, I'm deadly serious. I truly think it best if you leave for Ceylon and take your code machines with you."

Still Alex looked doubtful and that made Lander take charge.

"As you appear to be unwilling to take advice, Lieutenant Murdoch, I am ordering you to protect those extremely important code machines and personally return them to the headquarters of Lord Mountbatten in Ceylon."

The formal tone set by addressing him as Lieutenant Murdoch indicated Lander would brook no argument.

"Yes, Major," Alex responded dutifully.

Later that day when they were alone, O'Shea took the opportunity to speak to Lander.

"I appreciate the only way to get Alex to go home was to order him. But you were a bit rough on the young fellow, Charlie."

"Yes it probably came out that way. Believe me, Arthur, it hurt to say those things to Alex. He's such a splendid chap. But I felt if I left the door open even just a smidgen, he would have opted to stay. I had to be curt."

"Yes, I suppose you're right."

Three days later as Alex sat alone in the hut he received a coded message from Ceylon saying in ten days he should be at the same place where he had arrived. There he should await another message telling him exactly when a submarine would pick him up. He sighed deeply still unconvinced he ought to leave Malaya.

"Well I suppose that's that," he murmured sorrowfully. "I've arrived at another crossroad only this time I didn't choose which way to turn. I was ordered. I hope it is the correct decision."

Abu Bakar and his men had already left the camp and Woon's men were almost finished preparations for their journey when Alex left camp with his two guards. They were carefully chosen by Lander. One spoke quite a bit of English. The other was a particularly tough individual who spoke almost no English. Both could handle a truck and would share the driving. Most importantly they were both brave men and good shots.

They had to trek five miles through the jungle to the small boat which took them downriver to where the truck waited. Alex had studied maps and knew they would drive north in the state of Terengganu, until the tip of it, then the road turned west through the state of Kelantan. Here the road would become narrow and tortuous as they traversed the mountains before arriving in the state of Perak. There, he was told, they must cross a lake in a rickety ferry. No one was quite certain if the ferry could carry a truck.

"What happens if it cannot?" he had asked Lander when they were planning the journey.

"You're an officer. Use your initiative," was the disconcerting answer.

Then realizing he had once again been curt, this time because he had no clue how to answer the question, he continued in a gentler tone.

"Once you're over the lake it will only take about half a day until you reach the state of Kedah. Then it should be plain sailing. The entire journey should take about a week. With everything I have witnessed you do, I have no doubt you will make it safely, Alex."

But Alex's emotions were still conflicted as he set out. On the one hand he was excited about the thought of going home, and on the other he felt guilty about leaving Malaya while the war was still going on. He believed it his duty to continue contributing in any way he could.

However such thoughts were temporarily banished from his mind as he focused his attention totally on trekking through the jungle and later as he sat in the small boat that bobbed perilously on the fast flowing river. It was only when he settled in his seat in the truck that they returned.

"I hope this proves to be the correct turning at this crossroad," he mumbled.

"What you say, Tuan?" asked the guerrilla who spoke some English.

"Nothing," replied an embarrassed Alex.

The guerrilla shrugged then a moment later he spoke again.

"No Japanese until in Perak. Then must be careful," he explained.

"How about Siamese troops in Kelantan?" asked Alex, knowing it was one of the four former Malayan states given to Siam by the Japanese.

"No problem," he said showing Alex the money he had in his shirt pocket.

Also recognizing their route through north Perak came very close to the Siamese border, he asked another question.

"Will there be Siamese bandits operating in Perak?"

Bandit was an English word not recognized by the guerrilla, and he looked puzzled.

"Bad men who rob us," tried Alex.

That message got through. The guerrilla grinned, raised his rifle and gave the same answer.

"No problem."

That was not the reassuring answer he was looking for. He had hoped for something like, 'Bandits never cross the border into Perak' and the thought they may get embroiled in a gun fight left him decidedly uneasy. However he adopted the only practical mind set possible – that of 'let's wait and see' and settled back in his not terribly comfortable seat.

It had been decided they would drive only in daylight for security and safety reasons. Maybe driving in the dark for the first few nights would not cause problems, but thereafter, truck lights at night would certainly attract attention – unwelcome attention. That night they parked just outside a village and one of the men went in to buy food. Alex was not to show himself. It was bad enough a Chinese would go into an almost entirely Malay area but a westerner would certainly set tongues wagging and local police could be inquisitive and troublesome. The guerrilla returned with chicken cooked in curried rice.

"Only Malay food," said the Chinese disdainfully. But Alex thought it delicious.

The next afternoon they began climbing the mountains. The truck's engine labored up the slopes and the brakes screeched as they descended into valleys. This would have been bad enough on a straight road but on the constantly twisting one it was hair-raising. To add to Alex's discomfort was the realization that the drivers appeared even more afraid than he was. They seemed incapable of blinking as they stared at the road. One of them constantly licked his lips with a smacking sound. It sounded like a metronome on top of a learner's piano.

By some miracle they survived. There had been several times they came perilously close to the edge of the road and Alex found himself staring into an abyss. But on the sixth day they arrived at the lake. The ferry was constructed of planks of wood strapped together. It had no guard rails and just managed to take the truck. Chocks of wood were placed under the tires in the hope they would prevent the truck from rolling off.

The guerrillas and Alex took no chances. They carried whatever valuable possessions they could and stood at the side of the truck, ready to dive into the water if the ferry foundered. Blessedly it was a calm day with virtually no wind. The ferryman was a wizened old man. He wore shorts, a sleeveless undershirt, a floppy hat and strapless rubber sandals. He clamped his few teeth on the stem of a pipe and appeared unconcerned about the crossing. He chuckled at the obvious nervousness of his passengers and spoke Malay to the guerrillas. The one who spoke very little English had a strong build with a pock-marked somewhat ugly face. When the ferry man stopped speaking this guerrilla's face suddenly took on a decidedly pasty pallor.

"What did he say?" asked Alex of the other guerrilla.

"He s-s-say this ferry number f-four," stuttered the guerrilla. "Other three sank. He say he no worry he is old but he good swimmer."

Alex couldn't contain himself, he broke into loud laughter. Later when he pondered his reaction he wasn't sure if it had been a nervous reaction or just the unreal comedic situation. His laughter changed the old man's chuckles into fits of cackling coughing. But the guerrillas only stared at Alex in complete disbelief at his reaction. The ugly one spoke to his companion in Hokkien.

"This foreigner is as crazy as the old Malay."

His companion nodded his agreement. Alex now understood sufficient Hokkien to get the gist of this comment.

'You may be right,' he thought.

Nevertheless they made it to the other side. Once there the strongly built guerrilla took over as driver. He immediately pressed hard on the accelerator as if to get as far away from the ferry as possible. This worried Alex all over again as the driver's hands were shaking as he gripped the steering wheel. After a few miles he slowed to a reasonable speed, and Alex took the opportunity to consult the map of northern Perak.

"This road turns at right angles close to Grik," he said to the English speaking guerrilla. "We should be very careful. I don't know if the Japanese rebuilt the camp we previously destroyed there."

The guerrilla had heard of the exploits of Lee Sheng's group. He had recovered from the ferry trip and seemed unperturbed about approaching Grik. He gave his stock answer.

"No problem," he said and gave instructions to the driver in Hokkien.

When they drove past the turning to Kedah, Alex protested.

"You missed the turn."

"No, we stay night in Grik. Maybe we get good Chinese food there."

To Alex great relief the Japanese had left Grik. He never found out if the guerrilla knew this or just didn't care. It could have been his blinding desire for his native food overpowered his sense of reason.

On the ninth day of the journey they arrived at their destination. They had taken the coast road and the truck stopped a mile from his initial landing point. That night Alex contacted Ceylon and was given the time of his pickup on the following day. They stayed in the truck until late the following afternoon when one of the guerrillas helped Alex carry his baggage to the coast. There he hunkered down to wait.

An hour later he spied two sailors paddling a rubber dingy to collect him. As they returned to the submarine, Alex took a long last look at the country where he had experienced war. It was a complex country with three predominant races; each with its own set of customs, cultures and traditions. A country he would have liked to have known in peace-time. The Executive Officer was standing on deck and greeted him with a salute. He returned the salute; then in an instinctive action he turned and saluted goodbye to Malaya.

As he did so he thought he heard a voice in his head say, "Well done son. I'm proud of you."

Chapter Forty Two

"I'm honored to meet you Lieutenant Murdoch. May I shake your hand?"

Alex shook hands with the XO feeling uncomfortable with his effusive greeting.

"Let's get you below we shouldn't hang around here too long. And the captain is anxious to meet you."

The captain was waiting at the foot of the ladder as Alex descended. He briefly acknowledged Alex's salute before grasping his hand in both of his and pumping his arm vigorously, as he added his own words of praise.

"I'm sure you'll remember the captain who brought you out here. He's now Commander Carson and he asked me to convey his very best wishes and congratulations for a job exceedingly well done. Also he said to tell you he has no intention of busting your nose. I suppose that's a private joke since Adam Carson did not elaborate. Your exploits in Malaya have made the rounds in Ceylon and I can't tell you how proud we are of your achievements. I've asked the crew not to pester you for details. I reckon you must be pretty exhausted. Get as much rest as you can. Now XO, get us underway as smartly as you can."

The crew did not pester him but Alex lost count of the number of times a hand was thrust out as he passed accompanied by a "Well done, Sir." He spent a lot of time in his bunk. He had not realized just how tired he really was. Perhaps his exhaustion was augmented by being utterly emotionally drained.

The day after he arrived in Ceylon he was ushered into the office of Lord Mountbatten who requested full details of his stay and news of the current situation. That took several hours at the end of which he was decorated with two medals.

The next morning his head was still spinning from receiving all those honors and from the previous night's celebratory dinner accompanied by many toasts. Nevertheless at ten o'clock he reported for his scheduled medical examination. At the conclusion the doctor reviewed his findings.

"You still have traces of a few jungle diseases. Your malaria is apt to flare up now and again but there is something else in your blood that requires attention but I can't quite pinpoint it."

Those words alarmed Alex.

"Can't you diagnose what it is?"

"No, we don't have the latest diagnostic tools out here. I am giving you a note to take to the Armed Forces Hospital in London. They will be able to help you."

"Is it something I should be worried about?"

The doctor gave him a smile that was meant to reassure Alex.

"Just have it checked as soon as you can."

His words cancelled out the smile of assurance. But Alex only had time to mutter his thanks to the doctor before a member of Lord Mountbatten's staff whisked him away and told him he was to be immediately flown home by the fastest plane they had.

"With the war in Europe going well, it will be a significantly more direct route than the one you had to take on the way out. But I've just been informed you will have to go through yet another debriefing as soon as you land in London. This time by the SOE; I believe the officer's name is Smith."

That was a name he could never have forgotten.

The journey to England was indeed much faster than his trip on the way out to Ceylon. Yet it seemed to drag on longer as Alex was constantly haunted by the words of the doctor. Upon landing in London he was met by a major from the Intelligence Service.

"I would like to go straight to the Armed Forces Hospital," he insisted.

"Sorry Lieutenant, you are ordered to report to HQ immediately."

Alex could tell by the officer's tone there was no point in arguing.

"Can I at least shower and change?"

"My orders are to get you to HQ without delay."

When they arrived he was not shown into the previous small room with the faded gray painted walls. He was asked to wait in a corridor while the major went through an unmarked door. Then when the major came out, Alex was told to enter. This time it was a spacious office. Sitting behind an enormous desk was Mr. Smith. He rose and greeted Alex warmly.

"You surpassed all my expectations. Your country owes you a debt of gratitude. Thank you for coming straight here. I know you wished to go to hospital, but that is not necessary at the moment. However you will be taken there following your debriefing and Lieutenant Murdoch will unfortunately die there in two days."

The shock of this abrupt death sentence caused Alex's legs to buckle. Smith quickly held him under the arms and lowered him into a chair.

"I'm sorry. I've been told I have a terrible bedside manner," he said gruffly. "Let me start over. *You* are not going to die. One of my men in Ceylon instructed the doctor to give you that worrying warning. In fact you are in surprisingly good health. Apart from your attack of malaria you have come through your experience very well. But Lieutenant Murdoch did not. I must ask you to return the medals you received. They will be buried with a body purporting to be Lieutenant Murdoch."

"I have no idea what you are talking about," responded Alex heatedly.

For the moment he didn't care a whit who Mr. Smith was or what high rank he held. He had travelled almost two days thinking he was seriously ill thanks to some cockamamie plan devised by Smith. And he was mad as hell.

"Calm yourself. I will explain everything."

"Yes, I think you had better," replied Alex in a distinctly non-reverent tone.

Smith held up his hand in supplication.

"Would you care for coffee before I begin?"

"Yes, please," said Alex reverting to his normal courteous self.

Smith pressed a buzzer and in less than a minute a man entered with a tray of coffee and biscuits and swiftly exited.

"You most probably learned in Malaya there were a number of fifth columnists operating there prior to the war."

Alex nodded his head remembering his conversation with Arthur O'Shea.

"Well we also had spies operating here in Britain, both for the Germans and the Japanese. And we have reason to believe there are a few in Ceylon. I don't know how much you learned about the Oriental mind but in some countries in the East, particularly Japan, there are people who never forget and forgive after a war. You no doubt learned of the Kempeitai, the Japanese secret police. They act as though they are a law unto themselves."

"Oh yes, I know of them. They committed acts of utter brutality that were almost unimaginable."

"When the Allies have won this war with Japan, many of the senior Japanese Officers will be tried as war criminals. Those criminals will include the most important men in the Kempeitai. However through my network I have learned that some of the middle ranks of Kempeitai, who are among the most fanatical, are already planning revenge on a large scale whether Japan wins or loses the war. To this end they have contacted their foreign spies to draw up lists of our men who inflicted great losses on them during the war. Not battlefield losses, which are considered honorable, but clandestine losses which inflicted ignominy and loss of face to Japan. I have no doubt the name of Lieutenant Murdoch will be on that list. That's why he must die and have a public funeral. And in that way you, as Alexander John MacMillan, can resume leading a normal life."

Alex stared in amazement at what he had just heard.

"I have built a complete cover story for you. When you left Bletchley you came to work in the Intelligence Service here in London, as an analyst: which you supposedly did up until now. This thick folder is a complete history of that supposed work. You can study it during your next two days in hospital. Don't worry you will have a well guarded private room. Then after the funeral of Lieutenant Murdoch you can return to your own life. You will receive a discharge from duty on spurious medical grounds with a generous final payment and a reasonable pension."

Alex believed he had learned quite a bit about spying; however after listening to Smith he realized he was still a neophyte.

"After you are quietly spirited out of the hospital, go to this address and talk to Colonel Harris. He will tell you what your options are. Any questions?" he asked abruptly, reverting to his usual curt style.

Alex shook his head – still in a daze.

"Good. Now let's get down to all you have been up to since we last met."

When the briefing was over, Alex had once again been advised not to mention his service in Malaya to anyone.

"You neglected to threaten me with being shot," he said impudently.

Smith had to smile at this and he was happy to see that despite all of the danger Alex had experienced in Malaya, he had not lost his sense of humor.

"May I ask a question now?" added Alex.

"Certainly."

"Will it be acceptable if I get in touch with Dr. Josh Kind?"

The doleful look on Smith's face immediately told Alex it would not be possible.

"I'm sorry to have to tell you he was killed in a bombing attack while visiting relatives in London."

Chapter Forty Three

Several days later he left central London for home. It felt strange walking on a street in Croydon. It seemed as though nothing had changed as he walked towards his house. He didn't have to unlock the front door; his aunt was waiting for him. He had called her the previous day. She had thoroughly cleaned the house and stocked his larder with a few essentials. There were tearful greetings before she managed to gain control of her voice.

"I've prayed for this day. The day you would return safely, but you are so thin. Have you been ill?"

Then her hand flew to her mouth.

"You've not been badly injured, have you?"

"No, Aunt Jenny, no injuries; I've been a little ill, that's all."

He didn't wish to detail the tropical nature of his diseases, so he changed the subject.

"I can't thank you enough for taking care of the house."

"Oh it was nothing. I'm sorry there's not much food, Alexander, but most things are rationed and this is all I was allowed."

"That's okay, Aunt Jenny. Look, I was given a ration book as part of my demobilization package. I think they even gave me extra coupons. So you take these for your own use. And here's two hundred pounds to cover all you must have spent."

"Oh! -- I couldn't take all that, Alexander. You'll need your coupons and your *money*," she protested.

She did this politely but when he persisted Alex saw the look in her eyes at receiving such a treasure. Two hundred pounds was indeed a huge sum in those days. A sum his aunt could never have imagined she would ever see far less own. She continued to stare at all this money as though mesmerized. It was only then it struck Alex how much the ordinary people must have suffered during the war.

"No, I insist. It is such little compensation for taking care of the house during all this time. Thank you so much, Aunt Jenny."

He put his arms around her and hugged her. He did this mainly in thanks but also by holding on to her he could truly believe this was all real and not a dream. He had survived the war and was at last home.

"I didn't know if you would want me to stay for a few days, Alexander?"

"Thanks, but I believe I will take me some time to adjust and perhaps I should do so on my own."

He walked her to the bus stop and promised to visit her in a week or so. Then he walked slowly back to an empty house. There was no father to talk to or to play chess with – he was all alone.

The next few days were full of trauma. Like all returning soldiers from active service, he discovered there was no on/off switch in his brain. He couldn't just shrug off the recent past as though it hadn't happened and resume life in Croydon. He constantly thought of his experiences and particularly of the men he had served with. And he couldn't stop seeing the carnage he had witnessed. He was experiencing the aftershock of war. He tried to read the books he loved but his concentration was persistently interrupted by those thoughts.

'I had better get a job, otherwise I may go mad,' he thought on the fourth day. It was then he remembered the doctor in London mentioned by Colonel Harris - the colonel who had interviewed him and tried to persuade him to remain in the army. When that had failed the disappointed colonel had given him excellent advice.

"It takes time to readjust following the type of action you have seen. This can be made easier if you talk to a trained specialist. Here is the card of an excellent one, Doctor Fleming. I would highly recommend you visit him in a week or so. He has been briefed on your situation and will be expecting your call."

"Perhaps I had better visit him sooner rather than later," he mused out loud, and immediately telephoned for an appointment.

Two days later he took the train to London. He felt uncomfortable as his suit sagged in all the wrong places. His aunt had been right, he had lost weight. Upon arriving at the station he took a taxi straight to his appointment.

"Ah, Lieutenant MacMillan, or should I say Mr. MacMillan, I'm delighted to meet you," said Doctor Fleming.

At first Alex looked a bit confused. After all the time being Lieutenant Murdoch, it was proving difficult to readjust to his real name.

Doctor Fleming was a tall, thin, slightly stooped man of fifty two. His head seemed too big for his narrow shoulders. But his most notable feature was his clear blue eyes. They seemed to shine with such intensity that they were almost hypnotic. And they instantly noticed Alex's confusion.

"Don't be too concerned Mr. MacMillan, you will soon be totally comfortable with your real name. I have been given a complete record of your life with special reference to your military service. From the study of similar undercover cases, I know one must live one's cover name if one is to survive. It is not a simple matter to come back to reality."

He smiled reassuringly at Alex who noticed for the first time the doctor's buck-teeth.

"Now then, I am recommending three sessions this week and a fourth two weeks from now."

At Alex's startled look he rushed on to explain.

"I have had a lot of experience in these matters. Yours is a bit more severe as you lost your father at Dunkirk. Oh yes I know about that too. You may not have realized it; however, the SOE did a complete background check on you. That, and your war record, makes up this rather bulky dossier."

He patted the thick file on his desk.

"And since you were very close to your father and now have no one to confide in, I am recommending four sessions. Oh, and before I forget, Colonel Harris has arranged for you to stay at his club while you are in London and has left this envelop with some money to cover your expenses."

"That was most generous of him."

"The army is not usually so magnanimous," said Doctor Fleming with his toothy smile, "but having read your file I can see why they consider you a most deserving case. Now let's get started, shall we? Just before we do, I want you to take this small bottle of pills. They are only to be used sparingly when you find it difficult to sleep."

When Alex walked out into the sunshine on Harley Street an hour later, he had to admit he felt much better. The session had been more like a chat with an old friend – no, not and old friend – more like talking to his father. There had been no tension. Doctor Fleming explained how the brain attempted to reset itself back to a time pre-war, but constantly found itself going back to the more stressful situations experienced in war. The trick he explained was not to fight this, let the brain slowly adjust to the present. He was charged with the task of taking an interest in current events.

'Well, the most significant current event is, I must buy a few more clothes,' he thought.

He had packed a small bag in case he had to stay overnight, but if he was to be in London for almost a week he would need to purchase a few more things. He stepped into a doorway to check the contents of the envelop he had been given and was shocked at the large amount of money it contained. This along with the money he had been given in Mr. Smith's office made him feel a very rich man. Rather than dash off to the nearest gent's shop he decided, wisely, to sit down in a café, sip a cup of coffee and think out a cogent plan.

Luckily he had brought a small notepad and pen with him and by the time he had almost finished his second black coffee, (sorry Sir, we have no milk, the waiter explained) he had an organized list. He reviewed it one last time and drank the last mouthful of coffee.

"Ugh!" he muttered.

Having been so engrossed in preparing his list of intended purchases he hadn't paid attention to the coffee. All he noted was that it was hot and black. Now he recognized it was also watery and tasteless. Probably the grounds had been used for several cups before his. It was now late afternoon and he thought he would defer his shopping until tomorrow. He set out looking for the address of Colonel Harris's club. Half an hour later he arrived at a very grand looking building with a liveried doorman. He entered with some trepidation however the doorman and the receptionist were very courteous.

"Yes, Mr. MacMillan, a reservation was made for you by Colonel Harris. Would you kindly sign the register? And you only have to sign a chit for anything from the restaurant or the bar. All charges have been arranged," he said with a friendly smile.

That night Alex had one of the best meals he had ever eaten, supplemented by an excellent wine suggested by the sommelier. It was capped by an excellent cup of coffee and a glass of delicious port. It was only when he finally laid down his coffee cup a pang of guilt came over him as the awful truth struck him.

In times of deprivation there was an even greater yawning gulf in this world between those who have and those who have not.

Chapter Forty Four

Next day he met with Dr. Fleming at ten o'clock.

"How did you sleep last night, Alex?"

"Not too well. I had a simply delicious dinner and the wine made me sleepy but I wakened at two in the morning. My brain kept returning to Malaya and the horrors I witnessed. By three I had to get up and read. I thought it would be too late to take one of your sleeping pills in case I overslept and missed our appointment."

"Then may I suggest you have a light dinner tonight and no wine. Go to bed early and take a sleeping pill. We will meet tomorrow at the same time."

During the rest of the session Dr. Fleming made several suggestions to Alex as he continued to explain the most probable course Alex's recovery would take.

"Have you thought of getting a job?" he asked.

"Actually yes, I think it would give me something to focus on and take my mind of the war; well at least part of the time."

"That's an excellent idea," enthused the doctor with an especially wide toothy smile.

As they shook hands at the end of the session the doctor eyed Alex.

"One more suggestion," he said, "you may have thought of buying new clothes. It's rather obvious your old ones don't fit very well."

Alex nodded his head quite vigorously.

"I would strongly advise against that. You will undoubtedly regain some of the weight you have lost. Then you will find your new clothes don't fit. I'd give it a month or so."

Outside on the street Alex muttered to himself in a highly agitated manner.

"How can I have been such an idiot? Of course I'll gain weight. That's so obvious. Has thinking of survival and plans of attack during my war service robbed me of my ability to use common sense?"

He swiftly stopped muttering when he noticed people staring at him and crossing the street to avoid him. But he hadn't lost his sense of humor. He concluded his muttering.

"In addition to being dense, I'm now a raving lunatic."

He took the doctor's advice and was in bed by nine o'clock. The sleeping pill worked well and he didn't waken until seven o'clock, but it was not a gentle wakening. When he did, it was from a vivid dream and he did so with a violent start.

"My God," he yelled. "I really am a hopelessly demented man. How could I not recognize that crossroad? Thank you, mum and dad - thank you! – thank you! – thank you!"

He bathed, dressed and went down to the dining room and enjoyed a hearty breakfast. The waiter hovered nearby in a state of nervousness, finally plucking up the courage to speak to him.

"Is there something wrong, sir?"

"No, nothing at all," he replied in puzzlement.

It was only when he stood and caught sight of himself in a mirror that he saw he was grinning from ear to ear. He still had a broad smile on his face when he entered the doctor's office.

"I have decided not to seek employment," he announced in a triumphant and preemptory manner.

The doctor's smile of welcome instantly disappeared to be replaced with a worried frown. But before he could speak, Alex rushed on in an exuberant voice.

"That would be stupid. I shall return to university!"

The doctor's frown evaporated to be replaced with one of his signature buck-toothed smiles. And Alex had a strong felling that somewhere his mother and father were smiling too.

Doctor Fleming was delighted with this session with Alex. It was apparent that having made his decision, Alex was now relaxed and fully engaged in their discussions. At the end of the session he shook Alex's hand.

"We shall not require the fourth session. At least not for a while; however should you feel it necessary to talk to me again do not hesitate to call. I suggest you return to the office of Colonel Harris and tell him of your decision. I think you will find he may be of great assistance in re-enrolling you at Cambridge. He has good connections which you will require as the term started quite some time ago. I wish you the very best of good fortune."

When Alex left, the doctor called Colonel Harris to apprise him of his progress. He was shocked when he was given a succinct and very strict instruction.

"Are you certain, Colonel? This is highly irregular. What if Mr. MacMillan should wish to see me again? ---- Oh well, if you absolutely insist."

He put the phone down and for a moment stared out of the window. Then he rose and complied with his instruction. He burned every shred of the thick folder that was Alex's life. Now there was no trace of his double existence.

Colonel Harris had indeed managed to have Alex accepted to Cambridge. He even had his previous scholarship reinstated. Alex left London and headed straight to Berkshire. First he visited the graves of his parents. He talked to them for a long time then he went to see his Aunt Jenny. He told her of his decision and asked if she would once again check on his house while he was at Cambridge. She was only too pleased to do so and attempted to refuse the additional money he offered her. At last she relented and Alex headed for home to collect his effects. Next day he was in Cambridge.

Some of his professors were not happy to have a latecomer interrupt their schedule. However it didn't take long for them to change their minds. Alex not only quickly caught up but sped ahead in most of his classes.

Halfway through his final year he suffered a recurrence of malaria and was hospitalized. For two days he was delirious. During this period he constantly saw an image of an angel hovering over him. When he recovered all he could remember was her red hair, slightly freckled face and bright blue eyes. Later that day he pressed his bedside buzzer to request a drink of water. Nurse Hamilton arrived and he found himself staring into the smiling blue eyes of his angel.

"I'm pleased to see you're back among the living," she said in a delightful Scottish accent. "Now, what can I do for you?"

"I would like a large glass of water, please."

She soon returned with a large pitcher of water and a glass and put them on his bedside table.

"It's important you drink as much as you can. Your fever has left you dehydrated and although we gave you fluids intravenously your body needs more."

"Yes Ma'am," he said as he sat upright and saluted.

When she stopped laughing she said, "If you need anything further, just ring." Then she left the room.

"Wow!" was all he could say.

Although he was extremely busy with his studies, he did manage to aggressively pursue a promise he made to himself before being discharged from the hospital. He sought out and persuaded Joyce Hamilton to have dinner with him twice a week. His biggest difficulty in seeing her was to avoid talking about his activities in Malaya. He had told her everything else about his life. He covered that particular period by saying he worked for Army Intelligence in London.

"Oh I see, very hush hush stuff," was all she had said. She knew he did not contract malaria by staying in London but was astute enough not to pry further.

"Yes, I'm afraid it was classified work," he admitted and left it at that.

Two weeks before graduation he received a visitor at the university. The man was tall, slender but very fit looking. His dark hair was tinged with gray at the sides and his brown eyes seemed to bore into Alex's. But they were not unkind eyes just ones that missed nothing. He smiled as he extended his hand.

"My name is Anderson and I am a friend of Colonel Andrew Harris whom you know. Allow me to give you my card."

Alex read the card.

Montague Anderson
Deputy Commissioner
Scotland Yard

"May we sit and talk, Mr. MacMillan?"

"Only if I'm not under arrest," responded Alex with a grin.

Anderson's brown eyes twinkled.

"No, Mr. MacMillan, quite the contrary. I am here to ask *you* a favor."

That intrigued more than startled Alex. Anderson got straight to the point of his visit. He was obviously a man who did not have time to waste.

"Since the end of the war, the Commissioner charged me with revamping Scotland Yard. We have to move into a new era using the most modern techniques. That means we must have new thinking and new officers; ones with high intelligence and not just long years of experience.

Of course we will always need our experienced men but the future demands new skill sets they may not have. You see we need the balance of the two."

Alex nodded, impressed with the intensity of this man's belief.

"Andy Harris has told me about you and suggested you may be an exemplary model of the type of man I need for my challenge. I would be very appreciative if you would visit me at the Yard. I understand this is a busy time for you. However a visit with me after your graduation will allow time for a thorough interview, both from your perspective and from mine."

He paused to let his next statement have the impact he desired.

"In order for you to comprehend the importance I attach to this proposed meeting, let me tell you that in my present position I have never been directly involved in recruiting anyone. That is always done at two or three levels below me. I only say this so you will understand how great a future you could have at the Yard. That's always supposing I agree with the glowing report Andy Harris gave me."

Alex could tell from this last remark that Montague Anderson was a no-nonsense, straight-forward type of man. He liked that. He had been approached by the university to consider teaching as his future profession. However there was nothing to lose in considering another option.

"When would you like me to visit?"

"Three weeks on Monday at ten o'clock."

Alex's opinion of this man was reinforced by this statement. This man's time was valuable and he never wasted it. He didn't have to consult his diary. He had come fully prepared.

"Very well, I look forward to seeing you then."

Chapter Forty Five

Alex graduated with first class honors. Immediately following graduation he visited the graves of his parents.

"I wanted to show you my graduation robes. It's thanks to both of you I was able to accomplish this. I'm going to London to interview with Scotland Yard, but I'm torn between a life as an academic and a policeman. I wondered if you had any advice."

He listened intently but there was no responding voice from inside his head.

"Oh, I see, this is one crossroad where I must make up my own mind. Very well, I believe I can do that. If I should decide to be a policeman I probably won't be able to visit you often. So if you don't hear from me for a while you'll know I'm in London."

He continued to talk to his parents for almost an hour before readying to leave.

"Goodbye for now. I love you both very much."

To some people, talking to a patch of grass in a cemetery may seem a little foolish. Not to Alex. He always felt better after doing so. Later that day he found discussing his plans with his parents was easier than with Joyce Hamilton. He had avoided doing so until now. But next week was his interview and he had to tell her the choices facing him. They sat in a coffee shop and he reached across the table to hold her hand as he struggled to find the right words. One of the many joys in being with his blue eyed angel was the almost telepathic relationship that existed. And this time was no different.

"Tell me what's troubling you, Alex. Is it something serious?"

"Nothing life threatening, but yes, it's serious."

Then the words came tumbling out. When he finished she sat quietly

231

for a while digesting all he had told her. Then she raised her head and looked earnestly at him.

"If you accept the position at Scotland Yard, I won't see you very much. Not that London is very far, but I am guessing the job there will demand significantly more of your time than a teaching position. And I know you well enough, Alex, to recognize you will throw yourself whole-heartedly into anything you undertake."

"I know," he agreed with a sorrowful look.

She leaned across the table and kissed him gently.

"You must do what your heart tells you is the right thing," she counseled.

"Anyway they may not offer me a job. This is only an interview," he demurred.

She merely smiled at this remark.

"Of course they will offer you a job. They aren't stupid enough to let you slip through their fingers. At least I hope not. I don't want to lose faith in the people who are supposed to protect me."

Early Monday morning she accompanied Alex to the train station. As the station master blew his whistle she held him close to her and whispered, "Good luck," in his ear. She released him just in time for him to leap into the carriage. He leaned out of the window waving until she was out of sight.

A sad nurse turned away with tears in her bright blue eyes. Her heart was heavy with the foreboding she was about to lose a very special man. The last few months had been wonderful and although the word was not yet used, she knew beyond doubt she truly loved this man. One of the reasons was his exceptional character. He wanted to do the best he could with his life to help his fellow man. This was not a hollow gesture. It seemed to be deeply ingrained in him. And while teaching at Cambridge could be construed as meeting that goal, she recognized that most of the students came from wealthy backgrounds and didn't need an excellent education to ensure a prosperous future life. Whereas serving the community by maintaining public safety came closer to his life's ambitions. She knew in her heart that Scotland Yard would prove to be an irresistible challenge.

She daubed away the tears, straightened her back and walked rapidly towards the hospital and her vocation. One of the many things nursing had taught her was how to face tragedy along with joy, in life. There was always great joy in seeing a patient restored to full health. And in that way her aims in life were aligned with those of Alex. Perhaps it explained the virtually instantaneous symbiosis that developed between them. The initial relationship had turned into love, for her part, and she believed Alex felt the same.

As she walked along an idea came to her.

"So you're going to the big city, my bonnie lad. Well two can play at that game," she murmured, and quickened her pace.

Alex reported at the reception desk of Scotland Yard at five minutes to ten.

"I would like to see Deputy Commissioner Anderson," he said.

The young lady, who was new, was about to say that the Deputy Commissioner did not receive people walking in off the street. However the sergeant sitting nearby heard Alex and intervened.

"And what might be your name, Sir?"

"Alex MacMillan."

"And do you have some identification?"

Alex showed him his discharge document and the sergeant consulted the visitor's log for that day.

"That's excellent, Sir. The Deputy Commissioner is expecting you. I'll show you the way."

"Ah, Alex. Right on time. How about a coffee?" said Anderson as he rose to shake Alex's hand.

"Yes, please."

Anderson only had to glance at the sergeant.

"Right away, Sir."

"Do you know you are quite a famous fellow, Alex?"

"No, not at all, Sir," replied a puzzled Alex.

"Well you are. Somehow word got out of our meeting, and I received a call from General Richard Howe. I am guessing his information came from Colonel Harris in whom I had confided."

Alex still looked confused.

"General Howe is Deputy Director of MI 6 - a very important and influential man. Perhaps you would have known him better as Mr. Smith during the war - his not very imaginative pseudonym."

Alex's face cleared up and he nodded his head.

"General Howe sternly told me not to pry into your service while you were under his command. So you don't have to make up a fictitious story to account for that time in your life. He did tell me your work for our country was superlative. You and I know he is given to affect a somewhat gruff nature much of the time. I've know him for a long time and I have never heard him give such high praise of anyone. He also said if I failed to grab you for Scotland Yard, he would snatch you for MI 6."

Alex looked embarrassed. A look noticed by the sharp-eyed Anderson and one he tucked away in his mind as a strong point in Alex's favor. Anderson had no time for egotistical men.

They talked for almost an hour. Alex found Anderson to be penetrating in his questions and perceptive in receiving the answers. Yet he was easy to talk to. Perhaps this was because Alex liked people who were direct without ever being rude.

"Well, Alex, I enjoyed our time together. I certainly concur with the appraisals of General Howe and Colonel Harris. I would very much like you to join us. Although highly unusual I would offer you a starting position as a Detective Inspector in our CID, the Criminal Investigation Department. You would report to Detective Chief Inspector Lowell, and to allow you to tidy up your affairs, I propose you start two weeks from today. What do you say?"

"Thank you for your time today and for the offer. If I may I would like to think it over for a day. Could I call your office tomorrow afternoon with my answer?"

"Of course you can. It's quite sensible to carefully consider this quite dramatic change in vocation. You have my card, call me directly."

Anderson paused and looked intently at Alex who sensed there was an unasked question hanging in the air. Finally Anderson spoke again.

"You haven't asked about the salary."

"I am certain it will be sufficient for my needs."

Anderson felt a surging sense of satisfaction in that response. A man must have a livable wage but a man who only thought of money was not made of the material he wanted. And he really wanted this man.

"It should be. Anyway here is an official letter of offer. Obviously I hoped our meeting would go well and had this prepared. It contains the salary details and all other benefits. I look forward to your call. I regret I don't have the time to offer you lunch. If you would like I could have one of my men take you."

"No, that's all right. Thank you, I'll grab a sandwich and head back to Cambridge."

Yet again Alex was impressed by Anderson's direct approach and his sense of urgency. He had been handed a critical assignment to rebuild Scotland Yard and such a task demanded immediate decision making. Nothing could be more poisonous to the success of any mission as a wishy-washy time wasting leader. That was one of the many lessons he learned in Malaya.

Alex was back in Cambridge by mid-afternoon and met his nurse at the end of her shift. They hurried to one of their favorite little restaurants. Along the way she asked, "Well how did it go? Did you accept their offer?"

"Let's talk about it at the restaurant," he parried.

He had barely sat at the table before she again asked, "Tell me everything?"

He did and it was obvious he liked all he had heard.

"When do you start?" she asked.

"I'm not sure I'll accept it."

"What?" she demanded in astonishment. "You clearly want the job. What are you talking about?"

"I thought about it on the way back in the train and decided I would be happier being closer to you. Therefore I'll accept a teaching position at the university."

"Well if you want to be close to me you had better move to London."

Now it was his turn to be astonished.

"Whatever do you mean?"

"I knew you would be intrigued by Scotland Yard, so during my lunch break I composed a letter of application to Guy's Hospital. It is one of the most prestigious hospitals in London. Then I consulted the Sister. She was extremely kind and understanding. She even game me a letter of commendation to go along with my application. I have everything here ready to pop in the mail box. Just say the word."

"Do it," he said with conviction, intuitively recognizing this was the correct route to choose at this crossroad.

Chapter Forty Six

The first two weeks at Scotland Yard were uncomfortable ones for Alex. It was abundantly obvious all of his team were unhappy at being led by an inexperienced man. He had been given a large group to supervise necessitating two sergeants. Both sergeants were the most resentful of his position. They believed the job should have been theirs and not given to a man straight out of university. Everyone had the feeling his appointment was due to some personal relationship with one of the big bosses. It must have been, they reasoned, as nobody ever started at the rank of Detective Inspector.

But after a month they had all changed their minds. DI MacMillan had learned at lighting speed. His intelligent analysis of situations was dazzling. And he didn't make the mistake of attempting to gain his staff's favor by pandering to them. On the contrary, although he was fair he managed to convey he expected their very best efforts. His insightful questioning often had them scurrying back to reassess a situation or to get information they had not thought of. Within six months his team's record of success was the envy of all in the CID.

His boss, DCI Lowell, who had come up through the ranks and was within three years of retirement, had harbored similar initial feelings to those of Alex's men. He was a rotund man and his florid, veined face told of his drinking problem. Worse still, he was of the old school, the school Deputy Commissioner Anderson was determined to replace. As a copper on the street, Lowell had no qualms over the methods he used to get a confession. If the suspect did not immediately own up to a crime, he did not hesitate to beat one out of him. Lowell did not believe in leaving a conviction to the vagaries of the court system. Consequently a few innocent men went to jail following their 'admission of guilt'. However since no serious complaints had been lodged against him, his dastardly deeds were unrecorded. Those whom he had coerced were too afraid of the consequences of protest once released from jail.

Lowell had only been promoted to his present position due to the great exodus of younger, more talented, policemen who joined up to serve in the war. Many of whom did not return. Much as he detested 'university boys' he was too long in the tooth to question Alex's appointment. Someone up there had thought him capable and it wouldn't be prudent to challenge higher authority. But he kept a sharp eye on Alex. One bad slip and he would take delight in putting this young whippersnapper in his place. However as Alex's team solved case after case he was quick to take the credit. At one of his Chief Superintendent's review meetings he said, "I saw the talent in young MacMillan right off. That's why I gave him some of the toughest cases to work on. Of course I've had to guide him a lot."

Chief Superintendent Cook knew Lowell was lying and this was his attempt to have the bright light of Alex's successes cast part of its glow over himself. Cook had the advantage of knowing Alex's appointment was ordered by Deputy Commissioner Anderson. In addition he had guessed the recent moves made by Anderson were part of a plan to upgrade Scotland Yard. The Yard had lost several good young men to the war. That tended to leave middle aged men, with years of service but no great talent, in positions for which they were unsuited. Cook was smart enough to realize the bright young Macmillan would only require a few years, if that, before taking Lowell's place.

Initially it didn't concern him. But after seeing Alex's incredible progress, he was truly afraid it may only be a few years before Alex would be considered for a significantly higher position – like Chief Superintendent! Cook was well educated and had a university degree. After a few years in London he had seen the opportunity for more rapid promotion by applying for service in the colonies. After several postings he had finished the war in India and returned to England a year ago with both his present rank and considerable wealth. Cook went to great lengths to keep the latter aspect a secret as the amount of his fortune could not legally have been acquired on his police salary alone. It had not taken him long to discover bribery was a way of life in the colonies. He had used a combination of talent, obsequiousness and devious guile to gain his present rank and had no intention of seeing it go to one of Anderson's bright young things. While overseas, he had used his Machiavellian skill to undermine a few of his superiors, making them look very bad and subsequently taking over their jobs. Unlike Lowell he had many more years before retirement. He would

have to think very carefully about this potential challenge, knowing all
too well that someone of Anderson's acumen could not be hoodwinked as
easily as the dinosaurs he had encountered in the colonies.

As often happens in life, an unforeseen and unexpected event can
change one's plans. So it was with Cook. He had believed he had several
years to devise a plan to ensure Alex would never threaten his position.
This was not to be.

One afternoon Alex happened to tell a colleague he was taking his
girlfriend to dinner at a highly rated restaurant in the countryside. Just as
he was doing so Cook's secretary passed by.

"I couldn't help overhearing you. Actually my boss is away today but
he telephoned and asked me to deliver a file to his home. It happens to be
quite near the restaurant you are going to. If you like I can give you a lift."

Alex gratefully agreed. He called to ask Joyce to take a taxi and meet
him at the restaurant and at the end of the meal they could take a taxi
home. That way they could enjoy a cocktail before dinner and a bottle of
wine with dinner.

When they arrived at Cook's house, Alex was impressed by its
stunning architecture and its setting. It stood gracefully on a large piece
of land. However when Mrs. Cook invited them inside Alex was not only
impressed, he was awestruck. The house was full of treasures from Asia
which she proudly described.

'These antiques must have cost a King's fortune,' he thought.

When Cook returned home late that evening and heard of Alex's
visit, his face darkened in anger. He knew Alex was bright enough to have
recognized the value of his prized possessions. He would have to speed up
his thought process to be rid of him. It was not only the far off threat to his
position that alarmed him, but should MacMillan tell anyone at the Yard
of his wealth, it would undoubtedly raise serious questions of how he came
by it. However, after several months without such a disaster materializing
Cook was breathing much easier. But once again fate stepped in and
presented an opportunity to possibly resolve his problem.

Alex had never met Cook and was blissfully unaware of the concern
he had caused him. Otherwise he might have looked much more closely
when after only fifteen months in London he was met with yet another
crossroad. It was cunningly set up by Cook. He had a meeting with Lowell
and succeeded in making him believe it was his own idea.

"Sit down MacMillan," commanded Lowell when Alex had obeyed
the summons to his office. "You are a most fortunate man. I am going to

present you with the opportunity of a lifetime. Do a good job and you may even get a quick promotion. You know I will retire soon."

He paused to let this sink in; and was disappointed at Alex not jumping up and down with joy. Alex knew Lowell all too well and did not trust him for a second. Nevertheless, although he remained cautious, he was intrigued.

"You probably know two months ago, I sent DI Connors to Malaya at the request of the Home Office. One of the senior officers at the Kuala Lumpur High Commission had been murdered, and they wanted someone from the Yard to investigate. Well unfortunately Connors was involved in a car accident last week and has died of his injuries. I am offering you the chance to take his place. With the work that Connors compiled it should not take you longer than a month to wrap things up over there."

No one at Scotland Yard knew of Alex's wartime service in Malaya. Therefore Lowell could never have guessed the effect his words would have on Alex. He sat in his chair nonplussed. Every nerve end in his body jangled. Whether it was with dreadful fear or joyous anticipation was unclear to Alex at that moment. He only knew the thought of going back to Malaya was causing him to struggle mightily to stop from shaking all over.

Lowell was perplexed at Alex's reaction and stared at him in confusion.

"Well say something you lucky bugger," he finally exclaimed loudly.

"May I have some time to think this over?" asked Alex.

"No you bloody well can't. This is Scotland Yard, not the Salvation Army. You do what you are told. I'll give you a week to finish up any loose ends with your present assignments. You can take this file of Connors' reports and study them. Report to the administrative office. They will fit you out with all the necessary travel documents and airline tickets."

With that Lowell slammed the file on his desk and then watched as Alex left his office.

"Bloody ungrateful bugger," he muttered. Then a smile crossed his face. "With any luck he might just have an accident too."

The very thought Cook had wished for when he manipulated Lowell into selecting Alex.

Alex told Joyce Hamilton that night. They were very much in love but wisely had decided to save as much money as they could before marrying. Also Alex wanted to be certain that police work was indeed the career he wanted. She took the news without crying although her heart was aching at the thought of not seeing him for a month or more. Alex sensed her upset.

"I have been thinking," he said. "As I may get the promotion Lowell spoke of, let's not wait any longer than we have to. Let's get married when I return. And I promise to propose properly - on bended knee and offering you a ring!"

She flung herself into his arms and now tears flowed.

Chapter Forty Seven

The next several days were hectic. Alex's sense of duty made him determined not to leave anything less than complete and detailed notes on all his cases. Lowell had not yet appointed a temporary successor. This was a terrible mistake as far as Alex was concerned. It would have been much easier to spend the remaining week with someone at his side to ensure a smooth transition. Lowell had given a weak explanation when Alex raised this point.

"It shouldn't take you long to complete this assignment; therefore there is no need to appoint anyone else. You will soon be back to resume your duties."

Alex thought this ludicrous. Someone had to be in charge of his team. Decisions had to be made and he was convinced Lowell had neither the time nor the skill to handle Alex's job in addition to his own. He had been tempted to go over Lowell's head to make his point of view known, but one of his sergeants, who had become an excellent advisor to him on the inner workings of Scotland Yard, had strongly counseled against this.

"To your intelligent brain it will seem utter stupidity not to have someone in charge. But, believe me, Sir; the Yard takes a very dim view of someone going over his boss's head. There are still enough old timers in senior positions who strictly adhere to this doctrine. It can only land you in trouble. And even if someone very high up agrees with you, he will find himself in the embarrassing position of defending you against many of his subordinates. And you don't want to precipitate such a confrontation, do you?"

Alex had no intention of embarrassing Anderson who was the only very senior person he knew. So he dropped his idea and instead was spending fourteen hour days in the preparation of his meticulous notes. He would give a copy to Lowell and as insurance give copies to both of his sergeants. And he would tell Lowell he had done this. He wanted this insurance as he didn't trust Lowell. His statement that Alex would soon return to his present position was at odds with his prior inference that a good job by Alex could lead to a promotion. He had a sneaky feeling that Lowell wanted things to go wrong while he was away. He may even attempt to ensure this by giving his team bad directions. Then he could say that Alex was really a poor manager and that he, Lowell, had been carrying him and in reality deserved the recognition for most of the excellent results. He hadn't just reached this thought on his own. His sergeant had hinted as much. And he had known Lowell for many, many, years.

What none of them knew was this thought had been planted in the not too smart brain of Lowell, by Cook.

The more Alex thought of his upcoming assignment the more he felt something was very wrong. Why was *he* being sent to Malaya? Even though he had achieved good results he was still a very junior officer. And surely someone above Lowell had to have approved this assignment. That someone must have raised questions over Alex's capability to adequately conduct a successful investigation in Malaya. As far as anyone at the Yard knew, Malaya was a far off land with widely different customs and cultures and a multiracial society, all of which were surely alien to Alex. No, there was definitely something that did not add up relating to this assignment.

As his mother used to say, 'If the fish smells bad, don't eat it', and this fish was giving off a distinctly foul odor.

'Still,' he thought, 'I do have an advantage in knowing something about Malaya and if I do pull it off it will be a feather in my cap'. With that he resolved to stop thinking negatively and look upon this as an opportunity.

Five days later Alex was again working very late and was finishing up a report on one of his cases. It was past midnight and he was the only one still working. He was standing in the outer office, bending over a filing cabinet as he searched for the file he required. Suddenly his sixth sense warned him he was not alone. He whirled around in time to hear a voice come from the rear of the darkened office.

"I hear good reports about you, Detective Inspector MacMillan. I'm glad you are proving as competent as you did as Lieutenant Murdoch."

The man came out of the shadows and Alex was astonished as he recognized Mr. Smith walk forward with an outstretched hand.

"I suppose I should formally introduce myself. My real name is Richard

Howe In reality I was Colonel Howe when you knew me as Mr. Smith. Now I work at MI 6."

"Yes, I know, you are Deputy Director; and you are now a General."

Howe showed no sign of amazement at Alex's knowledge. He had long since ceased to be surprised at Alex's talent. He merely smiled and nodded his head.

"I assume Deputy Commissioner Anderson told you that. I have stayed in close contact with him and have followed your career with great interest. He recently told me that DCI Lowell has ordered you to Malaya and I wanted a private chat before you go. Oh, don't worry; Montague Anderson is fully aware of our meeting, but not its purpose. No one at the Yard, including Montague, knows anything of your past activities in that country. I came to warn you to be most careful while out there. As your work will be in Kuala Lumpur, I am hoping you will not meet anyone you knew from the past. And you must studiously avoid looking up your wartime acquaintances. There is one exception to that."

Alex looked straight into Howe's eyes.

"And who might that be?" he asked softly.

"I am certain you will remember Arthur O'Shea."

Alex nodded his head vigorously.

"Indeed I do."

"Well he has returned to his previous position as Secretary for Economic Affairs in the Kuala Lumpur High Commission. In reality, he is a member of MI 6 and works for me. Recently he has been busy tracking down traitors who were in the employ of the Japanese before the war. His assistant, also part of MI 6 was working with him and he was the man murdered. I requested the assistance of the Yard to find out who did it. Presumably you were told the man previously sent to Malaya to investigate this case, Detective Inspector Connors, was killed in a car accident while out there. If I were you I wouldn't assume that it really was an accident until I personally checked. I don't think O'Shea believes it was an accident and neither do I. So be very watchful, MacMillan."

"I will, Sir," said a thoughtful Alex.

This warning seemed to confirm his own suspicions about his assignment. But he said nothing of that to his visitor.

"I have fully briefed O'Shea of your coming," continued Howe. "He was initially stunned. He had read of the death of Lieutenant Murdoch and apparently had mourned his passing for quite some time. Once I explained the situation he became unreasonably irate in my opinion. I had no idea you two were so close. Anyway he cursed me for not taking him into his confidence. And he did so in a manner which would have gotten him instantly sacked in other circumstances. However I decided to overlook his insolence in this case."

He said this with a chuckle which was probably the closest this rigid man could come to admitting he had been thoughtless in not telling O'Shea.

"Needless to say he is delighted you are going out to Kuala Lumpur. But I have instructed him not to inform anyone, not even the High Commissioner, of your past. When you conclude your assignment and return to London come and see me. I want to hear first hand what you uncovered."

"Yes, Sir," was all a dumfounded Alex could reply.

"Remember your training, MacMillan, trust no one and never, never, turn your back on anyone. I don't need to remind you that you almost forgot this warning and had your side slit open. I have come to the conclusion there is something decidedly evil about this affair. O'Shea is convinced the head of the spy ring before the war was in a position of great authority either out there or even back here. And he also believes this man is still very much alive and has a competent and deadly group at his command. You will find it much more difficult to survive an assault by such a man than it was to evade the attacks of the Japanese. Skilled traitors are extremely difficult to uncover and should it become apparent you are getting close, he will have no compunction in immediately ordering your death. Two excellent men have lost their lives in an attempt to unmask this villain. Therefore be on constant alert. However, I have high hopes your intelligence combined with the training both in Malaya and here at the Yard will help you succeed. So I will only finish by saying good luck. Call me at this number immediately upon your return."

Howe tossed a card on the desk next to Alex.

"Thank you, Sir,"

He bent to pick up the card then turned to say goodbye. But he couldn't - Howe had disappeared into the darkness.

Old spy habits are hard to break.

Chapter Forty Eight

It was early evening when Alex arrived at Kuala Lumpur airport. Initially he was mildly disappointed that O'Shea did not meet him. Instead he was greeted by a middle aged Malay in a bright white uniform wearing a songkok on his head and holding up a sign with his name on it.

"I have been sent by the High Commissioner to take you to your hotel, Sir, and to give you this letter."

"Thank you."

"My name is Abdul Ali. Welcome to Malaya."

On the drive to the hotel, Alex read the letter. It was a rather stiffly worded one of welcome; and it indicated a car would pick him up at nine the following morning to take him to the High Commission.

'Not a terribly warm welcome,' he thought.

Then his policeman's brain was supplanted by his wartime one. He understood O'Shea was not ignoring him, he was protecting him. The man who authorized the murder of the two men must surely know of O'Shea's pursuit of all in the spy ring. O'Shea was convinced the leader had held a senior position before the war. That's why he was so useful to the Japanese. And holding such a position would have made him aware of O'Shea being Head of Intelligence and not merely involved in economic affairs. Therefore O'Shea may well be under regular observation and that's why he had not wished to be seen with Alex at such a busy place as the airport. With his mind now at ease, he leaned back in his seat and enjoyed the rest of the ride.

He checked in at the hotel and no sooner had the bellboy left after depositing his suitcase on the bed than there was a knock on the door.

"It's so good to see you again, Alex," said a beaming O'Shea giving Alex a long welcoming hug.

"And good to see you, Arthur. How are you?"

245

"I'm well, and I feel even better now you are here. That bugger Howe could have told me the death of Lieutenant Murdoch was a staged affair. I was furious at him. I believe I vented my anger a bit too virulently. I'm surprised I still have a job."

"He spoke to me before I left and I got the impression he realized he had made an error in judgment."

"Well I quickly forgave him. I can't imagine how grueling his job was during the war. The stress must have been horrendous. And I have no doubt he's carrying just as heavy a load in his present position. Actually although I lost my head for a minute and cursed him vehemently, I really do admire the man."

"As do I. He is quite concerned about the dangers of your current undertaking. It looks like you're facing some pretty tough opposition. I'm sorry about the death of your man and DI Connors."

"Yes, but let's see if that extraordinary brain of yours can help find this bastard. Oh by the way, it's safe to talk here in your room. I had it swept for listening bugs just before you checked in."

He held out his hand to show Alex the device he had used.

"You had better keep this and check your room every day. And don't say anything of importance on the telephone. Better safe than sorry. Did you happen to bring a code book with you?"

Alex grinned and nodded his head.

"I worked this one up before leaving London just in case I have to leave you written messages. You can have this copy."

"Excellent. I won't stay long, you'll need rest after your long journey and I must get going. I did want to tell you one thing. Before he went home after the war, Simon Chesterton kept his promise. He dug up our dear friend, Tony Benson, and gave him a proper funeral with full military honors."

"I knew he would if at all possible. I would very much like to visit Tony's grave."

"We can arrange that at a suitable time. You are meeting the High Commissioner tomorrow at nine-thirty. He will introduce you to me and the rest of his staff. I'll do my best to remember we are supposed to be meeting for the first time: also to remember not to refer to you as Lieutenant Murdoch. I must get used to the name MacMillan. I think it will be safer to always call you Alex. After you have been introduced we can review all the files I have. Goodnight my friend and sleep well."

"One thing before you go, Arthur. Have you kept in touch with Steve MacDougal?"

O'Shea gave him a quizzical look.

"I am pretty sure my boss in London strictly told you to avoid all contact with anyone who knew of your past service in Malaya."

"He did. But it's my life that's at risk in this mission, not his. And I think I'll have to use my initiative to complete it successfully and safely. I just need a contact number for Steve. I don't want to get you into hot water with Howe by asking you to call Steve."

"Why do you want to contact him?"

"I'm guessing you are probably being closely watched by members of the old spy ring. Their boss must have believed both of our men were getting too close for comfort and authorized their killing. However unless those spies are total idiots they must also be thinking there is one other way the ringleader can protect his identity."

"And that is?"

"To permanently sever all connections that could lead to him."

"In other words to kill them too."

"Yes. It seems reasonable to assume that the leader would only allow communications with one man. That man would then pass on his instructions to a few others and so on. It would be a pyramid system. But just to be certain of absolute security he would have to eliminate some layers in case there have been leaks in his system. Can you have the local police give you details of all recent murders?"

"Of course. And if we find local thugs among them it will give us a place to start."

"Precisely. I am assuming you would be aware of the murder of any foreigner."

"We haven't heard of any except our two men."

"Perhaps you could also check on resident foreigners appearing to leave the country for good."

"I see, just in case they disappeared before reaching their supposed destination."

"Exactly. So between the investigations into the murders of our men and the anxiety over the spymaster's possible intentions towards them, the members of the ring may be a little nervous. That's to our advantage. Nervous men make mistakes. But I need someone to watch my back; someone who knows Malaya and is not known to the bad guys. I can think of no one better than Steve."

O'Shea stared at Alex for some time then let out a long sigh.

"I've talked to Steve a few times but not recently. His plantation is about seventy miles from KL. I'll give you his telephone number tomorrow. God save me if Howe ever finds out."

"But it's peacetime, therefore he can't have you shot," said Alex with a grin.

"I wouldn't be too sure of that. At the very least he can fire me."

"If it's too much of an imposition then forget I asked you. It may take a little time but I'm sure I can find out Steve's location on my own. My only reason in mentioning Steve to you is I will not hide anything from you on this job and I wanted you to know I need Steve."

O'Shea's worried look disappeared and he smiled.

"I appreciate that. But don't worry; I'll still give you Steve's number tomorrow. Actually you're wise to want someone to work with you. Contact between us will mainly take place inside a safe room in the High Commission. And you're absolutely right; the danger to you will be on the streets where we can't be seen together. You see, you've started using that brain of yours to great advantage. You've already thought out a plan of action. But I had better call Steve before you do. I'll tell him I have just learned about the fictitious death of Lieutenant Murdoch and you are alive and well. I won't tell him you are here. I'll let you surprise him. Once again, I'll say goodnight, Alex."

"Goodnight, Arthur," replied Alex as they shook hands.

Alex sat in a comfortable chair and began adding to the notes he had compiled on the plane. He now had a clear idea of how to proceed. He would check this with Arthur tomorrow to be certain he hadn't overlooked anything. Then he would contact Steve and get started. He had no doubt Steve would help him, he was that type of man. He would always come to the aid of a good friend.

Comforted by this thought, he had a shower then tumbled into bed.

Chapter Forty Nine

Alex woke up with a start. He was bathed in sweat from his nightmare. In this horrible dream he had been shouting, 'It's my fault, I should have seen this coming. I missed something, I missed something!'

He looked over at his alarm clock which he had set for seven o'clock. It was only five-thirty. Nevertheless he decided to get up and once again had a shower. Then he called room service for coffee and a light breakfast. While he waited he again reviewed his notes.

'Have I really missed something?' he worried. But nothing leapt out at him. Nevertheless he was shaken by the vividness of his nightmare. And like many dreams which culminated in an explosive fashion he could not remember how it started. But it had sown seeds of doubt in his mind. It took a considerable time for Alex to regain his composure and confidence. Happily, by the time he arrived at the High Commission those doubts were completely banished.

After the necessary introductions and verbal pleasantries, he was taken by O'Shea to his safe room. It had been recently remodeled and was now completely sound proof, windowless and air-conditioned. It also housed the latest in safe communication capability: this giving rise to the stenciled name on the door – 'Telecommunication Room'. It had three desks, a carpeted floor, and on one wall there was an enormous blackboard. There was also an easel with a large pad of paper and a variety of thick felt writing implements. On one of the desks was a large pile of files, several notepads and a collection of pens and pencils.

"Am I correct in assuming you have reviewed the files sent to Scotland Yard?" asked O'Shea.

"Yes."

"They were only edited versions of my files. Therefore I suggest you begin by looking at my files relating to the two murdered men and their activities. Then study the pre-war files compiled by Tony Benson and me on the spies we managed to round up at that time. High Commissioner Graham is hosting a group of prominent businessmen from Britain this morning and unfortunately I must be in attendance. It will conclude with lunch so I won't be able to rejoin you until early afternoon. But I have arranged for lunch to be served to you here. There is a plentiful supply of coffee and if you press this buzzer a young man named Walter Halliburton will appear. He is my new assistant and is familiar with all these files but knows nothing of you past service in Malaya. And last but not least here is the telephone number I promised you. The white telephone over there is completely secure. Well, all of that should keep you out of mischief until I return."

The last sentence was said using a broad Irish accent and with a twinkle in O'Shea's eyes. Then he returned to a more serious tone of voice.

"I am truly grateful that you came, Alex. I have a feeling you will be of invaluable assistance in tracking down the bastard who has caused so much damage."

The door hissed to a complete close behind him followed by a distinct clunk of the secure lock.

'First things first,' thought Alex as he picked up the receiver of the white telephone and dialed the number he had been given by O'Shea.

"Hello," said the distinctive voice.

Alex felt a warm glow fill his entire being at its sound.

"Is that the MacDougal who was banished from my bonnie Scotland for sheep stealin'," he said in his best, though somewhat inadequate, imitation of a Scottish voice.

"Aye, it might just be one an' the same. Although whoever ye are, ye're no Scotsman. No whae such an atrocious accent. Ye should be ashamed o' yerself for attemptin' to mimic ma hame one. Who the hell are ye'?"

MacDougal was laying on his Scottish accent much thicker than Alex had ever heard before.

"Hello, Steve, you've no idea how your voice is music to my ears."

There was a moment of absolute silence before Alex heard a loud gasp.

"Is that you, Alex?" was the breathless response.

"Yes, my friend. How are you?"

"I'm just fine. Last night Arthur called to tell me of you're faked death. It was a nightmare when I heard you were dead. But after hearing from Arthur I haven't been able to sleep. I was so excited and I kept thinking of our time together during the war. But tell me, how are you? And where are you? And how did you get my private line number?" tumbled out the questions.

"I'm very well, thank you. And I am in Kuala Lumpur. And I desperately need you help."

"Are you in imminent danger? Just tell me where you are and I'll leave immediately."

"I just arrived yesterday and am not yet in danger although I could be in a couple of days. I think it best if you take care of the arrangements you will undoubtedly have to make to cover your absence from your plantation and, if possible, travel here the day after tomorrow. We should meet at the British High Commission. But do not ask for me or Arthur O'Shea. Just say you wish to renew your passport. Someone will be on the lookout for you. And Steve, it's vital that no one knows you are meeting me and more importantly no one sees you with me or Arthur."

MacDougal was sufficiently sentient not to ask questions.

"I understand. Say no more. I'll arrive in the morning at ten o'clock. See you then, Alex."

The line went dead. Alex hung up the receiver and stared at it for quite some time with a smile on his face. The dreadful feeling he had experienced this morning was completely gone, overtaken by one of immense relief and great hope. He removed his jacket and sat at the desk piled high with files.

He worked assiduously, making copious notes as he went. He only stopped occasionally to refill his coffee cup. He was so engrossed that it startled him when he heard the hiss of the door opening. A young man stood in the doorway with a tray of food.

"Excuse the interruption, Sir, I brought your lunch. My name is Halliburton. Arthur O'Shea instructed me to bring you lunch at twelve-thirty."

"Oh yes," said Alex recovering and looking at his watch. He found it difficult to believe so much time had elapsed. "Thank you very much. It's Walter isn't it?"

"Yes, Sir. Is there anything further I can do for you?"

"No, no, thank you. I appreciate the lunch."

"Just press the buzzer when you have finished and I'll remove the tray. I think I should bring another container of coffee."

"That would be most welcome, Walter."

The door hissed close and the lock clunked into position.

Alex bent over his task once more while attempting to eat his lunch. It was then he recalled the advice of Josh Kind, his mentor at Bletchley Park.

"You can eat your lunch or work but not both. Should you be foolish enough to attempt this, three things will happen. First, you will be so absorbed by work that you will miss your mouth and impale your cheek on your fork. Second, you will experience the most painful bout of indigestion. Third, you will be so frustrated at you efforts; you will completely lose the ability to concentrate on your work, and lose you train of thought. So eat your lunch!"

He put down his pencil and for the first time took note of his lunch. It was a steaming bowl of char kway teow. He had had this Chinese dish before. It consisted of stir fried rice noodles, with bean sprouts, prawns, eggs, chives and slices of preserved Chinese sausages. All spiced with slices of red chilies. He had been given chopsticks and the thoughtful Halliburton had also supplied a fork in case Alex was unfamiliar with chopsticks. In addition to a large glass of water, a pot of jasmine tea was also served to wash down the local food. He recalled this was excellent not only for its taste but also to offset the oiliness of the food. For desert Halliburton had reverted to a British treat of a large slice of spiced gingerbread. It was one of the most delicious meals Alex had enjoyed for a long time. He sat still for several minutes, allowing his taste buds to relish this delightful lunch. Then being eager to recommence his work he pressed the buzzer.

Almost immediately Halliburton appeared with a fresh pot of coffee.

"How was your lunch, Sir? I thought you might enjoy trying one of our native dishes."

"It was delicious but a little spicy," he replied. Then remembering Halliburton did not know of his prior war time experience, he asked, "What was it exactly?"

Halliburton rattled off the name and the ingredients.

"I'm pleased you enjoyed it. Now I'll leave you to continue your work. But if you should need anything do not hesitate to call me."

Alex finished the last of the files then again studied the notes he had made. Next he drew a large organization chart on the blackboard. In the bottom two rows of boxes he put in the names of the locals who had been caught. He left several boxes empty as he was sure the locals had not all been found out. In the next two rows of boxes he had no names, but where he could, he put in questions based on the known relationships between some of the locals. The fifth row had four boxes, all without names. He surmised there could not be more than that number of senior men. Those four had a connecting line to one box and that one in turn had a direct line to the final box – the top man. Then, he drew connecting lines between boxes where there was a relationship. Some of the known locals had belonged to a same gang or association. And some had worked for the same company.

Then he stood back, scrutinized his handiwork and put his brain to work. After considerable thought he drew up a list of questions he wanted Arthur to have checked; either through his connections or by using the police. He was still poring over the files once more when O'Shea entered and looked at the blackboard.

"I see you *have* been busy."

Almost as though he had not heard him, Alex blurted out, "I would like answers to these questions if that's possible."

This came out more tersely that he had intended. But O'Shea showed no sign of umbrage.

He read the long list and whistled. "It hasn't taken you long to analyze everything. I'll do my best to get as many answers as possible. Did you contact Steve?"

"Yes, he'll be here the day after tomorrow at ten. I thought it best we have our first meeting here."

O'Shea nodded his agreement.

"Oh by the way, you were very astute to use a fork for your lunch and not the chopsticks. This combined with the fact that you pushed most of the red chilies to the side of the bowl has totally convinced Halliburton you have not experienced Asian food before. You're always thinking, Alex, aren't you?"

Alex shrugged his shoulders.

"Well let me get a cup of your coffee then I'll start making a few calls to get answers to some of the questions on this rather daunting list."

While he was doing this, Alex kept going over and over all he had done. Looking for anything he may have missed.

It was then thoughts of waking up from his nightmare came flooding back and a quiver of fear ran down his spine.

Chapter Fifty

Two days later Alex was deep in thought in O'Shea's safe room. The information O'Shea had gathered so far had allowed him to make a few more connections between the boxes on the blackboard. O'Shea had left him to his deductions while he took care of a few matters. When he re-entered the room he immediately saw the semblance of a smile on Alex's face.

"What have you discovered?" he asked eagerly.

"This organization was cleverly constructed on a tripod cell system."

"What the hell is that?"

Alex walked over to the blackboard.

The information you got has confirmed this theory. I was able to identify more relationships which I have now color coded. Where two or more boxes shared a relationship I colored them red, yellow or green."

"But several of the boxes are not colored," protested O'Shea.

"That's right; I need more information to see where they fit. But let me explain the organizational set up. Obviously the box at the top is the mastermind. He is connected to only one box, his trusted second-in-command. Originally I guessed he would control no more than four subordinates but now I see it is only three. By doing so, the three have no idea of the identity of the mastermind. These three cell leaders probably do not know each other. That forms a completely compartmentalized structure. And each of these three cell leaders controls three men – most probably foreigners I would guess. And each of these three foreigners controls three locals who most probably have responsible positions where they have access to sensitive information. Also it is these locals who hire the thugs to do any dirty work required."

"I see, so now you can track the people Tony Benson and I caught to one of those three cells."

"Correct. And with a bit of luck I should be able to begin identifying some of the upper levels of this organization. I can definitely say that one of the cells was military. Perhaps another was too, but as yet I'm not sure. However the third appears to be completely civilian. This structure was very well thought out and may have been suggested by the head of Japanese Intelligence."

"That won't lead us anywhere. He was executed as a war criminal so we can't interrogate him," said O'Shea wistfully. "What do you propose doing next?"

"Obviously the only way to get the mastermind is by identifying his second-in-command and the only way to reach him is through one of the cell leaders. I propose going after the civilian cell on the basis those who were in the military have probably been demobilized or transferred. We may be lucky and discover some military names, if so perhaps they can still be made to talk."

"One thing troubles me, Alex. This organization you talk of is pretty large. After catching some of the lowest levels, we had thought there may only be another handful of spies."

"I believe this idea was created a long time before war broke out. And it was painstakingly put in place piece by piece over one or two years."

"How did you reach that conclusion?"

"Well the Japanese would naturally start by recruiting the top man. And either he was completely disillusioned by the British colonial system, or badly treated in his work, or he was compromised and blackmailed. I agree with your supposition that he held a senior post somewhere out here. I feel pretty sure he was put in a compromising position and was blackmailed."

"You mean he was set up with a woman?"

"Or he may even have been in a homosexual relationship. Either way I feel sure he was a married man and would not wish his wife to find out. Even more important to such a man would be the ruination of his position of power in the social strata. You see it is not only the Japanese who dread losing face. That's why one of the questions I gave you was to find out if a photographer had been murdered in three years prior to the war. And you found two cases. One of them was in late 1938 and one in 1939. Based on that I guess the top man was the first to be blackmailed and he then arranged the incriminating photography of his selected second-in-command in 1939. Both photographers then had to be murdered to maintain absolute security."

"Excellent work, Alex," exuded an admiring O'Shea. Then he glanced at his watch. "I asked Halliburton to be on the lookout for Steve and to bring him straight here, but not to come into the room himself. He ought to be here any minute."

And right on cue the door hissed open and in strode the tall well-built MacDougal. He went immediately to Alex and ignoring his outstretched hand enveloped him in a tight bear hug. Alex returned the hug then a little later tapped MacDougal on the shoulder, indicating the hug was over.

"Don't kill me yet, Steve, I've still got work to do," he gasped.

"Sorry laddie, it's such a pleasure to see you again."

"It's wonderful to see you," he wheezed in return.

Then turning to O'Shea, MacDougal held out his hand in a greeting. "And how are you? You Irish reprobate."

"Very well. And the top o' the mornin' to you, you Scottish scallywag."

They grasped hands and grinned at each other.

"How about a cup of coffee, Steve?" O'Shea asked.

"That would be great. Then perhaps you'll tell me your new name, Alex, and what this is all about."

Alex took his time and gave a fully detailed explanation to MacDougal. He covered the time since they last met up to his current assignment.

"As usual you've been busy, laddie. Now what would you like me to do?"

"Be an adviser and a bodyguard," replied Alex succinctly. "My presence will not yet be known to the bad guys; however, as soon as I start poking my nose into the past of some of these spies, my chances of meeting the same fate as the other two murdered men will escalate. And you will have contacts inside some of the larger British trading houses that could be very valuable."

"I see. And presumably Arthur can't go around asking too many questions as the bad guys, as you call them, know of his real position out here."

"Precisely," said O'Shea. "But I can still provide insights that could be of use."

"There is no doubt about that," responded Alex quickly, sensing O'Shea was beginning to feel left out. "You already have by using your contacts to provide answers to the many questions I raised. And your work allowed me to construct this," said Alex pointing to the blackboard.

MacDougal stared at the diagram and immediately realized its implications.

"There are three cells and the names in some of boxes in the lower two levels are those whom you have already caught, Arthur. Aren't they?"

"That's correct. Unfortunately the chart is anachronistic as they were all discovered before the war. There could still be other men we didn't catch or new recruits to fill the spots of the ones we did get."

"And I suppose the next level up must be mostly Europeans?" mused MacDougal."

"You catch on fast, Steve," agreed Alex.

"How do you propose penetrating that level?"

"The cell to the far right must be all civilian. Therefore I intend questioning people at the two companies which employed the locals in the second lowest level. Hopefully I will rattle enough cages to cause significant concern to one of the Europeans in the third level. Could you arrange those meetings, Arthur?"

"No problem. But remember the local spies we caught were immediately put in prison and then shot. Their families and places of employment were never informed. To them they simply disappeared off the face of the earth."

MacDougal's face showed his concern at Alex's plan.

"In other words you are going to dangle yourself as bait. That's really dangerous, laddie," he said. "Could I not do some cage rattling for you?"

"No Steve. I need your involvement to be kept secret for as long as possible. That's the only way I can feel safe. So long as no one knows you are acting as my guardian, you may be able to spot someone tailing me. And as soon as we catch someone new we should be able to move up the chain of command."

"I see; but nevertheless I intend staying close to you at all times. History has shown these people don't hesitate to permanently terminate anyone who poses a threat."

Those words turned out to be prophetic quicker than any of the three anticipated.

A few days later it was early evening when Alex left the High Commission, shadowed by Steve. He collected his room key at the front desk of the hotel, waited for the elevator then took it to the third floor. As he approached his room he was juggling his briefcase, the evening newspaper and his key. In doing so he dropped his key and rapidly bent down to retrieve it. He heard two thuds as bullets fired from a silenced pistol imbedded themselves in his door. Before he could fling himself on the floor the explosion of a revolver deafened his ears. He turned to see MacDougal at the end of the corridor with a smoking gun in his hand.

Halfway between them was the body of a Chinese with a gaping, bleeding hole in his head. He was clutching the silenced pistol in his right hand. MacDougal had raced up the stairs and taken up his position behind a partially open corridor door, before Alex exited the elevator. He ran to Alex and quickly gave him instructions.

"Get in your room and call the police, then call Arthur, and then inform the front desk. I have to disappear. I'll come to your room later tonight. Remember, when the police question you, you didn't see who shot the Chinese."

With that, he was gone, leaving a badly shaken Alex to do his bidding.

Chapter Fifty One

At ten o'clock Alex answered the knock on his door to admit MacDougal. O'Shea was in the room with Alex.

"Are you okay?" Steve asked anxiously.

When he received a nod from Alex he said, "I brought you some medicine," and produced a bottle of scotch.

"Couldn't you have had the decency to bring some Irish whisky?" demanded O'Shea indignantly. Then with a smile he added, "I suppose that'll have to do. I'll get some glasses."

"What did the police have to say?" asked MacDougal.

They recognized the assailant as a member of a gang of thugs. And they found it hard to believe I hadn't seen my savior. I kept repeating I was face down on the corridor and saw no one. Finally they left me about nine."

"Yes, I know. I was keeping an eye on them. They finally finished with the hotel manager and left about half-an-hour ago."

When he had pored generous amounts of whisky into the three glasses, MacDougal, continued talking.

"What have you and Arthur come up with?"

"Our unhappy conclusion is that one of the traitors still works in the police department," said Alex. "Some of the questions I raised earlier with Arthur were answered by the police. They were the only ones who could have known we were back on the trail. But how they connected me with the search is a mystery. I'm glad you were my guardian angel, Steve. Thanks. Did you suspect trouble tonight?"

"I wasn't sure. But when you took the elevator there were only three other persons who got on with you. One was an elderly lady, one a young European man and the Chinese. He had attempted to dress in a manner that suggested he was an affluent businessman. But it was his suit that gave him away. It was exceedingly ill fitting. It looked at least two sizes too big for him. That was a sign he must have borrowed it from someone. And that rang an alarm bell. However I must admit I didn't believe he would be bold enough to attempt murder in a first class hotel. I though he was only tailing you."

"Lucky for me you were prepared for the worst," said Alex.

"Do you remember I gave you a similar warning regarding always being prepared for trouble when you were first in the jungle? Well we must treat this city as a jungle and constantly be on guard if we are to survive."

When his guests had left, Alex took a shower before bed. MacDougal's words were still rolling around in his head.

'I seem to be back in the jungle,' he thought. 'This time it's a concrete jungle.'

But he couldn't sleep. He switched on the light and began again to study his notes and the files. Finally something he read clicked into place and the satisfaction of his discovery permitted him to fall asleep.

Next morning the three of them met in O'Shea's safe room.

"You said you wanted to visit two British trading houses. Which one do you want to start with?" O'Shea asked Alex.

"Something has been troubling me. I even had a nightmare over it. Last night I restudied DI Connors' notes and something came to me. He visited several foreign firms; however there was only one he called on twice - Thompson Trading Company. I don't believe this was the cause of my nightmare but it has to be significant so I'll start there."

"I'll call and set up an appointment for tomorrow," said O'Shea.

"And I'll be right behind you," chimed in MacDougal.

Noticing a concerned look on Alex's face, he quickly added, "Don't worry I won't blow your cover. I've used Thompson on several occasions to export rubber from my estate. Therefore it will appear natural for me to drop by when I'm in KL on other business."

The meeting was set for ten o'clock. Meantime Alex returned to studying his notes. Steve caught Arthur's eye and motioned him to join him in a corner of the room.

"Listen Arthur, I'm afraid Alex could stir up a hornets' nest when he visits Thompson. I know you don't want to be seen with Alex in public but I need you to be around during his visit. Either wittingly or otherwise he may uncover one of the spies. That could trigger an immediate reaction; should that happen it will require both of us to protect him. With all the fancy dress parties the foreign community has, you must know of a shop that deals in such items. Go there and get yourself a disguise. A wig, moustache and fake thick glasses should do the trick. And get a panama hat to cover your face. Wait for Alex to leave the Thompson building and follow him. I may have to stay behind at Thompson to see if Alex's visit causes a reaction. Keep your car nearby in case he hails a taxi to get back to the High Commission. Can you manage that?"

"No problem and I know just the shop to get a disguise."

Next day, Alex arrived promptly at ten o'clock. He didn't notice the man with the thick glasses, moustache and Panama hat standing in a nearby doorway. Nor did he see MacDougal alight from a taxi just behind his. Steve nodded an acknowledgement to Arthur and followed Alex into the building. Alex was shown into the Personnel Manager's office on the second floor. He showed his credentials and explained he was interested in the disappearance of two employees prior to the war. Both were Chinese and he gave their names.

"I'll have my secretary search our files. I wasn't here at that time. I only joined the company six months ago."

It didn't take long before the secretary retuned with the files of both men and Alex studied them then asked if he could talk to their supervisors.

"Well one of them worked in the general trading section. However James Green who is in charge there also only joined the company recently. Therefore I doubt he can be of much use. But the other man worked in the car import section and Lesley Marsh, who runs that area, was here before the war."

"Oh, was he a prisoner of war?"

"No, luckily he managed to get out of Malaya in the nick of time. Several of our senior officers were not so lucky and they were interned at Pudu prison. From what I have been told it was very unpleasant. Lesley returned to Kuala Lumpur shortly after the war and has done an excellent job in rebuilding our business. Would you like to talk to him?"

"Yes please."

"I know he is in today. I'll call him then take you to his office. It's on the first floor."

The first floor was a large area packed with desks. Malayans of various ethnic groups occupied those desks. Around the outside were a number of glass enclosed offices, one of which was occupied by the head of car imports.

Marsh turned out to be a stout, middle aged, man. His brown hair was thin and turning gray at the sides. His expensive suit, made of light weight material, was freshly pressed with a red handkerchief flowing out of its breast pocket in a show of pretentiousness. Along with his ostentatiously large gold watch and his diamond cufflinks, he appeared for all the world like a highly successful car salesman. And as if to prove his self esteem, he waved a long cigarette holder in the direction of Alex.

"Do have a seat and tell me how I can assist you," he purred with a wide smile.

"Thank you for seeing me."

"Not at all, dear chap."

"I am making enquiries about a Lim Eu Tok who used to work in your section. He disappeared before the war."

"Lim? Lim? Ah yes, I think I remember him. As I recall he just seemed to vanish. One must remember, things were very confused at that time. I seem to recollect we reported his disappearance to the police but they came up with nothing."

He waved his cigarette holder as he spoke. His face had turned solemn as though reflecting the sad incident.

"Did you know him well?" asked Alex.

"Not really. I can check his file but I believe he had only been with us a few years."

"Actually he worked here for ten years and you promoted him twice. He was your assistant at the time of his disappearance," responded Alex in an intimidating voice.

The façade put up by Marsh cracked momentarily and he hastily attempted to repair it by smiling again. It didn't quite work. Alex was too keen an observer not to notice.

"You seem very well informed," said Marsh in a low tone.

"I just read his file in the personnel office."

"Then I'm sure you are correct. You must forgive me It was quite some time ago and I had no knowledge of Lim's personal life. I'm sorry I can't be of any more assistance. Now if that's all, I must get back to work."

The cigarette holder waved in the air as though to dismiss the subject.

"Just one more thing if I may. As a matter of interest, how did you manage to get out of Malaya just as the war started?"

This time the waving of the cigarette holder was so violent, the cigarette fell out.

"My mother was seriously ill and I had to go back home," he said testily. "I really can't see what that has to do with Lim."

"Sorry, I was just curious," said Alex in an apologetic tone.

His false contrition seemed to be accepted by Marsh. He rose and extended his hand. That was a grave mistake. As Alex shook it he could feel Marsh's sweaty palm.

Alex was deep in thought as he left and failed to notice MacDougal talking to an Indian at a desk on the far side of the office. He had positioned himself to be able to observe Marsh's office. Within a minute of Alex leaving, Marsh came bustling out of his office, walking as rapidly as his pudgy legs would carry him, towards the stairs. Steve politely but quickly brought his conversation to a close and followed Marsh up to the third floor. There was a glass door marked Executive Offices. Marsh rushed through this door and then directly through a door marked 'John Gross, Assistant Managing Director.'

As he followed through the glass door, a receptionist asked Steve if she could help him. He had to put on his best act.

"Sorry, I'm a bit lost. I'm looking for the rubber export section."

"That's on the first floor, Sir."

"Thank you," he said with a feigned bewildered shake of his head and left as quickly as he could.

Once outside he couldn't see either Alex or Arthur. He took a taxi back to the High Commission.

"Well, Alex you certainly rattled a few cages," he muttered to himself.

"What you say?" asked the taxi driver.

"Oh, nothing, nothing."

Steve sat back with a contented smile on his face. Things were beginning to move.

Chapter Fifty Two

Back at Thompson, John Gross was livid.

"You blithering idiot. Why did you have to say you hardly knew your own assistant? Didn't you stop to think that sounded suspicious? Then, to crown it all, you came charging in here! He may have seen you!"

"No, no, I swear he didn't. He had already left the building. I made sure of that," wailed Marsh, as he wiped the sweat from his brow.

"Get back to you office and for God's sake try to act normally."

Marsh attempted to walk out calmly but the receptionist noticed he continued to mop his face.

Gross sat contemplating his dilemma. He stared at the three telephones on his desk. One was for inter-office communication. One for outside calls and the third was very, very seldom used. He selected the third and dialed a number.

Sometime later at the High Commission there was elation.

"I can almost be certain Marsh is a member of the spy ring," said Alex.

"And if that's the case we must consider Gross to be involved," added MacDougal.

"This could be a most significant breakthrough," breathed O'Shea. "I know John Gross. He is a respected member of the Selangor Club. In fact he is on the board, and he and his wife mix in the highest social circles. Furthermore, he is a regular golf partner of the Deputy High Commissioner."

"That could qualify him as a candidate since he must know many influential people," MacDougal opined.

"Perhaps," O'Shea said with a trace of doubt in his voice.

"What's troubling you?" asked Alex.

"Well, he served on a key businessmen's council before the war and was very vocal about his strong anti-Japanese feelings. And perhaps because of this he was speedily sought out and captured when the Japanese arrived. He did not spend the war in Pudu prison here in KL, instead was sent to the more infamous camp at Changi in Singapore. Prisoners there were treated terribly and many didn't survive. I heard he was kept in isolation for great periods of time and pretty badly beaten."

"Okay, then I'll only put Marsh's name on the chart and leave off Gross for the present. However I must say Marsh didn't strike me as being too clever by attempting to deny he knew Lim well. And there was no doubt he was really rattled when I probed how he got out of Malaya. Therefore to me, Arthur, it is suspicious the first person he ran to was Gross. If his spy boss *was* someone else why didn't he go to his office or if he worked somewhere else, why didn't he telephone him?"

"I can't answer that. Let's agree it casts John Gross in a bad light and keep an eye on him. Anyway I must attend another of High Commissioner Graham's luncheons. If I get the opportunity, I'll carefully ask him about Gross. Don't forget you have an appointment at Cowan and Company at two this afternoon."

While eating lunch Alex and MacDougal went over the blackboard chart once again. They ignored the lowest level of the chart as they were only hired thugs. And on the next level the only remaining known connection between the names in the boxes was two of them had played rugby for the same team. One of the two had worked at Cowan and was called Kwok Hee Mun. Alex had to hope he could find a connection there.

Cowan and Company was a smaller trading company than Thompson and had no personnel manager. Alex was shown straight into the Managing Director's office.

"Hello, I'm George Hill. Arthur O'Shea asked me to meet you. Please come in. I hope I can be of some assistance to you."

Hill would turn out to be a gregarious person who welcomed the opportunity to chat to people. He was in his late fifties and walked with a bad limp. His face was deeply lined but his blue eyes smiled in welcome. Making the assumption the Managing Director was a busy man, Alex got right to the point.

"Good afternoon, Mr. Hill. Thank you for sparing the time. I'm looking into the disappearance of Kwok Hee Mun just before the war."

At the mention of the war Hill's face clouded and its lines deepened even further. He paused for a moment and hung his head.

"Sorry, but those Jap bastards caused me to lose my leg. Now I hobble around on this wooden one. You see my company owned several tin mines and the Japs believed we had hidden a lot of our tin. They didn't believe me when I told them it wasn't true. And when they finally found our tin, they beat me so badly my leg had to be amputated."

"I'm so sorry," said a distressed Alex.

"No, no, it's over now. But it's an interesting coincidence you asking about Kwok. He was the most senior Chinese we had. He came from Ipoh, the center of the tin mining in Malaya, and was the manager in charge of all our mining. And as you said he just disappeared and the police could find no trace of him. We never found out what became of him."

"To whom did Kwok report?"

"To Johnny Beecham. That was rather a delicate situation. You see Johnny is the son of one of our main board directors back in London. He was sent out here in the middle of 1940 to learn the business. Before he came, Kwok reported to me, but I was instructed to make Johnny my deputy. Poor Kwok didn't take it too well. As it turned out Johnny was not cut out for management and was recalled to London in August of '41. Lucky for him - he missed the Jap occupation. After that Kwok reverted back to reporting to me. But he was not the same. He had a definite chip on his shoulder over his treatment. You see loss of face is a very serious matter out here."

Intuitively Alex knew there was no way Hill could have been Kwok's boss in the spy ring. He prepared to take his leave.

"I'll take up no more of your valuable time, Mr. Hill. Thank you."

"Oh, that's okay. I have plenty of time," said Hill, displaying his gregarious and perhaps lonely nature. He appeared happy to have the conversation continue. "All I can do out here is work until I retire in two years. No more sports for me. You may not believe it but before the war I was quite an accomplished tennis player. Sadly those days are long gone."

"I'm sorry. But I can still see the build of an athlete in you."

Alex was not merely flattering the older man. He was still slim. Alex could well believe he had been a good tennis player. But the response his kind words evoked from Hill almost made him fall out of his chair.

"Yes, I was good back then, but the real athlete at Cowan at that time was, and still is today, one of my directors, Geoff Sampson. He's a first class rugby player. He's also a lucky chap. You see he has turned into a really smart investor, and recently has made himself quite rich," he added conspiratorially.

Hill's pleasure at having a new person to talk to had made him indiscrete. He had given more information than Alex could ever have hoped for. Nevertheless it was time to end the meeting.

Alex shook Hill's hand and again thanked him. Then he almost ran out of the building and grabbed the first taxi he could find. Even in his haste he had time to notice the tall, well built Scotsman get the next taxi and follow him.

Arthur O'Shea was waiting for both of them, in a state of high excitement.

"I've got some very interesting news," he gushed.

Alex wanted to tell them of his news but O'Shea could not contain himself and continued talking.

"I had the opportunity to spend thirty minutes with the High Commissioner and his Deputy before the luncheon. And I found out two important things. First, as has been his habit recently, the High Commissioner asked how our investigation was coming along. In the course of our discussion he happened to mention he had had a meeting with several of the top police officers several days ago. Unfortunately he told them of your assignment Alex. This explains how that thug was put on your trail. There is no way to know which officer gave the order to have you killed. However it definitely confirms our suspicion about police involvement. Secondly I judiciously introduced the subject of Gross, by inventing a story of intending to host a dinner party and asking Graham what he thought of my intended guest list. He thought Gross would be an excellent choice but warned me that he was very class conscious and only accepted invitations from the very crème de la crème."

"Snobbish bugger," interjected MacDougal.

"Yes, but the really important thing is Gross is now displaying extreme affluence that was not evident before the war. Recently during one of their golf games he told the Deputy High Commissioner he made his fortune through skillful investments. I believe the Deputy will be reprimanded over divulging this. The High Commissioner is old school and it was obvious he didn't like his deputy breaking Gross's confidence."

"Well, well, things are really falling into place," said Alex, who proceeded to relate his meeting with Hill.

"Here we have two men who were judicious enough not to show their ill-gotten gains before the war. And who must have safely stashed away the blood money they received for spying. And now evidently feel secure enough to splash their money around; both claiming to have made their wealth through skillful investments."

"Gotcha, you traitorous bastards," exuded an ecstatic O'Shea.

Chapter Fifty Three

Alex walked over to the blackboard and entered the names of Gross and Sampson in the appropriate boxes.

"By God, look at what you've accomplished, laddie," shouted a gleeful MacDougal, pointing a wavering finger at the blackboard. "You've identified Gross as being a cell leader and Marsh and Sampson as being two of his three subordinates. Now we just have to find Gross's boss and we'll only be one step away from the mastermind."

"In theory that's true," admitted Alex, "but we still don't have a shred of evidence."

"The evidence will come," stated a confident O'Shea. "The structure of the spy ring has started to crumble. We just have to find another name or two and the rats will begin to desert the sinking ship. That's when they'll make mistakes and we'll nab them."

"What do we do next?" asked an eager MacDougal.

"Well we have one more clue," said Alex. "We have deduced a senior member of the police is involved. He must either be a cell leader or even the second-in-command. Arthur, is there someone in the police you trust implicitly?"

"Michael Strang. He worked closely with me before the war and was a member of Force 136 fighting in the jungle just as I did. What do you want him to do?"

"Ask him to look out for a senior police officer who has suddenly become rich like Gross and Sampson. Or, one who is either a ladies man or a homosexual. That would tie him to the death of the photographer. But for goodness sake tell him to be extraordinarily careful. I believe the second-in-command will act like a cobra – striking immediately with deadly effect."

"What can I do?" asked MacDougal.

"A difficult job, Steve. I want you to spend the weekend shadowing Gross. I suspect he is cunning enough not to be seen in contact with the second-in-command. But you never know. He may just be rattled enough to do so. This could turn out to be an extremely boring job sitting in a car waiting for Gross to make a move – a move he may be too clever to make. Will you do it?"

"Of course, laddie."

"What about you, Alex?" asked O'Shea.

"I have to do more thinking. Things have happened very quickly. With the details we have gathered, I want to go back through every file and all the notes I made in an attempt to glean further information."

He didn't say it but he was still haunted by his nightmare. Now, more than ever, he felt there was something of vital importance he had missed. And if he didn't recollect it, the dire consequences would be his fault.

In his hotel room he went over and over all his information but came up with nothing new. That night he did not sleep well and was restless the entire weekend. He rose at dawn on Monday and arrived at the High Commission just as O'Shea was opening the back door.

O'Shea was quick to notice Alex's haggard look.

"No luck?" he guessed.

"Nothing," grunted Alex disconsolately.

"Well I have something. No, it's not critical," added O'Shea immediately upon seeing Alex's eyes light up in anticipation. "It's a note from Steve. I arranged for Walter Halliburton to keep in touch with him and collect any messages from him. Walter was given this at six o'clock this morning by Steve who was still outside Gross's home, sitting in the car I loaned him

'You were right, laddie. This is the most boring thing I have ever done. Gross hasn't left his home. Nothing further to report except that damned Irishman gave me the most uncomfortable car he could find. Send more coffee.'

That brought a smile to Alex's face and briefly relieved the tension he had felt. O'Shea knew this is exactly the effect MacDougal intended.

"He's a really good man, even though he is a Scotsman," he said in a voice filled with admiration.

They were sitting in the safe room two hours later when the white telephone rang. O'Shea quickly grabbed it.

"Oh hello, Michael," he said recognizing Strang's voice. "What? When? How? Thanks for letting me know. Keep me updated if anything further shows up."

Alex looked at him expectantly.

"The organization structure *is* crumbling. Marsh was found dead last night. His throat had been slit. We can only assume Gross authorized it."

"Or his boss, the second-in-command," said Alex.

"True. But does this help us?"

"Most definitely," averred Alex. "It means the top of the tree is trembling. More mistakes are bound to follow. The only snag is – just like Marsh - more limbs may be lopped off before we discover their identity. We have to move fast."

"But how?"

"I wish I knew the answer, Arthur. Hopefully further events will give us a clue."

Early that afternoon such an event occurred.

The door of the safe room hissed open and in strode MacDougal. His eyes were puffy with black rings underneath from lack of sleep. But his pupils shone brightly. Before either Arthur or Alex could speak, he held up his hand.

"I know, I've deserted my post, but I've got something."

Alex jumped up to get him a cup of coffee. MacDougal nodded his thanks and sat down.

"All that sitting around in the car gave me plenty of time to think. And something came to my mind: something that had puzzled me some time ago. Near my rubber estate is another one that used to be owned by one of the largest companies in the business. Before the war it was managed by Ian Burchill; a man who went to all the right schools. However, in my opinion, he wasn't a good manager. And he was an even more ineffective husband. His wife led him around by the nose. She hated living on the estate and finally moved to KL where she enjoyed the high life and ran up huge debts. She escaped court by suddenly departing the country, leaving Ian burdened by her debts. He was slowly paying them off when war broke out."

He could see the impatient look on O'Shea's face.

"I'm getting to the point, Arthur. He returned to Malaya after the war and bought the estate from his old company. I used to wonder how he managed that. It must have cost a packet. This morning I called my assistant who is looking after my estate and asked him to make some discreet enquiries through his opposite number at Burchill's estate. The answer he was given was that Burchill had made some very astute investments."

"That reason is too much of a coincidence," said Alex excitedly.

"You're damned right, laddie. Then something else came to mind to clinch the deal. As you know, I trained with Force 136 just before the war, Burchill didn't. But he joined the Self Defense Force for the State of Selangor and because of his education, but mainly through his well placed university chums, was appointed Deputy Head. In that position he would have attended all military briefings. And that would have given him knowledge of the position and strength of all army units in the state. KL is in Selangor and many important army units were camped nearby. Burchill's knowledge would have been invaluable to the Japs. As far as I'm concerned you can fill in the third box below Gross with the name Burchill!"

"But again we have no proof, Steve," argued Alex.

"We will have. Trust me. Just let me have a few hours sleep then you and I will pay him a visit. I'm certain I can sweat the truth out of him. He's not built of strong material. Believe me, he is a weak, cowardly man."

At two o'clock the next morning they arrived at Burchill's estate and Steve banged on the door until an irate Burchill answered.

"What the hell do you want, MacDougal. It's two in the morning."

"Just a little chat," said Steve as he barged into the house dragging Burchill with him.

"This is a man from MI 6 in London and he would like to ask you a few questions about your wartime activities."

Alex managed not to roll his eyes at MacDougal saying he was from the British Secret Service.

"I haven't the faintest idea what you are talking about," Burchill said with false bravado.

"We already know all about your traitorous activities, we merely require you to fill in a few details. The bank the Japanese used to deposit your blood money has been most cooperative. We even know your co-conspirators. I just need you to confirm some things," said Alex brazenly.

"You're crazy. This is all a pack of lies."

Burchill's voice was now betraying his fear.

"I was afraid you would take that attitude, Burchill. But if you don't co-operate I can't protect you from a slow painful end," said Steve in a low threatening tone that sent a shiver of panic throughout Burchill's body. "You and I well know that strange things can happen on a rubber estate."

"You wouldn't dare harm me. And even if you did beat me, you'll answer to the police when I report you."

His voice now indicated his trepidation at being severely hurt. But this sense of trepidation was about to turn into uncontrollable terror.

"Oh the police won't be able to listen to a corpse. But I don't intend to do the actual killing. I think it better to bind you to a tree on the edge of the estate, close to the jungle, and cut you a little here and there. You know how acute the senses are of jungle animals. Something's bound to catch the smell of your blood - most probably a panther. It must be terrible to have a panther eat you alive, tearing off chunks of your body one piece at a time. I wonder how long it would take before you die."

"Shut up, shut up, you bastard," screamed a petrified Burchill. He had looked into MacDougal's eyes and had seen the dullness of a cold killer. It was then he believed this was not an idle threat. "What do you want?" he whimpered.

"Write out a confession and include the names of all known accomplices, particularly your boss."

"I never knew my boss," lied Burchill.

"Come now, how do you think we got your name. John Gross has already confessed and *he* gave us your name," said Alex.

At the mention of Gross's name, Burchill's eyes widened in shock.

"He told you?"

"Of course. All I need is your confirmation to finalize my report."

Burchill's brain worked overtime. It was no longer wartime; therefore he didn't believe he could be shot. The worst that could happen would be a long jail sentence. With a sense of self preservation, a completely demoralized and defeated Burchill picked up his pen and began to write.

"Thank you," said Alex. "Now you had better get dressed."

The walls of the bungalow were thin and from his bedroom Burchill could clearly hear the two talking, even though they were speaking in low voices.

"You weren't really going to feed him to a panther, were you?" asked Alex with a wink.

"Oh yes I was. And I still am. I'll be damned if I am going to let that traitor get off easily. Jail is too good for that bugger. He will suffer a slow, excruciatingly, painful death," replied MacDougal in a strident tone, as he returned the wink.

Burchill's knees buckled and it took whatever strength he had left to walk to his bedside table and open the drawer.

They heard the loud blast of the revolver.

"Well that's over, let's call Arthur and have him contact Michael Strang to take care of things ---" MacDougal's voice trailed off as he noticed the far away gaze on the face of his friend.

"No, I have a better idea," said Alex with a thoughtful look.

Chapter Fifty Four

On the drive back to KL Alex was silent for a while before he asked, "Did we do the right thing?"

"No, we didn't," was the startling reply from MacDougal. "We *did* let him off too easily! That traitorous bugger caused the deaths of hundreds and hundreds of our men. And the wounding of many more that finished up in POW camps where they were tortured unmercifully. No, a quick death was too good for him. I saw our boys as they were rescued from the POW camps at the end of the war. Those skeletal men would eventually have their bodies heal but not their minds. I should have fed the bastard to the jungle animals."

MacDougal's vehemence shook Alex. And he was eternally grateful he had not witnessed the same sights at war's end as had his Scottish friend. After another few minutes MacDougal shuddered as he tried to dispel the images which still plagued his memory. Once he was calm again he glanced at Alex.

"Now tell me about this better idea of yours."

"The one thing worrying me right from the start has been, even after we manage to identify the second-in-command, how we can we make him identify the mastermind?"

"And you've now come up with an answer?"

"Yes, but you may not like it."

"I think you had better tell me, laddie, lest I feed *you* to the panthers."

"Well, you are going to be an assassin."

"What?" shouted MacDougal as his grip on the steering wheel tightened and the car swerved violently.

In the trunk, the wrapped body of Burchill banged around loudly before the car was righted.

"You had better have a good explanation, Alex."

"Okay, this is how I plan to catch our mastermind. When we get back we snatch Gross and keep him safely hidden. Then we arrange for Strang to 'find' the body of Burchill. Strang should then report he recently received a tip that a trained killer had been sent from England on a contract to eliminate certain people. But initially Strang did not have a name for the assassin. Now he is confident the combination of Burchill's body and Gross's disappearance, presumably killed and buried, must be the work of this killer. If my plan works, the second-in-command will believe the mastermind has decided to cover his tracks permanently by sending this assassin, and he, the second-in-command, will be next."

"And then what?"

"You grab the second-in-command and tell him you have been sent by his boss to kill him, just as you killed Burchill and Gross. I hope he will curse his boss by name for his duplicity."

"I can see two problems with your idea. First, how do you intend finding the second-in-command? And second even if you do, suppose he doesn't reveal the identity of his boss?"

"As usual you're correct, Steve," replied Alex wistfully. "I've recognized the same two problems. I'm hoping Strang has managed to find incriminating evidence against one of the other police officers to identify him as the second-in-command. As for the other problem – I don't have an answer yet. I'm sorry but it's the best outline of a plan I could come up with at this stage."

MacDougal raised his eyes to heaven as if in prayer.

"You're a bright man, Alex. I only hope you're lucky too," was all he said.

Once back in KL Alex checked his room for listening devices. Satisfied there was none he called O'Shea. He wasn't best pleased to be wakened at four-thirty in the morning but dutifully rushed over to the hotel. He listened agog at Alex's plan including the part that he must acquire a quick acting drug to knock out Gross. Mumbling his misgivings he left to 'acquire' such a drug from the hospital. Following the successful acquisition of the drug, he called Strang and asked him to come to Alex's room.

They all met there at six o'clock. The meeting started out badly when Strang said he could not find a single scrap of evidence against the other three most senior members of the police force.

"What now, Alex?" asked a disappointed O'Shea.

"We go ahead. The second-in-command must be a highly skilled man. He is probably sufficiently skilled to have covered his tracks. Perhaps when

Michael makes his announcement of an assassin, it will shake something loose. We have to give it a try unless someone has a better idea."

There were shakes of heads.

"Okay, then at eight o'clock, when Gross parks his car behind his office, Arthur will greet him in the car park. Gross will be so surprised to see him there he will be completely off guard. That will allow Arthur the few seconds he requires to inject the hypodermic into his neck. Michael will be parked close by in his car and both of them will quickly load Gross into the back seat and cover him with a blanket. Then Michael will take him to a safe place where he will be kept securely bound. In the afternoon when Gross's disappearance is reported, and Burchill's body is found, Michael will then make his announcement about the assassin. And then we wait to see if someone rises to the bait. Steve and I have been up all night and must get some sleep, so I suggest we all meet at the High Commission at around six-thirty tonight."

While he still had reservations over the efficacy of Alex's plan, MacDougal admired his 'take charge' style. From great experience he knew that strong leadership was a key ingredient to the success of any mission - strong leadership *and* luck. He prayed again that Alex would be lucky.

Alex fell into his bed in a state of exhaustion. Not so much physical exhaustion although his body ached, but mental exhaustion. He tossed and turned but couldn't sleep. His mind kept going over and over and over every aspect of this case. In his nightmare he had called out, "I missed something, I missed something," and these words again echoed around in his head. He must have finally gone into a deep, deep sleep for he wakened from a dream at four o'clock. In his dream he had been driving a car through a thick fog. The windshield wipers were arcing furiously but couldn't clear the mist. Then for a split second it evaporated and he could see clearly. But now that he was awake he couldn't bring the clear image back into focus.

"What was it I saw?" he yelled in frustration, but to no avail. The mist had enveloped it again. "Damn! Damn! Damn!"

Thoroughly discouraged he showered and dressed. After ordering a light meal to be served in his room, he grappled yet again with the ethereal miasma. Nothing!

"I hope this isn't a harbinger of total failure," he muttered.

He arrived early at the safe room. It was only five-fifteen. O'Shea was busy so he sat alone with his lingering frustration. At five-forty Strang arrived.

"I hate to be the carrier of bad news, Alex, but there was not a flicker of guilt or fear in the eyes of my colleagues when I mentioned the assassin. I have to assume your target is not a senior policeman."

"But it must be - it must be! Those bullets were meant to kill me. They were real and no one other than the police knew of my role. No one - No one ----."

His voice trailed off as a corner of the thick blanket of fog lifted and he saw a little of the picture which had eluded him.

"Oh my God, surely not. It can't be, can it?"

Strang was looking at him with alarm as Alex almost ran around the room; his wide open eyes staring into space. He seemed like a man possessed by some evil spirit.

"Can it be possible? Can it be truly possible?" he said in a cracked voice.

"What is it, Alex?" Strang cried out.

"You'll have to excuse me. I have to make a call and it's exceedingly private," croaked Alex as he unceremoniously ushered Strang out the door.

He picked up the white telephone and dialed a long series of numbers.

"Hello," answered a voice that Alex recognized immediately.

"General Howe, This is MacMillan. I need you to get me some confidential information. And I need it immediately!"

Chapter Fifty Five

Howe was accustomed to giving out terse orders, not to receiving them. But years in the intelligence business had taught him to recognize high stress situations. He didn't waste a second.

"Tell me," he commanded.

Even with all his experience he found it hard to believe his ears. He stood up, gripped the telephone as though he wanted to crush it into a thousand pieces.

"Are you certain of this, MacMillan?" he snapped.

"Not certain - but more than eighty percent sure. I just need the information I requested to be one hundred percent."

"Where can I call you back?"

"I said I need it now!" almost screamed Alex. Then realizing to whom he was speaking he lowered his voice. "My apologies, Sir. If you don't mind I'll stay on the line while you use another phone."

Howe didn't rebuke Alex. In fact he smiled.

'This young man has really turned out to be quite a forceful character when he wants to be,' he thought.

"Hold on, this may take a while."

Alex waited for half-an-hour to get his answers. He hung up the phone and sat back in the chair. Magically the mist cleared and he saw the whole picture.

At six-fifteen MacDougal and O'Shea arrived simultaneously only to find Strang standing outside the room.

"Didn't you ask Halliburton to let you in?" asked a surprised O'Shea.

"I *was* in and then something very weird happened. Alex suddenly appeared to lose his marbles. He kept shouting and striding rapidly around the room. Then he almost threw me out saying he had to make a private telephone call."

"This is ridiculous, I'm going in," said O'Shea testily.

"I wouldn't, Arthur," responded MacDougal barring the door with his large frame. "I've known this young man for quite some time and if he needs privacy there must be a very good reason for it. Once he gets deeply into a problem he's like a dog with a bone – he won't let go. Something critical has entered that massive brain of his and I suggest we wait."

O'Shea looked appraisingly at MacDougal.

"Not that I could shift that huge body of yours anyway," he concluded. "However, your tiny Scottish brain may just be right, it's probably better we wait," he added in an accentuated thick Irish brogue.

MacDougal merely grinned at this jibe. They didn't have long to wait. Five minutes later Alex opened the door. He seemed to be in a trance. He had a dazed look on his face and staggered back into his chair.

"There's brandy in that cupboard on the left, Steve. Get him some for God's sake. Alex, Alex, what's wrong with you?"

"Me? Nothing at all. I've got it. At least almost all of it. I just have to ask you a couple of questions, Arthur."

He stopped to sip the brandy MacDougal had thrust into his hand. The others waited in agonizing anticipation, hardly daring to breathe. Alex's dazed look vanished; his face took on the most serious expression with his eyes almost closed in concentration. His words came out slowly as he carefully pronounced each one.

"Was High Commissioner Graham interned at the POW camp in Changi? And do you know if he was subjected to solitary confinement?"

"The answer to both questions is yes. The bastards tortured him and refused to allow him to mingle with the other prisoners. At the time the war broke out he was Deputy High Commissioner. The then High Commissioner was so badly tortured and beaten that he died."

Alex's face showed no emotion. He simply nodded as though it was the answer he expected.

"And before the war was there a policeman serving here by the name of Cook?"

"Yes, that's right. He was Deputy Chief Superintendant. But he was transferred just before war broke out. I believe he was sent to India."

"Aah!" Alex let out a deep breath and his face lit up in a broad serene smile.

"For God's sake take that silly grin off your face and tell us," cried out O'Shea in a voice filled with strain and impatience.

"Sorry, I was just savoring the moment."

"Hurry up and share your feast with us, laddie," growled MacDougal.

"From the beginning my training focused my attention on connections. What linked those spies together? The one obvious link was money. Then I recognized they all must have been counseled not to flaunt their wealth until after the war. My meeting at Thompson led me to the extravagantly dressed Marsh. And he in turn led us to another rich man, the allegedly astute investor, Gross. By chance I learned of another allegedly astute investor, Sampson. By now the pattern was set and Steve remembered yet another recently wealthy man, Burchill. None of them had been wealthy before the war. Their wealth came from the money paid to them by their employer – the Japanese Intelligence Service."

Alex paused to take another sip of his brandy. That only heightened the tension in the room. They already knew all this. They desperately wanted more information.

"Something has been nagging at me since the beginning. I even had a nightmare about missing an important clue. Today it came to me. Before this assignment, and by pure chance, I was at the home of my boss's boss. He wasn't there but his wife showed me around. One could not have avoided being struck by the grandeur of the building and the beautifully landscaped large grounds. But it was the inside which was truly awesome. It was packed with the most gorgeous Asian antiques. The whole thing must have cost an absolute fortune. But all that was swept out of my mind as I concentrated all my attention on this mission. It was only the discovery of the link of wealth which brought it back to me. My boss's boss's name is Chief Superintendent Cook! He is the mastermind of the spy ring!"

There was a stunned silence in the room. It was as though this deduction was too good to be true. If it were true, it would be the end of the hunt. Finally Strang voiced a doubt.

"That's quite a leap to take in drawing such a conclusion. And without any real evidence or reason why he would become a spy," he countered.

"When I asked you to leave the room, Michael, it was to call General Howe, the Deputy Director of MI 6. I asked him to get answers to several questions."

"One of the answers gave me the reason, which I firmly believe was blackmail. General Howe found out that Cook had the reputation of a notorious ladies man."

"I remember hearing rumors to that effect," confirmed Strang.

"That's why you got me to research the murders of photographers," interjected O'Shea.

"Correct, that's the reason you are looking for Michael. And once Cook was photographed with one of his ladies he was blackmailed. I would even bet she was supplied by the Japanese. Given his thirst for social and professional power he would have done anything to prevent the publication of those photographs. Now to your point regarding evidence, Michael, my assassin will get that for us."

"Your assassin?" exploded O'Shea.

"He means me. Although I haven't the faintest idea what he is planning," intoned MacDougal in a voice filled with unease and resignation.

"It's quite simply really. You will get the second-in-command alone and tell him you are about to kill him on the orders of Cook - just as you supposedly killed Burchill and Gross. I'm quite certain he will curse his betrayer for his disloyalty, thereby giving us our evidence."

"But you would have to identify the second-in-command first," objected O'Shea strenuously.

"Oh, I already know who *he* is. You see, Arthur, we both made a terrible mistake by assuming he was a policeman. But Michael is certain he is not. All the traps we laid for policemen failed. So it had to be someone else who ordered my death."

"But I swear I didn't tell anyone else," protested O'Shea.

"Yes, you did, Arthur."

"I tell you I didn't. Only the police – and of course the ---."

His voice trailed off as a look of horror came over his face.

"That's right, Arthur. You told the High Commissioner."

"The High Commissioner?" echoed MacDougal and Strang in utter astonishment.

Chapter Fifty Six

"Yes, the High Commissioner. I requested General Howe to have the Home Office check their records of the interview with Graham in 1937 before he was selected as the Deputy High Commissioner. One of the questions asked at that time concerned an unsubstantiated rumor of homosexuality. Of course he stoutly denied everything and the Home Office accepted this. But I feel certain that Cook somehow found out his proclivities and had him photographed in the act. That's how he was recruited; that, and the money. And that ties in with the second murder of a photographer discovered by Arthur. The other incriminating thing uncovered was this. In preparation for his retirement next year; Graham recently purchased a large, very expensive, home on the south coast of England. In addition he bought an even more expensive estate in Scotland with a river that is well stocked with trout. And Graham is an avid fly fisherman."

"That all sounds very damning, but it's hardly conclusive evidence the money came from spying activities," said O'Shea.

"Right, but the redoubtable General Howe tracked down the source of his wealth. The money came from a numbered bank account in Switzerland. The first deposit was made in late 1939 and the last in August 1941. All together a total equivalent to eight hundred and fifty thousand pounds was paid into that account. The funds came from the Mitsubishi Bank in Tokyo."

"Damn, how could he? He always seemed such an honorable man," cried out a badly shaken O'Shea.

"Don't they make the best spies?" suggested Alex.

O'Shea nodded his reluctant agreement, and then a thought struck him.

"But if he worked for the Japs, why did they treat him so badly in the POW camp?"

"They didn't. I restudied DI Connors' notes. He interviewed an ex-POW prisoner, a senior army officer, who informed him a guard he was bribing once told him a few white men were living in a large house guarded by Japanese soldiers. Those men must have been Graham and Gross. They were never in solitary confinement and were never tortured. Probably they were knocked about a bit just before Singapore was retaken. It would just be enough to show a few bruises before they were returned to their cells.

"The bastards," said Strang heatedly. "So it was the money that led you to all of them?"

"That, and finally Howe's invaluable information."

"How could the general get all this information so quickly," asked a puzzled MacDougal.

"He is the Deputy Director of the British Secret Service. When he asks for something, people drop everything and get answers," responded O'Shea austerely.

His longtime desire to catch the top spies had overcome his past mistaken loyalty to Graham. Now all he wanted was to punish the traitor. "What do we do next?" he demanded brusquely.

He had the scent of his prey and he wanted blood.

"In your daily meeting with Graham, tomorrow, you must mention you heard an assassin arrived from London and is believed to have killed Burchill and Gross. Tell him the police still believe he is here and are looking for him. They think the only reason he is still here is he intends further assassinations. Say you will get an update from the police at four-thirty and if Graham is interested you can brief him immediately afterwards. That should keep him in his office until then. Steve, my trusty assassin, will enter his office at around five-fifteen and do his act. Michael, you have to set up the spurious four-thirty briefing. But be on hand here to arrest Graham following Steve's performance."

Strang, who had not known Alex until recently, gazed at him in wonderment.

"You really have all this incredibly well orchestrated," he marveled.

"One final thing for you, Arthur: I know how much this spy hunt has meant to you and Tony Benson. Recognizing how your emotions must be at this time, you probably would like nothing better than to strangle Graham. But you must curb those emotions. Graham is a highly intelligent spy who will be on edge at the news of the deaths of Gross and Burchill. If you give even the slightest sign of your true feelings, he will sense the danger. You must act as though you know nothing of his true identity for this to work."

"I understand, Alex. You can count on me. I'm not going to blow it now that we have the bastard in our sights."

And true to his word – he didn't.

High Commissioner Graham was astounded as a big man entered his office, leaving the door ajar. He was even more astonished at seeing the large pistol fitted with a silencer.

"What the Dickens is this? Who the hell are you? And how did you manage to get past security?"

"Too many questions," responded the man laconically. "All you need to know is a certain Mr. Cook sent me. He told me to tell you he regrets this action but he must terminate your relationship. There must be no loose ends. You have allowed people to get too close to him. However I will give you the same opportunity I gave Burchill and Gross. Any last words?"

Graham attempted to open his desk drawer to reach his revolver, but MacDougal moved like a cat and slammed his pistol on Graham's hand.

"Don't even think about it. Your death will be a quick one but if you try anything like that again, I promise you it will be slow and painful."

Graham was a highly skillful spy, one who worked best in the shadows. But now that he was in the light, he turned out to be just a frightened man.

"I can pay you. I have money," he pleaded, almost in tears.

"Mr. Cook is already paying me well. Do you have any last words?"

Seeing there was no way out, Graham's demeanor totally unraveled and he began shouting.

"Tell Cook I hope he roasts in the fires of hell. He deserves to. After all I did for him, the risks I took in obeying his every command – the ungrateful bastard."

Graham was ranting uncontrollably now. Spittle was flowing down his chin. In his rage he failed to see the two men enter his office.

"Okay, that's enough. I've got all that on tape," said Strang as he and another senior officer stepped into the room. "High Commissioner Graham, you are under arrest for espionage against Great Britain resulting in the countless deaths of men serving in her armed forces. And complicity in several murders to be fully defined at a later date."

He completed the rest of his caution as he handcuffed a completely bewildered and stupefied Graham, who now realized he had been tricked. As the High Commissioner was led from his office, Alex had to put his arms around O'Shea otherwise he would have finally lost control and beaten Graham.

"You filthy bastard, you will definitely roast in the fires of hell," he hissed at his ex-boss.

Later at the bar in Alex's hotel O'Shea had downed two large Irish whiskies in rapid succession.

"Take it slowly, Arthur," counseled MacDougal.

"I can drink you under the table any day," retorted a still highly distressed O'Shea. But, in truth, his anger was directed at himself for being fooled by Graham.

"I have no doubt about that, my friend, but since you have forced me to join you in drinking this Irish imitation of real whisky, let's sip it and do our best to enjoy it."

O'Shea turned his troubled eyes on MacDougal.

"My apologies, Steve, my dear friend. You're absolutely right. May I propose a toast?"

"By all means but don't make it too long. I need several more drinks."

O'Shea's eyes brightened at MacDougal's remark. He had needed his Scottish friend's sense of humor to stop him from completely breaking down. The adrenalin had gone from his system now that his long pursuit of traitors had ended in victory. He threw an arm around MacDougal but his eyes were on Alex.

"I propose a toast to Alexander MacMillan; the greatest detective and code breaker in the world. But more importantly the most wonderfully reliable comrade-in-arms that anyone could wish for. A man who will never let you down."

They drained their glasses, and MacDougal ordered another round. They were half way through this drink, (it was going to be a long night), when O'Shea suddenly sat bolt upright and stared incredulously at Alex.

"Did you truly ask Steve to say to Graham, 'Any last words'?"

"Yes, Why?"

"Why? Despite my toast to your brilliance, that's the stupidest thing an assassin would ever say!"

"Well it worked, didn't it?"

There were a few seconds of silence before they startled all the others in the bar as they let out the most colossal roar of laughter.

Chapter Fifty Seven

After a few more rounds the singing began. It started with the Irish favorite 'Danny Boy' followed by the Scottish 'Loch Lomond' and so it went on; one country's song after another. Obviously the patrons of the bar were musical ignoramuses, or perhaps, it was only the fact they possessed ears unaccustomed to a raucous, off-key, drunken, racket. For whichever reason, and to the night manager's chagrin, the bar soon emptied. When, finally, the barman insisted he had to close, the manager was astute enough to find them lodging for the night.

Alex awakened late the next morning to a loud thumping noise. He was half way to the door before he recognized the noise was coming from inside his head. He had two large glasses of water and went back to sleep. Two hours later he was once again wakened by a loud thumping noise. This time it was the door. Strang stood in the doorway.

"I'm pleased to see you are still alive. I saw your two friends and I'm not certain they are. I left them with large glasses of Epsom salts as a starter. Now if you don't mind I'll use your phone to order for all of you, the best hangover cure I know – tomato juice, lemon, Worcestershire sauce and a raw egg. Then perhaps you'll be able to clearly understand the latest news."

After they had all assembled and taken their cure, they started on two large pots of coffee. They were still obviously under the weather and Strang waited until the groaning had reduced to a tolerable level before holding up his hand to get their glassy-eyed attention.

"Early this morning Graham took his own life by hanging himself with his belt."

"What? Didn't the jailers have the sense to take away his belt?" burst out an aggrieved O'Shea.

"Perhaps they did and perhaps they didn't. Or maybe they just forgot. Some of those jailers were POW's who were tortured by the Japanese.

However I found it strange when I noticed Graham had severely beaten himself before he committed suicide," replied Strang with a knowing look.

That sobered the three.

"They should have had more sense," lamented MacDougal. "Better to have him spend the rest of his life in prison, where he would have undergone beatings from his fellow inmates every day of his miserable life."

There was a moment of silence as they each had their individual thoughts on an appropriate punishment for Graham. Strang finished his coffee before breaking the silence.

"Also, Arthur, General Howe would like you to call him immediately; and to have Alex with you when you do. I told him you had suddenly taken ill. He said he perfectly understood how such an 'illness' could occur. He left this telephone number and asked you call him the moment you recover – no matter what the time."

"Oh Lord, I suppose we had better get to my safe room," mumbled O'Shea.

"Are you finally sober?" asked Howe when O'Shea called him.

"Yes, Sir, I am – sort of – not entirely. But enough to obey your instructions to call you."

"Good, then listen carefully. Is MacMillan with you?"

"Yes, Sir."

"Ask him to wait outside for a few minutes."

After Alex left, Howe requested a concise briefing.

"He's one of the brightest men I have even known," said an admiring Howe when he had heard everything.

"Yes, Sir, I wholeheartedly agree with that."

"Don't tell him this, but I tried for a second time to steal him back from the Yard, but they wouldn't hear of it. They intend promoting him when he returns. He will be the youngest Detective Chief Inspector in the Yard's history. Now you can call MacMillan back in and put this conversation on your speaker. Oh, and get a pen and paper."

"Alex is here," said O'Shea a few moments later.

"After my conversation with you, MacMillan, I informed Montague Anderson of your success. Then I had Cook arrested as a spy. The man had no guts whatsoever. He cracked like a walnut and gave us the names of his co-spies. Some of the military men had been transferred back here and we picked them up. Here are the names of three men still out there. Have them arrested, O'Shea."

O'Shea wrote down the names. His eyes were shining with the deep satisfaction of finishing the job he had started so long ago. He then gave Howe news of Graham.

"I gather you don't believe it was suicide?"

"No, Sir, I don't. But I do not intend doing anything about it."

"Quite right. Now, MacMillan, I must say you have astounded me once more with your ability: my congratulations and my most sincere thanks. You have done your country yet another great service. I can't award you any medals from MI 6 but I believe Scotland Yard will honor you in some way."

"Thank you, Sir, but it was very much a team effort," replied Alex in embarrassment.

"When are you planning to return?"

"I have a few things to do here. I should be back early next week. I shall inform DCI Lowell when I have a final date."

"Remember, I still want to see you, so call me."

"Yes, Sir."

O'Shea hung up the telephone.

"What do you still have to do, Alex?"

"I want to visit Tony Benson's grave and I must buy a ring."

"A ring? You didn't mention that. Are you getting married?"

"As soon as possible after I get back."

"That's wonderful. You can get a good deal on a ring in Singapore."

"Singapore?"

"Perhaps I didn't mention. Singapore is planning a very large, beautiful, war memorial parkland for all the fallen allied troops. It will be at Kranji, near the Woodlands district. The bodies of some troops have already been exhumed and reinterred there. Tony is one of them. I'll go along with you and I suspect Steve will wish to come too."

It took another two days to finalize the other arrests and to complete all the reports. Then early in the morning the three men boarded a Malayan Airlines DC3. The old plane flew at a low altitude all the way to Singapore. Alex had a window seat which gave him the most wonderful view. He gazed at the sight that lay before his eyes and thought he could never tire of its tranquil majesty. Memories of London seemed like the imagination's thoughts of a distant planet: so far away and surreal. Only this view of Malaya's spectacular scenery was real and he wished it were possible to stay longer.

But in his mind's eye he saw the freckled face of a red haired beauty.

She was calling him home and that was a much more compelling scenario than even Malaya's beauty.

"Maybe one day we'll come here together," he murmured.

"What'd you say?" asked the almost sleeping MacDougal.

"Nothing, Steve."

They checked in at the Raffles Hotel. Shortly thereafter they went to the cemetery. They stood with arms around each other at the foot of Tony Benson's grave and were unafraid to allow tears to run down their cheeks. Each took a turn to say a few words. Probably each would have liked to have been more eloquent and lengthy in saying their goodbyes; but he emotion of the moment restricted their words.

"Thank you, professor, for your wise counsel and friendship. You will never be forgotten," was all Alex managed to say.

Then, as if by some unspoken command, they stood at attention and saluted their fallen comrade.

Later they visited a jewelry store recommended by the concierge at the hotel. It was large and brightly lit so that its wares gleamed invitingly. The Chinese manager promised a good discount since they were sent by the hotel. Being a good salesman he brought out a case of his best rings. Alex took one look at the prices and shook his head ruefully.

"Something less expensive," he suggested.

O'Shea took Alex aside.

"I told old man Howe of your impending marriage and he instructed me to buy the very best ring possible. He said he would inspect it personally when he saw you and if it wasn't the best, he would have me shot."

"That sounds like him," admitted Alex. "But I couldn't allow MI 6 to spend so much money."

"Alex, believe me, you have earned much more than any amount of money we could spend on you. Anyway Howe said it was his wedding present to both of you. And you don't want me shot, do you?"

Alex shook his head with a rueful smile. Then, after some considerable time due to the initial conflicting advice of both of his friends, they all finally reached an agreement. They settled on a stunning diamond surrounded by sapphires. Alex didn't dare look at the price tag; anyway O'Shea quickly covered it with his hand. Then when Alex's back was turned he peeked at it. The Irishman was unable to keep a jolting look of astonishment from his face at the colossal ransom being asked.

"Not to worry," said the Chinese, noting his look. "I give you fifteen percent discount."

MacDougal, whose knowledge of the local customs was extensive, put his arm around him and held him in a firm hug.

"How much?"

"Okay, twenty five percent," gurgled the small man.

MacDougal's hug tightened.

"Ah don't think ah heard ye properly, laddie. How much?"

The manager had no idea what a 'laddie' was and had no intention of finding out in case is was the most terrible thing imaginable. He looked at the giant and gulped.

"Okay, forty percent."

MacDougal smiled benignly at him and patted him on the back.

'Now I only make ten percent profit,' calculated the manager in his mind.

Before dinner that evening they went to the hotel's famous 'long bar' and had the obligatory Singapore Sling.

"Not bad," opined O'Shea. "But let's have a real drink."

"Oh no! No! Not again. My head couldn't stand all that pain once more," said a determined Alex.

"Oh, very well," responded MacDougal regretfully. "I don't suppose it would do to send you back to your fiancé reeking of Irish whisky."

They settled for two bottles of wine with dinner.

Next morning they stood at the airport, awaiting Alex's flight to London. No one quite knew what to say. With hugs and back slaps, goodbyes were finally spoken. The Irishman and Scotsman looked forlornly as Alex boarded the plane.

"I could do with a drink," said Arthur.

"Maybe even two," agreed Steve.

They knew of no other way to drown their sorrow.

Chapter Fifty Eight

So many thoughts crowded his mind as Alex drove west under cloudy skies. He couldn't help smiling at the most pleasant of those thoughts. His fiancé had met him at the airport and almost knocked him over as she flung herself into his arms. He disentangled himself and fell to one knee, fumbling for the ring in his pocket.

"Oh, Alex not here in the terminal in front of all these people," she whispered, glancing anxiously at the gathering crowd.

"Yes, here!" insisted Alex. "I can't wait a second longer. Joyce Hamilton, will you make me the happiest man on earth and marry me?"

It seemed that everyone in the terminal stood still, looking at the man on his knee. There was a hush until she said softly, "Yes, I will." Then the crowd erupted in a roar of approval.

She had been so embarrassed she hadn't even looked at the proffered ring. Now she did and the terminal echoed back her scream of thunderstruck delight at its dazzling beauty.

"Oh, Alex, Alex, it's absolutely gorgeous," she gushed.

She addressed her words to him but her eyes remained transfixed on the glittering ring. Suddenly something clicked in her brain and her face clouded in doubt.

"But, but, but how could you afford it?" she at last managed to stammer.

"Don't worry, it didn't bankrupt me. It was a gift to both of us from General Howe for my work in solving the case. I'll tell you all about it later. Look, it's almost noon, let's have lunch here at the airport before going back into town," he suggested.

Her crestfallen face told him this would not be possible.

"Oh, my darling, I'm sorry I can't. There has been a bad case of flu sweeping through the hospital and many of our nurses have come down with it. Sister kindly allowed me to meet you but on the condition I come straight back. But we can celebrate tonight."

"That'll have to do. I'll pick you up at six."

After dropping Joyce at the hospital the taxi took him to his flat. He was in a state of exhaustion after his long flight but there was something he had to do. And now, as he drove along on this windy, cloudy day, he thought what a difference this weather was to that of Malaya; the far away country which held so many vivid memories for him. Malaya, where he had often feared for his life during his war service – Malaya, where lived Steve MacDougal and Arthur O' Shea, two very dear friends he might never see again – Malaya, where his other dear friend, Tony Benson, had lost his life – Malaya where the mountains and jungles were as different as could possibly be to the terrain he was now passing - the rolling grassy hills of Berkshire.

His daydreaming ended when he reached the cemetery. Alex carefully arranged the flowers he brought on each grave, and then sat on the grass facing the headstones.

"I want to thank both of you for all you did for me," he said softly. "And most particularly for all you taught me. You may not have fully realized the impact you made on my life. Not just by the advice you gave me but even more importantly by the example you set in all your everyday actions"

Being a little self conscious at speaking out loud, he paused to allow a couple to pass by.

"I have come to appreciate the struggles you must have faced in your lifetimes. I have learned it is the working class families around the world who deserve to be called heroes. They, just as you did, face unending challenges. Yet for the most part they manage to overcome them. I have often wondered what their secret is. Perhaps faith helps some of them, but maybe it is a sense of belonging that aids most; belonging to some group important enough to propel them forward. And surely the greatest such group must be family. Members of a family depend on one another, look out for one another and care for one another."

Alex stopped speaking to look upward as a few sprinkles of rain fell gently on his face. He smiled as he contemplated his next words.

"I doubt if there are too many families who recognize the endless journeys they undertake in their lifetimes. The many times they encounter a crossroad and choose a path. Most times such encounters are minor and so go virtually unnoticed. But they all accumulate. How many times does a person silently indulge in a game of 'what ifs' and fantasize over possible different outcomes to his or her life if only a different route had been taken? I was one of the most fortunate persons to have a mother who explained the vital importance of recognizing oncoming crossroads, and thinking carefully before choosing which path to follow. I was further blessed by having a father who instructed me on how to handle the consequences of such choices – whether good or bad."

Once again he paused and his smile broadened.

"I came today to tell you I have reached another crossroad, this time a major crossroad. And after serious thought, I am certain I have chosen the correct path. This path will most assuredly lead me on yet another series of life's journeys. And it will be one of my happiest journeys. I am going to be married. Her name is Joyce and she is just like you, Mum, a truly lovely person. And Dad, I am sure you will be pleased to know that your father would whole-heartedly approve – she is Scottish – and has the most adorable brogue. I'll bring her next time I come to visit you. Until then, remember, I always have, and always will, love you both."

Alex stood and as he walked away he turned up the collar of his raincoat in preparation of the rain intensifying. He had not gone fifty yards when Britain's erratic weather once again displayed its contrariness.

The sprinkling rain stopped, the clouds parted, and the sun peeped through.

Printed in the United States
By Bookmasters